FLESH AND BONES

By David Pyle

-BOOK TWO-
BETWEEN LIFE AND DEATH

Flesh and Bones. Copyright © 2014 by David Pyle.

First Edition

Library of Congress Cataloging-in-Publication Data has been applied for.

ISBN-10: 0692313583
ISBN-13: 978-0692313589

Designed by david@pentwist.com

www.pentwist.com

*HELL FROM BENEATH IS MOVED FOR THEE
TO MEET THEE AT THY COMING:
IT STIRRETH UP THE DEAD FOR THEE...*

ISAIAH 14:9

FLESH AND BONES

PROLOGUE
NATCHEZ, MISSISSIPPI – 1977

A house is only an empty building without its inhabitants; equally not a home without a family to occupy it.

In the recent past, the Ames Estate was only a wistful museum visited monthly by one family member, who by a strange turn of events had become proprietor of both the estate and curator over the family's vast financial affairs.

These monthly inspections made sure that the caretakers were performing their duties and that the place hadn't fallen to vandals or the rot of time.

None qualifying as a family member had any desire to live in such a huge home of eight monstrous bedrooms and many other rooms of social and utilitarian design. Even the aged servants' quarters stood vacant and unused save for a few errant cobwebs.

Though entirely alone, Martiel Ellington's diligent oversight for repairs and renovations rendered the building a true historic testament of time. However, to pronounce the house entirely uninhabited in the strictest sense was incorrect; this factor directly contributed to the lack of willing occupants.

For several generations the Estate was both host and confinement for the spirits of several specific Ames descendants.

The Estate had earned a reputation as a place with an abundance of bumps, clinks, and whispers, for perhaps a century.

But now, through an evil turn of events, those spirits were also gone and the rightful living descendants had taken ownership. Remarkably, it was a death in the family, which brought life to its structure.

James Earl Williams was the next intended recipient to bear the torch as family curator and at seventeen years of age was poised for a lengthy formal education as well as a *spiritual* education from his great Aunt Martiel Ellington to prepare him. His unique qualifying trait setting him apart from all the others was his awakening to a family genetic ability to read minds.

At the same time this and other unexpected abilities became evident, an evil adversary awakened, and through torturous events hurled him into a world trapped between life and death.

Between Life and Death Continuum...

The voices were quiet now and what should have brought a moments' consoling peace, instead brought a crushing emptiness.

His thoughts, previously drowned in a sea of chatter, had spoken and like the last dying embers in the hearth had grown cold.

James Earl Williams, first-born son of Robert and Catherine Williams, rehearsed each of his triumphs and terrors one by one, looking for that place, that point of irreparable error bringing him to this current destination.

Once again, he listened throughout the Family Estate, saddened that there was no one with which to share the loneliness eating at his soul, maddened that he would want to share it with anyone.

If only he could sleep and forget.

For the first time he understood why some people chose drugs and alcohol to deaden or turn off their minds and despised his own past judgments toward them.

His memories had become inescapable hounds of hell, replaying every horror over and over in a steady cadence. Even the miraculous events of healing he had somehow performed; how he had snatched his Aunt Martiel Ellington from the very chasm of death could not soothe his presence of mind.

Was this both his future and his end?

If he could cry, his tears would be an eternal river. He prayed for an end, begging his own thoughts to stop playing that incessant slideshow from the beginning of his end.

First were the nightmares..., then the wreck..., and the sight of frigid water washing over his mangled body. The days of torments that followed replayed one by one. And then..., it started all over again.

Insanity was inevitable.

Insanity at seventeen years of age.

James Earl Williams laughed softly..., *"seventeen."*

He found a flicker of consolation that by losing his life he had saved his family and the love of his life.

But where was his victory?

Here he sat..., dead. You can't run or hide from dead..., not at seventeen, not at any age.

Suddenly the empty silence returned to torture him. He choked back a scream to spare the houseful of sleeping relatives his rues.

Somewhere in the darkness, he heard the thermostat click, shutting down the cold air, and....

'No. Not now,' he thought.

It was the whisper of tender bare feet cautiously approaching.

"James?" whispered a gentle voice.

Jolie Dimanche walked into the darkness of the family library where James was seated in a motionless stare before the fireplace.

"What are you doing awake?"

4

He heard the smug tort in his voice and cursed himself further.

"I was dreaming of you, dreaming of being close to you. When I woke, I listened for you, but didn't hear anything.... I had to come find you.

"Come sit with me?" her voice asked, but her heart begged.

Jolie sank into the huge chesterfield, leaned against its comforting arm and curled her feet under her gown for warmth.

Her presence was such blessed relief, but he couldn't tell her; could not give in to the temptation of letting her know how much she had come to mean to him.

James rose silently from the floor and pushed closely beside Jolie in the darkness of the early morning. His heart caved in at the desperation in her voice and thoughts.

How easy it would be to allow her to fill that emptiness, that cavern inside himself; and all he had to do was give in to her need.

He fought it; fought his desperation. He couldn't, it was all wrong. Those selfish thoughts were the very reason he had spent the last several hours tied to his own personal internal whipping post.

He had to think of what was best for her, the right thing to do for her and he was the farthest thing from right for Jolie.

Somewhere in the distance, he heard the faint cry of the eastbound train, instantly turning on the rehearsal of memories.

'Oh God, not again,' he thought.

"Hold me," Jolie whispered, feeling the sudden coldness pour from the strange spectral body beside her.

As his arm encircled her shoulders, the sensation was electric and became warm as usual. At least she could feel him when he initiated contact. It was far better than never feeling anything at all. Since his victory over the Bokor Lyda Brown, since his emancipation from Syrus Earl Ames and his love Ellie Rosalie, it was nearly impossible to be that viable, tangible, flesh-like person Jolie needed.

She reached to take his hand, hoping, but like so many times before, there was nothing to touch.

"How can you still love me?" asked James.

"We aren't going to have this conversation again are we?" she pleaded. "Just this once, sit with me."

"You deserve so much more...," he began.

"Kiss me," she said, leaning toward him.

Her lips were warm and sweet, soft as a feather, so enticing, so much love, yet so wrong....

In that moment, as soon as their lips parted, he knew what he had to do; he had to try once more.

CHAPTER 1

The sounds of early morning life began to echo throughout the house and soon the enticing scents of coffee and breakfast swam through the air.

Catherine walked into the sun-goldened library and stopped by the entrance, a trickle of steam rising from the cup in her hands. Their Siamese cat, Tommy padded silently across her feet into the room, startling her.

Jolie lay on the grand sofa, loosely covered in a soft thick blanket, yet tightly bound in the grip of sleep.

Catherine Williams chose the thickly padded loveseat near Jolie and sat down, memorizing the shape and curves of the young girls' face, peering over her cup of coffee.

Jolie was such a tiny thing and despite all the recent events, still desperately in love with her son. Her long black hair cascaded in waves over the verge of the seat, radiating colorful hues from shards of morning sunlight.

Somewhere inside her, Catherine envied the love Jolie felt for her son James and empathized her pain.

Each day James was becoming more reclusive since the threat against their family was vanquished. It was as if his purpose for existing had somehow been misplaced. The avalanche of events had left little time for him to consider what the future would hold, or its vague consequences.

Each blind choice, each blind decision, forced him

further down a road where angels could not tred.

Where *was* her son?

Catherine didn't have to wait long for an answer.

Her Aunt Martiel's voice came bounding down the stairs in a heated conversation with James Earl.

"Someone has to talk to her," gritted James, lowering his voice.

"Well, it's not going to be me!" said Martiel. "I've been around the chicken yard long enough to know not to get between two people in love. You're on your own James."

In a futile attempt to interrupt a verbal train wreck, Catherine quietly slid through the house, following them into the kitchen.

"Would you two please keep your voices down?"

"Jolie's still asleep," snapped James. "I have to find somebody to talk some sense into her. Maybe you can have Jolie's Aunt BeBe talk to her again?"

"James!" Catherine surprised James at her outburst. "That little girl in there loves you and I won't sit by and let you crush...."

"I love her too," said James, in a blunt declaration that raised everyone's eyebrows. "Am I the only one with any sense left around here? Mother, I'm dead.

"What kind of future does she have with me? She hasn't left this house in two weeks. She just..., mopes, like she's waiting for some..., miracle to take place."

"You've got to let this work itself out naturally, James," said Martiel. "You better pull your britches up and finish what you started. If you try to force Jolie into reality, you'll only break her heart and it won't be pretty."

Martiel's crude version of southern allegory was the last straw.

"My britches were never down!" he hissed angrily. "Jolie's not a...."

James desperately wanted to finish, to put them all in their place, but closed his eyes as if in a moment of contemplation.

"She's awake," said James, sighing quietly.

He heard Jolie's heartbeat step up one beat faster, then another, then her first deep waking breath. It was as if they were conjoined at the soul. Jolie drifted back into a peaceful pre-awakened dream state and James relaxed.

"It's not only Jolie I'm worried about," he said, his voice almost a deep growl.

They were forcing his hand, despite his attempts to isolate them from his rabid worries. He sat down backwards in one of the chairs and leaned forward with his hands gripping the top posts.

This was evidently going to take some time.

"How long do you think it'll be before another monster like Lyda Brown discovers me?"

If nothing else, he finally had their undivided attention.

"*Miss Lyda* did this to me..., to our family, to..., to those ancestral ghosts you were so fond of Aunt Martiel. I should have died in that car wreck and went on to..., I don't know, heaven, somewhere, but not this half-in, half-out existence.

"Martiel, you think this is perfectly normal because you've dealt with others like me since you were a little girl.

"Trust me when I tell you. This..., isn't..., normal," he whispered angrily.

His grip tightened on the posts of the wooden straight back chair and they crushed, splintered, powdered between his fingers.

He stood quickly, "I'm..., I'm sorry. I didn't mean to do that."

Catherine slowly squatted down, watching James, scooping some of the destruction up into her palms, then realizing the absurdity, dusted it from her hands back down on the kitchen floor.

James turned his back on Martiel and Catherine before he continued, "I have a target on my back. It was there when I was born, and it's still there now. Somewhere out there, somebody knows way more about me than I do.

"Lyda Brown knew exactly what she was doing to me. She's gone but there's no undoing what she's done. Now, if another monster comes along, and discovers me, who do you think they'll use to force my hand?"

He looked between his Aunt and Mother waiting for another one of their ridiculous rhetorical answers. Surprisingly, they were both quiet. Good.

"This last monster tried to kill Jolie, Gramma and Grampa, you..., Aunt Martiel, then she tore me in half and left me like..., this. What will the next one do? Who else has to die before you understand me?"

It was one of the few times James could remember, that Martiel was without some pseudo intelligent sarcasm.

Catherine began staring down at the table between them with heavy eyes, "It's hard for a mother to let a son go James. Even when it's the right thing to do."

"I know it is mom," he said quietly.

Maybe they were listening. Of course they were listening. They didn't know what to do anymore than he did. At least he had given it that one last chance. Now he would do what he was forced to do; all other logic and discussion was inconsequential.

"Something's on your mind," said Jolie. "Do you want to talk about it?"

How could he tell her? It was impossible and cruel.

"I've got a lot on my mind," James said, then smiled. "Let's just enjoy today together."

He took her hand, something he knew she loved..., making himself real for her, substantial.

The morning air was still cool, despite the rising heat of the sun. July in Mississippi was only the precursor to the coming furnace of August.

Natchez lay in the crux of the Mississippi River, an hour away from the Gulf of Mexico; most locals referred to it as the Delta.

The combined heat, humidity, and fertile soil could make anything grow. Throw an apple on the ground and next spring, a tree would be sprouting where it fell.

The private road in front of the Ames Estate called to the young couple today as it had for several days, to walk and contemplate; to talk of things that might have been and possibilities of what might still be.

Jolie quickly noticed that today was somehow different. James deferred all conversation of the future and turned it toward Jolie's possibilities for a happy life.

School, a family, children, endless intricacies of where life would take her, places she would see and things she would do.

Finally, when Jolie had enough diversions, "I wish you had some faith in yourself. You know I'm not blind. I know where we are, you are. It's not some mystery. I lived through everything you did James."

"Not quite," he said, turning a quick smile to offset the glum comment.

"Aw, James. You're still here baby, can't you see it? Feel it? It's not over for you. I just know it. If it was all said and done, I wouldn't be here walking beside you, holding your hand, and talking to you."

For once James didn't give into the anger that frustration sometimes brings and kept his gentle hold of her hand.

"Do you remember back when we first met? I saw you sitting there in the Natchez Library with a huge stack of books taking notes like a drowning Psych Major. You looked as out of place as a Jock trying to dance ballet. Your ink pen was cutting grooves in your notepad, did you know that?"

Jolie glanced up at his face and James dodged her gaze in silence.

"I walked past your table and you were so zoned out you didn't even see me. I had to rap my knuckles on the table just to get your attention. Talk about a hit on a girl's ego."

"I remember," said James, barely above a whisper.

"I was so nervous I could hardly breathe. Did you know that? But when you didn't even notice me, I..., kind of got mad at you.

"Then you looked up at me and my heart dropped into my stomach. You looked exactly the way I'd seen you in my dreams..., for three nights running."

James looked away and kicked at a rock, tumbling it down the road ahead of them. He hadn't forgotten the look in her blue eyes, not once. Not ever.

Jolie hoped she was finally making him remember something worth living for.

"Then you spoke," she laughed and rolled her eyes. "The boy from my dreams had a voice like a foghorn!"

Her laughter rang out; it sounded like music.

James looked away once again, begging for some self-control. She was doing it again, ripping his heart in half.

"I'd never heard a boy with a voice like yours before. It wasn't like anything I expected. I don't hear things in my dreams you know, voices and such. I kinda just know what's being said if you know what I mean. Music is different, but not conversations.

"And you should'a seen the look on that haggy Librarian's face...."

"Jolie..., what are you getting at?" asked James.

"Nothing, James," she frowned. "I'm just talking. Remembering the good stuff I never told you. You know. How I felt when we met and stuff."

He gripped her hand a little tighter and swung it in a gentle arc with her footsteps.

"I thought I'd never get you to kiss me. Then I just gave

up and kissed you first. That was a little weird for me, I have to admit. Most of the guys I've known tried to get a kiss from me before asking me out on a date. But not you. I even took you to my favorite spot in town, my private thinking bench in the Garden District, away from all the traffic. I have to admit I was getting a little upset with you, until I realized what was going on in your mind, besides me that is.

"Do you remember our first kiss?"

James seemed to loll back into the conversation. Jolie was being patient but what she couldn't know was that her words had become the blade of a razor inside him.

Of course he remembered their first kiss.

That moment was as if he saw Jolie for the first time and his heart beat its very first thump in his chest.

He turned quickly to confess everything, to tell her how much he loved her, to give in, to vow never to leave her side for as long as..., she lived..., then looked away, broken.

When James didn't answer, she continued.

"I had such a good time that first day we spent together with your family. Except for that crazy neighbor, Ms. Straw. I didn't like that so much," she mumbled

Her eyes glanced his direction, watching closely, "But when we finally got away from there and it was just us. It felt like everything in the world was right.

"Then I had to suggest we stop by my special place in the Garden or you would have just dropped me off at Aunt BeBe's. "What is it about some guys trying to get up the nerve to kiss a girl?"

Jolie's face fell into a frown, then softened again.

"It was worth the wait though. Do you remember? I know I do. It was like..., the world stopped turning."

Jolie stopped in the road; she needed his full attention. It might have even been nice to hear him agree....

"That was when I knew for sure," she said, the words choking in her throat.

"I know," said James.

He raised her hand to his lips and she closed her eyes waiting to feel something, anything.

It was brief, a touch, nothing more.

She started walking again, looking at her feet, away from James, hiding the welling in her eyes. Was she reaching him? At all?

"That was when I knew I couldn't live without you."

"Jolie...," sighed James.

How he wanted to rant, drop her hand, and recall every detail of what he was; more importantly, what he was not. She already knew how he felt. It had been the daily conversation between them for weeks now and it wasn't worth hurting her anymore.

Instead, he now wanted her last memory of him to be a good one.

He smiled at her finally and raised her hand to his lips and kissed its soft olive tanned skin and she felt what she had been waiting for. That too was wrong; to give her false hopes that she was changing his perspective. This was the final confirmation he needed.

He had made the right decision.

CHAPTER 2

Nightfall brought blessed relief from the summer heat. The low humming fans of the central-air units began cycling off, giving the north side of the Estate some peace and quiet.

The silence was soon replaced by the low chatter of cicadas rising and falling in waves from the surrounding trees, competing with the somber tone of crickets.

It had been impossible to insulate every part of the walls in the old structure, even though it had a substantial vacant wall space between the inside of the house and the outer shell.

It was a frequent habit of older homes of the south to have those tiny crawl spaces in the walls, access places that made upgrades to plumbing and electrical wiring a much easier transition from the days of kerosene lamps and candles. It was as if the designers and builders could see into the future and knew that someday that space would be used for more than a place to hide their young daughters and valuables from the ravages of civil war.

To the credit of Martiel Ellington, the house was retrofitted into the twentieth century without losing its charm of dark panels and slowly whipping ceiling fans so prevalent of the previous era.

"Doesn't anybody know where James is?" asked Jolie,

storming around the outside porch.

"He's always with you, Hun," said Maime Ames.

The southernmost porch-swing creaked and Martin Earl Ames grunted his affirmation of the same.

"You can sit here with us if you like," said Maime. "Martin, move over and make some room for Jolie."

Reluctantly he crunched over, patting the empty spot between them and gave the swing a gentile nudge with his feet, making it sway slowly.

"That's okay, I want to find James. I need to ask him something," said Jolie as she scooted up on the porch banister in front of the older couple.

"I'm sure he'll turn up soon," smiled Maime. "You're welcome to wait here with us. It's such a nice evening."

"Maybe for just a minute or two, I really need to talk to him."

Maime noticed Jolie's anxious fingers tapping the edge of the thin rail, "Would you remember to invite your Aunt over for cards this weekend?"

"She'll like that," said Jolie, twitching her feet. "I'll see if I can get her to bring some fresh shrimp from this week's delivery. I know you like those."

"She'll think I put you up to it," said Maime. "Better not."

"If it's that big a deal, order some, Maime," mumbled Martin.

"It's not a big deal," she bit back. "I don't want to impose on BeBe."

"Impose? Maime, she runs a Café for goodness sakes," he murmured. "If we asked her to come over and cook a whole meal, now that would be imposing."

"Well then we should quit imposing on Jolie then," Maime said, shuffling in the swing to widen the gap between them.

Martin was silent, weighing his next words very carefully.

"You do have a pretty good flair for spicing up the food, young lady," he said.

"I only help," said Jolie. "Catherine's the real cook."

"Now you're being modest," said Maime.

Jolie impatiently twitched on the banister, listening for signs of James and the faint murmur of his thoughts.

She hopped down and turned to look out at the quiet of the encroaching night just as the front lamp on the lawn blinked on.

"I'll go see if I can find Martiel. Maybe she knows where James is," said Jolie, impatience written across her brow. "And don't squabble about the shrimp, it's not any trouble at all."

She tucked her fingers into her back jeans pockets as she quickly disappeared around the corner the porch, suppressing the urge to speed up her gait.

"That girl sure is unsettled," said Maime.

"Can you blame her?" Martin mumbled. "She's held up pretty good if you ask me."

The both slid slowly back next to each other in the center of the swing, Maime leaning her head on Martin's shoulder, "I don't know what I'd do if I were in her situation."

After an exhausting interview of faces, no one knew

where James was. Jolie hurried to her bedroom, looking for a quiet place to confirm what she felt earlier that day.

It must be true.

Her suspicions were a churning engine inside her.

She told herself that James was off on one of his expeditions to learn something about himself. That wasn't the truth and she was angry that it didn't take a premonition or a dream to let her know.

It was the very idea of him leaving her.

It had been right there in front of her in full display, getting plainer each day, until today. It was like a thinly covered painting, and now the canvas was exposed, its veil thrown back.

Surely he wouldn't leave without telling someone, the least of all her, not without saying goodbye.

Surely.

The night air was still, quiet, even peaceful. James was perched quietly outside Heaven's Gate Cemetery, not far from his physical body's resting place.

He glanced up at the stars and the cloudy scrim over a waning moon hovering above the horizon. During last summer's trip to Natchez, he had ventured roughly a mile down the railroad tracks near his grandparents' old house.

Seated on the rails in the dark, he had pondered the moon and stars and other things that bewildered him at the time. His life seemed such a mystery, full of promise, even with the chaos in his life back then.

Heaven's Gate Cemetery inhaled his phantom's laugh as

he yearned to return to that summer of '76, the year he turned sixteen.

Last summer - so far away.

A gentle tug woke him from his nostalgic pining and he turned to look deeper past the head stones and listing moss bagging from the trees.

There was something unnatural about his desire to return to his grave. Far too much had happened to him revolving around what lay six feet under the ground, beneath a large white crypt with his name emblazoned on a brass plate.

It held no secrets, only misery. He didn't need to walk up and touch the stones to remember the cold grain of their touch or the yanking sensation, pulling him downward.

His memory was a recorder. He only needed to prompt his thoughts and a replay of the experience would begin.

Again, he was reminded; he was here to decide, not rewind.

His choices were few. If he strayed too far from here in daylight, his strength faltered, his strength drained like a cheap battery.

The night however held that mysterious quality he had yet to understand. He could travel anywhere, as far away as he wanted, but if he stayed until daylight blossomed, he would have to wait there until darkness to return home.

If he could get far enough away during the night, when the sun came up he might..., who knew? He might just fade away into nothing.

It would be better than being stuck in the dark trap of

his grave, possibly alive and awake until judgment day.

Then he remembered his own words of warning to his family.

What if someone saw him? What if there were others like the voodoo woman out there somewhere?

There was a place he could go to ask and even though he probably wouldn't get answers about who he was or where to go, he could get one last impartial opinion and it was within walking distance.

CHAPTER 3

There was a hissing old radio tuned to a jazz or a blues station with its volume down low and the clear words of *Cry Me a River* pouring like cool water into the room.

The old man was wearing his usual black dress slacks and those huge shiny black oxfords James remembered from his last visit to the Holiness Cathedral Church.

The only thing different about the old pastor's looks was the relaxed thin white jersey undershirt instead of the hard starched white dress shirt, and maybe a few more gray hairs on his head.

The Pastor was humming along with the radio and sloshing some dishes around in a sink full of hot soapy suds in the modest kitchen.

The last time James visited the aging Pastor Baskin, he feared that he would kill him from fright, another blotch on his undead record.

Tonight was no different. He would knock on the door and announce himself.

The last time, he appeared at the front pew of the church and the pastor asked him if he was an angel; that was a scary thought.

The light above the outside parsonage door flicked on, instantly attracting a crew of moths to flitter and bang themselves to oblivion against a bare light bulb.

James heard the door-latch click and waited patiently while the old pastor decided to open his door.

"You!" he said instantly, his face turning pale.

"Please, don't be scared," said James, surrendering open palms.

Instantly James regretted coming and the phrase almost sounded biblical; *don't fear* echoed in his head.

"I suppose I should invite you inside?" the pastor asked reluctantly.

"Only if you have a few minutes to talk," said James, giving the old man an excuse to refuse.

"No, no, I got nothing pressing. Come on in," he sighed, drying his hands on a small dish towel.

Pastor Baskin walked over to the nearest chair and sat down.

James closed the door and joined him across a little round dining table, suddenly without a clue where to start.

"I did some praying since we last met," the pastor admitted.

"Get any answers?" asked James, to encourage the hopeful line of conversation.

"Some," he answered, nodding. "I've thought a lot about you since our last meeting, young man. So what brings you here?"

"Well...," James faltered, "I had several questions, but they don't seem as important as they did earlier. The main thing I'm trying to figure out is..., how to move on. You know what I mean? I'm stuck here Pastor."

"Have you asked anybody besides me?" asked the aged face, the implications were obvious.

"Yes," said James. "Several times. I got nothing."

Again, he declined to mention that he probably hadn't heard anything because of the whirlwind of events.

The pastor grunted, "Hmmp."

The old man sounded so much like his grampa Martin Earl it was eerie.

"See…, I'm not doing anybody any good," continued James. "In fact, there are others that know I'm here and they're having a hard time letting go of me."

"You feel those people that love you are holding you back?" he asked.

"No. I mean, I don't know," said James. "Maybe I'm just too scared to let *them* go. I can't decide. But it's not just them, Pastor, it's like…. I feel like some little ant running full speed in the red hot sand and something evil is chasing me around with the dot of a magnifying glass."

Pastor Baskin chuckled at some childhood memory, "I've felt the heat from that dot a few times myself, son. It can disorient you, trip you up, even knock the breath out of you. But even worse, it can cause you to make rash decisions you wouldn't make if you stopped and thought it all over."

The pastor looked at James somberly, the face of a father.

"Do you remember me telling you that you might have a mission or some unfinished business?" asked the Pastor.

James had replayed the recording of their exact detailed verbiage of their conversation many times over the past few weeks, verbatim.

"Yeah, I remember, but I don't want to rehearse all that. I just want you to tell me how to finish this. Do I go jump in my grave and lay there awake like this?" asked James.

"No, no, I believe the grave is supposed to be a peaceful sleep. That's the way my bible reads."

James stood up and wandered past the kitchen window, thinking he had made a mistake coming back to talk with the old pastor.

"You said you got a few answers," said James. "What kind of answers did you get?"

"You have a purpose," he said slowly. "Everything and everybody has a purpose..., a destiny. Including you. There are vessels of honor and vessels of dishonor but both are necessary in the Master's house. Even if you feel like you're nothing but the chamberpot, you still have a reason for being here and if you don't get too impatient, you'll eventually see what that purpose is."

"I'm not real good with patience," admitted James.

"You'd better get well acquainted," he chided. "I'm guessing that if you stay like you are, you're going to be here a long time, young man."

It sounded almost like something his Aunt Martiel had said.

That was the entire reason for coming here, to find out how to end this, not to prepare for the next hundred, five hundred..., or thousand years.

His heart sank into a puddle as he realized he was only seventeen years old trying to contemplate hundreds if not thousands of years..., alone.

This wasn't the answer he was looking for and this was going nowhere.

"Think of this as a gift," the pastor continued. "Use your time to help others."

"A gift!" James laughed sarcastically, before he could restrain himself.

Oh how he was sick of hearing that word.

Pastor Baskin jumped, obviously a little scared at the boy's reaction. The soft expression on his face quickly turned serious.

"You need to leave," said the pastor, struggling to stand.

His frustration began to weigh more than his curiosity concerning this strange apparition of a boy.

"I don't know who or what you are for sure, but I've given you the best advice I can with what I know. If that's not good enough, you need to leave," he said, pointing at the door.

"I..., I didn't mean to scare you," mumbled James.

Suddenly, the old man paled and coughed. He slid back down in his chair and his breathing became shallow.

'I knew I shouldn't have come here,' bounced inside James thoughts.

Suddenly, the old man wasn't moving and was breathing in small gasps.

"Hey," said James. "Are you okay?"

There was no answer from the pastor, verbally or from his thoughts. James drew close and listened to the old man's body. His heart was barely thumping and his mind was almost still.

He was dying.

It wasn't fair. He would go to that peaceful place and leave James here stuck among the living.

Not today.

James didn't understand how it worked or even if it would work again but it was worth a chance. He grasped the old man by the shoulders and concentrated, going inside himself, pulling out some of what he was and placing it in the pastor.

Pastor Baskin coughed, softly at first, then harder and gasped in a deep breath of air. His eyes popped open and he stared at James, realizing what had happened.

His heart was giving up on him, but somehow this boy, this ghost, brought him back.

"Can you hear me?" asked James.

"You're right in my face. Of course I can hear you," coughed the old man.

"You gave me a scare," said James. "If you think you're going to be okay, I'd better go."

"You brought me back," he said. "I was almost gone and you brought me back. I told you if you were patient you'd see who you are."

"I'm glad you're okay, Sir, but what if it was your time to go and I messed things up?" asked James nervously.

"Son, if it was my time to go, there's nothing you could have done to stop it," said Baskin.

James found something in his words. Hope, minuscule as a pinprick, and yet it seemed to soothe his indecision.

As soon as he relaxed, ugly foreign arguments crept in.

-Had he been looking for an excuse to stay all along?

-Was he looking for someone to agree with him?

He'd ruined his own life with decisions he'd made. This was his opportunity to step away and let Jolie live her life. Now, was he looking for someone to nudge him toward what he already wanted, so that the decision, right or wrong, would not be his responsibility?

James groaned it was so obvious; the decision was made. He was going to stay.

"I guess I could try to have some patience," griped James.

If he stayed, it meant going back to face Jolie, and it meant he would have to keep this visit a secret.

Could he go back and give into the desires of everyone around him?

James disappeared, leaving the pastor to his thoughts and experiences, ...and both of them a new heart.

CHAPTER 4

Jolie was seated alone in the upstairs bedroom that now bore the unofficial title of *Jolie's Room*, wondering if she should bother calling to James. It was a simple process. Light a single candle, envision the face of James swimming in the flame and call his name.

But why should she force him here? He obviously didn't want to be here. He didn't even have the courage to say goodbye to her. Everyone else was tired of hearing her pine over James; she was even tired of it.

Why couldn't she let go?

She couldn't seem to shake free of her feelings for him, simply because she really didn't want to be free.

Love was being hateful to her.

This other side of the coin was despicable, vile, disgraceful; even embarrassing.

She had locked her bedroom door, cleared off a little table and retrieved a candle to help her focus on the face of James. It didn't take much to picture him, she could probably call him, summon him without the tiny burning candle flame to drift into.

"No!" she spat.

She snapped the candle in half and threw it on the floor.

If he was so determined to rid himself of her, she wouldn't give him one more thought; not one single more.

Hardly a moment later, as her temper cooled and her passion rose, she scrambled to the floor retrieving the wax and began to try to squish the two stubby halves back together.

Hot tears dripped on her hands as she twisted and pushed at the wax until the candle was a crooked replica. She carefully lit a match and tried to seal the rejoined halves, burning her fingers with the flame.

She dropped it all on the table and kissed her scorned fingers.

How she wanted to curse, to stomp, to throw it all against the wall. How she missed James…, already.

"You won't need that," said James.

Jolie spun, startled and heated.

"Where were you?" she asked angrily, hiding the candle behind her.

"Getting some advice," he said quietly.

'He's been listening to my thoughts,' she thought angrily.

She felt exposed and empty with embarrassment.

"I'll knock next time," said James.

"You do that," she gritted, instantly wanting to pull back the hate in her voice.

"I thought you left," she said.

Her breath was short and she tasted the salt from her tears; she scraped at them in two hard swipes - further embarrassment.

She hated his indifference. How could he just choose to leave her despite her love for him, her need for him? Hadn't she exposed every last raw emotion? Splayed her bare heart out on the floor for him, for the whole world to see?

Was he now having second thoughts about leaving her? Was he showing her some kind of pity; an afterthought? Was that all she was to him, an afterthought?

She spun and dropped the candle in the wastebasket by the door.

"I came back," said James.

"Why?" she asked. "So you can bounce me on the ground again?"

"I was trying to find out how to stop..., bouncing you on the ground," said James.

"By leaving?" she smirked. "That makes perfect sense."

"Maybe," said James, carefully placing his words. "Maybe not."

"Errr," she gritted, knotting her fingers into fists.

James smiled despite himself.

He had taken a mental photograph of her standing in the middle of the open floor, feet apart, arms stiff at her sides with little knots for fists; and the look on her face was priceless.

She was as beautiful as the day he first met her at the library. What was he thinking? How could he exist without her?

It would be misery.

His growing smile was not construed as one of admiration by Jolie.

"Get out!" she yelled.

"That's the second time I've heard that tonight," said James.

"You'd better get used to it then," she said.

"We can talk tomorrow," said James.

"Maybe…. Maybe not," she mumbled.

'Patience,' thought James, as he disappeared without a whisper.

She stood for a moment listening to the silence in her room, then reached in the wastebasket and retrieved the battle-scarred candle, placing the pieces back on her dresser.

She wanted to call him back, to run calling his name down the hall, to bring him closer.

Jolie flung herself on the bed and buried her face in a pillow, to hide a squeaking growl.

She wanted….

Martin Earl Ames, the sole surviving patriarch of the Ames family, sat in solemn concentration on the front porch swing reading the Natchez Gazette. The subtle mention of "Under New Ownership" was hidden amongst many headlines on the front page, yet it drew a slim smile on his aging lips.

Imagine that…. His family owned a newspaper and the chief editor had to pass any controversial headlines through him for approval. No more heated phone calls or emblazoned letters to the editor….

"What are you grinning about?" asked Maime Ames, her hands busy with some knitty craft.

"I'm not grinning," barked Martin, almost to himself.

"I saw it," confirmed Maime, her eyes darting back down.

"Hmpf," he mumbled back.

The crackle of tires on the pea-gravel drive interrupted their would-be controversy.

"Oh, Lord. Not Bethany, not now," said Martin.

Bethany Monroe was Martin and Martiel's older sister and after her most recent visit, the welcome mat had been completely removed from the front doorsteps. Then it dawned on him..., Bethany would have no discernable reason to return, not after....

Martin Earl dropped his paper on the hanging porch swing and stood, watching the gleaming black limousine pull up and park near the front of the Estate. This didn't look like his sister Bethany.

As soon as the long car stopped, the chauffer, a slim young man, jumped out of the drivers' seat and briskly headed to the rear passenger-side door. His black suit and cabby styled hat bounced as he engaged the door handle for the passengers inside.

The frown deepened across Martin Earl Ames' forehead.

Out stepped a short middle-aged man in what looked to be an expensive gray suit. Before moving, he turned his face this way and that, exploring the lay of the property, then peered upwards along one of the many Greek revival pillars to the expanse of the looming veranda above.

Another suit-clad tree of a man emerged from the car behind him and became an iron statue with folded arms.

"Martin, is this someone from the newspaper?" asked Maime.

"It sure isn't my sister," said Martin.

A troubled look flashed across his forehead for another instant. Could his wife be right? The quick purchase of the Natchez Gazette had taken everyone by surprise. Martiel Ellington was noted for making rash decisions without consulting anyone. Had she yanked the local newspaper out from under someone else's disgruntled vying bid? A second glance, Martin decided not. These men didn't look like they were here to discuss anything.

The stranger ambled thoughtfully across the expanse of the front lawn, then slowly climbed the first two porch steps just below where Martin Earl was standing and halted as if testing the air.

The visitor looked up at the gray haired older man looming above him who seemed nonplussed by his sudden visit; obviously this old man didn't know the meaning of respect. It didn't matter. He'd spent most of his lifetime teaching others the meaning of respect.

"Are you Mr. Ames?" he wheezed.

Martin Ames noted the air of authority as well as a shallowly hidden and unfamiliar accent.

His ice blue eyes were burning into Martin and for a short moment, Martin wished he had his new shotgun resting in his arms.

"Yes, I'm Martin Ames," he answered. "How can I help you?"

"I understand you have a young lady, Jolie Dimanche, residing with you. May I have a word with her?" he asked, but it sounded more of a demand.

He pulled out a handkerchief and dotted his forehead, waiting. The old man hadn't budged from his blockade above him; it was such an irritation.

"And you are...," said Martin.

"Damien Dimanche."

His chin raked against the knot of his necktie and he cleared his throat, "Her father."

His face was hard and his smile had long forgotten the path to his piercing eyes.

'That's right, *balordo vecchio*,' thought Damien.

"Her father? What a surprise. Jolie's a wonderful young lady," said Martin cautiously.

Something told him this wasn't the usual social call. Otherwise, he'd have automatically stepped down, offered a hand, and began a barrage of casual questions. Instead, Martin Earl stood his ground and looked around at his wife who was already on her way to find Jolie.

"Would you like to come inside where it's cooler?" offered Martin.

"Here is fine, thank you. I don't intend to take up much of your time."

CHAPTER 5

It was Samuel Earl Williams who heard the vehicle's tires popping along the drive and hurried into the library to peer out one of the many front windows.

James was already planted there when his brother Sam arrived, and had been since the limousine stopped and regurgitated its passengers onto the lawn.

"Ho-lee crap!" barked Sam.

It was James who suddenly seemed concerned, hushing his younger brothers' excitement.

"Keep your voice down," said James.

He was thankful that his grandfather couldn't read the visitors thoughts.

"It's Al Capone, minus the fedora and pinstripes," whispered Sam.

A bitter cup of revelation began to pour into James as he concentrated on the stranger in the expensive suit. His Aunt Martiel had offered to have a similar one fitted for him..., back when he was still breathing free air.

James nodded, "He may not have on the garb, but that's not far from the truth little brother."

He probed past the first level of the man's conscious thoughts, searching.... It was mix of English and some other tongue, something European, but the meanings were universal.

James backed away from the window slowly, still listening, yet dumbstruck into a stupor.

Why didn't Jolie tell him?

Yes, her parents were divorced.

Yes, they lived at separate ends of the continent, but that was where the truth of her life derailed into a phenomenal catastrophe.

Maime walked in the front door and scuttled nervously to where the breakfast club was still mingling in the kitchen.

"Jolie?" called Maime.

Her eyes scooted frantically across the room, her voice stressed beyond the last few days of peace in the Ames household.

"Mother, are you okay?" asked Catherine. Something had her mother on edge, sending out an alarm.

"Where's Jolie?" she asked again, waving away her daughter's concern.

Jolie walked in from the other door, her flushed cheeks betraying freshly wiped tears.

"You have a visitor," said Maime. "Your father is here."

Maime's dark eyes buried themselves in a concentrated stare almost as quickly as Martiel's expression went pale.

"Her father?" said Catherine, in a desperate attempt at an explanation. "That's wonderful...! Isn't it? Jolie? Sweetheart, are you alright?"

Catherine walked closer to support Jolie's wobbling frame. One hand on her shoulder, one on her back - the young girl was shaking. Catherine wanted to retract her impulsive comments and offer some sort of refuge when

Jolie's frightened blue eyes went blank.

Jolie's face fell, "My..., My father is here," she repeated Maime's words, letting them heap into something flat.

Maime glanced at her daughter Catherine and with a quick shake of her head insinuated this particular visit probably wasn't the wonderful reunion she had initially envisioned.

Jolie began moving leadenly toward the door, unmistakably as a prisoner to the gallows.

"How did he find me?" she whispered to herself, suddenly her thoughts flashed to her Aunt BeBe.

"Jolie, what's wrong dear?" asked Catherine. The young girl had already won a place in her heart, quickly becoming a daughter.

Jolie turned and looked at the trio of women for an instant. It was as if she wanted to say something; to have them make her feet stop walking. She knew it was too late for that – *he* had found her. By now her father knew she was inside the house.

Martiel listened intently with her other worldly sense, her *gift* as she called it, an inherited genetic ability to peer into the thoughts of others. She probed the unbridled clatter radiating from Jolie's mind, but couldn't believe the spew.

The herd of women slowly followed several paces behind Jolie as she zombied toward the sound of Martin Earl's one-sided conversation drifting in through the open front door.

Martiel gently tugged Maime and Catherine to a halt, back where they could listen and observe, instead of interrupting what was about to take place.

The beaming golden sunlight pouring in the front door gave Jolie the illusion of a portal into another world.

"Daddy?" she said timidly, the moment she stepped out onto the deep front porch.

"*Mia Fiore, My Flower,*" he repeated in English, as if his daughter wouldn't understand his wheezy Italian dialect.

He opened his arms in an uneven stance waiting for her to come to him. It was as cold, stiff, and as rehearsed as a vaudeville scene.

A puff of breeze whipped her long hair across her face, but she didn't seem to notice. The mind-numbing reality of who had shown up on the doorstep had her locked in evil memories.

Jolie came out of her momentary stupor, wanting to turn and run back inside the house. Damien's sapphire blue eyes locked with his daughter's, drawing her feet forward into another trancelike motion.

They met halfway up the steps in a hug; the expensive suit crunched against his iron tight chest and the scent of stale cologne brought back even more memories.

She dodged his kiss after feeling the press of hard metal holstered tightly against his left side.

Jolie pushed back and the embrace was over much too quickly for feelings to pass between them; far too quickly considering the many years they had been estranged.

"Are you ready to come home?" he asked, sweeping his hand grandly toward the stretch limousine.

"Maybe visit with your *mamma*?" he grinned sarcastically.

Jolie felt her insides turn to jelly and managed one step back up toward the porch. Somewhere behind her was safety.

A charred smile was pasted on Damien's face, but his thoughts spat, '*Entrare le dannato limousine!*'

Jolie heard him think, "*Get in the damn car*" and felt as if she had been slapped, barely managing to keep her surprise from showing.

One of the many things her father didn't know about her was the passing on of the family torch, her supernatural gifts, the thing which had drawn her to James Earl.

"Home?" asked Jolie. "What do you mean? I am home."

"With me, *sìa già*," he feigned a hurt look.

"Daddy, my home is with Aunt BeBe now," she said. "We discussed this before *mamma* and I left. Don't you remember?"

Actually, Jolie barely remembered the conversation herself. She was just a little thing when her mother escaped the clutches of this overbearing man.

The quite demeanor exited and her father's business face emerged with that same voice Jolie had heard many times as a little girl.

"*YOU*... discussed this right before *YOU* and your *mamma* ran away," he choked out, coughing some spittle. "*Pensaci*! That's what I remember! *Tu e vostra mamma*...."

He stepped back in anger, his Italian accent becoming vicious, betraying *his* particular *family* heritage.

"Leave *mamma* out of this," said Jolie, also retreating another step of the stairs. Terror began to grip her heart;

it was her childhood all over again. Her father, screaming at her mother, backhanded slaps, but to show any sign of weakness to him was a deathblow.

She was now looking downward on her father's face, something that she remembered he despised. More evil memories resurrected and Jolie hardened her heart.

Damien Dimanche dotted his forehead once again as his frustration arose with the morning humidity, then he looked down at the division of steps between them in contemplation.

One by one, the other Ames family members began to assemble behind Martin Earl.

"*Ficcanaso e balordo*" he mumbled, grasping at the hair on the nap of his neck.

He had too many witnesses to the forthcoming potential exchange between father and daughter to allow any indulgence and put away his handkerchief.

"Okay," he smiled at the gatherers.

Sunshine was illuminating their assorted faces in the last hues of morning sunrise – all were trained on him – he'd have to kill them all if he lost his patience this easily.

Jolie felt the small hairs on the back of her neck rise as another memory accompanied the smiling expression on her father's face. The look she'd seen once, just before he reached beyond his suit and retrieved a killing weapon.

"Look…, uh…," his right arm waved in little circles. "I'll be in *città* for the day. *Ci Pensati*, I'll be back, uh…, *domattina* to pick you up," said Damien.

"I've thought it over already, *Daddy*," said Jolie, unmistakable contempt in her hardening voice.

"Talk to your *Zia* BeBe. She'll explain things to you," he grinned.

'That's right,' he thought, watching the expected shock come over Jolie's face, 'I'll play your silly little game for a day.'

He turned to walk away, bringing an end to their confrontation.

"Aunt BeBe isn't going to change my mind," Jolie flung at his back while he was retreating. "You're wasting your time."

He shook a hand in the air as each man slid in rehearsed order back into the limousine. It sat there idling for several moments, its blackened windows hiding everyone but the chauffeurs nodding head.

As soon as Jolie stumbled up the last step behind her, close against the throng of the Ames family, the coach eased out of the driveway.

The family gathering stood frozen in time, gradually turning their gaze from the exiting limousine to Jolie.

"Oh... my... Gaawd," whispered Martiel, clasping her hands under her chin. "Out of the fire and into the frying pan."

The conversation in the limousine was practically non-existent, but there was enough clatter going on inside each passenger's mind to paint a sordid picture.

Also inside was an extra passenger, listening carefully to each word spoken, each fletched thought waiting to be launched at the slightest provocation.

James felt that same cold inching up around him, the

chill of death which was clinging to the men inside the circular lounge. It was Jolie's father he was most interested in, he was the threat.

Damien Dimanche's thoughts were a blathering stream of his native tongue, but his thoughts were visceral, leaving nothing to the imagination. Damien Dimanche had seemingly arrived for one single-minded purpose, to retrieve his estranged daughter, and use her to regain something he had lost.

That's where Damien's thoughts turned bloodthirsty, but James couldn't root out that all-important something. As he listened to the choppy banter, there was no mention of his desire to reunite himself as a parent and father to Jolie. The entire meeting was a ploy, some odd diversion, something to do with Jolie's mother, Regina Dimanche.

Finally, the limousine pulled up the incline in front of a floating hotel and casino along the waterfront.

The first man slid out the back passenger door before the chauffeur killed the engine, looking around in a quick expert sweep beyond the emerald green covering of the valet drop.

Damien stepped out next, a row of diamond-studded rings flashed brilliantly on his left hand against the overcast sun as he straightened his lapel, then his tie. He smiled at his reflection in the tinted car window and slipped on black sunshades.

His apparent vanity screamed money and the desire to flaunt it. The rest of his envoy slid out into the hot sun, including a fourth man that had not shown himself at the Ames Estate.

Three bodyguards made their relaxed pretense of vacationing gamblers realistic, but their eyes were trained in every direction, watching for anything out of the ordinary.

It was impossible for a man such as Damien Dimanche to go anywhere without someone of his opposition being informed. He was a powerful man with powerful enemies, which meant that whatever he had lost, whatever he was after, was also very valuable to him.

Sadly…, it wasn't Jolie he deemed of such great worth although his daughter was definitely the focus of this conquest.

CHAPTER 6

Inside the old Ames mansion, the stares from each face around the crowded living room were as tangible as needles delicately pricking Jolie's nerves.

Jolie waited, hiding behind a sad attempt of a mask, until she could stand the torment no longer.

"You called him?" Jolie burst out in a whine. "Why on earth would you call *him*?"

"You were kidnapped at the time, remember?" said Martiel. "BeBe thought your father could help."

It was suffocating. Instantly Jolie was back in the derelict boat where James had found her, dangling by her wrists in oily water, her blood-matted hair glued to her face, waiting to be eaten by....

"Oh, God..., no Aunt BeBe *didn't* think," said Jolie, unconsciously rubbing her wrists.

The rope burns from her ordeal had left an ugly discolored reminder below the skin, even though the pain was gone and the scars healed.

Martiel frowned for an instant, "When your mother didn't call us back, we tried to reach your father. We didn't know...."

"Aunt BeBe knew," whined Jolie. "She knew my father was nothing but trouble. James dealt with the situation. What was she thinking?"

Memories erupted once again; that crooked little stick pressing behind her neck, forcing her chin to her chest.

If it hadn't been for James she would be dead. He became her savior; found her, somehow..., in her desperation, and rescued her from a gruesome end. Now she was wishing he'd been a little late....

"We love you Jolie. We're all here for you," said Catherine. Then after watching Jolie's desperation lift, she decided to offer a voice of reason. "You can talk it over with BeBe when she gets here."

It was endearing, even sweet, but Jolie didn't need *sweet*, she needed to get away. She had no other safe heaven than her Aunt BeBe at the moment..., even distant cousins would be easy enough for her father to track down. Then he'd start watching her again, from a distance, as if she didn't know or couldn't feel the eyes on her.

"There's nothing to talk about," said Jolie, as she stood and began to pace in a circle. "I've got..., to get..., out of here," she mumbled. She was struggling for each breath and making herself dizzy in the process.

Her heart plunged. What was James going to think about her now? It was obvious he was already trying to find a way to free himself of her.

"I'm confused Jolie. Ten minutes before your father arrived you were crying about staying here with James," said Catherine.

"What else are you hiding?" asked Martiel. "I never suspected you for a conniver!"

"I am *not* a conniver!" snapped Jolie. "It was safer that

no one knew about that part of my family. You saw him! What do you think I should have done? Hey everybody, meet my father. Oh by the way, he makes people *disappear* from time to time, just part of the family business."

Her mind was spinning, making her stomach churn, "I'm wasting time. I need to get far away from here before he comes back tomorrow."

Jolie suddenly froze with dread when she heard James walk in the room. Her body jerked softly, then her stomach clenched as she hid her involuntary desire to break into tears.

"Jolie, calm down," said James.

She was near fainting and as he placed a hand on her shoulder she felt warm, even comforted.

"Didn't you know you could tell me?"

"No James, I couldn't. I was hiding from my father."

Her heart was still racing and she still couldn't look James in the eyes.

"So all those things you told me...," said James.

"I *had* to lie to you. Don't you see? After everything you told me that happened to you and Sam. I was afraid you'd hate me, just because of my family, and who I am."

"Well you certainly are full of surprises," said Martiel. "I think I may need a drink...."

She glanced innocently over at her brother Martin and his wife Maime, then smirked, "*Of tea*, I suppose...."

"Do you want me to deal with your father?" asked James.

Catherine sniffed and then began to laugh, hands raised

in the air, "Did I hear you right? Did my son just ask permission to get involved?"

Martiel fought back a snicker at the irony of the situation.

Out of nowhere, Sam blurted, "Wow, your girlfriend is a daughter of *the family*? From our old neighborhood? How cool is that?"

Jolie slumped down in the nearest sofa as the last of her strength abandoned her legs. She glanced quickly around, facing their accusations in silence.

A distant rapping at the front door became the focus of attention and the two eldest of the group left the gathering, temporarily saving Jolie from the stack of building questions damming up in the living room.

Moments later, Martin Earl and Maime escorted BeBe Cavalier in among the awaiting group.

The elders drawn faces spoke volumes, but surprisingly kept silent, cautiously listening as if testing the temperature of the room.

"Your mother just called me," said BeBe, dropping her heavily bangled purse beside her. "She's on her way."

"No! Call her back, now!" Jolie yelled. "Before she leaves, you have to tell her. That's exactly what my father wants. He's using me to find *her*!"

"Your mama could slip through a crack in the wall if she wants to see you, Jolie. You already know that," BeBe said, frowning.

"Aunt BeBe, my daddy will be watching everywhere I go from now on."

"Jolie's right," agreed James. "Damien was barking all

kinds of orders about watching the house when I left his hotel room."

BeBe grunted, shaking her head, then grabbed her jingling purse and dug out a notepad, hurrying toward the telephone. Moments later she was on the phone with Regina Dimanche.

"Here, talk to your daughter," said BeBe into the receiver.

Jolie slowly raised her forehead from her open palms in tearful resignation.

"It appears that my benefactors failed to forewarn me of someone with your particular talents, Miss Dimanche," scowled Martiel.

Martiel Ellington dazed off into memories of her lifelong training from the recently *twice* departed family and the generational gifts thrust upon her.

It was tiring to recall her initial reluctance of accepting the ability to see their departed family at first, at only five years of age. She remembered the sad look on her father's face when he understood that his youngest daughter was next in line instead of her brother Martin Earl. Knowing that his little girl's life would never be normal, never having regular friends, all because she would know what others were actually thinking about her.

Then there were all the secrets.

She was destined to have many secluded conversations in an upstairs bedroom with the ghosts of several generations of Ames. During those formative years more gifts developed and became stronger, especially the more prevalent one of hearing the thoughts of others.

She sighed over her feelings for nephew James, who was destined to be her protégé and replacement. James Earl Williams was developing such potential before his - *incident.*

In a moment of revelation, Martiel realized that the subject of Jolie's past and family..., simply never came up.

Was BeBe really her aunt?

Martiel snapped back into focus the moment that BeBe stepped directly into her view, demanding her attention.

"I can only hear bits and pieces of what you were thinking. To answer your question.... Yes, I am her aunt," said BeBe. "I don't have the ability to hide my thoughts like Jolie *and a few others here,* so I kept myself focused on other things."

James was getting tired of the merry-go-round of questions and accusations that were leading nowhere and offering no solutions. He placed both hands on Jolie's shoulders, trying to diffuse her discomfort.

"That's why you don't sound Cajun," he whispered in Jolie's ear. Surely Jolie would remember one of their lively conversations from when they first met.

"Cajun on my mother's side," said Jolie timidly. "Italian on my fathers'."

It was working. The tension in her shoulders softened until....

Sam had been hovering, quietly containing his excitement to the point of explosion while exploring Jolie's every feature.

"Wow, she's from one of the families that ran the

streets where we grew up," hissed Sam. "The same ones!"

Sam stood brazenly, inspecting Jolie, the canary in a cage. He and James had seen a few members of the crime families several times during their childhood.

"Of course, the black hair, and blue eyes!"

"Samuel, *please*. Settle down," said Martin Earl, embarrassed and even blushing at his grandson's outburst.

He skewed a glance over at James to keep him from exploding on his brother Sam. It was time someone put an end to this kangaroo court.

Martin Earl had participated in far too many railroad sessions in juries, town council meetings, church board meetings, and unfortunately family gatherings. It didn't take special gifts to see that Jolie was on the brink of crumbling. His heart suddenly poured out for her broken spirit.

"Young lady, we don't choose our family like we choose our friends. We are who we are, we don't get to pick. Nobody's blaming you for anything. Lord knows this bunch kept plenty of secrets and told enough lies over the years. We've got no stones to throw."

He looked directly at his sister Martiel in emphasis.

Martin sighed breathily before continuing, "We all see you as a part of our family now."

Jolie felt herself sweep the room, at each of the faces and saw their expressions shift from questions to concern, but it was more than that. Suddenly, she didn't feel the cold distant rejection that always persisted during the family conversations of her childhood.

"When Jolie was missing and Damien didn't show up, I assumed…, actually I hoped, that something had happened to him, you know, maybe…. I know that's wrong," BeBe said, shaking her head. "Jolie was almost nine, such a tiny little thing when she and her mother left Damien. He was just promoted to *capo bastone* in the organization."

BeBe grinned at the private joke. *Capo* in Italian meant boss, but in her native Cajun, *capo* meant coward.

"Gina, actually its Regina, that's Jolie's mother…. She knew it was time to get out. The abuse was getting worse the deeper Damien got involved with the family business. So, she divorced him and took Jolie with her. Damien never recognized the divorce, neither did the family. It wasn't the *family way*."

"Let me get this straight," said Martin Earl, trying to understand every detail before offering any elderly wisdom. "Jolie and her mother were in hiding from the Dimanche family?"

"Hiding with extreme prejudice it seems," said Martiel, sipping her fresh glass of iced tea.

"Martiel, that's enough," said Martin.

"My mother was hiding," stressed Jolie. "My father knew where I was the whole time, watching me from a distance. He just left me alone."

CHAPTER 7

The vast cavity of the living room had cleared and the feeling of suffocation was beginning to lift from Jolie's mind. James waited directly across from where Jolie was seated in an attempt at consoling her and to get as much information about her father as possible.

"I rode with your father after they left," admitted James.

Jolie sat blankly, unaffected.

"I assumed as much," she sneered. "I can just imagine what you heard."

Angered embarrassment flushed color into her cheeks, but if it took embarrassment to compel Jolie to open up, then it would be worth her momentary discomfort.

"He doesn't intend to take no for an answer, Jolie," said James. "I just want to help. I couldn't really understand their conversation but his thoughts were.... They were so violent and..., *creative.*"

"I can't believe you would use *creative* to describe my father's methods," she replied, still angry.

"I'm not sure how to get them to leave town, but I did make their visit less comfortable. I took their luggage and their guns and tossed them in the river," said James. "They're not likely to report them stolen."

"That's only going to make him mad," sighed Jolie. "And more cautious and more determined."

"We have to do something and we have to do it before tomorrow morning," said James.

Damien Dimanche had visualized several alternatives of making BeBe and as well as all the Ames family disappear so that it would look like an accident.

What was even crazier, he could possibly pull it off, knowing how ill-equipped the local law enforcement really was.

James recalled one of his conversations with Jolie. Was it only a few weeks ago? The warm summer night in front of his grandparent's house was so peaceful and the intimacy he felt with her sitting on the sweet smelling lawn by his side. It seemed a lifetime ago and indeed, for him, it was.

The short weeks before his death, he had poured out his most private secrets to Jolie, revealing his childhood and the evils of the New Jersey neighborhood gangs. It had been an intimacy of events intended for Jolie to understand who he was and....

No wonder she didn't seem disgusted the way he believed she would. Jolie had been so understanding; so quiet.

The gruesome details of his childhood he was so reluctant to describe to her..., she must have heard many similar stories. Even at her young age, she must have heard rumors and whispers about her fathers' business.

She had to know, how could he have been so stupid? Then he remembered he wasn't exactly in the frame of mind to notice anything but his own despair at the time. His life had just been thrown in a blender set to "high".

Jolie remained silent, listening to James' thoughts and emotions. Silent because she knew that sometime in the future she might have to give an account to James for much more.

Suddenly an epiphany of the situation confronted James.

For the last several weeks, he fought an evil, a curse so diabolical that it had claimed his life and left him as something not quite dead and not quite alive. Thoughts flashed furiously in recollection of the ages old hoodoo woman Lyda Brown and her deceptions.

All of those events were foreign to James, an unknown so strange that he groped through it blindly; those deadly decisions altered his future forever.

Normally, the gloom of those battles would start the ever-present replay of darkness he had no desire to endure.

Not this time!

He and his brother Sam cut their baby teeth with the streets and gangs, under the very noses of their unobservant parents.

Dirty cops and judges, paid to look the other direction were a way of life. Cut throats, thieves, drugs, hiding places....

This time he had the advantage.

When he looked back at Jolie, at the intensity of her stare, she was trying to get inside and almost succeeding.

"What were you just thinking?" asked Jolie. "Are you keeping me out, out of your thoughts now?"

"For now," he answered, kissing her on the forehead.

Martin Earl Ames took a tentative sip from his cup of coffee as the front porch swing creaked beneath him. He wanted a few minutes of privacy to think, but everyone seemed to be following his every step. It was annoying; just as well, they might as well understand what was on his mind.

Maime and Catherine, increasingly concerned over his welfare, had followed him out to his usual escape.

After several moments of contemplative thought, he raised his bushy eyebrows and began to speak privately with his wife and daughter.

"You know, I've come to terms with what's happened to James
Earl, as much as I can that is. I've even begun to accept the fact that our family history was tied up with some backwoods black magic voodoo."

He became silent and stared blankly into the distance.

Another sip of coffee and his brow drew deep painful furrows, then he continued, "But the fact that almost everyone around us reads minds, sees future events, and God only knows what else, is more than I can handle."

Martin looked over his shoulder to see who might be lurking just out of sight. When he was reasonably sure that they were still alone for the moment, he silently wished that he had burned down the Ames Estate years ago. He had so many chances to rid himself of his childhood fears, to rid himself of the inexplicable feelings while inside the old mansion.

The years when he was a child growing up in the old

house, he knew things weren't right. Things were off; noises, voices, and happenings were commonplace. As a child, he wouldn't dare venture upstairs for any reason.

Then came the day when his little sister Martiel Ames became strange and reclusive. He thought something bad had happened to her, and he was always questioning her. The not knowing was bad, but he now realized that the knowing would have been far worse!

Another sip of coffee and he grunted and shook his head.

"But it sure explains a lot of things."

Maime and his daughter Catherine sat quietly listening to the ramblings of the last surviving male Ames in their estranged family.

The chain of the porch swing creaked again and broke their trancelike state as Martiel walked out onto the porch, with a spry expression on her face.

"How about a vacation?" she asked, looking at her brother Martin.

"Someplace warm and sunny, with a cool breeze," she elaborated.

"Didn't you say that we could take a vacation?" asked Maime, looking expectantly at her husband.

Martin Earl stared down at the swirls in the bottom of his coffee cup, remembering the circumstances surrounding his earlier promise. Vivid memories of his wife lying against the wall in their dark hallway, bleeding from a deep cut on her arm. How close he came to losing her swept over him.

"Daddy, that's a wonderful idea," agreed Catherine.

Apparently she caught the gist of what Martiel was trying to accomplish.

It was his daughter Catherine's voice that snapped Martin back to attention.

"I have a friend that can book you a cruise today to see places you've only heard about," Martiel prodded further.

Martin Earl grunted and leaned forward in the porch swing.

"You may have abilities that I don't understand, Martiel, but I wasn't born yesterday. I know when someone is trying to get rid of me."

"Not get rid of you, exactly," whined Martiel in her southern drawl. "It's just to make sure that you and Maime don't have to go through another nasty ordeal like the one we all just went through."

"I can't up and leave here with this Damien character..., running around like he owns everybody he meets. Jolie and BeBe are just like family now. They need my help; they need all our help."

"That's exactly why I want you both to get away from all this, stretch your legs, get out and see the world," she nudged further.

Martin Earl's eyes became steel as he glared at his younger sister.

"I see..., you think that if Maime and I stay, we will be a liability."

Martiel sighed, "I'm saying..., if you really want to help, it would be best if you took Maime on a nice long *safe* vacation."

"So your answer to all this is for our family to scatter

like a covey of quail?" asked Martin.

"Sometimes, Martin Earl, a show of numbers and a show of force is a liability. The smaller the numbers, the smaller the target."

Martin studied her words carefully, "A smaller target...."

"A smaller target," she repeated.

Martiel visibly relaxed when older brother dropped his petulant stare.

"Are you suggesting that there will be more violence?" asked Maime.

Her question was answered with acute silence.

Catherine waited quietly, watching the expressions on her parents' faces. Her father would not give in easily, but if anyone had a chance of persuading him, it was Martiel Ellington.

Once she had begun her suasive rant, she rarely lost a debate if given enough time to employ all her wiles.

Martin Earl stood and stretched, handing his empty cup to Catherine's outstretched hand.

"I need to talk to James," said Martin, glaring at Martiel. "Alone."

As the front door closed, Martiel spoke toward him, "There's more to life than Natchez, Mississippi, Martin Earl."

CHAPTER 8

Samuel Earl had become his brother's keeper, whenever Jolie wasn't crowding his attention. That was the majority of the time. Having his brother back from the grave in any form was acceptable at this point. James had been the only person alive which shared all the trials of their youth, even the unspeakable ones.

"What do you have planned?" asked Sam.

"I don't know. I'm still working on it," said James quietly. "I can't really do anything until we get Grampa and Gramma in a safe place. Aunt Martiel promised to work on that."

"What about Jolie and her aunt?" asked Sam.

"I'm working on that with mom. Don't get too carried away Sam. If I've learned anything in the last few weeks, it's not to get in a hurry and spread myself too thin."

"Yeah, but dude, you're like the ultimate spy."

Sam struck a boxers stance, pulling his fists up, and popping at the air.

"You can just go in and wipe'em all out," gritted Sam excitedly.

"Sam, you don't know what you're talking about... death is...," James fell silent.

"Sorry man," he mumbled. "Open mouth, insert foot."

"Hey, it's okay bro, no harm done," said James. The last

thing he wanted was to cause a rift between him and his brother. Sam was the only other person on the planet that had always taken his side and always accepted him as he was without question.

"Do you remember back when we watched the older members of *The Hand* beat that kid to death?" asked James. "It's like that same feeling, that helpless feeling, only when it's you that's dealing the beating, a kind of rage takes over...."

"When you know you can do it..., kill somebody that is.... Once you let it in, it's like a drug. You start justifying what you want to do; you tell yourself you're right, even when you know you're wrong. You understand? I've seen it, felt it. And that my friend is messed up."

James didn't want to remind Sam that he was referring the moment before he almost killed the gang member that had Sam pinned to the wall in an alley. It almost cost him years of his life in a juvenile facility, but instead he got several years of probation, thanks to his Aunt Martiel.

James had nightmares reliving that moment. But silently he was always more terrified at the thought of what could have happened to Sam if he hadn't seen him being dragged into an alley.

"It's uncontrollable," said James after some thoughtful hesitation.

"Bummer," said Sam. "So how do we stop them without..., you know?"

His younger brother's insistence was becoming a frustration. He'd stepped away from the others to have a few minutes to reflect and plan, but as always..., "I'll just have to be creative Sam. As Aunt Martiel would say, there's more than one way to skin a cat."

"That's gross," snarled Sam. "And you're worried about me?"

"Figure of speech. You let me worry about what to do with them. You know how they operate on the streets, it won't be much different."

"Fear tactics," nodded Sam. "I remember when..."

"Fear tactics was their way of recruiting and controlling," said James, cutting him off. "This will be different."

Before Sam could blurt the next of an endless list of questions bubbling up in his mind....

"Grampa's coming," said James. "He wants to talk. Do you care if I talk to him alone?"

Sam nodded his head about the same time that Martin Earl called for James.

There were lines of age beginning to show on his grandfather's face. That was something new. The speckled gray in his hair and wiry eyebrows had always looked the same to James Earl, or they had crept forward so slowly that he never noticed until now.

Martin Earl strolled slowly toward the back of their property, with James at his side. It was one of the few places he felt he wouldn't be pestered by his new following.

For several minutes, there was only the bright orange glow of the late afternoon sun and the sounds of nature between them.

As a child, Martin Earl Ames took this same walk, bringing to mind several man-to-man talks with his father, John Earl Ames. Some talks were good, some were troubled, but all a part of the learning process. Funny though, it still seemed that he was the one in search of answers.

Martin looked up from the path, toward the pond where he and Sam had gone fishing recently. That jaunt was cut short and replaced with the memory of the hard thump on the back of his head and darkness, as he fell face-first into the cool dark depths of the pond water.

Martin Earl rubbed the back of his head subconsciously.

"Grampa, don't worry," said James, breaking the silence.

Martin continued his walk around to the pier and found a comfortable place to sit on its gray weathered boards.

"It's the nature of the beast," said Martin. "Worrying is just something that us old folks do from time to time."

Before James could start trying to answer all the questions he had heard from his grandfather's thoughts, Martin Earl caught James by surprise.

"What's it like, James?" he asked. "In the afterlife I mean."

"I don't know," said James. "I'm still here with you. I haven't seen anything of an afterlife like I thought I would."

"You know you're messing up my theology, James," grinned Martin.

"Nothings like I thought it would be either."

James struggled with the urge to reveal some of the things he had experienced, but wisdom won the battle.

"Grampa, is that why you stopped going to church the last few weeks?"

"Of course not James. My religion may have taken a beating, but my faith hasn't budged. I needed some time to sort things out, to see what's really important with my life."

Martin Earl returned to his line of questions.

"Have you had any encounter with God or..., you know...?" he asked cautiously, his eyes becoming round.

His query was almost verbatim to the old pastor James had nearly frightened to death on a couple of occasions.

"The only thing I've met after what happened to me, I don't want to tell you about, Grampa," said James.

"Ghosts?" he mused, with raised eyebrows.

This made James grin as he shook his head no, "Not really."

It wasn't a huge lie. He hadn't cavorted with any spirits of the dead since the battle over his soul. Silently James was thankful his grampa didn't have a penchant for zombies. He had seen a few of them, and was actually responsible for a few.

"Hmmmpf," grunted Martin. "So it's not all it's cracked up to be..., life after death I mean."

"Grampa, this isn't...," stammered James, getting frustrated. "I don't know how to tell you what this is like. This isn't the afterlife. I'm not quite dead..., at least not yet."

Martin looked at James, "...and not quite alive. I can see that."

It was then he remembered to have patience.

"As best as I can figure, I'm kind of stuck here, in between." His grampa didn't seem to understand what he was trying to tell him or he wasn't good at explanations.

Martin took a few moments and gave the answer some consideration.

"Can you protect Jolie and her Aunt?" asked Martin. Then out of nowhere. "Have you ever hurt anybody, James? You know you might be forced to do something *permanent* to this fellow, to keep him from coming back."

"I can keep them safe, but I don't plan on killing anybody," said James.

"These people, Jolie's father and such. What kind of people are they?" asked Martin. It was more of a rhetorical question. James knew where he was heading.

"Bad. The worst kind," James admitted, his voice falling.

Martin had been avoiding looking James in the face, but finally their eyes met in sincerity, "Worse than that voodoo woman and her hoodlums?"

"I know what you are driving at, grampa. I know this kind of people. I didn't have any idea what I was doing with Lyda Brown. In fact I don't think it would have mattered if I had known. I don't think it would have changed the way everything turned out."

"But you think you do know these people?"

"I grew up dealing with these people," said James.

Martin sighed deeply with sounds of regrets.

"If only I could have convinced your mother to come back here when all that trouble with you and Sam started."

"It wouldn't have changed a thing, grampa," said James. "The fact that I did have to deal with the street gangs back then helps me now."

Martin grunted a little as he stood back up on the creaky boards.

"Your Gramma and I are going on a vacation," he said finally, with some reluctance. "Are you going to be able to take care of Martiel and the rest? She's not as unbreakable as she thinks she is."

CHAPTER 9

The front bedroom was lit with the warm yellow glow of several lamps, and the ceiling fan the only sound breaking the silence.

"Pack light, Maime. You can pick up whatever you need on your vacation. Martin, don't be a miser, spend some money on your wife. You can't take it with you, trust me, I've asked."

Martiel Ellington opened the overnight bag with certain experience and began to fold in items as they were handed to her.

Martin sat in begrudged quietness, his feet propped on top of a suitcase containing his basic necessities.

"Explain to me one more time exactly why we need to leave tonight," sighed Martin.

Martiel noisily zipped the lid of Maime's luggage, whipping her comment over a shoulder, "Martin Earl, if you weren't my brother...."

She stuffed the case up against Martin's, bumping his feet from their resting place.

"Here's a card to buy whatever you'll need," she said, handing her brother Martin a solid black credit card.

"I've got money," he barked back at his sister.

She ignored his male ego and dropped it in his lap, "Try not to lose it. It doesn't have a limit."

Martiel looked him in the eyes to make sure he understood the depth of her meaning, then handed him a thick envelope. "Here's some traveling cash. Don't use the card until you are out of country."

"Out of the country?" he asked. "I thought this was a cruise down the coast."

"You'll be making a stop or two," she corrected. "Your passports will be waiting at Bethany's house, by the time you get there."

"Exactly why do we have to go by there?" asked Martin. "We didn't part on the friendliest of terms in case you don't remember."

For the sake of time and argument, Martiel bit her tongue at the sheer volume of crow she had to eat by calling their elder sister in the first place.

"Bethany was thrilled that you were coming by. You've never been to Washington to see her home in all these years. Besides..., better you than me," she added.

The women hugged and Martiel assured her sister-in-law that they were going to have a fabulous time.

"It's time we left," said Martiel, snatching a glance at her Rolex. "The car is already outside. If..., *when* we have visitors in the morning, I want them to find an empty house."

The steps on the front porch creaked as the young couple sat down together, side by side. The two antique carriage lights on either side of the door behind them cast their odd shadows out into the yard. The shadows attached to Jolie stretched into a long thin X, but the trails cast by James were translucent as if the light was passing through a smoky screen or the light was actually bending around a clear glass of water. James noticed immediately; it seemed that everything around him was a constant reminder that he was not real.

"Are you sure you want to do this?" asked Jolie.

"It's not going to be the *first meeting* of your parents that I imagined," said James.

The sly grin disappeared as quickly as it formed on his lips.

Jolie shuddered, "You won't actually be meeting them will you?"

"Why? Are you ashamed of me?" asked James, almost playfully.

Jolie smiled and pushed at his arm in an instinctive reaction, but her giggle died the instant her hand swam through mist.

James observed that at that exact moment they were being watched from a distance by one of her father's spy's.

Jolie noticed that her boyfriend didn't react, didn't make some snide remark reminding her of his illusive condition. Where was his mind?

Jolie probed and listened toward James but got a brick wall of silence. Why the wrestling match? She needed a way inside his thoughts.

"I never saw my daddy do anything bad to anybody other than my mother," said Jolie. "But I heard a lot of stories."

"We weren't so different then," said James, nervously.

Jolie waited for more of an explanation of his childhood,

but there was that strange gulf between them again; a preoccupation. Try as she might, he had completely shut her out of his private thoughts.

Jolie stared at the distant light from the yard lamp, mentally pacing his perimeter, waiting for the slightest opening. The lamp was glowing brilliantly against the backdrop of the enormous magnolia tree opposite the driveway. Its perfect taper and huge splay of flowers glowing with incandescence, gave it the feeling of Christmas in summertime.

James quietly picked up Jolie's hand and began a steady vigil, feeling each tiny finger. His concerted effort allowed her to feel his body next to hers, hoping it was keeping her mind off his status quo while he was listening to other things in the distance.

Jolie became restless with his silence, frustrated that she was shut out; something she wished she'd never helped him understand how to do.

Fine, if he wanted to play that game, then she'd play by her own rules.

"I actually think it's sweet that you don't want to keep me hanging and I know you think it's best for me to move on James. But I still want to take things one day at a time and see what happens. I wanted to tell you so many times before...."

"Before I was murdered," finished James, almost absently.

"Why do you do that!?" she whined, snatching her hand away from him. "Every time I start to tell you how I feel about you, you find a way to kill it."

"It's my new nature," said James, darkly.

"Why can't you give it some time? If it is to be, then it will be and if not, well, we can cross that bridge then."

James couldn't help but laugh, "Are you sure you're not related to Martiel Ellington?"

Jolie smiled, "It's good to hear you laugh again."

"Jolie, I would give anything to go back in time, do things differently, but what's done is done."

Jolie stood from the front porch steps, looking out into the blackness of the evening.

"Why didn't you tell me we were being watched?" she asked.

"I didn't want you to know. How did you get in my head?"

"It was easy. I got your mind occupied on emotional things and finally got past that *thick head of yours*," she spat.

"So all of that was just to *distract* me?"

"I didn't say it wasn't the truth," she confessed. "You were just so preoccupied. I had to know what was bothering you."

"Jolie, you have got to quit playing mind games with me."

"I know..., I know," she whined, then plopped back down. "That's why I've decided to go with your mother to your aunt's house in Biloxi tonight. Aunt BeBe and I will be leaving with Catherine when Martiel takes your grandparents to the airport. I really am going to miss you."

"Good," he said absentmindedly, snapping back her

direction once again.

He remained beside her, ignoring her misdirection, just as the spy in the distance viewed them through a pair of binoculars. It was disconcerting watching himself and Jolie seated on the porch steps through the mind's eye of the stranger.

"James, I really didn't lie about how I feel. Baby, are you even listening to me?"

He looked at her and nodded, "Yeah, of course."

He pecked her on the cheek with a kiss, "I'm glad you're going with them. You'll be safer with them for the next few days."

Immediately his thoughts turned away and she was alone again. It was futile, he was oblivious and in another world. His wall was back up and Jolie continued looking for another venue back inside.

"I don't understand why I was drawn to you or why I had the dreams about you, but I still believe we have a future somehow. You have to believe me. You're the first person to ever mean this much to me."

"Alright, I guess that'll have to be good enough for now," said James.

"You're impossible!" she blurted, her open palm slapping at the vapor of his face as if swatting a gnat.

With her last imagined moments of intimacy dashed, she angrily stomped back into the house.

CHAPTER 10

Everyone was huddled in the foyer with their meager suitcases stacked in a row, each with imagined destinations and trials awaiting them. It was Martiel wearing her heels to nubs just inside the door, waiting for the okay from their sentry.

Finally, her nephew appeared behind them all and shuffled through their muttering figures.

"We're ready to leave, James," said Martiel. "Are we still being watched?"

"Just like we expected, but I can take care of that when you're ready."

"I have to stop by the Sheriff's house on our way out of town," she continued. "I'd like to let him know that the estate will be empty, without telling him too much. Maybe I should ask him to stop by and check on the place tomorrow. Oh..., I don't want him to get hurt though."

"Really Aunt Martiel," he laughed quietly. "Why don't you invite the Sheriff over for dinner?"

Her face flushed pink. "Hush, James!"

"You know you like him. I don't see what the problem is."

Martiel's expression turned dark, "I should be allowed a little privacy concerning the affairs of my heart, don't you think?"

"I guess…. Too bad you don't see mine the same way," he prodded.

"Touché," she smirked. "I don't *really* mean to be such a busybody James. The future of our family is resting on our shoulders. I can't see complicating it further with some type of romantic entanglement."

"Like mine, you mean?" spat James.

"Exactly like yours," she replied. "The road I'm on is narrow and a little lonely at times, I have to admit. But that's just the way it has to be."

She turned and began to fuss with the zipper on Maime's luggage and thrust it at James.

"Aunt Martiel, I'm…," whispered James.

He wanted to apologize, but she was already searching for a way to distance herself.

"Go take care of our nuisance and get back here. It's time for us to get on the road," she ordered.

No sooner said, James faded from their view.

The old sedan was parked in high brush about a hundred yards up the private road from the Ames Estate. A heavyset man was perched on the passenger side of the wide bench seat, binoculars in one hand and a lukewarm cup of coffee in the other.

James noticed the pockmarks on his cheeks and forehead and the receding hairline.

Just a common goon. Damien had sent a mindless minion that couldn't be trusted to do anything other than menial tasks.

James invisibly slipped into the back seat of the car and

carefully immersed himself into the round bellied man's thoughts. His immediate concerns were food, and his current wager at the Louisiana Downs, and wishes that someone else had been chosen for this evening's duty.

James listened intently for other stray thoughts in the area and scanned the darkness with his otherworldly vision.

There was no one else.

Damien Dimanche had obviously underestimated the Ames family. That was the best news he'd had all that day.

James reached around and ever so gently pressed a finger to the side of the man's neck. The gentle throb, throb, of his pulse beat steadily against James Earl's fingertip.

'Don't worry, you won't feel a thing, I hope,' thought James.

James pressed slightly harder against the rhythmic vessel delivering oxygenated blood to the man's brain.

As expected, he yawned, lolled his big head around in a circle, rubbed his neck, and took another sip of lukewarm coffee. It was anybody's guess how long it would take for him to nod off into unconsciousness.

James continued to constrict the blood vessel until he heard the binoculars thud into the car seat and watched his big head thump over against the doorframe.

James caught the cup of coffee before it spilled and placed it on the dash. After listening to make sure the odd fellow was asleep, he slid forward and flashed the headlights on the sedan to signal his family, which went completely unnoticed.

"He won't wake up for at least 15 minutes," said James. "But you need to go now just in case my timing is off."

"And you're sure he's just taking a nap?" asked Martin Ames from inside the car.

"Yeah, I'm sure," said James. "You two have a great time with your vacation, okay? Don't worry about stuff here."

James heard the fake condescension in his own voice and cringed, wishing he knew when to shut up.

"We need to make sure he wakes up right after we're gone, so he can report our lack of activity to his fearless leader," said Martiel quietly.

"I know..., I know what to do," said James a little impatiently. "My memory is pretty much infallible now days."

"Infallible," she whispered.

Martiel rolled her eyes upward, "Okay, stick to the plan."

She slid into the front seat of her BMW and in an instant, it purred to life.

Moments later, BeBe's car cranked noisily and James cringed, listening back toward their unwanted visitor for signs of life.

"Jolie, honey? Will you please get in the car?" asked BeBe.

Jolie stood in a huff waiting outside the open car door in expectation.

"Jolie, I'm sorry," he whispered. "What do you want me to say? I'm a jerk. It was for a good reason though."

Jolie had imagined quite a different scenario in those

few private moments with James. All she felt now was scorn.

James hesitated before darting a kiss on her cheek.

"I don't think so," she hissed, and her persistence got her the kiss she was waiting for.

"That's what I'm talkin' about," said Sam, his head barely visible from inside the back seat.

James quickly leaned in the car and gave Sam a well-deserved thump on the head.

"Boys," corrected Catherine. "We're wasting time."

James heard Jolie mumble, "That's a matter of opinion."

"Call here to the house when you get to Biloxi," said James.

"I know…, I know…," she smiled. "Two rings."

"Love you mom."

He returned her smile and faded from view.

A moment in time later, James silently reappeared in the back seat of the watchman's car as his family drove slowly past.

When they passed, everyone's concerned and frightful faces were staring into the car James was guarding. As soon as their taillights disappeared onto the main highway, he focused back on the sentry.

"Time to wake up sleeping beauty," said James, and began to whisper repeatedly into the man's waking thoughts, offering dreamlike explanations to what he would see upon waking.

"They must have gone to bed. The house is all quiet."

James patted the big man on his floppy jowls until he snorted.

"Oh, Jeez!" he sat bolt upright. He snatched the binoculars from the floorboard where they'd fallen and smacked them to his eyes.

"They must have gone to bed, the house looks quiet."

He had no way of knowing that two vehicles were missing from inside the closed garage doors.

He nabbed his coffee cup from the dash and took a sip.

"Cold," he whispered, and dashed it out the window, cursing himself for dozing off.

James bounced back inside the estate, opened the front door and made an appearance. When he was satisfied that Damien Dimanche's observer had seen him, he walked back inside, turned off the porch lights and secured the house.

For a fleeting moment, James actually felt sorry for the overweight fellow in the car. If he knew Damien Dimanche, tomorrow wouldn't be a good day for him, not a good day at all.

Sam Earl sat crunched next to the whistling back window of BeBe's car, nervously watching utility poles passing by in the darkness, angrily listening to the chatter between Catherine and BeBe. The trip already seemed an eternity.

Jolie remained both distant and silent in the back seat, holding her family journal close in her lap, drifting in and out of sleep.

"You know it doesn't do any good to sit there all mad," whispered Jolie.

Was she listening to his thoughts? That wasn't right.

"I wanted to stay and help James," fumed Sam. "I'm not some little kid that has to be watched."

"Can you at least calm down? I can't sleep over here, with you.... Oh, never mind," she moaned.

She sat up and stretched.

"What?" he blurted. "I'm bothering you?"

"Hmm, since you asked...," hissed Jolie. "If you had a problem why didn't you just come out with it?"

"You know why. You're the mind reader, aren't you?"

Sam turned away, staring at the black night outside the window. Instantly they both noticed that the front seat of the car had become quiet and they were being observed.

"If I didn't know better, I'd think you two were brother and sister," said Catherine.

BeBe turned her head away into the dark to hide her grin.

"We'll be in Biloxi in a little over an hour. Does anyone need a bathroom break or snacks?" asked Catherine.

Silence ensued for a solid minute, until Jolie spoke up.

"He does, but he's too mad to admit it."

"I'm too mad? Quit that mind reading crap with me. You..., you stay out of my head. I don't care if you are James Earl's girlfriend, that's just not right."

The moment all chatter died away to the sound of the highway, Jolie sighed loudly. "He has to pee," she grumbled, causing a round of giggles.

CHAPTER 11

The St. Augustine lawn was uniformly manicured with the exception of a few telltale dandelions randomly asserting their rights to the morning sun. The warm early rays reflected off the vivid white face of the old mansion making it loom gigantic from the distant private road.

At seven o'clock sharp, the Adams County Sheriff pulled through the gates of the gravel drive leading to the Ames Estate and circled to park around behind the two-story carriage house, now used as a three-car garage adjacent to the house. This was his usual routine over the last six or seven years, looking in on the vacant old estate for Martiel Ellington while she was out of town or on business trips.

Sheriff Howard squinted at the blazing sun rising threateningly on the horizon; wiped his brow and dropped his hat back on his head.

Martiel's strange visit to his home late last night and the weeks of unorthodox troubles the family had recently endured had him more than a little on edge with this particular visit.

The grass crunched softly under his boots as he walked around to the front and pulled out his key to the door. He slid it home and the lock turned easily enough, yet something wasn't right.

He had served as sheriff for almost twenty years in

Natchez Mississippi, the county seat, and in those twenty years, he had learned to trust his instincts.

The door eased partially open and he stood on the threshold listening into the cavernous living room. There was nothing but silence; still, something wasn't right.

He pulled the door closed and stepped back out onto the porch, shrugging away the cold chills clawing his spine.

Was it his imagination getting the best of him?

He walked the outside perimeter of the house quietly, still listening, his hand resting uneasily on the holster of his revolver.

The .357 magnum was not the standard issue, but despite its reputed firepower, he didn't feel the usual reassurance of knowing it was there. He wouldn't admit it to Martiel, but this place gave him the creeps, especially with its recent history.

His mind flashed back to the row of headless black chickens that were strung above the front steps - Their putrid dark blood drying in rivulets from some filthy ritual..., and the flies.

He felt cold chills returning like an army of ants as he wrestled with the memory, reinforcing his determination.

He decided to go back to his county vehicle and radio dispatch to send another officer to meet him. Better safe than sorry.

As he rounded the corner of the house, a black limousine pulled into the long gravel driveway with the blazing glare of sunlight reflecting off its top into his eyes. It slowly crawled up the long pea-gravel drive, finally halting as the sheriff stepped in front of the garage.

The driver holding his cabby hat bounced out and all but snatched the rear door open. The entourage exited the back of the vehicle with rehearsed flair, similar to the previous morning.

The sheriff stood watching as a skinny little man, in a suit costing maybe half his annual salary, took his time sauntering boldly to stop in front of him. Two other men followed closely behind and halted on either side with arms folded.

Sheriff Howard snickered at the cliché, then quietly mumbled, "Martiel Ellington, I swear, you're going to be the death of me yet."

"Can I help you gentlemen?" asked the Sheriff.

The man in the suit looked away from the front porch and stared at the ground for a moment as if deep in thought.

Looking up, he painted a quick smile on his face, "Hello," he wheezed. "Yes, I'm looking for my daughter. I'm supposed to pick her up this morning."

Somehow all evidence of an accent had disappeared from Damien's voice.

"I'm not sure who you're talking about," said the Sheriff. "But I just checked; there's no one at home."

"I see, I see," the man strained out, looking back down at the ground. A frown began to deepen as he focused his attention back on the sheriff.

"So, would you be so kind as to tell me...," he drug out the last word, "where they might be?"

His hand carefully followed his words, making nervous

little swipes and curious circles in the air.

"I suppose I could. If I knew..., but I don't."

"I see," he said again, looking mildly agitated.

"So are you this little town's private security service?" he asked.

"I'm the Sheriff of this *little* county, Mr...?"

"Uh, Dimanche," he wheezed out, and coughed.

Suddenly he threw both hands in the air and dropped them back down, turning on the charm. "Well then, if no one's home and you don't know where anyone is..., I guess our business here is concluded. Have a good day sheriff."

No sooner said than done, they quickly reassembled back into the limousine and exited the circle drive.

Sheriff Howard felt that nudge again. He was about to ask for some identification from them when that little voice inside warned him to let it go. Nevertheless, he stood in place, arms folded, until they turned out the front gate onto the private road before strolling back to his car.

"Dispatch, this is Sheriff Howard. Can I get you to send backup out to the Ames Estate for a routine check?"

"I trust you slept well?" asked Bethany Monroe.

Martin Earl's elder sister had first knocked, then peeked through the offered crack in the bedroom doorway.

"I can't believe you would succumb to Martiel's ridiculous idea of last minute travel plans. Morning flights are much more pleasant, especially when you get to be our age."

Bethany was now standing in their open bedroom

doorway with an elusive grin on her puffy face.

"I know we parted on less than…, amicable terms, but I say we let bygones be bygones. I want you to enjoy your stay. I can't tell you how happy I am for you to be here."

Martin Earl Ames was already regretting stepping inside the threshold of Bethany and Moreland's home. The rumble of thunder mingled with steady rain pattered on their array of windows.

"There are robes hanging on the warmer in the bathroom and, …well I think you'll find everything you need. I'm sure you'll appreciate the cooler weather here once you get used to it."

Martin and Maime sat bleary eyed against the tall headboard, wondering what time it was.

"Breakfast is in twenty minutes. I'll see you then," she chirped and walked away.

"How long were we supposed to stay here before the cruise?" asked Maime in a hoarse whisper.

"I thought Martiel told you all the details?" he grunted. "I'm ready to call a taxi as soon as we get dressed."

"Oh Martin, we can't do that," she whispered. "It's just Bethany here alone in this big old house. How bad can it be for maybe a couple of days?"

"Couple of days?" groaned Martin, sliding out of bed. "Come on…. We do this together or not at all."

He extended his hand to Maime and grinned. It was the closest thing to a smile she had seen on her husband's face in several months.

"Do you remember where the dining room is?" he asked.

"I think we should ask for a map of the place," she answered.

They hurried through their morning routine and stepped into the hallway.

"It's bigger than it looked last night," said Maime.

"I told you," grunted Martin.

At the end of the hallway, the upstairs view opened, revealing the expanse of the ground floor below. With only the hardwood banister to hang onto, Maime looked down at the opulence below.

"It looks like a hotel," she murmured.

"Aren't you glad we didn't let Martiel talk us into a bigger place?" asked Martin.

"I..., I suppose it's pretty," she said. "Doesn't have the feeling of home to it though."

A bell began tinkling below; from the echoes, probably originating somewhere underneath where they were standing.

"I guess we'd better hurry up," he grunted.

CHAPTER 12

At the Sheriff's earlier arrival, James stood quietly and invisibly as Sheriff Howard opened the front door. Directly behind that same door was the intruder that James had been watching skulk around inside the Ames Estate since just before daylight. He was a tall auburn haired fellow with linebacker shoulders and the gun holstered under his left arm looked tiny in comparison to his mass.

He had to admit, this guy was good, a pro.

Had James been a normal human, asleep that time of the morning, he would have never known the intruder was inside the house. No glass was broken, no pry bar was used. A simple set of tools opened both dead bolt and door lock to the back storeroom door.

He walked on the balls of his feet with the stealth any housecat would have envied. Simple, quiet, professional; nothing like the amateur sent to watch the family's activities the night before.

This concluded his Aunt Martiel's instructions for watching the house and he was itching to put his own touch to the situation.

Even though he didn't always agree with Martiel, and even though she rarely shared entire scenarios of her dreams and visions, they were almost always exact in every detail when events ran their course. This houseguest included.

Had the sheriff entered the door that morning, Adams County could have possibly been looking for a replacement after the current one apparently "surprised an intruder" in the commission of a theft.

End of story. End of Sheriff Howard.

But for some reason the sheriff had hesitated and relocked the door.

Of course James would have happily kept any harm from being propagated on the sheriff and had in fact been coiled to strike the intruder, just in case. He had to make sure Sheriff Howard was safe; even if it ruined the plan. He still owed the sheriff an unpaid debt for the untold hours protecting his family.

As soon as Dimanche's entourage left the property in the flashy limousine, the auburn haired man hurried to the back of the house mirroring the sheriff's movements, understanding it was time to make his exit.

But, there was something else. The intruder's first purpose was to make sure the transition of Jolie to her father was smooth and quick. Instead he had found the house empty and as in times past knew what was now expected of him. His secondary mission was to find out where everyone had gone.

He scrambled to the living room first, then the den, looking for signs of life and activity. Ending up in the kitchen by the telephone, apparently the congregating place, where he looked for discarded scratch paper. He collected a notepad on the counter, then quickly dumped the waste paper basket on the floor and examined each and every tidbit of paper, grocery receipt, and newspaper page, looking for scribbles and phone numbers.

He carefully flattened two scraps of notepad, placing them between the pages of another notepad in his pants pocket. He carefully cleaned up the mess and was trying to decide whether he had time enough to search the bedroom nightstands and bathroom trash bins. There were too many rooms and he knew from experience that he had about ten more minutes before he would either have to leave or find a suitable hiding place at the risk of being caught – getting caught was not an option.

James watched him take the nibble of bait offered him, but with the Sheriff outside, he couldn't afford to scare the intruder into leaving just yet.

The gunman pulled his fingers through his auburn hair, thoughts blazing, clear and concise preplanned steps, practiced, an easy read for James.

He ran for the stairs, while picturing his search of the upstairs bedrooms.

Somewhere near the midpoint of his ascent, James sped forward and closed one of the doors in the upstairs north hallway.

The intruder froze in his tracks and crouched low, listening. James gave him something to listen to. Footfalls from his footsteps began echoing toward the top of the stairs, just above where the skilled intruder was standing.

It produced the intended results and James was pleased with himself. James reappeared downstairs, forcing another door open and closed. Feeling shocked and cut off, the auburn haired man assumed that the sheriff had entered the downstairs and he now would have to hide somewhere upstairs.

The last noise he heard was from the north wing, so he headed left, down the hallway of the south wing of upstairs bedrooms, looking for access to the estate's attic space.

Every old large house of this era had an attic big enough to house an entire family of migrant workers or store three bedrooms worth of furniture. Concerning this house, maybe both at the same time.

He targeted the first bedroom on the right, reaching for the doorknob and James opened it for him.

The man snatched his hand back as if burned and froze in his tracks while watching the door slowly open on its own. In that same instant, he produced a thin six-inch metal spike much thicker than an ice-pick from somewhere unknown, gripping it firmly in his right hand.

James saw a dizzying slideshow of thoughts with this man pushing the metal spike into the face and up the nose of some unassuming blank faced victim.

The man was truly evil; his thoughts were mechanical with no hints of remorse or hesitation. This was his preferred method of silent eradication.

Martiel's plan was to let this intruder go, so that he could also report his meager findings, but should he let someone of this caliber of evil continue to breathe?

There was the rub. Could he allow himself to entertain the thoughts of taking a life and becoming just like this assassin?

Was his grampa right?

It was almost as if his Grampa Ames had known..., no..., not a chance.

James quickly brushed away those ideas, then quieted his senses and relaxed; stick to the plan – his plan.

The intruder assumed that the weight of his body on the hallway floor had caused the door to unlatch itself and cautiously entered the bedroom.

Time was running out and if either the sheriff or one of his deputies entered the house, James would definitely have to intervene to some extent to keep them alive. That would be unfortunate, because they needed this killer to get away unnoticed and report back to Damien without incident. Still, he had no right to plunder the home of his family.

As the man walked into the room, James placed both hands on the intruders back and thought, 'Behind you!'

Icy shivers poured down the intruder. The man spun like an attacked animal and pushed the steel spike deep into the solid oak bedroom door behind him. The sound was no more than a thud.

When he saw no one was there, he yanked the spike free and shrugged his shoulders a few times to shake off the cold, never uttering a word, although plenty of curse words were flowing in his sealed mind.

This guy was not going to be easy to freak.

Again, the intruder started looking for a paper trail, fast and meticulous.

James pulled out one of the drawers of an ornate maple dresser at the opposite end of the room.

The intruder stopped cold, then twisted his head to one side and stared at the dresser drawer. James slammed the drawer back in its place; a nice loud whack, causing the pulls from every drawer to jingle at once from the force.

Finally, progress.

"What the...?" he whispered, then scourged himself for breaking some cardinal rule of absolute silence while on a job.

James pushed the bedroom door wide open behind the man, bumping its final travel against the wall.

The intruder swore to himself and cautiously headed toward the veranda windows. He held his breath beside the thin curtains and peered down at the Sheriff, waving at the arrival of another vehicle in the distance. There was an iron ladder, some kind of fire escape attached to the outside wall, but it was in plain sight.

That meant there was no one downstairs to block his escape.

James saw him imagine leaving out the back door as he slid out of the room and downstairs toward the back storeroom door.

James created footfalls that matched the cadence of the man and he began to run for his exit. The fellow spun his head in jerky movements looking behind himself for an unseen pursuer.

The back door opened in concert with the opening of the front as the Sheriff poked his head inside.

"Hello, anybody home?"

"My goodness. I don't understand all the secrecy?" said Bethany.

Her fork seemed to be absently chasing a piece of food around an otherwise empty plate.

"It's not a secret. Martiel didn't give us all the details because she wanted to surprise us," mumbled Martin. "We want to keep it that way if you don't mind."

Bethany was already plucking the last of Martin's nerves, trying desperately to know every detail of their vacation.

"You should have let me plan you a vacation," she chirped. "I could have set you up a daily itinerary of the most wonderful places. Paris is just wonderful, especially this time of the year. Oh, and then there's Athens. Oh my."

"We're not exactly the world travelers that you are Bethany," said Maime.

"If Martiel wasn't so *greedy* and *secretive* with the family funds, you could have already seen the world by now," she said in her best smug tone. "Why if I...."

"In Martiel's defense," said Maime, cutting her off. "She has done everything but try to force us to go places over the years."

"Well it's a pity that she didn't plan something like this before what happened to little James. Maybe he and..., what's his brother's name? Samuel. Yes, he and Samuel could have gone with you and averted that horrid tragedy. By the way, how is Catherine taking her loss? I know she was beside herself when we last spoke."

Maime watched as her husband clenched his jaw and she answered before Martin Earl came unhinged.

"Catherine is coping quite well, thank you," said Maime in her best upbeat tone. "She and Samuel are visiting with us for awhile and it seems to be helping quite a bit."

"I don't suppose her husband is in the picture much. I can't say as I blame him either. After all, it's the woman's duty to hold the family together during transitions like that," she grunted.

Martin and Maime both sat in silence. Maime's cheeks were hinting pink hues and she was quite willing to let her husband take the next volley. Maime ducked her head and took a drink of coffee, glancing at her husband.

"Can you bring us some fresh coffee?" boomed Bethany toward an empty doorway, seemingly satisfied with the lack of response.

Martin gripped the leg of his trousers along with part of his leg before he spoke.

"A transition...," he huffed.

Bethany glanced up and shrugged her frail shoulders. "Life is full of transitions," then began to move a few things across the table to make room for the delivery of a new carafe.

"A transition might be if you changed out your china or you moved to another bedroom in this mausoleum.... The death of my grandson was not something I would consider a *transition*, you insensitive...."

"Martin," Maime shook her husband's shoulder cutting him off. "Honey, don't get your blood up."

He wiped his face with a palm and released a pent up breath along with the painful grip to his leg. That was going to leave a bruise, but it was better than biting his tongue.

Bethany turned, as a young lady in a gaudy uniform sat down a brightly polished carafe of coffee on the table and quickly disappeared without a word. Servants..., yet another goading thorn that Martin Earl had to whisk away. An employee or two was one thing, but to require an air of muted subservience was repulsive.

"I wasn't trying to be insensitive. I'm more of a..., realist Martin. That's all. Which is probably why Martiel and I never quite got along."

Bethany poured herself a cup of fresh Brazilian coffee in the sudden silence.

Marin Earl saw no reason to restrain his thoughts, "You never got along with Martiel because she was more qualified to manage the family's financial affairs."

It was Bethany's turn to crest pink as she stirred sugar and cream in her cup.

"You really believe I was jealous of my little sister?" she laughed, taking a sip from her cup.

"Without a doubt," mumbled Martin.

For the first time in years, since they were infants, he wanted to goad Bethany beyond her smug plateau of arrogance. Instead he let his staring contest die away.

There was one item of recent events that would send her right over the edge where he wanted her. The investment statements Martiel had shown him only weeks ago was living proof that she had obviously been the rightful choice as curator of the family estate. Not only did Martiel have an impartial view of the family as a whole, she would never risk the family fortunes for personal gain. Unfortunately, he was bound by a promise to Martiel to keep his silence.

"Is Moreland going to be home soon?" asked Maime.

"Martiel was always stuffed under daddy's arm. He never made time for anyone other than his little jewel," Bethany chirped, ignoring Maime.

"I'm sure he had his reasons," grinned Martin.

For years, he had served as peacemaker between him and his two sisters..., but no more. The years had changed Bethany into something greedy and ugly that Martin Earl hardly recognized.

"I'm certain of that," she mumbled. "I remember all conversation would cease as soon as I entered the room."

Martin Earl ducked his head and gave it a shake. Was it possible that Bethany couldn't recognize the need for privacy in a conversation without her jealousy turning it into something personal?

Then there was the problem with their father, John Earl. He always was a bit of loose cannon, never hiding his true feelings concerning life..., or his children.

Bethany turned to Maime, "No. Moreland won't be back for another week. He's on a business trip."

"I haven't seen your son Harold, will we get to see him before we have to leave?" asked Maime, hoping to keep the conversation moving away from the mounting explosion.

"Harold...," she frowned. "He seems to have taken ill, some strange episode, right after we left Natchez, after the funeral. He's..., such a delicate child. Some fright overtook him."

Bethany glared at Maime, waiting for some hint of knowledge, then seemed almost violently disappointed when there was none.

"He's convalescing in..., Northern California, near the ocean."

"I'm so sorry to hear that," said Maime. "Is it serious?"

Bethany clattered down her cup into a saucer and sat upright.

"Martiel left me the number of the travel agency. Would you like for me to call and see when your cruise is scheduled to arrive in Seattle?" asked Bethany.

"The sooner the better," barked Martin.

CHAPTER 13

"So..., you what?" demanded Damien Dimanche.

"You sit there all night, you drink your coffee, the only *thing* you have to do is *watch*, and you can't do *that*? *Ingenuo scimunito! Non capisco!*"

The heavyset man stood, uncomfortable and silent, knowing that he was damned if he did, damned if he didn't. It was just *how* damned that had him worried at the moment.

Damien paced back and forth across the floor of the hotel room looking down at the floor and rubbing the back of his neck.

"I should be back on a plane, headed to Liberty Airport, with my daughter. It was a simple thing, *semplice cosa*. First, I spend months trying to find her. Jolie shows up here and she's living with her *Zia* BeBe.

Now, out of the blue, I get a phone call. Jolie *needs* me. BeBe *needs* me, because Jolie's missing. The bumble-head I have in New Orleans knows nothing. He's getting his information from some stupid local cop and guess what? It was some kind of boyfriend problems, she's fine, nothing but a few bruises. All I want is good information. Is that *troppo chièdere*, ...too much?"

The men's *capo* was agitated. They'd seen it before, but when Damien talked to himself it meant he wanted to be heard. He never spewed his private thoughts to his underlings without reason. Damien wanted them to know without any hint of a doubt that he wanted results.

The knock at the door interrupted Damien's dissertation of woes.

"Ah, my best man," he exclaimed, clasping his two hands together.

"Rooster, what did you bring me?" asked Damien.

"Two phone numbers," said the auburn haired man. "But it wasn't what we were looking for. One is to the local newspaper, the other to the local Sheriff's Department."

"Another disappointment," wheezed Damien.

"Boss," said Rooster. "There's another thing. My visit was cut short. I need a little more time in that house. It's old. It might be one of those old places with fake walls where people used to hide during the Civil War. Someone was hiding in that house. I know it."

"Hmmm, that would explain why *Fatso* here didn't see anybody leave," said Damien. "What makes you think that?"

"I heard noises, saw stuff happen in the house that I couldn't explain," said Rooster.

"What. So now you believe the house is *infestato*, haunted?" laughed Damien.

"No Boss. Stuff don't move by itself. Someone had to be in the house," said Rooster.

"Bah! Parlor tricks. Some of that Cajun mumbo-jumbo Gina always tried to push off on me. I guess, like mother, like daughter," scoffed Damien.

Why was Rooster so strangely quiet?

"Can you figure it out by yourself?" asked Damien.

"Boss, I been taking care of business since I was twelve. Since I been contracting for you..., how many times I let you down?" asked Rooster.

"Never. Go..., do what you have to. Bring me something. I'll get my connections busy looking at where they might be, just in case you don't find anything. If you buy a ticket, rent a room, rent a car, then you leave a trail."

"So, what are you waiting for? Go! *Esci!*"

Both men turned to leave as quickly as possible.

"Fatso," said Damien. "Where you think you're going? I'm not through with you."

As the door closed, Rooster heard, "...if you weren't a blood cousin, I swear I'd make you disappear...."

"How did it go?" asked Martiel.

"It went just like you said it would," said James. "Damien sent a tough guy to sure up his bets, but he found the house empty."

"Tough guy?" questioned Martiel. "What kind of tough guy?"

"The toughest," said James, trying to avoid a long explanation. "No one to fool around with. You were right to get the family as far away as possible until they quit nosing around. But I don't think that's going to be good enough. Something tells me Damien won't drop his search for Jolie or her mother this time. He's got something to prove and the trail is warm again."

"We know it's not Jolie he's after. It's her mother,

Regina," said Martiel. "He only wants her to draw Regina into the open. He's known for a while that Jolie is living in Vidalia with her aunt. The question is, how long has he known, and who's been keeping tabs on them? But my list of questions keep getting longer the more I think about it."

Martiel sunk back into the couch, staring out her hotel window overlooking the Mississippi River, wishing she'd kept her mouth shut. She rattled her glass of tea in a swirl and took a sip, realizing that once she posed the questions, it would only be a matter of time before the headaches would come. The dull headaches were her early warning that an answer was about to sit her down and grip her senses, then flood her with pieces of what the future held.

She preferred dreams instead of visions, but dreams too often were mixed with her own emotions and vivid imaginings that could sometimes cloud or distort the truth.

Her visions were clear, concise, and like a shot in the arm; painful, but over quickly.

"How long are you going to hide here?" asked James.

The Vidalia Hotel had been her choice of refuge from time to time and she had a long-standing relationship with the management and owners. She was not a registered guest, but a floating nameless patron that paid very well for her privacy. She liked keeping things simple.

"Aunt Martiel? What is it?" asked James. "I can't keep up with what you're thinking."

She wasn't trying to hide her thoughts from him, but her thoughts were beginning to avalanche into a blur.

"I was just wishing that fool old woman Lyda Brown

had kept her filthy self away from you," she mused.

"But not just because I ended up dead in the process. You miss your family counselors, those spooks that used to live in that old house, don't you?"

"You shouldn't speak ill of the dead. Those spooks as you call them were your ancestors, our family, your family. And yes, they would have proven quite helpful in this particular situation. That much is true," said Martiel.

"Sam pointed out something to me, you might be interested in," said James. "Now that the living family is out of harms reach for the moment, I could make sure they don't come back...."

Martiel began to laugh, purposely cutting him off.

"You could what? Become a murderer and slaughter the whole bunch?"

"I didn't just decide I want to be a killer, but it's better them than our family. I like the direct approach. I hate these cat and mouse games."

Martiel leaned over on the couch arm and looked at James.

"You scare me James. I thought we were past this conversation. Murder begets murder and violence more violence. You know that James. Besides, these cat and mouse games are the spice of life."

"Not when our family's the mice," grunted James.

It was useless to mention what his grampa said concerning the matter.

She stood and stretched, realizing why James did not fully agree with her.

"It's time we get back to work on our little problem,"

she said. "Let's you and I give that nest of rats some cheese, so you can get back to watching the house for the next visitation."

Biloxi Mississippi was scripted beautifully on the front of the postcard, while the illustration focused on white salty beaches, clear water, and bright sunshine. The postcard couldn't describe the peaceful steady breeze that defeated the humidity or the wispy sound of soft waves singing to the beachcombers strolling the waters edge. Sam crunched the card in the back pocket of his soggy cut-off jeans. It wouldn't be much of a souvenir by the time everything dried out.

"What are you doing with that?" asked Sam.

"It's private," said Jolie. She continued to scribble thoughtful notes into her thick leathery book.

"So are my thoughts, but you don't mind poking your head in there all the time," argued Sam.

He inched around behind her where he could sneak a look over her shoulder.

"Jolie... Lefleur... Dimanche," said Sam, reading her name from the open page. "What's your name mean?"

"Pretty Sunday Flower," she answered in an annoyed drone.

Not exact, but close enough to shut Sam up.

"That a picture of your mom? Wow, she's really pretty. Isn't that a picture of our family and James?"

Sam's curiosity was forcing him to lean over Jolie's shoulder.

"Hey, where'd you get those?"

He reached across to pluck one of the pictures.

With the force and accuracy of a cobra, Jolie slapped the back of his hand.

In an instant she shut the book and looked intently at Sam. Her bright blue eyes flashed and darted at several points of his face - A cat deciding where to place its claw.

"If you weren't James' brother," she gritted.

"Sorreee," grinned Sam, as he backed away.

His hand stung but instead of giving her the satisfaction of showing it any attention, he grabbed a shock of long dark hair and feigned combing it out of his face.

She almost laughed at the similarities between Sam and his brother. His eyebrows twitched and lowered after every comment, drawing attention to the steel gray of his eyes. The thick black unruly hair, wide shoulders, and narrow waist unmistakably linked them as brothers. Even the way they both set their jaw when making a point.

Jolie stood and began to shuffle the white sand out of her flats. The breeze pouring in from the Gulf of Mexico brushed her long black hair to and fro, hiding her face. She was already missing James and this younger version of him wasn't helping matters. She missed his emerald green eyes and the way they always seemed to change colors when he was angry..., nearly matching the color of Sam's.

She tapped the last of the grit from her shoes and slid them back on her feet.

"Your Aunt Martiel has a beautiful place. I see why she chose here to settle down."

"Ha, settle down?" scoffed Sam. "You don't know my Great Aunt Martiel very well. Settle down is not part of her vocabulary."

"No, I suppose not.... It's a family journal," said Jolie.

"What is? Oh, the book. Then why are *you* writing in it? It looks ancient. Who made you god of your family journal?"

"Too many questions, Sam. I'd gladly give it to someone else to keep, but there aren't many of us left."

"I thought you had lots of cousins that worked at your aunt's café?"

Jolie rolled her eyes and exhaled deeply when she saw that Sam wasn't going to give up.

"They're all distant cousins from family that are no longer living. That's enough question and answers for now."

"But...."

"Sam?" She tilted her head and cast him a dart or two.

He threw up both hands in submission.

"When did you get the pictures of...?" asked Sam.

"Oh my God...," she whispered tiredly.

Jolie turned quickly and began the walk through ankle deep sand back toward Martiel Ellington's house.

"Hey! Wait up! I was just wondering...."

She spun back to Sam, "My Aunt BeBe took that picture right before what happened to James, Okay?!"

"I'm sorry," said Sam. "I'm just trying to figure it all out. I know how you like James and everything, but we're pretty tight, you know? He's always been there for me as long as I've..., existed. You only had him for a couple of months, he's my brother."

Jolie retracted her verbal claws for a moment after understanding his perspective.

"You know James as a brother, but I know him on a completely different level. Let's just leave it at that, okay?"

Sam let that thought settle for only a second, he wasn't going to let *that* go.

"You know that no matter what you write in that book, it won't bring James back to life," said Sam angrily.

Jolie's emotional claws extended fully, "Don't you *EVER* say that again!"

Jolie quickly dragged through the sand back to Sam, reaching no higher than his chin, and glared up at him.

"*Never*...! Is that too difficult for you to understand?"

CHAPTER 14

The door would have slammed shut with gale force behind Jolie, if not for Sam's quick reflexes and stinging palms.

"Oh, good," said Catherine. "I was about to come look for you two. It's lunch time."

Sam smiled sheepishly as Jolie huffed away, toward the restroom. She passed in such a blur Catherine only caught a glimpse of her.

"Is Jolie not hungry?" asked Catherine, as she began setting out their food.

Sam wasted no time walking toward the large half-atrium dining room.

"I'm sure she'll be back," said Sam. "Can I go for a swim after lunch?"

"Nope, it's probably going to rain anyway so don't unpack, we're back on the road tomorrow morning."

"Aww, crap, mom," whined Sam. "I thought we'd get to stay at least a week here."

"Just a precaution," she continued, her nose wiggled as she chewed on a bit of carrot. "Low profile."

"So are we going to be spending the last of my summer vacation driving around? I didn't get to stay and help James. I don't get to spend anytime at the beach, and school's gonna start in a little over three weeks. I sure don't want to go back to Boston. I don't care how great the new place is."

Sam cut off the conversation as quickly as it spilled out of his mouth. It was too late to say sorry for the brutal reminder.

BeBe reversed her step and backed from the hallway into the bedroom where she could listen. Catherine was so tight with her feelings, no matter how BeBe tried; Catherine wouldn't open up to her. Catherine's two boys were a different story. They always seemed to cut straight to the heart of the matter and knew how to pry past the chinks in her new friend's armor.

"Consider it a road trip," said Catherine, "...and you're not going back to your dad's. So you'll have plenty of chances to swim later."

"Yeah," said Sam quietly, and began to shovel food onto his plate without looking back up at his mother's expression.

Catherine quietly walked out of the kitchen, bumping into Jolie just outside the room.

"Oh baby, I didn't see you," she whispered, grasping Jolie's slim shoulders.

Jolie instantly ducked her head. Catherine's hands felt like her own mother's grasp.

"It's okay, I'm okay," she sputtered, and let the comfort continue to linger on her shoulders. Catherine pulled Jolie to her in a quick hug and for the first time, Jolie noticed how much shorter she was than Catherine. Not as tall as James, but taller than her; so much for genes.... She was barely as tall as her father.

"I didn't mean to eavesdrop, but..., have you heard from Robert, I mean, your husband?" asked Jolie.

The hallway was suddenly cold and Catherine closed her eyes.

She slid past Jolie to hurry away, "No, not since the funeral."

BeBe felt Catherine's discomfort building and turned the corner of her hiding place, her raven hair still wet from a shower.

"Jolie, that's a little too personal, don't you think?" she scolded.

Catherine flashed back to the night after her son's funeral. James was gone; at least that's what she believed then.

The stinging words of her husband, Robert Williams slapped her in the face once again. Then there was the revelation that her marriage of so many years had been a sham.

What a faithless liar he turned out to be.

Catherine turned around, but not before swiping the extra moisture from her eyes. "No, it's okay. It wasn't too personal. Really, Sam was the one that caught me off guard. I know Jolie was just concerned."

"I'm very sorry, Mrs. Williams. I didn't mean to upset you," said Jolie.

"Oh please Jolie, don't revert back to Mrs. *anything*, it's still Catherine."

Another quick hug and peck of a kiss on Jolie's cheek sealed the scar and Catherine's armor quickly closed ranks.

"Martiel called while I was cooking," she continued, diverting the subject. "Why don't you two go eat and I'll fill everybody in when you're through."

Nearly sunset, James was prepared for the next uninvited houseguest. The manufactured information was already in place, but James had checked it multiple times already.

Despite the years of reparations and upgrades to the old structure, the Ames Estate creaked and groaned at every possible occasion. It seemed to add a warm character to the old place. If James didn't know better he would have thought the structure itself was haunted. Then he quickly subdued a laugh at the irony. He still saw himself as alive.

Maybe he hadn't been dead long enough for the facts to settle inside his hard head.

James looked one last time at several slips of paper. He and his aunt had worked on a believable list of destinations, fresh bait for Damien and his men to chase. Martiel warned him to never play the distraction game for long or risk ending up like Samson in the biblical tale of Delilah, so they agreed to keep it short and sweet.

Now was the part that James hated above all else, the waiting.

The Sheriff's Department had long gone, leaving the house and the entire area deserted for several hours. Hopefully, this would provide the desired false sense of security and freedom to roam about the house.

At twilight, James heard a slight jingling at the back

door of the house. It was that same entry point used by the previous intruder. Again, despite obvious assuredness that the house was vacated, this intruder moved with smooth stealth. It was the one that called himself Rooster again.

James heard the familiar voice of Rooster's thoughts before he went to meet him. Rooster definitely needed to get out more.

He had that same reverberating theme playing inside his thoughts. The big fellow considered himself a *cleaner* with a finely tuned and experienced response toward his job. It was a no hesitation policy of kill first, as cleanly as possible, and dispose of later. James didn't like the idea of allowing this snake access into the home of his treasured family, no matter how necessary it was.

Back in New Jersey, he and Sam had walked the knife's edge day after day while dealing with the old neighborhood streets and the gangs. Standing here before him was the perfected version of that ilk walking on tiptoes, where generations of his family grew up. It took all of the self-control James could collect not to do something he'd regret. A thief in the home would have been unforgivable, but here was an experienced murderer desecrating the sanctity of their privacy.

He also knew from the rule of the streets that this man was not part of Damien's or any other *family*. To be *bonafide*, to be *made*, he would need to have the family bloodline. This meant Rooster was a contractor for Damien; a trusted contractor that had proven his ability and trustworthiness. There was a name for that too; he had earned his *bones*.

The intruder swung a tiny pen light in precise arcs across each room, looking for signs of life. He inched around the polished mahogany grand piano into the sitting room, the chairs and end tables looked completely unused.

Half an hour and several rooms later, he settled in front of a roll top desk in the front study. The slide was pulled down and locked. Locked was good. It meant there was something to hide. He quickly picked the single tumbler lock, slid up the cover and found what he might be looking for - information.

This was going to be too easy. A stack of recent looking items were neatly paper clipped together beneath the stationary slots.

A travel voucher with telephone numbers for a hotel in Las Vegas, and the reservation information in the name of Smith. All current dates.

Rooster smiled to himself. They had used one of the most generic names possible as their cover.

The next was an itinerary for a tour of San Francisco, again for a family named Smith. Again, all current dates. He carefully scratched through the rest, just a few paid utility receipts. It was the end of the breadcrumb trail, but it would be enough for an experienced tracker to follow.

These items he quickly stuffed away in a pouch.

James saw that he was about to overlook one more bit of information and puffed a little air at the desk.

As the intruder was pulling down the lid, a piece of paper flittered to the floor at his feet.

Rooster quickly picked it up to replace it in the desk, when his light flickered across the heading. He frowned and stared at the pamphlet from the James Earl Williams memorial service, revealing a recent loss in the family. It too was added to Rooster's collection. He dutifully relocked the cabinet and meticulously wiped his prints from every point of contact.

Satisfied that all the bait was fully delivered, it was time for Rooster to leave before he stumbled upon anything of quality.

His penlight began to swing in an arc across the room, carefully avoiding direct contact with any windows or reflective objects.

There was suddenly the sound of a person running along one of the upstairs hallways.

Frozen in time, the light flicked off and Rooster walked in almost total darkness out of the room. An excellent memory of items and furniture guided him silently toward the stairs. James began to wonder if this man had his version of night vision, but that would have to be proven.

The water faucet in the kitchen sink came on, ran for a few moments and turned itself back off. To get there, meant crossing the enormous expanse of the living room.

On clicked the penlight and crouching down, he almost ran the full distance toward the kitchen door, in silence. There he waited patiently, guarding his every breath with the metered practice of a killer.

Rooster's thoughts were ablaze. Someone was in the house with him and he determined to find them, question them, and possibly eliminate them.

A toilet in one of the upstairs bathrooms flushed as if it was finishing its duty, the downstairs washroom door opened and closed. That was his point of entry, but more importantly, it was also his planned exit. Didn't he lock that door behind himself?

Rooster's mind was reeling.

Upstairs and downstairs, both? That meant there was more than one person in the house with him.

Wait, no, it could be a leaky seal on a toilet that refilled whenever the tank got low, but that didn't explain the footsteps.

A grandfather clock began to chime from behind him in the living room making him spin on the balls of his feet. It gonged out nine hard hammering blows. Then he realized that it was the first time he had heard the clock in either of his visits. As he squinted through the darkness he noted that the long brass pendulum was perfectly at rest.

A cold chill went up his spine with the help of James blowing air across the back of his now sweating head.

'Get a hold of yourself Rooster,' he commanded. 'Okay, two noises in the kitchen and washroom,' he thought. 'Two noises upstairs. I'm down here, so here is where I look.'

He unholstered his gun and began to gently thump the walls around the kitchen with the rubber handgrip, stopping often to listen for more movement. He opened the broom closet adjacent to the door of the storeroom. Tommy roared out as soon as the door cracked open, past Rooster's legs and into the abyss of darkness. Rooster kicked and missed, then relaxed when he realized it was probably the cat plundering inside the house the whole time. He sighed heavily, about to replace his firearm before he turned to close the broom closet door. There he saw the back of a dark haired man leaning against the back wall with hands splayed.

He fired his revolver instantly, just as the man disappeared. Rooster, wild with adrenaline, flicked the penlight back and forth, but the only evidence of the event was the gulf of hovering blue smoke and a huge hole in the back of the closet wall. His ears were still ringing from the confined blast of the .45 caliber revolver.

He stumbled backwards and stopped.

So much for stealth. He jumped to the doorway and flipped on the kitchen lights. Someone or something was there and that same someone or something knew he was there.

He quickly went back to the broom closet and checked the back wall to see if it was a false wall or doorway.

Again, the kitchen faucet turned on, and he spun to see..., nothing but water running into the empty sink.

Rooster steeled his nerves and walked to the sink and watched as the dull brass spigot turned itself off.

"Parlor tricks," he said, remembering what Damien Dimanche had told him.

"Parlor tricks!" he yelled. "You gonna haveta do better than that!"

One of the chairs by the kitchen table slid smoothly across the floor in front of him and stopped.

"Sssit," commanded a hissing voice.

"Hell no, I prefer to stand," said Rooster, now inching

toward the storeroom exit.

James turned off the kitchen lights and instantly began poking the big fellow in the chest with a rigid finger.

Blaze after sparkling blaze of deafening muzzle fire lit the dark kitchen until only an empty click, click, click, came from the revolver.

Rooster found his exit door already unlocked and open and waiting on him.

CHAPTER 15

"**Funny how the strongest** of wills can be rattled when facing the unknown," said Martiel. "You didn't hurt him did you?"

"Did I hurt *him*?" laughed James. "Only his pride, but the kitchen's gonna need some repairs."

Before his aunt could chide him about getting rough, he explained that it was the six rounds of bullets from the guy's cannon that did all the damage.

"Good, they won't be back inside the house anytime soon," said Martiel. "They'll be chasing their tails for at least a week, and that will give me time to find out more about Mr. Dimanche."

"Did you consider telling your friend at the Sheriff's Department about the break-in?" asked James.

Martiel looked stunned that he would even bring up the idea.

"You know, just in case one of Dimanche's men is willing to try and hurt someone. Oh, wait, that already happened."

"Your sarcasm is noted," she said glumly.

"At least you admit it," he argued.

"I didn't admit to anything, only noted."

James shifted to look Martiel directly in the face, "Then let me spell it out for you. His gun had real bullets in it.

He fired them at random in all directions in my family's house, while trying to kill me. Damien Dimanche wants us out of the way and you better wake up before he gets past me and kill's somebody. I already found out I can't be everywhere."

Martiel sat dumbfounded at his uprising.

"It's for your own good, James," she countered. "No killing."

James was visibly angered at her nonplussed attitude. Had she lost her mind or was she the one on the verge of losing contact with reality?

"Why do I suddenly feel like *Jiminy Cricket* here?" she asked. "Do you not have a conscience anymore?"

James turned his head and walked away. There was no solution to their argument.

"Have you heard from gramma and grampa?" asked James.

Their disagreement was being postponed for another time, despite her willingness to contest her nephew's hardened will until the bitter end.

"No. I gave them strict orders not to call here for any reason. I told Martin that if he needed me, to call his beloved Natchez Gazette and place a personal ad in the classifieds that only he and I know about."

Martiel grinned, "He kind of liked the idea of that. Said it was like being a secret agent. I guess we all have some latent childhood imaginations hiding in us somewhere. It just takes the right circumstances to make it surface."

She immediately began to make notes of the next few days' tasks leaving James to an impatient bout of pacing the room. She scribbled incessantly. Did she think this was some sort of grand test of wills or a game? James raised his usual inner wall, giving him the privacy of thought and solitude he needed. He'd let his aunt make all the plans she wanted, but he needed to be the realist. All her plans pivoted on him and his ability to move about with impunity.

Waiting..., again..., and it was stretching his patience as tight as a banjo string while he shuffled around the room.

"Oh for heaven's sake!" scolded Martiel. "Will you please stop that? I'm trying to think."

"I can leave," said James.

"And go where?" she asked. "You know you'll only get yourself in trouble. Ah..., Jolie..."

"She hasn't summoned me," said James. "I don't know where she is."

Martiel sighed heavily and set down her notepad. He knew exactly where Jolie was at that moment. Who was he trying to kid?

"James, you're as fickle as Jolie. One minute you want her to let go and move on, 'cause it's the *right thing,* then, the next minute you want to see her. You can't have it both ways. You got to make up your mind what you're gonna do."

"You make it sound so easy," said James. "I tell myself what to do, but I can't make myself do it."

"So you try to force her into making the decision for you," she snapped. "That's not fair to Jolie."

"I don't know how to let go," he whispered.

"They're all still at my place, for now," said Martiel,

finally, looking back down at her notes. "In Biloxi. As if you didn't already know."

James walked over to the window and looked out at the blackness of the night outside. Something else was calling him. He was actually feeling the horrendous surge of the Mississippi River only a mile from where he stood. Slowly his thoughts began to drift along with that same current. Then his mood darkened and his thoughts locked onto a memory.

"James.... James?" called Martiel. "That's not a good idea, don't go there...."

The room was already empty and silent.

"Oh James," she sighed.

It was almost ten o'clock. James had been standing at the entrance to Heaven's Gate Cemetery for half an hour. That same old drawing to the resting place of his bodily remains called to him. He expected all of that to end when his ordeal with the voodoo woman was over; it didn't. In fact, the call was getting stronger every day. An inexplicable urge to be near his cadaver, the desire to feel the soothing and pulsating energy called him at the oddest times. The battle of wills had prevented him from entering, falling to the crypt, and diving into the earth beneath. His list of reasons not to yield to that unknown, had grown shorter and shorter until only one remained burning bright.

That was Jolie.

The drawing was as strong as his feelings of love for her, maybe stronger, he couldn't tell, but so far his love for her was still winning the strange tug of war.

A healthy dose of caution and fear kept him from putting his hands in the flames he felt dragging him downward, back to his grave. The same old questions gnawed at his resolve, especially now that he had decided to stay.

If he touched his corpse, would he be trapped there? Isolated from the world, asleep? Would he be awake and stuck in his grave, in the cold darkness of his own private hell?

He remembered the pastor's advice of patience and his aunt Martiel's words of wisdom.

"What will my fear of the unknown make me do?"

James walked inside the gate but didn't hear or sense anything with rational thought. He grabbed a rusted cross on the first grave he came to matching iron for iron. Did anything in this place have any answers?

"Get up!" he hissed loudly, almost embarrassed with himself.

Lazily, a spirit obeyed him and sat in human form on top of its grave. James looked on, as the form of a man appeared bodily before him.

"What's your name?"

Vacant eyes with a yearning sadness turned to look James in the face. The eyes were as empty as the coffin that once contained a carnal body.

Disgusted, James said, "Sleep," and the fleshy apparition slid slowly back inside its resting place.

Again, he wandered around looking at the ancient graves in the old cemetery. Anger and bitterness rose from so many unanswered questions. These last few days were nearly unbearable with want and desire, something itching inside where he couldn't scratch.

"I need answers," he growled. "Surely, someone here has something left inside them...."

There was no way he would admit to his Aunt Martiel about this, especially after berating her for leaning on all of the ghostly family ancestors.

He raced to the entrance and turned facing the graveyard, a storm of power building inside. He placed both hands on either side of the iron archway and yelled, "Get up!"

He rattled Heavens Gate trying to wake the dead.

Groans and muted noises began coming from deep within the cemetery grounds. In minutes, a hoard of ghoulish creatures began moving toward him - angry, complaining, questioning where and what was going on.

James walked among them. Long past the horror of seeing the dead rise and walk. He looked and listened to each one of them, looking for something rational from at least one.

There was nothing here.

Each had awakened lost to the present time. There was no secret understanding flowing out of any one of them concerning the living or the dead. They were all nothing more than animated death, empty shills awaiting instructions from their overlord.

He felt the sensation of tears welling in his eyes, and emptiness filled him, a morose sadness began to tear at him, ripping him. Such grief..., and agonizing sorrow.

"It's them," he groaned. He was feeling their empty emotions.

"Sleep...," he barely whispered, desperate to rid himself of the multitude of parasites draining him of his strength.

Strength he desperately needed. His energy had raised them, but his energy was also needed to maintain their vigilance, and now apparently, it was also necessary to put them to rest.

Trying to speak brought only a dusty rasp from his throat.

What a fool.

This was surely the end for him and he was fading fast.

Where was his grave?

He had to find his grave.

If this was to be his end, he wanted to find his own, to lie down in peace.

James staggered back through rows of tombstones and markers, pushing the grasping throng out of his way until he saw the ghastly white monument his aunt Martiel and mother had conspired to have erected above his gravesite. It called to him.

The host of the dead continued to press behind him, touching him, draining him further of the energy that sustained him.

He fell forward with his hands outstretched against the cold white stone of his crypt.

Electric jolts shook him.

He crawled back to his feet as ripples of energy filled him, revived him, and soothed his weakened state. He turned to face his obedient followers and found those closest to him with their cankerous bodies in the process of restoration.

There was intelligence behind the eyes, recognition, and understanding.

"Do you know who you are?" asked James.

"Who I am," the creature repeated with a loud raspy whisper.

James read its simple mind and it was repeating, 'Who I am,' over and over inside its thoughts.

"You're empty," sighed James, "...they're all zombies."

He felt a sudden compassion for the throng of the dead, replacing their overwhelming despair. His desires to understand had outweighed his better judgment and now he had to right this terrible wrong.

"It'll be okay," he said, disgusted at the lack of information, relieved at his sudden rejuvenation.

"Sleep!" he commanded loudly across the meeting of faces.

The ground exploded with blue tendrils of light flowing outward from his body toward his followers. In a moment's time, all was quiet and James was once again alone in the dark graveyard.

The alone was absolute.

He stood for what seemed like ages clutching the stone of his grave, soaking in the power coming from his cadaver somewhere below.

"Lesson learned," said James. "Almost my last."

CHAPTER 16

The elemental body was pulsing with energy, rebuilding, strengthening itself..., and something completely unknown to James Earl was also taking place inside, shaping his will.

"James?"

A calming voice jolted him from his stupor of raw power. How long had he been standing here?

"James?"

He felt the pull, that irresistible yearning..., as he faded away.

"I'm here," said James. "You shouldn't be awake."

"You know me, I can't go to sleep without you near," said Jolie.

"I see you're still at Aunt Martiel's place." James had recognized the surroundings from his own summer visits as a child. He reached out and took her hand in his.

"You're hot," said Jolie. His touch produced a static shock.

"What have you been doing?" she whispered, as she withdrew her hand in fright.

"What I'm always doing, trying to understand myself. I'm tired of finding out everything by accident."

So many secrets, even from the one he loved. She simply wouldn't understand; he didn't expect her to.

Jolie rubbed her hands together in a frown, "Is it something I should know?"

"I always seem to be revisiting my past," he murmured, not really a lie. But it was far more than that; the power he'd been soaking in was like a wonderful drug, an addiction, filling and empowering him.

"That's dangerous," said Jolie, alarmed at his response.

He sounded odd and disturbed. He was hiding something from her..., as usual.

"Not as dangerous as not knowing. If you have my instruction manual, hand it over. Otherwise, I'm only left with trial and error," he said turning to the window.

"Always an attitude," said Jolie. "I don't know why I called you."

"I can leave if you want."

"Just like that? You can leave?" She stared deeply into his eyes. Gone was the emerald green she loved, replaced by that dead shade of gray she was afraid of. Another thing that she noticed immediately was his size. What was it? He seemed a little taller, filled out, something..., yes, something was different.

"You know I can't leave you," said James. He turned and paced the room. Upon closer inspection, he saw several small stacks of worn paperback novels, seashells, and a score of memorabilia from his visits. How convenient; Jolie was in the same room that he used when visiting his aunt.

A single candle illuminated the room, casting strange shadows in contrast with his smoky blue-gray night vision. And now, after the visit to his grave, the colors were a miasma of exotic rhythms.

There was a glow just on the outline of Jolie flowing from violet to bright blue in a pulse and it was hard to keep his eyes away from her, her every movement was hypnotizing.

"What have you done to yourself?" she asked. "I can't see in your thoughts at all. It's like you're not even here."

"Nothing that I know of. Maybe my distance from home or you simply can't see there anymore. It's probably better that way."

"Then I'll have to ask...," said Jolie.

"Ask what?" he snapped back.

His attitude was sharp, even hateful, and his words were just as cutting, but all this energy was causing him to have trouble controlling himself.

"What's been happening back in Natchez with you and your aunt? Has my father..., done anything?" she asked.

"Aunt Martiel called here. Didn't she give everybody a report?"

Before she answered his hate, "Jolie, I'm sorry. I'm having a problem controlling what I say. It's coming out all..."

"Choppy? Bitter? Hateful? Mean?" she offered.

"That bad huh?" James lowered his head in shame.

For a fleeting moment, he sounded like the James she cared for. James sat down on the edge of the bed and Jolie followed. He picked up her hand and held it gently. Jolie twitched at the static sensation, but didn't offer to pull away again, even though that same flow of energy was making her dizzy.

Martiel's words rang true in his memory; it was wrong to force Jolie to be the strong one.

"It's not easy being away from you," said James. "I know what I say, that it's best for you to move on, but I'm just as selfish. I still want you too, Jolie. I still need to be around you. Until I understand what I am, I can't promise you another minute. If something happened to me and I..., was gone.... I don't ever want to hurt you like that."

Jolie leaned up to kiss his cheek, knowing there would only be air.

"What have y..you d..done?" she stammered. "I felt you, you're solid."

She ran her hands across his chest, gripped his arms, frantically drawing him close to her, sensing that this was a fleeting moment and he would return to vapor at any moment. He *was* taller..., bigger.

She greedily pressed herself into the warmth of him. Her body took on a mind of its own, remembering everything she had wished for but was denied the chance while he was alive. Her arms slid up his back, pulling him even closer, as she let out a soft moan.

"Sssh, keep it down," said James. "You want to wake the whole house?"

"The whole town," spat Jolie.

James grinned and gazed into her eyes, cupping her face in his hands. The slim blue outline of light around her had turned pure clear red.

"What? Now you think it's funny?" asked Jolie.

"Not at all," said James as he pulled her into a kiss.

Jolie pushed back gasping for air before returning for a

second kiss, as wave after wave of electricity pulsed through her entire body.

James sat propped up against the wooden headboard, with Jolie curled around his chest, simply enjoying holding him close and feeling a real body. His warmth radiated through her like a heater and she gloried in the glow of the moment.

The sound of wind driven rain began pelting the window and she sighed, hugging James closer. He was here and she was already devising selfish ways to keep him right where he was for as long as possible.

"You never answered my question," said Jolie. "You didn't tell me what my father has been up to."

She didn't need to know about the vile aggressor who had paraded through his home in search of clues.

"He..., sent a visitor to the house to find out where everybody went. I misled him and..., ran him off," said James.

"That's all?" asked Jolie.

"Pretty much, we're waiting to see how your father reacts to the bait we fed him. How are things here?"

Jolie stiffened for an instant and then relaxed.

"That good?" snickered James.

"Aunt BeBe and your mother, *Catherine*, seem to be joined at the hip. Sisters no less," said Jolie.

James frowned and looked her in the face. Would Jolie rather the two women were at odds with each other? Surely Jolie wasn't jealous of BeBe's attention.

"And that's a bad thing?"

"No. No, I guess it's not, of course it's not," she whined. "But while they're having their private talks and chitchats, I'm stuck babysitting Sam most of the day. He follows me around like some stray puppy."

When James chuckled, his bare chest vibrated against her, "Jolie..., you're beautiful. You can't fault my little brother for having good taste. What did you expect?"

Jolie smacked him softly on the chest with her fist.

"I think there was a compliment somewhere in that. It's just that..., he's such a pain and he asks so many questions. He's nonstop."

"I'll have a talk with him," said James. "The girls his age chatter nonstop. He probably feels awkward when you keep your thoughts to yourself. You're an enigma."

"No. Don't do that," she said, sitting up. "That would be just... awful."

"I might as well. He's awake in the next room," said James. "He's been trying his best to hear what we were saying."

"NO!" she yanked at his hair. "Why didn't you tell me?"

Her face flushed hot at the very thought of Sam hearing....

"Don't worry, he didn't hear anything..., verbal," said James.

Jolie leapt from the bed, tying her gown around her waist. Her intentions were ready to break down the adjacent bedroom door and tear into Samuel Earl Williams.

"Wait, wait," said James, laughing at her version of damage control.

"I'm just kidding. He is awake..., but he just woke up."

"Errr...," gritted Jolie, smacking him on the arm. She couldn't keep from touching him, abandoning all self-control. She relished the corporeal solidity of the one person she had longed to feel near her once again. Then at once she grabbed him in a tight hug, smothering her face into his chest.

"It's so good to feel you," said Jolie. "Is this permanent?"

"I don't know," he answered. "Its part of that trial and error thing I told you about."

"I know you need to go," said Jolie.

"It's really late," said James.

Their synonymous announcements made them smile.

"You'd better leave before I do something I might regret," she sighed, "...or I might not ever let you go."

Jolie's eyes seemed to glow as he looked down at her face.

The heat of their last kiss was still on her lips as James faded into air leaving her with empty longing arms.

"Dang-it bro! You scared me." Sam's voice blared through the wall from the next room.

"What's a spook supposed to do, knock?" asked James.

Jolie muffled her amusement at Sam's fright, while she crawled back into bed, completely discarding the multitude of warnings going off inside her head. She pulled the chain on the little lamp beside the bed and drug out her journal from under her pillow. Finally, she had something good to record on its weathered brown pages.

CHAPTER 17

Rooster was awake with the dawn. The mirror's reflection confirmed what he already felt all over his body. Several deep bruises glared at him as his fingers smoothed over his bare chest.

The little round bruises ached. Not like being punched with a fist or hit with a pipe, those were feelings he was accustomed to. These were deeper, like his ribs were bruised from inside him.

He was a man of reason, accustomed to giving pain, and on occasion receiving it, but never from some invisible entity. That was crazy thinking and he threw it out, but it came right back in with the ache as he carefully stretched to put on his button-down shirt.

He threw back some aspirin and washed them down with a palm full of water from the faucet.

What would he tell Mr. Dimanche?

"A parlor trick attacked me and left me covered in bruises?"

He listened to the absurdity of his own voice.

"I unloaded my .45 on whoever it was and it didn't slow them down?"

Whoever? Or was it *whatever*?

Rooster composed himself and resigned to work "other jobs" for a while, maybe take some time off. He'd give

Damien the travel information on this weird family and get busy elsewhere. A man with his record was always in demand. Maybe he'd work the west coast shipyards for a while.

He wasn't going to ruin *his* reputation on some spook house. Nobody would hire him if word got around he was crackin' up.

"Just the facts," said Rooster, as he walked out the door.

"Smith, huh?" said Damien, smiling. He scratched through the travel brochures Rooster had offered him.

"And you found them in a locked desk," he continued his commentary, not looking up from the table top.

Damien sat thinking for so long that the men in the room became antsy and nervous from the silence.

Damien picked up each item he'd been given and assembled them like a poker hand.

"I don't like it," he finally blurted out.

He smacked them down on the coffee table in front of him.

"It's too easy. It sounds like something Regina would do, but..., I don't know these people..., so. Arthur, get two of your best men. Put them on the next plane to Vegas and check this out."

"Yeah boss. Do it now," came the response and his soldier turned to leave.

Damien arose from the sofa, impatience building inside him.

"I'm sick of this little podunk town and their historical societies. Let's get this over with. Anything else you want to tell me, Rooster? You didn't find any of those hiding places you told me about?"

"Nothin', just a creaky old house," said Rooster, subconsciously rubbing his chest.

"*Bene, bene*, well…, I'll contact you when it's time to clean up," said Damien.

"Sure thing, Mr. Dimanche."

Rooster left as soon as he was dismissed, but as soon as the door closed behind him, Damien snapped his fingers at his men to get their attention.

"You, Fatso. Earn your keep. Follow him, find out what's bugging Rooster," he ordered. "And don't screw up this time."

Damien picked up the pamphlet from James Earl's funeral announcement and studied it carefully.

"James Earl Williams."

He looked at his notes.

"Martin Earl Ames."

"Earl. Could be a grandkid," he pondered. Damien snapped his fingers once again. "Get the car. Before we leave we're going to pay our respects to this James Earl Williams."

The weather in the Twin Cities had turned foul overnight and a steady soothing drizzle pelted against Martiel's hotel windowpane. She yawned healthily and flipped on the television for company, then sank back down in the couch, sipping her coffee while waiting on room service to arrive with breakfast.

The headache crawled up and bit her moments before

the slideshow began across her muted vision. As soon as it had finished playing what little it wished to share with her, the headache left and her body relaxed once again. The visions were coming more frequent now and the ones about James were conflicting with one another; something that had never happened before.

"James?" she called out quietly. "You here?"

Her southern dialect turned her urging to *heah*.

"Yep, you're up early," said James.

It was strange of her to ask. Usually she could tell the instant he was anywhere near her.

"Yeah, ...early to rise and all that," she sighed.

"Are you okay?" asked James.

He knew something was wrong before he asked. But pressing her for the truth felt hypocritical, considering his constant objections to her probes.

"Yeah, that rain..., its sleepy weather," she commented. "This is one of those days I'd like to curl up under the covers and hide for a few more hours.

It wasn't a lie..., but it certainly wasn't the whole of the matter. James held his thoughts. When she was ready, she'd share what was bothering her.

"After breakfast, we need to head on down to Natchez and pay a visit to Heaven's Gate Cemetery. I expect our friendly mobster has been nibbling on our bait."

"So you found some information about him?" asked James.

"Yes, I'm afraid I did. Damien Dimanche is hell on wheels. One of his men roughed up somebody I know in New Jersey. Someone I sent to find out about him. Mr.

Dimanche probably knows my name by now."

"You seem so calm about that Aunt Martiel. How close do you want to let him get?" scoffed James. "Please don't use yourself as bait. I don't want to risk you getting hurt again. I'm tired of my family getting beat up on."

"It's not going to be like that James," she said, dismissively.

"Right. So you tell me how it's going to be," said James.

"You don't know these people like I do. You don't know what they're capable of. If you don't start working with me on this, it's not going to end well, Aunt Martiel."

She nodded somberly in agreement, then explained her thinking, "You do something to one of his people. He'll do something worse to one of ours."

Didn't she get it? He had free access to Damien Dimanche and his entire horde without any ties back to his family.

"It doesn't have to be that way. I know you think I'm some bloodthirsty, power crazy nephew, and well..., some parts of me might be, but that's not what I'm made of. I love my family."

Martiel looked at James for several minutes before commenting. "I had another one of my premonitions," she explained. "Last night."

She sipped her coffee and became quiet once again, not mentioning her most recent enlightenment.

"And?" he asked. "What does that mean?"

She raised both hands in the air, "Scrambled eggs. It doesn't mean anything right now, and they are subject to change. Time will tell."

"It looks *fuor di luogo,* out of place here." Damien railed on, waving his hands like a conductor at a music hall.

Droplets of rain were pelting his umbrella, dripping onto the fringes of his new suit. It was cheap and he despised it hanging across his shoulders. He imagined the pleasure of breaking the knees of whoever stole his favorite charcoal Armani.

The umbrella shook as he swatted at a mosquito running a strafe from out of the steam hovering just above the ground.

"This old cemetery, these old markers, and then there is this big white monolith with its big brass plate in memorial to this teenage boy," he coughed out the last words. "It doesn't add up and I'm not buying it."

The ropes of Spanish moss hanging from the trees glistened from the fresh rain, turning their mass of cascades from drab gray to sea green.

Damien fanned his hand in the air at the tomb of James Earl Williams in an odd display of disgust. "This was a trap for someone," he said quietly. *"Esca* - bait, a Trojan horse, or a big show for someone. I don't know. I can't quite put my finger on it."

Another car pulled up in the parking lot by the gate of the cemetery. It was quiet, and almost went unobserved, but one of Damien's men turned to listen into the distance.

"A car. You want I should run them off?" he asked.

"We don't want to attract attention. Let's see who visits an old place like this on such a dreary day."

In through the gate walked an attractive middle-aged

woman, wearing a knee-length beige wrap, gripping an oversized black umbrella and holding a small shock of bright flowers. Locked onto her right arm was a fellow at least a foot taller, maybe six foot two or six-four, dark jeans and t-shirt, wearing an enviable tailored blue jacket. His shoulders and arms strained the coat into an impressive "V".

Damien secreted glances and watched every nuance of the pair as they neared where he was standing. Somehow they managed to keep their faces askance not allowing him to view their features.

The young man had wavy black hair that was almost shoulder length but it didn't seem affected by the steady misty drizzle.

They walked down an adjacent row in the distance and stopped no more than fifty feet away with their backs to Damien and his entourage, at a relatively new, yet simple grave marker.

The young man placed the flowers on the grave and touched the stone for a few moments, and then they turned and left.

Damien watched them closely until they were out of sight.

"Let's go see the bereft grave," urged Damien, the moment they heard the other car leave.

His men were growing impatient of the humidity, the persistent drizzle, the mosquitoes, but obedience was a lifesaver in their line of work, thus there were no verbal complaints.

Damien looked at the headstone and read the name

aloud, if only to get their attention, "Wema Smith."

"*Smith*," he repeated, until the light of recognition flickered in their dull eyes.

"Smith," he gritted again.

"Let's go. *Andiamo!*" he pointed toward the exit.

His facial features hardened into stone and if the rain had met his skin, it would have turned to steam.

When he reached the limousine, the driver jumped out to open the doors for his passengers. Damien stopped in front of the driver, who was obviously annoyed at the rain batting his eyelashes.

"Did you see the car that pulled in here? Or the two people that got out? Or maybe which way it went?"

"I saw…," he bumbled, with reddening face.

"No, of course you didn't."

CHAPTER 18

The drizzle on the windshield was turning into fog as the BMW purred peacefully onto the exit to the River Cities Bridge, but inside it contained an atmosphere of anger. It wasn't the weather or the unusually heavy traffic that was causing the confusion.

"Now please tell me why you made me take you right up to the jaws of the lion. Those men were killers."

"We were sending Damien Dimanche a message," she explained. "It had to be this way James and if I had told you, you would have never taken me there. Now he knows that he can be played, he can be tricked, by his own cunning. We drew him out into the open, vulnerable, he won't like it. No sir, he won't like it one bit, which gives us the advantage. Now he won't trust any information he gets without double and triple checking it. We just threw a monkey wrench in his gears."

"If you're so confident we did all that, then why don't you sound happier?" asked James.

The sign reading: "You are now entering Louisiana," flew by unobserved in the silence.

"Because now, our job gets harder," she confessed. "Up until now, we've been shuffling pawns. We just placed Damien's King in check and now it's his move."

139

The first thing Damien Dimanche did when he entered his hotel room was rip off the cheap suit jacket and shove it into the hotel waste bin.

"Where's Fatso!" railed Damien. His voice cracked as the door flew open.

"He's trailing Rooster, Boss. Like you told him," said Arthur.

"I told him to trail Rooster and get some information, not marry him and have his kids. Find Fatso and get him back here, and call the hanger. Tell them to get the plane ready, we're leaving this mosquito pit."

"Yeah Boss..., right away Boss."

"I ran the plates on that car you gave me," said Detective Floyd. Floyd's eyebrows arched and he tipped his head, letting the Sheriff know it was for his ears only.

The lines on Sheriff Howard's face curled and straightened in expectation. Detective Floyd immediately noticed how the edge of gray hair was accelerating up the sides of the Sheriff's head these last few weeks. Hard choices and death had worn away the youthful dark brown hair that was always so neatly trimmed.

The Sheriff's office was already humming with activity, an oddity for this early in the morning, and Sheriff Howard shooed off one of his men from inside his office and closed the door.

"Have a seat, Floyd," said the Sheriff.

"The limo is leased by a corporation up on the east

coast," he began, not waiting for an invitation to speak.

"I think they're *connected*, if you know what I mean," said the detective. "I made a few calls for detailed information and got flagged to some FBI office. Basically they stonewalled me, they won't talk, but they sure had a lot of questions for me. So, I gave them the same professional courtesy. I didn't know anything either, it was a *routine traffic investigation*," he grinned.

The Sheriff looked puzzled and began thinking out loud.

"What were they doing at the Ames house? And what did he mean, pick up his daughter?"

The detective turned pale and sat back in his chair.

"That's where you saw the limousine? You didn't tell me that."

"Does that mean anything to you, Floyd?" asked the Sheriff.

"No, uh, no of course not, it's just after that kidnapping incident and all the bad trouble we had out there recently…," he stammered for an explanation.

He referred to the death of James Earl Williams as well as the attacks on the family as *trouble* and the Sheriff noticed the obvious downplay.

"The kidnapping, right," mused the Sheriff, as he remembered the foray of names and faces he'd interviewed after the recent crime spree. "The girl. The young girl that was kidnapped by that cult. What was her name?"

He reached inside his bottom desk file drawer and pulled up a thick manila envelope and fanned through the stack of papers.

"Dimanche," he muttered, barely a whisper.

Sheriff Howard remembered those eyes, those piercing eyes he had seen only two or three times in his lifetime as an officer of the law. The man that stood before him in the Ames driveway, the man that faced off with him, was a snake.

If truly the eyes are the windows to the soul, this man had nothing that resembled one inside. His ice blue eyes spoke of those he had ordered or personally sent on to the great beyond.

"Thank you Floyd. Let's keep this between us for now, okay? I'll get back with you after I make a few phone calls, detective. What's your case load like for the next eight or ten days?"

Sheriff Howard closed the manila file and put it inside a leather folder on his desk, while Floyd watched his every move.

"I'm working another homicide on that damn floating casino again. You remember, the one from the Fourth of July? Then there're two burglaries near the waterfront. Is there something you need help with Sheriff?" asked Floyd, his tone becoming cautious.

"Maybe..., probably," said Howard. "I'll be sure to keep you in the loop."

There was a peck on the glass door and Sheriff Howard waved the pair of peering eyes inside his office.

Detective Floyd waited anxiously, eager to leave and try to understand what just happened. He heard the sheriff's door close behind him and hurried along the wall to his own office.

Visions of the unspeakable rolled through his mind and his hands began to tremble. He closed the door and crunched down into his chair. Even though the events with the Ames Family had ended on a positive note, and his relationship with James Williams ended well also, the events were not on his top ten list of good memories. He knew what a bad cop was; he knew intimately. He had been that bad cop, until a seventeen year old boy gave him a chance, a chance to make a good choice.

Now it was inevitable; he new it was only a matter of time before he would get a visit. One that he never wanted to get again, not as long as he lived.

"Gone but not forgotten," said Martiel. "I certainly hope Damien's men appreciate their free vacation to Las Vegas."

"He's not going to like being made a fool of, Aunt Martiel."

"That's why I told Catherine and BeBe to come home, now that Damien has left," she replied. "You'll be able to watch them better here. They'll be hiding out in the open, so to speak."

"It sounds more like you're using them as bait. Is this another one of your plans?"

She didn't want to answer that question and applied one of her usual diversions.

"I expected more of a protest, James. Has something changed that I don't know about?"

He hated when she answered his questions with more questions. But he specifically didn't want to answer *that* question. It meant that he had conceded to allow Jolie as more of a permanent fixture and more importantly, that he desperately wanted her.

Was that such a bad thing? She somehow filled that void, even controlled and quieted his thoughts of insanity. After all his protests, he would look stupid if he admitted that he needed Jolie like most people needed their next breath.

"No, you're probably right," said James. "I think I can watch them. If you won't restrict how and when I choose to shield everyone, I won't protest."

"If you mean, will I give you carte blanche to *whack* somebody, then no." Martiel was already prompting for a heated discussion.

"Where did you hear that word?" laughed James. "*Whack*. Besides, I'm more resourceful than that."

She urged forward and gazed into his eyes, "And that bothers me."

"Everything about me bothers you now," spat James. He turned his back, rubbing his arms, hiding the hateful expression on his face.

"And it also bothers me that you seem to be larger now. Taller maybe? Thicker across the shoulders? I can't put my finger on it. You barely fit into your blue blazer the other day."

James laughed, "It's my new diet. Besides, if you hadn't made me wear the real thing, I could have probably put it on myself from memory."

"Be serious James," she scoffed.

"Fine. I'll do my best not to -*whack*- anybody, barring

accidents."

"I saw what your accidents look like in the kitchen," griped Martiel. "That's gonna take a week or more to repair and even harder to explain to Martin and Maime."

"Hey, I didn't do it. You want me to send Rooster a bill?"

"Just be more careful James. You might be bullet proof, but we aren't."

Martiel was proving his point for him, despite her objections, "And that's exactly why there might be accidents."

CHAPTER 19

The private office in the high-rise building was quiet and had been for several hours. Damien Dimanche demanded privacy while inspecting items of information his team had worked tirelessly to gather over the last few days. His huge desk was littered with bits and pieces of scraps of paper. There were fresh tiny grains of the life of his daughter Jolie, her Aunt BeBe, and her new friends. Damien made it look like he was assembling an abstract jigsaw puzzle from several different boxes of puzzles.

This was just the kind of challenge he enjoyed. He watched as one little trail of bread crumbs intersected with another, throwing himself into the mindset of each person for each character in his little imaginary play. Inventing the possibilities and scenarios and interactions until even more of the crumbs lined up into a solid trail. He had used this process many times to discover the actions of rogue enemies and over the years it had proven to be his saving grace; once thwarting his own execution.

He stretched back into his comfortable leather chair, and rubbed his tired eyes. A crystal decanter spilled amber liquid into a tumbler and he held it in the light streaming in through the windows behind his desk. For once he was ever so glad to be back in native New Jersey territory. Already his allergies were subsiding along with the congestion and he was breathing easier.

Abandoning the scraps for a moment, he focused on two stacks of papers on the corner of his desk. The letterhead on top of the first stack had the logo of the Federal Bureau of Investigation, with its official crest and watermark.

"Ellington Investments, LLC," he muttered.

He flipped through a few pages of printed material.

"Quite a portfolio..., and old money. The dame has brains and balls. I'm impressed."

For a fleeting moment, he didn't feel quite so foolish, that he had allowed himself to be manipulated so easily by a stranger, a *woman* no less.

He gripped the first few pages and bounced them on edge in a neat stack and began creating another fragile sequence.

The next stack had a funeral brochure clipped to the top.

"Robert and Catherine Williams."

Interesting.

He let his thoughts ramble as he read through the pages.

'They've lived all over New Jersey. What was wrong with this picture? Who moves their family this much? People with troubles, that's who. At least they tried to move away to Boston, but now they're over in Lincoln Park. And they just moved there?'

He crunched back in the chair with a grin, "I'll be damned. It *is* a small world."

He looked again at the long list of previous addresses.

"Huh..., some of the old neighborhoods."

The information on Robert Williams was colorful. Damien barked out a coughing laugh as he read about his journey from roughneck turned security expert on the coattails of his wife's money. Apparently, the only thing he was an expert at was concealing his many clandestine affairs. His wife was the real breadwinner.

He tossed those sheets aside as useless. A man like that couldn't be trusted for information, even if he was paid.

Next were the two children, listed as James Earl Williams (deceased), and Samuel Earl Williams.

"Wow, the dead kid had a record. A long one. I wonder...," he said, laying the paper aside.

He punched a button on his interoffice intercom and held it down.

"Mildred, look in the safe. Bring me the folder of names marked *FED*," he said, then released the button with a snap.

"I need a fresh name. Someone that hasn't proven his loyalty yet," he mumbled, putting away the rest of the stack of papers. "If it was your money I wanted, Ms. Ellington, this would be easy. I just need to find my ex-wife and you happen to be standing – in – my - *WAY*." His face became stone as he pounded his desk in emphasis.

"So. Now we play some nine-ball, Martiel Ellington. Let's see just how good you really are."

"I don't care!" said Catherine.

James sat with a somewhat whipped look on his face.

"Sam is only a kid. You don't need to be telling him

your wild stories about what you did to that burglar."

She looked around at the destruction of the kitchen walls and ceiling.

"If it's the stupid holes in the kitchen you're worried about...."

"No, James. I'm not that shallow," said Catherine. "Sam is still impressionable and you are..."

"Wait, stop right there," snapped James. "I don't want to hear another sermon about how I'm his *role model*. I'm freakin' dead here. I'm nobody's *role model,* understand? I'm not staying away from Sam just because you think I'm a bad influence either. He's my brother. Besides you already tried keeping us apart and see how that turned out."

It was obvious his mother had struck the deep vein of an old painful grievance.

"I'm just asking you to tone it down, James. Don't glorify violence around him. Haven't you both seen enough of that?"

James lowered his eyes from the staring contest with Catherine and regained his composure.

"Yeah, I guess you could be right, maybe a little," he conceded.

Catherine realized that this was the first rational argument that she had won with James since he was four years old. Something was different, something was changing about her oldest son. Satisfied that the confrontation had ended, however fragile the peace might be, she exhaled slowly, looking at her boy.

"And what's up with the growth spurt?" she asked,

diverting the conversation. "You didn't think I'd notice?"

James shrugged his shoulders, knowing there was no way he was going to tell her about his recent nocturnal graveyard visit or the side effects. It was funny to him that only Jolie had bothered to notice that he was now solid as a tree whenever he was visible.

"Well..., it looks good on you," she added cautiously. "James, I'm sorry too."

She waved her hand at all the splintered holes in the walls and cabinets. "I guess I'm just scared at all this."

"It's okay Mom. Have you heard from dad?" asked James.

She quickly changed her expression and turned away, but not for the reasons he assumed. She walked over to the counter and picked up her purse. After fumbling inside it, she reluctantly snatched out an envelope and half tossed it to James.

"Is this what I think it is?" he asked.

She didn't answer, but she wasn't crying either. Her face was fixed with a strength James hadn't seen in many, many years.

James held the envelope to his forehead and rolled his eyes upwards.

"Divorce papers," he blurted, feigning an old *Carson* scene.

Catherine pursed her lips and finally let out a laugh. It was a good tension breaker.

"You want I should pay him a visit," said James, using the voice of his old neighborhood; which incited a few more smiles.

"No. I don't need you to *pay him a visit*," she smiled.

"What does he want?"

"Nothing. That's the strange thing," she answered.

"Not even joint custody of Sam?"

Catherine shook her head and shrugged.

"No money, no custody, a clean break. Do you think he's up to something?"

"Or someone," said Catherine blandly.

"Aunt Martiel handed it over to one of our lawyers. Martiel said..., well..., I won't repeat what she said."

Catherine arched her eyebrows and released a long tense breath.

CHAPTER 20

The aroma inside The Cajun Café drifted out into the sidewalk traffic, luring several groups inside and creating a busy evening. One of the family employees had strung chili pepper lights around in various places, giving the dining area a festive hue.

"It's a good thing Maime doesn't know what she's missing," said Martiel.

She sipped at the sweating glass of sweet iced tea noisily, cooling off the fire on her tongue. The other two nodded as they fought over a heaping platter of appetizers.

Sam Earl buzzed past and grabbed a handful of food before scurrying back to the lone pinball machine. For him, visiting the restaurant was like a reprieve from prison and he was making the most of his freedom.

Jolie, Catherine and Martiel were seated at a corner table waiting for BeBe to relinquish her duties to the hired help so she could join them.

An invisible James sat crunched in an empty chair near Jolie. She could feel his warmth near her side. Thankfully, they could share a silent conversation between their thoughts that wouldn't alarm the other Café guests.

The waitress eventually brought out their order of Cajun grilled shrimp and steak fajitas, with colorful peppers and onions sizzling on the platter.

BeBe spun by, making another circle through the full capacity crowd.

"She just can't let go, can she?" said Martiel.

Jolie smiled, "She built this place from scratch. We practically know everybody by name. Even the tourists come back here every year."

"Mmm, this is so good," said Martiel, sneaking a piece of sizzling steak from the heap.

BeBe walked by on her return circuit placing both hands on the table. She blew a puff of air through her pursed red lips and relaxed into a smile.

"I just flipped the switch on the neon to 'closed'. I'll drop in as soon as my cook finishes with the last table's order."

BeBe looked at the circle of faces, "You aren't waiting on me I hope. Eat while it's hot. Oh! You need more coolant. Tea's on the way."

She quickly turned and disappeared across the room.

"I admire BeBe's energy," said Catherine. "I wish I'd had her working with me several years ago."

"She'd have been out of her element with those hoity-toity clients of yours," Martiel clipped. "This is where she flourishes. Besides, where would we find...," her voice drifted away just as she lifted a battered french-fry, her eyes slanted across the table at Jolie.

"Is it just the fajitas or is it getting warm in here Jolie?" asked Martiel, suddenly fanning herself.

Jolie's face flushed three shades of red, as she instantly remembered that the private conversation between her and James wasn't as private as she had hoped.

Catherine sat staring between the two of them and finally asked, "Did I miss something?"

"Who-wee. I'll say," Martiel mumbled, stuffing the squished french-fry in her mouth.

BeBe sat down at the table with a pitcher of tea before Catherine had time to pry deeper into Martiel's vague answer.

"It feels so good to be back at work," BeBe said. "I know you think I'm strange, but I feel out of place when I'm not busy."

Talk was as light as their mood and it didn't take long for the food to disappear from their table. Very soon most of the tables began to thin out.

"Down to business," said Martiel. "Do you two ladies mind staying with us until we get a handle on what Jolie's father intends to do next?"

"You sound like you're already sure that he's going to be back," said BeBe. "If that's true, why don't we send Jolie out west with Gina? She's hidden herself pretty well these last few years. Surely we can find a way to pack her out of here without anybody seeing her."

"Regina's been lucky," said Martiel. "And that's what Damien wants us to do. He wants someone to lead him to Jolie's mother."

She leaned toward Jolie, "We *will* have a little conversation about that later, in a more private setting."

Instead of Jolie responding to Martiel, she turned abruptly toward an invisible James.

"Aunt BeBe, James wants to know who the guy is over

by the front window seat."

"Just a new customer," she said. "Comes in here about the same time every day, for about a week now I'm told. Law enforcement, I think."

Jolie's hand lifted from her lap and plopped on the table and she looked up.

"And you didn't tell me?" asked Martiel. "I'll have Sheriff Howard check him out."

"Don't bother," James whispered in Martiel's ear. "He's the one."

James moved across the room to the table where the man was seated, busily scraping at his nearly empty plate in hopes for one more bite. His suit of clothes looked cheap, as if plucked out of a government issued closet.

With the recent unstoppable influx of everyone's thoughts, James was becoming increasingly fascinated by the way people made sense of their life. Some people's thoughts were simple and clear, easy to read, and others were jumbled. It wasn't that he couldn't listen in, it was the fact that they were conflicted inside and thinking out pro's and con's of their life or several tense situations. The man at this front table was one of those people; heavily conflicted. The person he'd been watching..., who'd been watching them.

The bulging, poorly concealed shoulder holster under his jacket, advertised his vocation as a law officer or maybe trouble; most likely both in James Earl's recent experience.

Jolie, who had the best vantage point, noticed as the man sat up and stiffened for a moment, then rubbed both arms with his hands. Moments later he rose to leave.

"James says he's FBI, but he'll tell us more later tonight."

"So Mr. Dimanche is already busy," said Martiel. "I'm so sorry darlin'. I know it must be uncomfortable for me to refer to your father in a less than friendly fashion."

"It's okay," said Jolie. "I've learned to separate my personal feelings for him as my father and from what he does. I've heard him referred to as a lot worse than that. I guess you could say he's earned his own reputation."

Special Agent Warner of the FBI quickly scurried down the sidewalk to an ugly navy blue car with black-wall tires, bulging from black steel rims. The Louisiana license plates were marked 'exempt', advertising its intended vocation. The wind-filtered shadows of an elm tree rendered the car barely noticeable under the dim overhead street lamps.

James Earl Williams deposited himself in the back seat and waited as the Agent slid behind the steering wheel and closed the door.

While Warner sat patiently, watching the door of the Cajun Café, James locked onto the stream of choppy garbage emanating from his mind in an effort to discover any hidden motives.

Special Agent Warner was assigned to a task force to monitor the activity of recently reported movement from organized crime in the New Orleans region. Obviously, he was out of the boundaries of the state of Louisiana and likely his jurisdiction as well.

His immediate interest and *unofficial* task was watching the movements of Jolie Lefleur Dimanche. Warner was nothing more than an errand boy with a badge.

James thought back on the long ordeal with Deputy Preston Floyd, now *Detective* Floyd with the Adams County Sheriff's Department. It must have been a weak moment, his own tragedy, or the hinted plea from Sheriff Howard that urged him to go through the agonies of reformation with Officer Floyd. Sheriff Howard still wouldn't admit, not even to himself, to colluding with the apparition of James on behalf of Floyd.

It was a true measure of forgiveness, considering Floyd participated in arranging the murder of James Earl.

However, he didn't regret his decision. Detective Floyd was truly a changed man. It actually reinforced his belief in humanity to see something good come out of the man.

However, he had no intentions of rehabilitating yet another corrupt officer of the justice system.

The mental conflict inside Special Agent Warner's thoughts was what brought James to his decision, his own conflicting decision.

Loud and clear, Warner was plotting how to abduct Jolie and if one of the friends or family had an accident in the process, it would be a bonus.

But why? Did he really need the money that badly? Or was it the thrill of getting to work with a crime syndicate? No obvious reason presented itself as to why and James quit trying to probe to find out. At this point, it didn't matter.

The Agent's plans were about to change.

Together, Warner and James watched patiently as the last of the patrons emptied out of the café, eventually followed by the working staff.

The lights went out, the neon *'closed'* sign already glowing brightly in the front window as the family walked out. Their buoyant chattering and laughing could be heard from across the street, huddling close to each other, waiting for BeBe to lock the door.

James had waited until the last minute to test and see if the FBI agent was actually going to follow through with his orders. At the very least he deserved the benefit of the doubt, but the agent settled his inner conflict and cranked the engine.

James made himself appear in the back seat of the unmarked car and stuck a steely cold finger up against the back of the agent's head.

"Have I got your attention?" asked James.

There was no answer except for a slight nod of the head and a desperate attempt at looking in the rear view mirror. All the agent could see was the silhouette of a large man with long dark hair and the voice was barely a deep growl. Warner slowly slid his right arm, already resting in his lap, upwards toward his holstered weapon. James twitched his ice cold finger once again against the base of the man's skull.

"Drive," James ordered.

"Wait, can we talk about this?" asked the agent.

"On the way," said James. "Go, make it quick."

As the car took off, James reached over the seat and flipped on the car's wailing siren and hidden grill lights.

"I always wanted to do that. Head for the Interstate, cross the bridge, then take the south exit toward New Orleans."

"You won't get away with this," said Special Agent Warner.

"I've heard that once or twice before," said James.

CHAPTER 21

Cold sweat was collecting on the ends of the agent's burred hair like morning dew and his voice was not the same self-assured steady one that he had been trained to use at the academy. That practiced voice was proven to show an adversary that a federal agent wasn't easily intimidated or out of control.

With the piece of cold steel pressed uncomfortably against the kill spot at the base of his skull, the agent was now considering his own short future.

"How much farther?" asked the agent. "What is it you want?"

A steady drizzle had settled in and the road was becoming an abyss in front of the dim headlights. Soon they were out of the Vidalia City Limits and the agent was getting antsy behind the steering wheel.

"What's the matter? You don't like using the siren and driving fast?" asked James. "I thought all you guys liked showing your authority."

'Play it through, wait for an opportunity,' thought Warner, taking a deep breath.

"Pull off at the next exit," said James. "This is far enough."

In an instant, 'Far enough for what?' reverberated in Warner's mind.

"See the road that leads down to the river? Take that one," ordered James.

"Look, we don't have to do this," said the agent.

"Yes we do," said James calmly, then pointed. "Over there."

The tires crunched and the car lurched through several slushy ruts.

"This is good. Stop here. Get out of the car."

James turned off the siren and lights, which warbled to a dead silent darkness. It was the exact type of anti-climactic dead quiet James wanted; a final curtain call.

The inevitable desperation of the moment overcame the agent's good judgment and he grabbed for his gun as he shut the car door.

James let him.

"Put your hands up!" he yelled, voice quivering. "Throw away your weapon!"

"You don't have to yell," said James calmly. "See? No gun."

James raised both empty palms then crossed his arms in a relaxed pose.

"Turn around, put your hands on the car," he screamed.

Warner's voice was shaking nervously as he realized how close he had come to meeting some unexpected terrible end.

"Let's talk instead, Special Agent Warner. You did want to talk, remember?"

"How do you know my name? Never mind, that doesn't matter. The only talking you're going to do is to the gravel in the river."

James needed information and this ignorant fool's thoughts were a mass of misdirected spasms of fear.

"Why are you following that family?" asked James in an effort to get Warner to focus.

The agent was now frantic that this ominous man was not obeying his orders, even at gunpoint.

"I have my orders, now turn around!" he yelled again.

"Who gave you your orders?" asked James.

James saw the picture of a face flash into the agent's mind for a split second.

"Ahh, the guy with the gray hair," said James. "What's his name...?"

James feigned trying to recall a disobedient memory.

The agent provided the answer.

"Yeah, that's it. Morrison, yeah, Morrison," said James, smiling at his flash of ingenuity. "He's the one that told you to kidnap the girl and you might even get a promotion if it went well."

Agent Warner had received his orders in a closed door session with Morrison. No one was supposed to know....

"What?" squeaked the agent. "Who told you...? How did you...?"

"You just did," said James.

Agent Warner was peeved, feeling he'd been tricked into confirming a guess.

"Which office do you work out of?" asked James.

Immediately the gun rose in a double-handed grip directly into James Earl's face.

"New Orleans," nodded James. "Special Crimes. That's impressive."

"Who are you?" asked Warner, shaking the gun for emphasis.

"Just a concerned citizen," said James, showing his palms.

"You're new aren't you?" mumbled James. "What a way to end a career. Did they tell you who to call if things got messy?"

James listened while Warner circled him, waving the gun and trying to force him to move toward the riverbank.

"They didn't. They left you high and dry," said James. "You were expendable..., and you wanted to work for people like that?"

"I'm gonna ask you one more time," he said, clenching the words. "How did you know about me?"

They faced off in the silent darkness for less than sixty seconds, which seemed like an eternity to the stunned agent. The steady drizzle of rain had turned into a mist that was beading up on his crew cut.

"It doesn't matter how you know. You and I are going to take a walk," he said, waving the gun again. "Out to the river, now! I don't want to have to carry your dead body, but I will...."

James flashed a hand out and took away the stunned agent's weapon, nearly snapping the man's wrist.

"Impressive, isn't it?" said James. "Didn't they teach you how to do that at the academy?"

There was no answer. The agent was too busy holding his wrist and grimacing from the pain. Then the devastating terror of the reversed situation settled back into Warner's mind.

"What are you going to do with me?" he asked.

"What would you do, if it was me?" asked James. "Oh, wait, you were about to show me what you'd do."

James took Warner by his good wrist and threw him back toward the car.

"Get inside, we're going for another ride, a short one."

"No, wait, I can pay you. I have connections that can set you up," said the agent. "All I have to do is make a phone call."

James tore the handcuffs off the agent's belt, fighting back offerings of anger.

"I..., I can get you anything you want. Don't do this! I..., I have a family."

James laughed, "No you don't. You're a horrible liar."

Once in the drivers' seat, James laced the handcuffs to both Warner's wrists through the steering wheel. Then the agent watched as James hurled the gun past the headlights of the car and his heart sank as it plopped quietly into the Mississippi River.

James walked around the car and slid in beside the agent, stuffed the keys in the ignition and started the car.

"You and me," said James. "Let's go."

A string of obscenities began to roll from the mouth of the agent.

"Are those going to be your last words?" asked James.

James stomped the gas and steered the car directly at the dark water. The evil of how James died flashed before his memory. It wasn't a death he could wish on any one, even an enemy.

The agent gritted his teeth as the car flew off the

shallow drop of riverbank into the Mississippi River.

The car hit the water with the impact of a brick wall.

As they began to submerge, James saw that the agent was unconscious from the force of the blow, not dead, but he would have one heck of a headache.

CHAPTER 22

Relieved that his Aunt Martiel was willing to share yet another of her visions, it had been a pleasure letting last night's events in the café play out exactly the way she had described.

Watching the special agent at the table, eating casually, while taking notes of descriptions of the people surrounding BeBe and Jolie was fascinating. He still didn't understand the necessity of the ruse to keep the others in the dark, other than keeping them from being afraid.

Now he was anxious to recall all the events of the rest of the story to fill in the uncertain portions of her vision.

"Take a note," said James.

Martiel retrieved her note pad that she was using to assemble all her information.

"The guys name is Morrison, stocky guy, close set eyes, and short gray crew cut. He works behind a desk at the FBI Headquarters in New Orleans."

Martiel scribbled as quickly as she could.

"The guy from the restaurant, his name's Warner, Special Agent John Warner."

He recanted the names and descriptions of several other co-conspirators garnered from his interrogation of Agent Warner, filling half a page, including a phone number.

When he was through, Martiel looked over the list, "James..., this is impressive. You didn't hurt him too badly did you?"

There was that same annoying question again. She was hiding something again as well.

"Naah, just a couple of bruises, but I predict he's going to have other troubles and a lot of explaining to do. It's gonna be one major fish tale."

"That's *his* problem," said Martiel. "I don't expect you to save the world, just our family. Understand me James. I really don't care what you do. I just don't want someone's blood on your hands. Hun, you're going to be around for a long time. A bad conscience and a long time don't mix too well. You'll thank me some day, long after I'm gone from this world."

James thought this over for a few moments. She was most likely recanting the memories and regrets from her latent group of ghostly advisors. He nodded in agreement, but only to avoid another long drawn out discourse.

"Now, before our Special Agent can construe a lie to tell his Mr. Morrison, we need to put a bug in Mr. Morrison's ear. We want him to know that Warner gave up his name and possibly more. He doesn't need to know that it was this long of a list."

She held up the notepad, still impressed at the number of names involved.

"I'm glad you're on our side, Aunt Martiel."

"Yes, well," she mumbled. "Likewise."

She licked her suddenly parched lips as she stared up at James, "I do have my devious moments."

She flipped the notepad's pages back over.

"Now we know who this Morrison character is. We don't really need to know the exact chain of command and all that. These are just names in no certain order. What we do want is for them to question the sanctity of everybody they report to, right up to the top of their food chain. It would be nice to have some idea of how deep and wide the corruption goes."

"Do you want me to go find this Morrison and follow the trail?" asked James.

"No, no, I have my resources too. You need to stay here and guard the fort. In my experience, devils tend to run in pairs. We have to stay alert, especially at the restaurant."

Martiel put the notepad down on the table and rubbed her forehead and eyes. She picked the pad back up and made another note with a heavy sigh. Her visions had not only increased in volume, they had also increased in intensity. She had her suspicions that it had something to do with her constant contact with James Earl. Whatever was happening to him was having some strange effect on her.

"Please, go take a nap," said James. "I'm the one that doesn't need sleep, remember? You're still human."

"So are you James," she said softly.

"Everybody out! *Esci!*" screamed Damien.

The room cleared in mere seconds without question. Every man that heard the report, that saw Damien's face, dreaded being the first called back into to his office.

When Damien went crazy with rage, their lives were

nothing more than a roll of the dice.

There was an unwritten, secret pact among his troops, a blood oath between the closest of his clan, the top eight that were not of the *family*. Their secret agreement said that if anyone heard about a contract on the other, they would give that person a chance to run before the hellhounds were sent after them. At least they could choose their method of death instead of the insidious imagination of Damien Dimanche.

This was Arthur's job - He was the ears closest to the throne. So there he stood, big arms folded in the office of Damien's personal secretary, Mildred. Cold, quiet, and collected on the outside, with an ulcer building on the inside.

They were all in too deep; there was no retirement from this job. If you were in, it was a permanent position.

Arthur was about to take a chair, when the door from Damien's office flew open and he snapped back to alertness. The fatigue in his legs faded with the instant jolt of adrenaline.

"Mildred, I'm going to the pay phone," Damien snapped, ripping his suit coat on as he went.

"I'll get the car boss," said Arthur immediately.

"No car, I'm walking."

"Yeah, boss," said Arthur, opening the door to follow him.

"Alone, Arthur," said Damien.

"But Boss, I don't think that's such a good idea, you going alone," said Arthur, close behind him. "If something was'ta happen to you on my watch, it'd be my head."

Damien spun back into Arthur's face, gun drawn, pointed down at Arthur's crotch.

"I didn't get where I am being a helpless little *coglione* that needs protection, *capisch*?"

Damien turned and continued his brisk walk to the elevator, holstered his gun, and began restlessly punching and re-punching the dull glowing call-button by the door.

Arthur stood silently in the distance, back against the wall, arms folded, and waiting.

The elevator door finally dinged its arrival.

"Arthur…, come with me," said Damien.

Arthur ran to the elevator door, just before it slid shut.

"Call me from the payphone on 13th Street in ten minutes," ordered Damien. He slammed the receiver back on the hook and lit a cigarette.

Arthur stood back away from the booth. He'd seen this a few times before over the years. Random payphones, cryptic calls, and all untraceable.

In ten minutes exactly, the phone rang.

"Somebody dropped a dime," he began. "I wanna know who and I don't care who gets squeezed, understand?"

Damien listened.

"I pay *You* to find out! If you need particulars, send your messenger."

He slammed down the phone and picked it back up. He dialed a special number, committed to memory.

"I need to order a pizza," said Damien. "Take out."

He waited impatiently for a different voice to get to the phone.

"You the one that wants a pizza?" said a slurry voice.

"Yeah, it's a *dono*, a present," said Damien.

"You want me to deliver a message with it?" the voice asked.

"I want to skip the message, let the pizza be the message. I want one with everything on it," said Damien, "...and I want a receipt, something *personalmente*."

"That'll cost extra," said the voice slowly.

"Twenty up front, plus expenses, plus twenty on delivery, if you can prove you watched him eat it all," said Damien.

"Pizza with everything on it, with a receipt. Uh, family jewels okay?" repeated the voice.

"I knew I could count on you," said Damien.

"It may take up to a week, since you want the works," said the voice. "Will my package be in the usual place?"

"The usual," said Damien.

"Tanks for da bidness."

The phone went dead in Damien's ear.

Damien walked out of the booth to where Arthur was, leaned against the wall and lit another cigarette, while the glaze of hatred in his eyes slowly cleared.

Arthur was glad to see the cold gone from Damien's face and glad that the transaction was over.

"Arthur, I want you to get a tap on the phone at these peoples house and that Cajun woman's restaurant," said Damien. "Record everything, every call, every word. I want it transcribed and on my desk every morning."

Arthur started to tell him that it would take some time to get it setup, then decided that too would be a bad idea.

"Sure thing, boss. I'll take care of it personally," said Arthur.

Damien dropped the stub of his cigarette on the filthy sidewalk, smearing it to a streak with the toe of his shoe and looked up at Arthur, just a glance.

It would be the only *thank you* Arthur received; Arthur nodded.

"Let's get back," mumbled Damien.

CHAPTER 23

Jolie woke up with a jolt of air rushing into her lungs. Another dream. The second one this week and the same dream.

"What is it?" asked James. "Another nightmare?"

"It's nothing," said Jolie. She stretched and faked a morning smile over at the chair where James was sitting.

His favorite way of occupying himself at night had become watching Jolie sleep, the expressions she made, the curves of her lips, the way her hair folded across her cheeks, and sometimes catching bits and pieces of her dreams. It took him dying to find out that dreams were nothing more than gibberish compressed into pulsing fractions of a second that seemed like hours in the mind of the dreamer.

"It's something, or you'd tell me," said James. "Do I need to get your Aunt BeBe or my Mom in here?" he asked.

"That's an improvement. Now she's your mom, not your *mother*," smiled Jolie, diverting his sad attempt at a threat.

"Don't change the subject," he said, kissing her on the forehead.

Jolie wrapped her arms around the firmness of his chest and squeezed him with a grateful sigh.

"There is no subject. I had a bad dream. End of story," she replied. "Now if you don't mind, I need to get dressed. Go. Shoo!"

"This isn't over," said James as he faded from view.

Jolie clutched her covers and sat on the edge of the bed.

"James, get out," she said. "I would have expected that from somebody half your age."

"Fine," A deep booming voice echoed from the room as the electricity of his presence faded.

She reached under her pillow and retrieved her family journal and with a pen from the nightstand began a new entry. Under *Dreams* she scribbled the date:

Second dream- a darkness I can't see past. It's happened once before, before James died. Maybe Martiel or Aunt BeBe can help. Questions: Can someone block my dreams? But who? Why?

Another question: Is the spirit of Lyda Brown really gone?

The Ames descendants were already at the kitchen table happily working on the breakfast that Catherine had placed before them.

"Where's BeBe?" asked James, as he sat down at the table. And in the same breath. "Man... I miss eating, that smells great."

Sam was still half asleep and poking food lazily into his mouth.

"Already gone to work," said Catherine. "I'm going to drive Jolie into town after she has breakfast if you want to go with us."

Then she remembered who she was talking to and cringed. "Is Jolie awake?" she asked quickly.

James was mashing and doodling a raspberry on the end of a fork and smelling the tart pink juice, oblivious to the conversation.

"Yeah, she'll be here in a second," said James absently, poking the raspberry in his mouth.

"Nothing...," he spat, dropping the fork to the table.

"What's up with you, Aunt Martiel? You're awful quiet."

She looked up at James, "Just a headache, didn't sleep much last night."

"You either? Jolie's been having nightmares, waking her up."

Martiel didn't reply, but kept stuffing a bite of buckwheat pancake into her mouth.

"If you'd let her get some sleep, she might not be having nightmares," said Sam.

"Talking about me again?" asked Jolie, her bare feet pattering on the floor.

"Somebody needs to let me in on what's bothering you two," said James, with no hidden sign of frustration. "If you're not going to tell me, at least talk to each other."

"We'll talk," said Martiel, after taking a sip of her coffee. She rubbed her forehead and closed her eyes for a moment.

Jolie sat down next to James and stole the plate he had started filling for himself.

"Hey," he mumbled.

"What?" she grinned. "You don't eat. That looks good."

He tried to taste another bite as the plate slid away,

then gratuitously spat it out.

"That is so gross," said Jolie shivering.

Sam chuckled past his overly filled mouth.

"You're both gross," she grunted.

Jolie frowned, trying to pose her delicate question in everyone's presence as a matter of regular conversation if only to avoid suspicion.

"Martiel," she began. "Have you ever had a dream..., one that you know was important but when you woke up you couldn't remember a single thing about it? Like..., I don't know..., it was interrupted and poof..., all gone."

Martiel raised her eyes warily over at Jolie and back down at her plate.

"I get those all the time," said Catherine. "You've been through a lot. I wouldn't worry about it."

"She's not talking about a garden variety dream," mumbled Martiel. "Are you Jolie?"

Jolie was frozen in everyone's headlights for a moment, angry with herself for assuming she could try to pass a comment like that without raising suspicion. She shook her head quietly and took a bite to fill her mouth as an excuse not to talk.

"Oh," said Catherine. Once again, something pertaining to the odd and unexplained was being avoided in her presence.

"Yes, Jolie," said Martiel. "We'll discuss it later if you want."

Jolie nodded her head, but something inside her was pushing, lurching forward for more answers. "James," she blurted. "Are you sure that Lyda Brown is gone for good?"

Catherine threw her fork at her plate, "How dare you speak that name in this house after all the pain she caused."

"I'm..., so sorry...," said Jolie.

"Catherine, it was a question that needed to be asked," said Martiel. "Don't snap at Jolie. I was wondering the same thing."

Catherine stood, "I guess I'm not as *spiritually in tune* as everybody else in this house. I'm surprised you'd have to ask the question. Any questions for that matter."

She quietly sat back down in her chair, staring at Martiel and listening to the intense silence around the breakfast table.

"I don't know what came over me," she said finally. "I just want things to get back to normal in our family. Will that ever happen?"

"Probably never," said Sam. "Did *you* really have to ask?"

There was a round of profuse apologies and the conversation became uncomfortably silent once again.

"Can I answer Jolie's question?" asked James, trying to avoid another round of confusion.

Catherine closed her eyes and nodded grimly.

"She turned to dust in front of me," said James; the rest he kept to himself. It was better that his mother not hear about the driving force behind Lyda Brown or what he had done with the evil spirit.

"But...." Jolie was about to dig deeper.

"If she's dead, *she's dead*," Martiel interrupted almost angrily.

James patted Jolie's hand to let her know they could talk about it later if she still needed details.

Martiel saw the gesture. She was already sleepless and bent to argue everything surrounding James.

"You're our muscle James. Keep your head clear and stay focused on the protection and let me focus on the strategy, okay?" she asked.

"That's fine. Just share information, that's all I'm asking," said James.

"That's really funny," said Sam. "Nobody gives anybody a straight answer around here anymore. I don't see how we've survived this long."

"You're alive Sam. That's all you need to know," said Catherine, but she silently agreed with her youngest son.

Sam spun toward Catherine, "Huh, well I don't get to hear anything, 'cause I'm too young and *impressionable*. I'm gonna take my plate and my *impressionable* ass in the living room to eat so I won't be *impressed* by all this, okay?"

This brought a smile to James' face, even if no one else appreciated the humor.

"Fine then. If you're all going to ignore me, I'll go watch cartoons while I eat, like a good little boy."

Sam scooped another portion of breakfast onto his plate and got up to leave.

"Pig," said Jolie, grinning; which earned her a quick snort from Sam.

The very instant Sam cleared the doorway Martiel began reciting her thoughts for the day.

"Catherine, when you drop off Jolie at BeBe's café, tell

her not to discuss anything over the telephone about where you are, where you're going, what you'll be doing, or anything that has to do with Jolie. Make sure she understands this. In fact, if she does talk about places or times, make up some wild lie."

Before Catherine or Jolie could ask why, "Just trust me. I haven't pinned down what it is yet, but I know something's up."

Sam spoke up from the living room, "Since I'm not supposed to know anything, does that mean that I don't get to lie about stuff?"

Catherine quietly walked into the living room and reappeared with an angry faced Sam in tow by his shirtsleeve.

Catherine and Jolie chatted lightly all the way to downtown Natchez. As she parked in front of the café, James got out from the back seat and opened Jolie's door.

"Is there a reason you're on display today?" asked Catherine.

"Yep, I want everybody that sees my girl get out of this car to know that she's taken. Also Aunt Martiel said it would be good to make a show of myself today for some reason. As she put it, I don't look much like my old self any more, whatever that's supposed to mean."

A quick kiss goodbye for Jolie and the two women walked up the curbside steps onto the sidewalk.

James slid into the front seat of the car watching and probing the thoughts of those in the café. It was almost a week since his adventure with federal agent Warner and his protection detail was getting boring.

A car slid up beside where he sat daydreaming, the door popped open and a short, thick-chested man slid a sawed-off double-barrel shotgun in James Earl's ear. It was no bigger than a pistol with two thumb-sized holes in the end.

"Come with me, pretty boy," said the man. "We don't want to do this here."

James tried his best to act afraid when the man rushed him into the trunk of the car. Mere seconds later he felt the car accelerate and turn the corner. So he was about to get *whacked*, as his Aunt Martiel liked to phrase it. Another bold move by some hired gun, but this time in broad daylight, which seemed like a sign of desperation.

James remained in the trunk to play the part of the helpless hostage, thankful that he had been alone in the car.

If this had been someone from his family or Jolie, it would have been the last time they were ever seen. The not-so-special agent must have described him and this was the result.

A contract was on him. He needed to have a long talk with his Aunt Martiel, especially if this was the reason she wanted him to be in focus today. There was no harm done, it was just another opportunity, but it might have been nice to know.

'I have to send my own message back upstream,' thought James, 'One that will be loud and clear.'

One of the few things that were common among his old neighborhood and on the street was bragging rights. It was a fact that bragging rights were in some cases more valuable than gold on the street.

If he turned this hit around and in fact stopped it cold, it would be a clear sign of incompetence on both parties of the contract.

There were two basic kinds of a hit; one you talked about, told everybody about, usually messy. Then there was the kind you never ever heard about – a signature hit.

James sensed that this was the latter of the two, one where he was supposed to just disappear, never be heard from again. This is what his family was supposed to get for interfering with Damien's business.

If he could deliver this thug back to wherever he came from, right on their doorstep, it would be the ultimate disgrace.

Then the word on the street to be loud and clear, Damien Dimanche *cannot* take care of business. Any sign of weakness would be deadly as high on the ladder as Damien was, especially when it was time to cut heads in the family.

CHAPTER 24

No more than thirty minutes of driving and the car stopped, turned, and backed up. There was no need to try to see where he was being taken, he would let it be a surprise even to himself, to help with his act.

He listened to a steady stream of single syllable filth pouring through the mind of this new killer. Compared to this man, Fatso was a kind hearted genius. This one was barely capable of any thought other than his assigned task of destruction. His one-track mind enjoyed, actually took pride in his task. He cursed, clanked with a tool in the back seat, struggling to free it from some snag. It had been a long time since James had used or heard the raw language of the New Jersey streets.

He heard a key being inserted into the trunk and thought, 'Finally.'

"Don't do nuthin' stupid," said a deep guttural voice. "I got my little helper pointed at you with two slugs. Get out slow."

The trunk latch clicked and James, who barely fit in the trunk of the old car, slowly climbed out and stood.

"What do you want with me?" asked James coolly.

There was immediately more of the silent stream of cursing. James gave him a vigilant eye, making sure to note every detail about his abductor for future reference.

The odd fellow grinned and said, "Here," thrusting a shovel toward James.

But before he could take it from his hand, James looked around to see that he was at the Heaven's Gate Cemetery! He couldn't help himself, it was all he could do to keep from laughing. Instead he used the surprise to enhance his act.

"No! Any place but the graveyard," said James, dully. He couldn't help feeling like *Brer Rabbit* taunting an overconfident and dull witted Fox.

The man pointed toward the gate and said, "Walk," totally missing the inference.

He pulled out a piece of paper and gave James directions until they were standing at the grave of Wema Smith.

"Wow, the Smith reference must have really pissed Damien off," said James.

"Dig," said the man.

"You're kidding," said James.

Both hammers of the sawed-off clicked back at the same time.

"Look like I'm kiddin'?" he asked.

James started digging, trying to decide how far to take this charade.

"Who sent you?" asked James, trying to see into his mind.

The ignorance was astounding. He wasn't visual in his thoughts and it was like digging around in a dumpster to find a piece of bread to eat. He was corrupt.

"Just dig," he repeated.

"You know you won't get away with this," said James, using the same words of Federal Agent Warner.

Then James heard very precise words loud and clear rolling from the man's thoughts.

'You'll make number one hundred twelve.'

They were the proud thoughts of a career disposal soldier.

"So is this your first time to do this?" asked James. "You know I can pay you twice whatever he's paying you."

"Just dig. It's a matter of honor," he slurred.

"You wouldn't know honor if it kicked you in the teeth," laughed James.

"Dig," he gritted, annoyed by the boy's lack of fear.

"You sound like you're from somewhere near Hoboken," said James.

This got his attention; it even rattled him a little.

He kicked dirt at James, "Don't matter who I am or where I'm from. You should be concerned about where you're goin'."

The square hole was now a two-foot deep body sized rectangle and James didn't relish the thought of unearthing the coffin of Wema Smith, his dear friend of many years past.

"Hows come you ain't even breakin' a sweat?" he asked James, swiping his arm across his own forehead.

"I'm used to the heat," said James.

"Good thing, where you're headed," he mocked.

After a few more throws of dirt, he stopped James.

"That's deep enough. Take off your shoes and socks," he ordered.

"My shoes?" asked James.

"I like'em. They look about my size."

James sat on the nearest tombstone wondering how this was going to work out. His clothes and shoes were part of the oddity of how he pictured himself in solid human form.

Slowly he removed his shoes and socks, laughing inside, as they slid from his feet.

"Wait! What's that on your foot?" he asked. "Show me your foot. Slow like."

James turned up the bottom of his foot where a distinct brand had been burned in it when he was much younger. A scar that even death could not erase from his body.

"I seen that cattle brand before," he sneered.

Where Rooster, the first killer, had displayed keen hunter instincts and extreme control, this killer was slaughterhouse raw.

"So *you are* from the street," said James. "Since you're going to put me down anyway, why don't you tell me who sent you?"

"You's should'a ask your girly friend," he laughed.

He raised the gun in James' face and without a moment's hesitation, pulled both triggers.

The blast from the double-barrel ten-gauge was loud enough to scatter every bird within half a mile and if it had been discharged at a normal human, it would not only have taken his head off at the shoulders, it would have turned it to mush.

James couldn't help but squint at the noise as the two slugs passed right through him.

"What the...?" squirmed the man. He frantically reloaded the homemade pistol with two more rounds of ammo as he stumbled backwards.

James walked forward quickly and snatched the gun out of his hands.

"That's enough," said James. "My turn."

He dumped the new shells out onto the ground and snapped the homemade pistol in half at the breech.

The hit-man turned to run and there was James in front of him.

"What? What are you?" he asked. "I didn't miss. I couldn't have."

"You're in a graveyard, you figure it out," smiled James.

In a flash, the man snapped open a knife and swiped at James, passing right through his midsection.

"You're some kinda prank, uh, uh, a joke. That's it, a joke," he stammered, a dullard trying to force a descriptor on the unknown standing in front of him.

James walked forward, drunk with the desire to kill, death swimming in and out of focus, until he saw the wild terror in the killers' eyes. The desire passed like a quick breeze and James regained control of himself, still determined to end the man's long murderous career.

He raised his finger and pointed it at the man letting the heat of his anger concentrate there. The air roiled and crackled with the stench of burning flesh as his finger prodded the fat man's heavily padded chest.

Before his assassin lost consciousness, he told James everything he asked and more.

CHAPTER 25

Dusk was falling on the sidewalk in front of the Cajun Café as James made a humanly entrance. The little brass bell above the door jingled a happy tune and caught Jolie's attention.

"Hey!" said Jolie sweetly. "We wondered where you went this morning. Your mom was worried. She's been calling all day."

Jolie reached up to thread his hair between her fingers and get a hug, when James hurried past her.

"I had an errand to run," he mumbled, looking back at her.

Thankfully, there was no blood splatter, no stink of sweat and flesh, no dirt sticking to his hands to betray his mornings' business.

"I don't like the sound of that," she said, trotting after him. "Tell me the truth; you want the truth from me."

James spun and closed his eyes, trying to hide some emotion.

"When I get all the truth from you..., then I'll tell you the truth," he said, obvious heat in his voice.

Jolie was stunned by the accusation and fell limp in the closest chair to collect her thoughts.

"What are you talking about, James?" she asked, tears were building from fear and uncertainty. Jolie had never seen James angry with her; never had he uttered a single unkind word.

"We'll talk about it later," he muttered, then turned his stare away.

"We can talk about it now," she said, her anger mingled with fear.

"No, Jolie, not here in public," said James, lowering his voice.

"Where is your Aunt BeBe?"

"She's in her office, but she's..., wait..., where are you...," she whispered, jumping to her feet.

Before Jolie could finish the sentence, James walked past the register into the back of the café.

He moved as quickly as he could without attracting more attention than they already had from the line of paying customers.

Jolie was moments behind him, but the door to BeBe's office shut and clicked loudly as the lock turned. She could see through the small window in the door as James and BeBe were locked in an animated conversation.

Jolie caught the words, "Mother..., liar..., thief...," then tightened her lips and banged her fist on the door to get inside.

James was pacing, talking, waving his hands with pointing gestures, then he looked over at the door in a cold stare at Jolie.

BeBe quit her reply midsentence and walked to the door.

"Jolie, there are customers that need taking care of," she snapped.

Furious, Jolie turned on her heels and walked back out to the business of the café. Then the heat of her embarrassment changed into fear as she turned to the line of questioning eyes of those trying to pay for their food; James knew something more.

"All I did was send them a message," said James. "And, I didn't whack anybody."

"That's one hell of a message," said Martiel. "Pardon my French."

"At least there will never be a number one hundred twelve," argued James.

Martiel put down her pad and pen, her hands quivering. Many pages of notes had been added as the result of a lengthy interrogation. Nearly all was explicit information about the Dimanche's and the crime families of the northeast.

"He was a wealth of information," she added.

"I was as surprised as you," said James. "I didn't think he could put more than three words together in a sentence."

James spun angrily once again, fingers rolled into tight fists, "At least we know what Damien wants with Regina and Jolie."

"James, you only know what was whispered in that killers' ear on the street. You know how rumors fly," said Martiel. "You know that's only Damien's side of the story and he has the character of a cold blooded snake. Please don't judge Jolie or her mother on the weight of street gossip."

She watched James relax his hands and felt him settle.

"Besides, even if Regina did steal from Damien, he's nothing but a thief and murderer himself. Jolie didn't have anything to do with it."

"I know," snapped James. "But...."

"Don't be angry with her, James," said Catherine. "She was only a little girl when all that took place. I know you love her. Give her time to open up to you."

"I thought I already had," he mumbled.

"What do you think they'll do now?" asked Catherine.

Her blood had turned to jello while listening to James recant all that had transpired. She knew that her son had watered down his part in what had taken place and it was still horrid.

"It'll take a day or two for them to get the message," said James. "I only take care of the protection. Aunt Martiel is the strategist, remember?"

"Don't you use my own words against me, James Earl," snapped Martiel.

"You really took out a hit-man from the old neighborhood?" mumbled Sam, from the darkness of the doorway.

"What are you doing up?" asked Catherine.

"Who's up? I'm not here...," said Sam, turning to go back upstairs.

"Wait, don't go," said Catherine, looking at a carbon copy of her son James; almost his size, but still fighting to remain a boy at heart. "You can't be tainted anymore than you already have by everything that's gone on in this family. You might as well stay."

"I didn't exactly *take him out*, Sam. I just put him out of business," said James.

"Not much difference, if you ask me," said Sam, hugging the doorjamb. "If they think he talked..., whew!"

The front door clicked open and shut as BeBe and Jolie walked in. The Cajun Café had obviously closed for the night and BeBe was wearing the usual satisfied yet tired look on her face.

"Who called this meeting?" asked BeBe. The smile quickly faded as she saw the serious faces sitting around in the living room. Jolie shrank behind her aunt in silence, then turned to hurry upstairs.

"I see you've been talking to James," sighed BeBe.

"No new customers?" asked James.

"No new customers," she answered glumly.

BeBe felt the absence of her niece and whispered at James.

"You should go talk to Jolie," she said, her voice pleading. "She's all tore up about all this. She feels like she's failed you. Could you do that? Could you just talk to her? For me?"

Jolie's tears had already stained her pillowcase by the time James knocked on her door.

"What?" spat Jolie angrily.

"Can I come in?" he asked.

"Why?"

"Because..., I need to talk to you," said James.

"Go ahead, you can talk from there," she mumbled.

"Jolie..., I'm...."

Why couldn't he seem to put two words together in a sentence?

"I'm sorry about today," blurted James.

It poured out in a stream, much colder sounding than how he meant it, but it was the only way he knew to get it out of his mouth. He listened, hearing her snub against her pillow and tried once again.

"Jolie, I'm sorry about how I treated you today."

That was much better, it sounded the way he felt.

It was quiet again.

"Okay," she whispered.

"Is that an 'okay, I forgive you', okay?" he asked.

Jolie smiled into her pillow, melted by the boyish sound of his voice.

"Yes…, I guess so. I mean…, I forgive you. Of course I forgive you," she sighed.

He heard her snub back a few more residual tears then she sucked in a deep gulf of air.

"James? Can we talk tomorrow? I'm tired."

One last thing, but most important.

"Jolie?" he said, as he knocked on the door once again, softer.

"Yes James."

"I love you Jolie."

"I love you too James."

CHAPTER 26

Mildred walked into Damien's office and dropped a brown overnight envelope in the center of his desk.

"Special Delivery," she said. "From New Orleans."

As the door to his office closed, he clasped his hands together and rubbed them briskly in expectancy.

"What kind of surprises do we have today?" smiled Damien.

He flicked open his special knife with *Rizzuto Estilet'* stamped into the steel blade, given to him as a boy by his father. It was one of the few memories he had of his childhood in Milano.

He slashed the end of the envelope, dumping the contents on his desk.

Out plopped a zip-lock plastic bag with two dirty dismembered human thumbs inside.

He picked up the bag and turned it back and forth, examining the bloody contents.

"Well, it's not the family jewels, but I guess it'll have to do," said Damien. "I need to have a heart to heart with the Pizza Man."

He dropped his prize back inside the envelope and wrote down instructions to have it cleaned, repackaged and sent to the Ames address in Natchez, Mississippi.

Then, he frowned; where was his receipt? The Pizza Man wouldn't turn down an extra twenty grand. He always gave him a Polaroid of his finished work....

The corner of Merrimack and Franklyn was already busy with noisy traffic as the freight truck pulled up to the receiving dock behind Martini's Ristorante and Pizzeria.

After the regular delivery of fresh produce and operating items, a large crate rolled out of the truck behind the struggling deliveryman. It was marked overnight delivery and the frame was covered in heavy black screen mesh.

The restaurant crew heaved the wooden crate, also marked "Danger - Live Animal," back on the loading dock out of the way.

Every so often, there would be a thumping against the side and some muffled grunts and noises. The morning manager assumed it was a wrong delivery and ordered everyone to give it a wide berth after calling the trucking lines about the mistake.

As the day grew longer, no one wanted to look in the crate, much less touch it. None of the helpers or cooks would dare to go near it. Surely someone would eventually miss their live animal and come looking for it, hopefully before it died and stunk up the place.

Just before noon rush, most the waiters were out on the docks taking their usual crowded smoke break. Each one daring the other to go take a look inside, until the bravest of the lot was goaded into tearing past the heavy seal to get a peek inside.

"Boss, you gotta come downtown and take a look at this," said Arthur.

"The Pizza Man, he don't look so good."

"Yeah? Put him on the phone," said Damien.

"Won't do no good, boss. He ain't talkin'," said Arthur.

"What do you mean, he ain't talkin'? Put him on the phone."

"Boss, he can't talk. He ain't got no tongue. The best we can make out, he keeps saying it was the devil himself had something to do with it. You want me to get the family Doc to take a look at him?"

Arthur looked on with pity and disdain as the workers disassembled the boards from the crate, their faces wrapped in cloth to mute the stench.

The Pizza Man was covered in fresh burn tattoos; the most profound scar was the one that scorched deep on his forehead, between his eyes, and traveled up on his scalp; one just larger and matching the scar on James Earl's foot. No amount of plastic surgery would be able to fix the deep-burned trough that now marked him. The scar alone would have put him out of business, but his missing opposable thumbs would make any future attempts an exercise in futility.

"At least some things are making sense," said Jolie. "Remember my dreams before I met James in the library?"

BeBe nodded, "Three nights in a row, I remember."

"But why Aunt BeBe?" she asked. "Why did things turn

out so wrong? I never intended for any of these things to happen."

Jolie snubbed back another flood of misgivings.

Jolie's room seemed darker now that the house was quiet and the silence pressed in where they huddled next to each other.

"I know, you just wanted to help, baby," whispered BeBe. "It's too late for regrets now, you need to move forward."

Jolie dropped her head back onto BeBe's lap, tears in her eyes.

"For some reason, I just couldn't walk away from him."

BeBe sighed and slid her fingers through Jolie's hair, "Fate found him, fate put you both together. It was no coincidence that he was raised where he was, born where he was, and from a gifted family. It was meant to be."

"When he told me about where he was from and the things that happened to him. I could have stopped it. I should have stopped it then," sobbed Jolie.

"He was the one that needed your help, remember?" said BeBe.

"There is no telling what horrible things would have happened to his family.... It could have been a lot worse."

"I didn't help him. I distracted him. All I did was get him killed," sobbed Jolie.

"You have to stop blaming yourself babe. Besides, you can't help it if you're a peach," said BeBe.

Jolie's sobs turned into half snubs until a small laugh emerged.

"Just when we were beginning to trust each other, this

thing about my mother had to raise its ugly head. Now I have to start all over."

They sat in silence.

"Maybe not. I could try telling him the whole story," said Jolie.

"I think it's a little late for that now," said BeBe. "He got an earful from Damien's hired killer."

"He knows my mother is a thief?" she gasped. "Then I don't know how to fix it. I'm so stupid, and he's so..., pigheaded."

"You're not helpless," said BeBe. "Use that built-in intuition of yours."

Jolie knew what her intuition was screaming at her, every time she closed her eyes, but it wasn't what BeBe was referring to.

There was another confession grating against her soul as she looked up at her Aunt.

"Three nights now, the same dream," said Jolie. "But I can't see what's coming Aunt BeBe. When I wake up it disappears like a puff of smoke and everything feels dark and empty and it's starting to scare me."

"Detective Floyd. In my office as soon as you get a chance, please...," said Sheriff Howard.

He smiled and kept walking down the hall.

The sheriff's voice shook him. Every corner of the Detective's world was making him jump. The one favorite trick of James Earl Williams was to show up unannounced and cause him to revert to idiocy. It was an odd friendship to say the least.

Now the sheriff was saying *please*? Sheriff Howard never said *please,* that he could remember.

This was bad; it was definitely a bad sign.

Floyd cleared his desk quickly and walked *cubicle row* to the sheriff's office and peeked in the door.

"Come in, shut the door Floyd. I need you to take a trip to New Orleans," he began. "I've already contacted the proper channels and you'll be meeting with a federal agent, Special Agent Morrison."

"Federal Agent?" asked the Detective. "FBI headquarters?"

"I've already explained to the N.O. Regional Director that this is only a routine information excursion and he agreed to give us his complete cooperation. Look at it as a break from your day-to-day caseload, Detective. You'll have a chance to relax in the evenings, mingle with the crowd, all on the department's dime."

The sheriff scrambled his hands around his desk and stuffed an envelope and handed it to the detective.

"I've explained to the FED's that we had a visit from some of the people that one of their groups, a special task force, is keeping tabs on. You should probably read through all this so you can get up to speed on who we're dealing with, just in case they decide to return to our fair city."

Floyd scanned quickly through the items and his face flushed.

"This *was* the mob, just like I thought," said Floyd. "What were they doing here?"

"That's why you are taking a trip to New Orleans," said

the Sheriff. "I spoke briefly with Agent Morrison, but he was reluctant to talk about anything concerning their ongoing investigation over the telephone.

I think you'll find that last page in there most interesting," said the Sheriff. "That last name, *Dimanche*, should ring a bell."

The sheriff stopped his extemporaneous movement and stared the detective in the eyes.

"I don't think I have to explain to you that the Ames family are very good friends of mine. This is important to me Floyd, so pay close attention to everything you hear and see. And do not *give* any more information than you absolutely have to, especially about Ms. Ellington. Do we understand each other?"

The detective nodded his head.

"Since you've had so much personal time in dealing with the family from that last debacle, I can't think of a better person to work on this."

"Debacle? Are you kidding?" asked Floyd, then cursed himself for blurting it out.

"Preston, I'm trying very hard to forget several things from that whole ordeal. I assume you are too?" said the sheriff.

"One other favor? Please be careful."

It had been months since the sheriff had called him by Preston. It had to be a bad omen. There was some comfort in knowing he wasn't the only one with scars from that *debacle*.

"Yes sir. You're right and I'll keep both eyes open," he answered, all the while wondering if the sheriff knew all the intimate details of his initial involvement in the Ames family *debacle*.

Detective Floyd dismissed himself and hurriedly closed out every pressing thing on his desk for the coming week. This was going to be a working vacation he was not looking forward to. In fact, anything associated with the name Ames, or Ellington, or Williams, meant trouble.

"I'm a piece of meat on a fishhook, all over again," sighed Floyd.

CHAPTER 27

The war room was now quiet except for the Colonel, his most trusted *Lieutenant,* and a single *runner.* All others had been blasted from the Colonel's presence with a hailstorm of orders.

"Arthur, who's my best inside man?" asked Damien.

"Rooster, without a doubt, boss," he answered.

"Besides Rooster, he's busy on something else."

"That would be *Slinky* then, boss."

"Slinky," mumbled Damien, lowering his head. "We got nobody besides him?"

Arthur saw the disdain in Damien's actions and quickly readjusted. "I..., I can't vouch for his ethics..., but he's like a ghost when it comes to B and E."

"Not like I can call in any favors at the moment either," spat Damien. "Fine. I got a job for him. Tell him I need to see him pronto, understand?"

Arthur turned and snapped his fingers at the man standing next to him and nodded toward the door.

"Now, back to business," said Damien, calmly.

"I want you and five of your best *soldatos* on a plane to New Orleans. Lift a car and go to that Café! I want you to make that Café look like a *hurricane hit it!*"

He slammed both fists down on the desk as he screamed his orders.

Arthur stood stiff; this was Damien. One second he was calm; the next in a violent rage.

Mildred heard the string of curses streaming out through the walls of Damien's office and shoved her rolling deskchair to a cubbyhole in the corner. The last time she heard anything close to this she had to rush in a clean up crew to bleach up blood and replace the double doors.

Arthur grinned and nodded, the anger wasn't toward him or his men, "What about the other house? You want me to take care of it too? A little gas and a match.... That old tinderbox would make for one big bonfire."

"Not until I have a heart to heart with the Pizza Man," mumbled Damien.

"Why the secrecy?" asked James.

The two family conspirators were locked away in the unused northernmost downstairs bedroom. Martiel didn't know how to answer him.

"Just because...," she whispered, rubbing her temples tenderly.

"You're head is hurting again," said James as he settled on his knees in front of his great Aunt.

"You weren't supposed to notice," she snapped. "We have business that the others don't need to know about."

Her voice cracked and James watched her stomach clench, barely noticeable.

"Martiel, please let me handle the rest of this," said James, clasping her hands in his. "I'll make the problem go away and you'll never have to know what happened. No one else will ever have to know."

He stared at her for an answer but her eyes and thoughts diverted him skillfully away.

"Another premonition," he gritted, standing suddenly. "Isn't it?"

"It's not that simple James," she swallowed dryly, wishing for something to drink.

He was forcing her to think about the conflicting information so he could piece the fragments of her thoughts together. She couldn't be angry at his attempts or his unwavering progress; she taught him how to do it.

"I know it has something to do with me," he whispered, close behind her, circling her. "Quit worrying about me. Start thinking of me as..., something disposable, or indestructible."

"I have to worry about you," said Martiel. "Lord knows somebody does."

She was still diverting, shuffling, so he struck home.

"If you know they're coming, why don't you let me go there and take care of business? It's only a matter of time!"

"I'm the strategist remember?" said Martiel, mockingly.

She sat back in her mother's chair by window, her mother's favorite, trying to look regal and commanding.

She was a stone wall again. His anger boiled while preparing for his usual rant but Martiel cut him off. Torn between two alternatives, one with almost no expectation of success, while the other would place James right where he didn't need to be.

"You're right..., it's time we do a preemptive strike."

James was flabbergasted and looked her in the face to see if he had heard clearly. Dumbfounded, he sank to the floor at her feet and listened in silence.

"How far can you travel safely?"

"Daytime or nighttime?"

"Either..., *both*," she replied. "I need to know our strengths and weaknesses. Don't exercise your ethereal testosterone and exaggerate your abilities. I need cold hard facts."

"Daytime, after I'm a hundred miles or so, I start to fade out," said James. "Nighttime? I can go just about anywhere on this continent, in seconds, especially if I'm summoned."

"Why not in the daytime?" she asked, sounding mildly curious.

"I'm..., I'm not sure," said James, hiding his secret.

"A hundred miles from *where* exactly?" she probed further.

He realized that she was not going to let this go, forcing a smile from his memory.

"You just reminded me of an old friend," said James, referring to his confidant from his childhood, Granny Smith. She was the only other person he knew of that could get him to spill the beans about himself.

"It has something to do with my grave," said James finally.

One little tiny secret, no more.

"Really," said Martiel, thoughtfully. "And you know this for sure? What about...?"

"Is this going to take long? You're starting to treat me

like I'm one of your long lost ghosts. Is that what I am to you now? An asset? A spy with a built-in gun? If that's how you see me...."

"Just because this house was inhabited by a number of family mentors for the last some odd hundred years, does not mean I know everything. And, as you well know, they're gone now. Besides, you're somewhat of an anomaly."

"Gee thanks!" "That makes me feel even worse than being dead somehow. I'm not only dead, I'm a freak."

"Focus, James," she commanded. "All our lives depend on the truthful information you give me."

Even though he still wasn't sure about her motives, his anger cooled. He did not want her to know certain facts of his newfound powers, but how could he avoid losing more ground?

"Quit locking me out, James," she said finally.

"Besides the usual stuff, I can see in the dark. I can appear and disappear at will. I can hit and not be hurt, burn, freeze, read minds – an entire room at the same time if I want to. I really like that," he interjected. "Travel.... My memory is a recorder."

"We covered that," she said. "Please continue...."

"What exactly do you want to know?" he asked, trying to divert her from the darker elements of his transformation.

He knew that this was not going to end until she knew far more than he wanted to tell. Did she really need to know or was it just her curiosity driving this inquisition?

'She's peeling the onion,' thought James, '...with a razor.'

Martiel didn't need to know about the aspects of his new existence that even he wasn't sure of, and he definitely wasn't proud of. Why was she insisting? Had one of her visions shone her something?

"Spill it, James," she barked. "It's getting late."

He spun and faced Martiel.

"I can basically command the weather, although I haven't tried that much. I'm pretty strong."

Here he paused, "And I can raise the dead."

There it was. One of his secrets. A peace offering.

"Are you happy now?" he mumbled.

There was a long ensuing silence in the bedroom. The last sentence somehow obliterated everything else he had spoken.

"Oh," said Martiel. "Oh."

"And tell them what to do," said James.

James felt a sudden relief from the sharing of knowledge, instead of the fear he had expected.

"Oh, my," she said.

'Good,' thought James, 'Maybe she'll stop asking questions now.'

She stood and looked out the window at front lawn inspecting the darkness.

"Let's keep that little secret between ourselves, shall we?"

He was glad the answer took her by surprise. Something in the back of her mind was refocusing and trying to get her attention. Something didn't make sense.

"One more thing. Just how strong are you, James?"

James shrugged.

"I'm tired James, please. On a sliding scale between a claw hammer and a nuclear bomb," she said, her arms stretched wide.

"I've broken an oak tree the size of your BMW in half," he mumbled almost ashamedly. "But I really don't know. I don't think I have any limits."

Martiel's face became pale as she sat back down in her chair.

"My Gawd," she said quietly. 'Holy Hell,' she thought. 'He's a force of nature.'

Martiel's mind was racing with the new information. This was probably only the tip of the iceberg of reasons the hoodoo witch Lyda Brown wanted James so badly. She was trying to create something powerful and knew his potential and how to harness it. It was mind boggling and the implications were far beyond her understanding. Martiel hoped that the trip she was about to take would help her figure it all out.

Her new persistent headache ebbed and flowed with yet another vision or premonition she was suppressing. One she did not want to affect her new decisions.

Martiel picked up the small valise propped neatly beside her mother's chair and pulled out some instructions.

"I need to make a few changes to this. If you'll be patient, James, I promise it won't take me long."

"You're head's hurting again," said James. "I can almost feel it myself."

"All the more reason for me to take my trip. Just be patient and let me finish this. I can't stress to you how important it is that I get this right."

"Trip? Where are you going?"

"I can't tell you. But I'm not going alone."

Anger fumed inside him over her answer. She'd just stripped more of his secrets from him and she wasn't willing to share her own.

Then he saw Martiel almost crumble as she sat back in the chair with her notepad. She was at the breaking point too.   The weight of the entire family was on their combined shoulders.

"Who?" he asked quietly. "Who's going with you?"

"BeBe," was her answer.

"Where am I going?"

"First…, to see your father…. Now hush while I make some changes to my notes…."

CHAPTER 28

For the first time in several days, maybe weeks, James felt that he and his Aunt Martiel were finally on the same page. He looked over the instructions carefully; if he could pull off this part of her plan, the rest would work like a charm. Apparently she understood the misgivings of his childhood far better than he realized.

His first stop was not so much to actually *see* his father. His father had absolutely no idea of the new status of James and didn't seem interested in Catherine or Sam which he had deserted.

He was to deliver a package and make sure that his father, Robert Williams, actually read it.

Then the list became strange and twisted, but it was exactly the kind of twisted that James would delight in performing.

He could still hear his aunt's voice in his head, "Follow the list as close as you can for the next two nights. Remember, there are far worse things out there than Damien Dimanche."

James wondered how the information he shared with his aunt would affect her decisions or for that matter how she would view her great-nephew from now on, especially after tonight.

It was still early by James Earl's standards, but

everyone in the house was occupied or asleep.

All except one.

Sam was chewing on the same old feelings that he and James dined on most of their lives. That feeling of being overlooked, ignored, and unimportant was still cursing him. Even though the location had changed, Samuel Earl felt the familiar pangs of rejection gnawing at him.

Lately, there was always some excuse of why he couldn't take part in some role of involvement in the family.

After listening to Sam's thoughts, James wished that he could thank his Aunt Martiel for suggesting something to include his brother.

James entered by the door instead of his usual scare tactics.

"What's up, Sam?"

"Bored as hell," he answered, turning down his radio.

"Whoa, better keep *that* down," warned James. "You know how mom feels about swearing."

He shrugged, "What difference does it make? I'm under the turd no matter what I do."

James ignored his belligerent remark, "I have a project for you."

"I'm sure it's colossal," said Sam, rolling over on top of his bed. He shuffled several books into a stack and set them on the floor on top of some sketch pads.

"If it wasn't for the few decent books in the library downstairs, I'd go crazy. Mom won't even let me take a walk in the back forty. The least they could do is let me go camping. Maybe I should write an essay on how my brother's girlfriend ruined my summer vacation?"

James waited patiently for his brother to run out of steam.

"What?" he said staring. "Is it time for me to take out the trash?"

"Come on, Sam. I'm serious here."

"Okay, what?"

"Since you can't sleep anyway."

"What?" he asked again, growing impatient.

"Do you still have the shotgun grampa gave you?"

This got Sam's attention, but his hopes fell just as quickly. He thought James was probably going to tell him to lock it away, or give it to someone else.

"Yeah, of course. It's in there," he pointed to the closet.

"Do you remember how to use it?"

"Duh, grampa put me through military training with it, remember?"

James led Sam through the paces of what he was to do during his absence over the next two nights. It wasn't dangerous if he did exactly as he was told. James added the incentive that if Sam took care of business exactly the way he said and didn't improvise himself into trouble, that he would make it up to him *somehow* later on.

"You ready to start tonight?" asked James.

Sam slid off the bed and retrieved his weapon like a good soldier, checked the safety, and grabbed a pouch of ammo.

"Not those," said James. "That's birdshot."

"It's all I have."

"Not anymore," said James, tossing a box onto his bed.

"Whoa, heavy duty," said Sam in awe. "Buckshot."

"Only for two nights. Remember to treat the house like a fort. Safety on…, finger off the trigger."

"It's better than laying here getting older and dumber."

"Time for me to go do my part," said James. "Are you sure you're going to be okay?"

Sam gave a smirky nod.

He handed Sam a small list of do's and don'ts with a note to their mother in case she woke up during the night and saw him cruising the house with a shotgun across his arm.

"I'm sorry you're stuck in the house. I promise this won't last forever Sam. I'll make it up to you."

"Okay," he nodded again, not really convinced.

"Back soon," said James, fading into the air.

"If I could do that…," said Sam.

James reappeared instantly, "You'd be dead. Careful what you wish for little brother."

An emergency vehicle screamed through the congested intersection, siren wailing, headed to some unknown destination. At least a dozen cars honked their horns in frustration after having yielded their rights to the momentary green light.

Two blocks away from the angry traffic, in a darkened doorway, James appeared. He shrugged as if adjusting the charcoal gray Armani identical to Damien's, his disheveled black hair dangling a few inches above his shoulders.

The night air was chill, buffeted by the steady traffic, and perfect weather for revenge. Not a single person noticed him as he stepped out onto the sidewalk.

"Ah..., the stink of the old neighborhood," laughed James. "Listen to all this noise!"

James pondered the address his Aunt had given him. It was different from where his family had moved to when he made his last and final trip to Natchez. That all seemed like a dream, so long ago, but this was not the time for mulling over past failures. It was a time for preventing future regrets.

He was early however, and early enough to visit his troubled past. Away from the noise he scurried, back toward where he'd spent most of his childhood. Cars were lining the streets on either side, decorating long lines of sidewalks and brownstones.

Very few windows still had that warm yellow glow he remembered, most were dark or corrupted. All the good neighbors had moved away, forced away before his father agreed to leave their "investment."

James felt a sickening sensation, remembering his parent's fight that day. He had just come home from court, after spending three hard nights in a juvenile detention center. He was facing two years in a facility for violent offenders and gang members, and would have died there, if not for his mother's aunt Martiel.

He had already given himself over to despair and yet somehow he got probation. That familiar itch on his foot was back, where he was branded. He felt that familiar swelling in his chest when he saw the lamppost he and Sam looked for when making a mad dash for safety. His pace quickened until he was standing at the bottom of the tall stoop rising to a familiar door.

Home..., but not one he had any desire to return to. The house was dark and empty, yet it was unscathed and none of the windows were broken.

There was nothing left for him here except foul memories. He heard footsteps and felt that familiar fear flood him as if he was still that lanky thirteen-year-old boy trying to dodge a club or a bullet. Even now, after all reason to fear was removed, it still bothered him.

He quickly shrugged it off and walked away, toward a darker memory. Minutes later he stopped and stared, bewildered. The building where *The Hand* used to congregate was boarded up and yellow tape draped around it like a Halloween house of horror.

So much for taking on personal vendetta's....

After needlessly walking in a daze for close to an hour and watching unfamiliar faces, he was standing at the next address on his list. His feet were planted on the edge of Lincoln Park in one of the better neighborhoods that he and Sam used to talk about.

This was where his father had moved? As soon as his family was extricated, he moved into a better, upscale place.

A few floors up, just above the street noise, only two tenants on the entire floor and one of the apartments belonged to Robert Williams.

James listened at the door.

The rattle of music was somewhere in a back room. He could just as easily enter, pass right into the room, invisible. James did not trust his emotions.

He'd heard the cold words hurled at his mother, after the funeral. How would he react if he met his father face to face? Would his anger and resentment take over and cause him to say or do something that he would regret?

There. He blocked out all ambient rabble around him.

There was what he was waiting for.

The clear thoughts of his father murmured, going over some detail, some trivial plan and meeting tomorrow. He was home and awake. This voice sounded so odd to James, coming from inside Robert's mind as opposed to the voice he heard all those mornings before his father left for work or parts unknown. He instantly tuned out Robert Williams' thoughts. He didn't want to hear any of the trivia that had to do with his life.

James stuffed the envelope in the crack of the door facing and rang the buzzer.

Moments later the door opened and the heavy envelope fell from the doorjamb at the feet of his father. The broad shoulders James used to admire and hoped he would someday grow into now seemed misplaced and disconnected.

Robert cinched the belt of his bathrobe tighter and stepped out the door.

James watched his father's steel gray eyes as he picked up the package and glanced back down the hallway towards the elevator, which was silent and still, then toward the stairwell door closed and dark.

He opened the envelope while propped in the doorway, shuffled through the first few pages with a pensive expression. Then scratching down in the bottom of the envelope, he held up a certified check, and laughed.

"Who is it, Robert?" asked a distant voice.

James listened; it was a woman, a stranger.

It was something he should never tell his mother.

"You're not going to believe this," he said, as he closed and locked the door.

It was time to leave, time to resist a violent urge to set things right. It would only be *his version* of right.

"A clear conscience is more important than revenge," he repeated, over and over, as he hurried away.

This was one of the hardest things he had faced to date, struggling not to go back, splinter the door, and finally get his father's attention.

He imagined the confrontation, the deathly look on his father's face at the sight of his son, the excuses he would make for crimes against his family. Then he began to imagine his response to his father, until his head became dizzy, his vision swam.

Anger was coming from everywhere inside his mind; it wasn't like him. The raw emotions were hateful, violent, and disturbing.

Why were they surfacing now?

The good of all the family weighed more than the scorned emotions of a son.

Despite the abandonment, wasn't his father family?

There would be somewhere else he could release his anger; it was at the next address on his list....

James wondered if his Aunt Martiel would know the turbulence inside him after making this his first stop, and use that fury.

He quickly found the address of the restaurant the *Pizza Man* had given him. It was truly what he and the old gang laughingly called a *dive*, a *joint*. Some place that he would never have been dumb enough to enter a few years ago.

Above it, just over the restaurant, was the dingy apartment of the Pizza Man.

James listened deliberately and found the familiar thoughts, the same string of single syllable perversions and profanity, now seasoned with something new – hardcore fear.

He entered quietly and invisibly. There was only one dimly lit lamp in the room with a large man sitting in front of the flickering light of a television. Bandages covered both his hands, scars, and the stench of fear; something new for the Pizza Man.

James forced himself visible and stood silently behind the man in the room.

"Hey Pizza Man," said James.

He heard a snort of fear and the man turned, clumsily holding a pistol with his remaining gauzed four fingers.

"I see you delivered my message."

The man uttered several unintelligible grunts and backed up, fumbling the gun and dropping it to the floor.

James made out the next few words through the man's thoughts.

"Are you the devil?" he blubbered.

"No. If I was, we'd be talking somewhere else," said James.

His face piqued and paled and he almost fainted.

"If you want me to go away and leave you alone, deliver one more message to your friends."

He stopped and let the spew of the television fill the room for a moment.

"Tell them Judgment is coming," said James. "What happened to you was a down payment. There's a new boss in town."

James walked toward the man and he reciprocated by backing up step by step. He picked up the discarded gun and slowly crushed it to a glob, then handed it to the Pizza Man and deliberately faded from sight before his eyes.

CHAPTER 29

At first glance, the office was massive as well as impressive. Four oversized leather sofas arranged facing each other contributed to a pseudo conversation pit and nearby a highly polished oak table with seating for sixteen members of Damien's crew. Next to the row of floor to ceiling windows, sat a presidential sized desk, sporting an enviable view of the Jersey skyline.

The office was situated high enough to overlook the gritty view of the rail yards in the distance below, yet low enough to distinguish the activities of his men on the streets.

This floor of the building was heavily guarded but always quiet after-hours and the ones staying the night inside were in dreamland. That was going to be temporary.

James looked at the instructions one last time. There was nothing specific. Martiel advised him to use his imagination, make a mess, and make a show. James looked at his aunt's handwriting and laughed, wondering if she knew what a vivid imagination he truly had.

After passing through the double wooden doors, Damien's desk was the obvious center focus of the room, standing out as a symbol of power and importance. That was what he wanted to challenge most of all, Damien's control and ability to rule.

One quick thrust of his fist and the top of the desk parted; splintering into two lumps on the floor.

It was loud.

James waited.

He was surprised that it took over five minutes for Damien's men to wake up and figure out the origin of the clatter.

The doors flew open and there sat James on top of the cloven remains.

The two men extracted their guns and walked toward James.

"You done made a bad mistake coming here," said one the guards.

"Do you know who you're messing with?"

"I think I know," said James. "Isn't this the Dimanche nest?"

"Then you know what we gotta do," grunted the other.

"You want to tell us who you are so we can tell your next of kin?" laughed the first.

"I can tell you who he is," grinned the other. "He's a dead man."

He raised his gun and emptied it at James, leaving six fractured holes in the outer sheathing of glass behind him, shattering Damien's picturesque view.

"That's right, smart man," said James.

James hopped off the desk as the two men stared in awe.

He turned his back, ignoring their stupor. With his finger, he made an exhibition of burning a note in the top of the shiny ruined desktop that read, "I'm coming."

The other man took aim and unloaded his gun toward James as he began to walk slowly around the room.

The room was thick with the smell and smoke of the spent nitrates.

"You must be the dumb one," said James. "What made you think your gun would do any more the second time?"

James calmly sat down on one of the plush sofas, looking at the men in awe as they both dumped their spent brass and reloaded.

The long seat was as comfortable as it looked, and he patted the arm and got back up. It was ignorance gone to seed as moments later, both were blasting at him once again. He strolled around the office to maximize their damage in and around the office as smoke filled the air.

The room was quickly a disaster at the hands of Damien's own. Multiple holes with puffed out marshmallow stuffing protruded from the sofas. Anything that might be inventoried as nice or expensive such as an enormous oil painting or exotic wall paneling was now in shambles.

"Pizza Man was right. It is the devil," said one of the men.

"What do we do?" said the other, crossing himself.

James walked past them, fighting a sudden overwhelming urge to destroy human flesh.

"Tell your boss, it's time to pay the devil his due," said James.

Both entry doors tumbled off their hinges and onto the floor as he left.

For the first time since his death, he wanted to talk to his Aunt Martiel about what was going on with his emotions. Never in his life had he wanted to hurt anyone, much less kill someone; until now. It was like some strange spiritual adrenaline pumping through him. That conversation would have to wait until he was finished here. He still had one more task to complete.

The next address on the list was unknown to James.

He hailed a cab after walking a few blocks away from the building complex, which seemed to be a novel idea.

James actually enjoyed the sound of the traffic as they neared the final address on his list, an uptown club. The front of the building looked both swank and cheesy at the same time, making him laugh. From the street, the façade was a roaring twenty's revival, quiet and respectful; giving no indication of activity, but inside it was very much alive with action, loud music, and revel.

James got out of the cab and started to walk away.

"Hey! You owe me twenty bucks, punk," said the cabbie, jumping out his door.

"Dimanche's men don't pay cab fare in this town, *capisch*?" said James.

The cab driver immediately began hurling a string of ethnic slurs and rearranging his turban. Then looking around and realizing where he was, he scurried behind the wheel, slammed the car door and sped off.

James walked calmly to the entrance of the club and was immediately confronted by the doorman - A man the size of the door.

He handed the guard five bills he had slipped from the cabby's till and was allowed to pass with a nod and a smile. Overkill, but he wanted to be remembered.

The office was above the main floor of activity, with mirrored glass lining for an exterior. Taking his time, he let himself be seen by those on the dance floor, peering over several card games, and inspecting the bar. Martiel's information was perfectly accurate in its description of the layout.

At the top of the stairs James saw two more men sitting on either side of the door to the office he was to plunder.

"Keep the show small," said James, reciting his task list.

With no effort, the two men lay unconscious on the floor, and he stepped inside the office.

"Where's Ronny?" asked the man. "Who are you?"

He leaned around a stack of boxes, looking toward the door.

"Don't know Ronny. I'm just a messenger," said James.

"Deliver your message and leave. I'm a busy man," he snapped, focusing his efforts back into a ledger on his desk.

"I'm the message," said James, lifting the edge of the desk. He slowly turned it over pinning the man against the wall. The man pulled his weapon from a shoulder holster, followed quickly by a trio of blasts. Only then did the downstairs become a flurry of confusion as footsteps started trampling up the stairs.

"Here's your message...," said James. "Dimanche says to join him or get out of town, you're all finished."

As soon as the words left his mouth, he realized how

James Cagney corny his warning sounded.

Not listening to James, the man resumed fire emptying the rest of the thirteen rounds from his Russian made 9mm handgun.

The shouting finally made its way up the stairs to the other side of the door and several bodies were trying to break inside.

"Did you hear me?" asked James.

"Wha…, what the…, what are you?" he asked.

"I've been called a lot of things lately," said James. "Devil, spook, make up your own. Just remember, there's only room for one *family* in this end of the city. Dimanche sends his regards."

"It'll be a cold day in hell when I give Dimanche a piece of my action," he spat back at James.

"Have it your way," smirked James.

He quickly found the hidden floor safe, ripped its door off, and pulled out a long heavy mail sack.

"Pay the devil his due," said James.

CHAPTER 30

Phone calls between three and six a.m. usually aren't harbingers of peace and good will. BeBe and Martiel were already dressed and hovering over a cup of early morning coffee while discussing the trip to and from Biloxi when the telephone rang. Martiel quickly handed the receiver to BeBe maintaining a casual expression and left BeBe to her phone call.

When the receiver dropped back on the wall hook, Martiel returned and casually refilled her coffee.

"My walk-in freezer went out," said BeBe, dropping back into her chair. "It's the craziest thing too. I just had it serviced. You'll have to forgive me. There's no way I can go with you today Martiel."

"But I need you with me. Close shop for the day," she answered. "We can still take our trip. Give everybody a day off and I'll call our repairman. He's always been fair to us, you can trust him."

BeBe gave Martiel a wary eye. Martiel seemed very calm and prepared at her sudden misfortune.

"I can't close down the place for the day," whined BeBe. "It was hard enough taking time off to go with Catherine, but...."

"They'll love you for a day off and I can have him out there in a jiffy. I'm sure it's something simple."

"But what if he can't? All my frozen foods...," whined BeBe. "It'll cost me a small fortune to restock."

"I'm sure your insurance would cover any losses, but he has a refrigerator truck. I bet I can get him downtown and have it fixed or at least all packed away before eight-thirty this morning. You won't lose a single itty-bitty shrimp."

Martiel took a sip of her coffee and waited for BeBe's decision.

"Okay..., I get it. You're not going to take no for an answer. What do you want me to do?" asked BeBe, giving up her argument.

"Make your calls. I'll make mine."

Catherine walked down the stairs half-groggy from a fitful night of sleep and heard the rambling conversation in the kitchen.

"Good morning BeBe."

Catherine gave Martiel a hug, "Why are you up so early?"

"Road trip," said Martiel.

"Oh, you should come with us!" said BeBe.

"Uh, I don't think that's such a good idea," said Martiel.

"Nonsense, she'll love meeting my friend Dominique," said BeBe.

It was eight a.m. before the receptionist in the lobby of the New Orleans Federal Building waved Detective Floyd up to her kiosk. She methodically handed him a large, ugly clip-on visitor's badge. A young man walked up beside Floyd and greeted him with a 'good morning' then waited for his instructions from the receptionist.

"This is the first time I've ever needed an escort to go inside a building," said Detective Floyd. "I almost feel like the criminal here."

"You'll get used to it," said the escort.

The detective wondered if he meant "being escorted" or "feeling like a criminal" - probably both.

On the wall outside the fifth floor elevator doors the less than impressive plaque on the door read:

Organized Crime Task Force
New Orleans Division

Inside the mini-lobby was a very busy young lady at a desk, two cubicles behind her and a few other doors, giving the entire setting a harsh claustrophobic feel. Floyd assumed the lady probably caught all the paperwork no one else wanted due to her disappearance when he entered.

Special Agent Morrison stepped out from door number three and greeted Detective Floyd. The agent appeared exactly as the dossier from Sheriff Howard had described him.

His handshake was firm and a couple of wild sprigs of his steel-gray crew cut wobbled with his exuberance.

"I'm Special Agent in charge, Morrison. Right this way, Detective Floyd."

The agent ushered Floyd into another tiny windowless conference room. A projector screen hung slightly askew on one end and two nearly wall sized whiteboards on the opposing walls. S.A. Morrison walked quickly to each and pulled down retractable screens to cover the mass of information scribbled on each of them.

"Please have a seat," he motioned. "Would you like some coffee?" he smiled.

Floyd instantly noted the sick-sweet hospitality engulfed with a smarmy southern dialect. For the first few moments, Floyd was consumed with picturing Morrison in a checkered suit, standing in a little used car lot strung with colored flags popping in the wind.

"Coffee? Detective?" he asked once again.

"Uh, sure, make it black please," said Floyd.

Detective Floyd flopped down a soft brown leather carrying case. It was weighty, having the illusion of an amassed amount of notes and information concerning his visit. Floyd had inserted a thick phone book inside for just that purpose. His motto was, always feign preparedness, but play dumb.

It was drawing Morrison's attention as planned, while he walked to the door to ask for their coffee.

"My director informed me of your visit. He said you were interested in getting some information on the ownership of a vehicle we may or may not have knowledge of," said Morrison.

Floyd began to dig and sort through a few papers from his collection.

"*My* superior tried to call to get the information, but there seemed to be complications..., so he called Director Carmange and cleared me for my visit."

The clown's smile on Morrison's face was beginning to cause Floyd physical discomfort.

"Well then, how can I help you Detective Floyd?"

"I understand you have an agent in your group...," began the Detective. He scratched into the first compartment of his attaché dragging out a legal pad and read, "Special Agent Warner."

He once again feigned skimming a sheaf of information which was not much more that the few pages Sheriff Howard had handed him.

"Special Agent Warner is assigned to your organized crimes task force and was recently in an altercation near the Natchez – Vidalia area, ...a little out of his jurisdiction."

Detective Floyd received another brick in the wall in the form of a toothy grin from S.A. Morrison.

"I understand he was found unconscious on the Louisiana side of the river, handcuffed to a steering wheel. The car on the other hand was discovered on the Mississippi side of the border. Interesting how that could have happened."

The Detective let the statement hang for a moment.

"Would you set up a time this morning that I can interview him?" asked Floyd. "Within limits of course."

"I'm not sure where you get your information, Detective, but S.A. Warner has been reassigned to another division," said Morrison.

Floyd wrinkled his forehead and shuffled a few more pages.

"Really?" said Floyd. "I must have been given some bad information. Is this Warner's photo ID?"

Floyd handed a photocopy of Warner's driver's license and FBI identification.

"It's a copy of the information that was filed by the

Louisiana Department of Safety."

"That surely does appear to be him, Detective, but I'm not privy to any accident he was involved in," said Morrison.

"I must have received the wrong information. Do you have a telephone I can use?" asked Floyd.

S.A. Morrison's smile took on a cold frosty glare, which Detective Floyd pretended not to see.

"Of course, of course, right over in the corner behind you," said Morrison. "But it won't do you any good, Warner was recently transferred out of state."

"So suddenly.... I wonder why Director Carmange didn't know that?" mumbled Floyd. "Can I have the number to where he's been transferred?"

"Surely," he sighed, his wan smile returned as he walked to the door and spoke to their department secretary.

"Could you give me the number to the Minneapolis Headquarters?" said Morrison.

"So far away," said Floyd. "That's a huge transition. I hope he adjusts."

"Agent Warner is very adaptable. I'm sure he'll be just fine," countered Morrison.

The secretary tapped the door and entered with two coffees and a slip of paper which she handed to Detective Floyd.

"Oh, by the way, S.A. Warner has taken some personal time to readjust to the move before he resumes his duties," smiled Morrison.

Floyd nodded and scribbled a note on his sheet of

information.   "Well if a telephone interview with S.A. Warner is out of the question, I suppose I'll have to schedule a flight to Minneapolis when I'm through here."

BeBe and Martiel mumbled several broken conversations between themselves in the front seat of the car, partially ignoring Catherine, alone in the back seat.

It wasn't the road trip Catherine had pictured after the excited outburst of an invitation. What had she been expecting anyway? In fact, even the scenery had turned horribly bleak.

"Where exactly are we going again?" she asked.

"To visit some friends of mine. We're almost there," said BeBe. "Just up ahead."

As they turned onto a little dirt road, a bulky white house resembling something from *Gone with the Wind* came into view.

"You're not serious?" said Catherine. "I'll bet this was an old plantation house. Oh, look at the flower gardens...."

The dirt drive turned to gravel immediately before ending at a path of flagstone steps, which seemed to wind aimlessly toward the front porch.

The three of them poured out and stretched, looking around at the solitude of the setting.

"Look at the oleanders, they look like they're on fire," said Catherine, just as a dark skinned lady dressed in what appeared to be a white sheet and turban caught her view.

"BeBe? Who is that? Is that your friend?" she asked, crunching closer to the group.

"Welcome BeBe!" said the lady, in a chirpy Caribbean

dialect. The two applied a generous hug to the greeting.

"And you must be Martiel Ellington," she continued. "BeBe has told me so much about you."

Martiel, still silent, smiled and extended a handshake.

"Oh, and you are the mother of James," said the woman excitedly. "The resemblance is amazing."

"Everybody, this is my good friend Mambo Dubois," announced BeBe.

"Ms. Dubois will be fine," she corrected. "I'm pleased to meet you both."

Catherine's pleasant smile froze in place; a knee jerk reaction from many years of dealing with assorted clients, when the smile on your face could mean the difference between successful negotiations or a total flop. How did this strange woman know James?

"Please come in," she waved. "I will bring you some refreshments."

Catherine slid to the back of the line entering the door and whispered through her teeth to her Aunt Martiel.

"What have you got me into now?"

"Hush, I *told* you not to come," said Martiel angrily. "Just keep smiling and help me remember everything that's said."

Detective Floyd, tired of the dance, pulled out a stack of paper with the FBI logo clearly emblazoned at the center top. He scribbled a few quick notes, attached the Minneapolis phone number, tapped them even, and slid it all back inside the attaché.

"Okay," said Floyd. "I suppose there's no other

pertinent information that you're anxious to share?"

"Don't get antsy Detective," said Morrison. "I understand you had a visit from some questionable people in Natchez that started your quest. I believe you mentioned a vehicle?"

"I didn't see anyone personally," said Floyd. "I'm only here to garner some information. Just trying to protect the good citizens of Natchez and Adam's County."

Floyd stood and flashed his best toothy grin back at Morrison.

"So you're just somebody's dog sent to sniff out information on an ongoing federal investigation," smiled Morrison.

Detective Floyd was weighing the cost of losing his badge and cleaning the old man's clock before he took a breath and relaxed.

"You don't have to be anybody's dog to smell the shit coming from this office," said Floyd.

"I believe our business is concluded, Detective," said Morrison.

Finally! The smile was gone.

"I'm done with you too," said Floyd, gathering his notes.

He latched his leather carrying case and walked to the door.

"Oh, by the way, the director asked me to check in with him when I arrived. I'm sure he will be thrilled to hear how well you cooperated. Thank you so..., much...."

The building escort, dressed like a department store manikin, came running up to meet Floyd as he exited the tiny office lobby.

"Which way to...," he looked down at his notepad, "Director Carmange's office?" bellowed Floyd.

Special Agent Morrison fled quickly back into his office and picked up his telephone.

The large delivery door behind the Cajun Café was pulled back down and locked. The walk-in freezer was repaired, a broken circuit breaker turned out to be the culprit. Something simple enough that the temperature never climbed high enough to cause a sweat on the heavily insulated door.

Just before noon, the repairman's truck pulled out of the alley behind the café about the same time the sign reading, 'closed today for repairs' clumsily fell down from the front door.

A fat Lincoln Continental rolled quietly through downtown, avoiding the town square and stopping a block away, in front of the Cajun Café.

"Boss said make a splash," said Arthur. "So's we make a splash."

"Ain't there supposed to be people eatin' in this joint?" asked someone in the back seat.

"Looks closed to me," said another.

The lights flickered inside the café and the neon 'open' sign came on.

"Sure makes me nervous, us not hearing from the boss before we left *Nor'leens*," said the man riding shotgun.

"He does his job, we do our job," said Arthur. "That kind of thinking will get you killed."

As soon as the Lincoln stopped at the curb, four men

rolled out of the Lincoln with synchronized swimmer accuracy. Each one raised their hardware and began to destroy the café, firing round after round of ammo into the cheerful lights. In moments, the front of the building was in shambles, and the already sparse streets were deserted.

"Just like the wild west," said one of the men, pumping another series of shots through the glassless windows, "...and we get paid to do it."

The reverse motion back into the car was about to commence, when the remains of the front door blasted down the sidewalk and out into the street.

James walked out from the inner sanctum of the café, his face and hands covered with dark red wet goop.

"What's that?" asked one of the men.

"Who cares? Cut'im in half," Arthur ordered.

The four gunmen emptied a complete rally on James, as he walked slowly toward the car.

As a last resort, one of the men swung his empty shotgun at James in a wild arc. James caught it, broke it in half, and threw it to the ground. Another came running up behind James as he approached the Lincoln. James spun and gave the large man a flying leap, caving in the top of the car, before bouncing to the street on the other side.

The two other men had reloaded and began another volley of fireworks. Now turned about in desperation, their crossfire began pelting toward the car and its driver, and the alternate driver.

Both men still inside the stolen Lincoln were screaming at them to stop, dropping down to avoid being turned into tenderized meat. No one could hear them above the roar.

With one last blast to end the nonsense; James came down with a well aimed fist onto the hood of the car.

The frame of the vehicle buckled and the undercarriage hit the pavement.

"Run!" was the only thing Arthur could manage as they all scrambled away.

The three women were still dawdling just inside the front room of the old house, afraid to touch the splay of antiquities at every turn.

"It is so good to see you once again BeBe," said Ms. Dubois. "I see that your circumstances have changed since our last visit, but there is still much confusion."

She walked BeBe to a wingback chair and waved toward two others.

"Please…, Ms. Ellington, Ms. Williams, would you take a seat over here. Please make yourselves comfortable."

Ms. Dubois was about to leave the room to honor her promise of drinks when Martiel reeled her back in.

"I would love to sit and chit-chat with you Ms. Dubois," said Martiel. "You seem like such a wonderful host, but time is of the essence concerning our visit. Please don't think me rude. So many things hang in the balance."

"Of course," she replied. "I completely understand. I have many skills concerning your questions, but you must understand I do not yet see into the visions of others for an interpretation."

Martiel looked over at BeBe as if to ask, 'Did we waste a trip?'

"However...," she continued, "my *Oungan* will be pleased to help you."

Mambo Dubois waved toward the door of an adjacent room, "This is Dominique, my mentor and wise one, also *Gran Met* to all who gather here."

After her rehearsed announcement, Ms. Dubois bowed her head as the man known only as Dominique poured into the room; a vivid smile glowing on his smooth dark face. He was dressed in brightly colored and decorated clothing from shoulder to shoe. Catherine tried to put a finger on his age, but his features seemed to swim from old to young as she studied him. As his smile smoothed back down, so did the deep crows feet around his eyes. His forehead sporting ruts deep enough to plant flowers slowly disappeared into a flat youthful caramel brown as his eyebrows lowered. Was he forty-eight..., or eighty-four?

Despite his thin appearance and ornate clothing, it was his blazing eyes that Catherine began to focus on. They were fierce and intimidating, yet something kind and unexplainable was still waiting there.

"Some things I will speak freely in front of all," said Dominique. "Others will require privacy."

His little high-pitched, almost feminine voice caught both Martiel and Catherine by surprise, yet still didn't give a hint of his age.

He placed his hand on Martiel's shoulder and she almost immediately fell into a trance state.

"You have carried many, many heavy weights on your back for many years. Yes. You still carry many burdens," he began. "I can help you with these, but you must also help yourself.

"This vision that torments you, causing you pain. It is not to be translated literally, it is a figurative revelation. Do you understand my meaning?" he asked.

Martiel nodded, with some visible relief.

"You must not blame yourself over past circumstances concerning the young James. It is clouding your abilities and distorting your gifts. You must cease that now. I have lifted that heaviness from you."

Catherine could see tears forming in the corner of Martiel's eyes as she sat quietly listening to what at first she considered a sideshow. This little man spoke in riddles that could have been offered to nine out of ten people off the street and deemed prophetic. Yet, why was her Aunt so emotionally engaged?

"The Fates have presided over the young James," he sighed. "But all is not lost. He is becoming a champion over his family. You must all give him room to grow. The gifts born in him will serve as his schoolmaster and as he yields to them, they will teach him what he must learn. Too much earthly wisdom would prove fatal to many you love. Even his childish ignorance will prove wise in the near future."

He took a deep breath and smiled.

As taught by her predecessors, Martiel listened for some confirmation inside Dominique's thoughts, but the harder she tried to listen inside him the more her persistent headache began to squeeze water from her eyes.

"The rest we will speak of in my private chambers," he said, while patting Martiel's shoulder.

He slowly wandered past Catherine and paused.

"You are a woman of many wisdoms. You have decided the fate of corporations, jobs, lives, yet you have struggled with those decisions closest to you. Many do not understand that these are the hardest decisions to make. You fret over the young James also. He has much to learn in the ways of life and understanding and the ways of love. He will learn. Simply allow him."

Quiet once more..., everyone listened as he took his time.

"You lost him, you regained him. It will happen once again. Your other son, a younger man, he is your concern now. He is much older and wiser than his fragile years. He has seen and experienced things...."

He stopped mid-sentence.

"I see that you are not ready to accept these things I say. Beware that you do not lose him to the foolishness of your indifference."

Catherine was indignant over the last few words that cut her to the quick, silently hoping that he would move on.

"Ah, yes, my good friend BeBe," said Dominique. "We have many things to discuss, but that will be for another time. Very soon I see."

He chuckled and sighed.

"Do not be disheartened when you return," he said. "Many things have changed since you have been away from home, but all will be restored."

BeBe looked up at him with a squinty Cajun eye and then over to Martiel, realizing that there was an ulterior motive to their trip.   She could already hear Martiel spouting one of her cute quips, something like, 'Killing two birds with one stone.'

Without hesitation, "Come quickly Ms. Ellington, we have further to discuss in private."

As they left the room, Catherine gathered herself to the front door. The sunshine and flowers did not seem quite as bright and welcoming as when she walked the flagstone steps up to the house.

How dare him accuse her of indifference toward Sam. He was a perfect stranger. So what if he made a few good guesses?

Something about this spiritual nonsense felt completely wrong. She replayed his hocus pocus speech until her thoughts became a lawn sprinkler spitting around inside her head.

Her palm pressed to the front door, anxious to leave.

Suddenly, she wished for a cigarette. A habit she had long forsaken.

Ms. Dubois spoke up suddenly from behind her.

"You are so much like the young James when he came here weeks ago. His stubbornness cost him his mortality. Please don't let yours cost you more than you are willing to lose."

Catherine ducked her head and stepped out onto the porch. She turned toward BeBe inside the house, "I'm going to wait in the car."

Ms. Dubois sighed.   "I might have handled that

differently, but she is a woman used to directness of speech. Anything less and she would not have respected my words."

CHAPTER 31

Surprised that the huge house was indeed empty, the little weasel-faced man had no problems finding an appropriate entrance into the Ames Estate. More experienced and much smaller, Slinky was better suited than Rooster for the task of breaking and entering; taking even less time.

He watched the place vacate, saw Dimanche's daughter, could have easily caught her and brought her back; that little bit of knowledge he would keep to himself.

Besides, that wasn't his assignment and he never did more than what he was contracted to do. His instructions were to pilfer the house and garner information for Damien to locate his ex-wife.

Slinky grinned to himself. He had been around back during all the troubles with Damien and he had seen the degradation heaped on him. Slinky offered once, only once, to track Regina down, but he was refused. That didn't stop him from keeping his ears open. After all, knowledge was power..., and money, when mentioned in the right listening ear.

The way Regina Dimanche had managed to evade her husband all these years was one little tidbit that Damien had not been able to live down since her disappearance.

Years had passed without a single sign of her

whereabouts. His ex-wife was like a ghost. That must have been easy enough though. Living off the three million-plus change in cash she had stolen from her husband. A levelheaded person could stretch three million dollars to last several years, even a lifetime, and living on a cash only basis made it easier for her to hide. Regina Dimanche had proven herself to be just such a person.

Slinky sat in a corner just inside an upstairs bedroom window and shifted the slight backpack on his shoulders. He started to light a cigarette while he assessed the room and the sounds of the house, then slid the little round stub back in the pack of unfiltered Camel's.

This house exuded the family way. A collection of possessions over the years that eventually became an anchor so heavy it was virtually immovable. Even the tidal rise and fall of years couldn't budge this much stuff. He closed his eyes and imagined the treasures hidden in the attic with a greedy shudder and a smile.

Slinky stepped about carefully in his soft-soled flats without a sound. At the bedroom door he paused, then waited in the hallway, still listening, still thinking.

Damien's parents and friends had told him not to marry Regina, but he swore he was *in love*. Choose someone from the *family*, they told him, meaning of course he should choose someone of his own kind. You can still have this Regina, for now, until you get tired of her....

Damien was hell-bent and blinded by passion for this hot blooded woman.

It was as if she had put a spell on him and trapped his

mind into accepting nothing less than a lifelong commitment of marriage. Then as Damien moved up in the family business, their relationship boiled away like water in a hot skillet.

Two years later the kid came along, Jolie. From what Slinky saw earlier, Jolie Dimanche had turned into a real looker, like her mother. Any woman that beautiful was a magnet for trouble. He unconsciously reached for a cigarette again, then pushed away his own suppressed misery and grimaced as he patted the vice in his shirt pocket.

The house had noises - old creaks and pops, two tree limbs scrubbed a south-side wall downstairs..., and there was a cat somewhere. Slinky didn't have to hear or see it. He scrubbed his nose and fought back a sneeze. As he neared the top landing of the staircase he casually sat down, memorizing the layout of the house and the antiques galore. This house was a veritable museum. Future reference only.

Poor, stupid Damien. Slinky grimaced as he recalled the drama.

Five years later came the ugly divorce, which Damien fought. When he finally consented, she disappeared with his daughter Jolie and a pillowcase full of Dimanche money.

A cardinal sin. A sin against the *family*.

Damien's reputation within the family and on the street was nearly destroyed. Damien slowly recovered, gaining a new reputation as the most bloodthirsty leader of all the families along the shipyards. And although his loss was still whispered about less and less over the years, by those few that dared, it kept the wound open and bleeding. The jilted husband still wanted retribution, over a decade later.

No one else cared that Regina was gone.

Ah..., but Damien wanted closure. Closure in the form of revenge, it was *personalmente*. About the time Damien's pride recovered, someone that remembered, someone that knew, would slip a casual remark. Even though Damien pretended not to hear, pretended not to care, he bled fresh hot blood on the inside.

This girl Jolie was his only link and he let her live her life apart from him, with her Aunt BeBe. He watched his daughter grow, from a distance, as Gina somehow filtered money to her sister BeBe and her daughter Jolie.

The very idea of Regina sneaking visits to Vidalia and Natchez to see her daughter was too much. The irony punched Slinky in the gut as he raised his chin in the air suppressing a belly laugh.

Now, because of some crazy person, Damien Dimanche had problems that made his personal family faux pas pale in comparison.

Damien Dimanche was on the brink of a family war....

Slinky stood up, looked at his watch and scurried downstairs, ready to pillage.

Bold, daytime break-ins were his specialty; most times right under the noses of the inhabitants of the homes and businesses he was paid to plunder. Some of his ventures were only for practice while exercising his voyeuristic twist.

He quickly isolated Jolie's bedroom and tumbled each drawer with precision, replacing every item back in almost photographic place of its origin, which was usually unnecessary. Close was good; most people attributed any changes to the motion of a drawer, or cleaning, or day-to-day activities.

Next came the closet, the valise, the chest of drawers, under the bed; the top, bottom, back of every piece of furniture, under the expensive oriental rugs covering the polished hardwood floors.

He almost drooled over some of the valuable jewelry on display, fighting the urge to place a handful of golden glitter in his pocket. That would have to wait for next time.

Inside books, under the bottoms of drawers, jars, vases, anything and everything that allowed air was visited.

Even the water tank behind the toilet seat in her bathroom was investigated.

Anxious, but not dissuaded, he realized that he was somehow making this too hard, especially since he didn't know exactly what he was looking for. It didn't matter how many trips or how long this took as long as it led him to Regina.

People that felt safe or secure in their surroundings didn't necessarily hide things; which was laughingly most everyone. They rarely placed their trinkets out of sight.

During his lengthy career, he had found that the hardest things to find were disguised and left right out in the open.

He had once found a hidden revised copy of a Will

stuffed into a pocket carefully sewn into the folds of a family's expensive draperies; right by their front door. That job had earned him a cool hundred thousand dollars after the massive estate was reverted to his employer.

He stood in the middle of Jolie's bedroom and dismissed his list of potential places, dismissed the urgency; took a deep breath and relaxed.

"Start there...," he whispered, pointing toward Jolie's bed.

He sat down on the soft white bedspread, closed his eyes and let his mind relax. He shrugged out of his backpack and eased down on her bed, head resting on her pillow and stretching out his feet. No one was as calm under pressure as Slinky while he was on the job.

He turned onto his side facing the window and slid his hand under the pillow.

Sam felt his stomach clench the moment his brother appeared in front of him. James was covered in bloody red goo.

"I think I'm gonna puke," he mumbled, about to heave.

He and Jolie had just witnessed the terrifying power of James Earl Williams from a distance.

"Don't try that at home," said James. An unusual glut of conceit seemed etched into his composure.

"Speaking of home, you both need to leave before all the law enforcement comes around to scratch their heads."

"Are you hurt James?"

James looked at himself and laughed.

"Oh, this? Just a disguise for effect. It's shrimp sauce. Best I could do on short notice. Kind of suits me, don't you think?"

James faded and reappeared two steps away, minus the slick red goop on his body.

"What if everyone had been working today?" asked Jolie, hurrying to her Aunt's car. "How did you know?"

He only shrugged, "You'll have to ask Aunt Martiel."

"I'm sure your Aunt BeBe has insurance."

"How do you know she's got insurance? Are you sure you're okay?" asked Jolie.

She seemed afraid to touch his arm, indeed to touch him at all.

James ignored her barrage of questions and began to usher them to leave, "Hurry, here come the troops."

The distant wailing of sirens signaled a rapidly approaching barrage of emergency vehicles.

"James, why didn't you trap them all in the car?" asked Jolie. "You could have let the police come and arrest them? Or...." She was about to discover another of several less risky alternatives other than the violent confrontation they had witnessed.

"Violence is the only thing they know. It's the only thing they respect. Besides, you can't buy advertisement like this."

Jolie wanted to accept his answer, wanted to believe his answer. She knew it wasn't the whole truth. He was acting strange somehow, enjoying this, inching out into a deeper darkness, stretching the length of his moral leash. The further he drifted, the farther he strayed from the

James that she had grown to love.

"You aren't going with us?" asked Jolie. "James? James!"

"Shhh..., I'm here."

Slinky felt a chill run up and down his entire body the moment his fingers brushed the cover of a thick book. Hiding under a pillow where the pretty one rested her head at night.

He eased it out of its hiding place and felt the tired old leather cover with a gentle swipe of his hand.

Possibly an old photo album? No, it was something else.

It could be valuable, it was obviously very old.

He continued with his ruse, happy that his instincts had shown him one of the girl's hiding places.

He opened the book and casually scanned a few pages.

"This is *wack*," whispered Slinky. He shivered violently, barely able to keep his eyes on the pages. It read like a play from the mind of *Alfred Hitchcock*. Instinctively, he skipped to the last entry in the book and began to skim backwards through its pages.

Cold chills ran up and down his spine.

"This can't be real," he mumbled, as a cold sweat beaded on his forehead. He completely dismissed the mission to uncover Regina Dimanche.

This had to be a young girl's strange imagination and her mind was long gone. But there were etchings and pictures of her family members long dead, stories, newspaper clippings, names, dates, epitaphs. If this was some fictitious rambling of a loony girl, she had gone through a lot of trouble to put it all together. Then he noticed that only the last few pages donned the young girl's handwriting. It had been authored over her entire family's lifetime.

He continued backwards through the book, looking for some kind of authentication and found far more than anything he had expected.

"Shit in a shaker," he mumbled, skimming an interesting page. "Pizza Man wasn't crazy after all," he whispered in awe.

Car tires began crackling slowly up the drive.

This was not the time to get brave, but he knew that if he came back empty handed now, especially with the impending talk of a street war between Dimanche and others of his ilk, his life might be forfeit.

Should he trust the book?

He ran downstairs; his short little legs leaping two and three steps at a time, throwing caution to the wind. He slid into the kitchen and began flinging open pantry doors.

There it was..., it was hard to believe that this just might save his life.

CHAPTER 32

James ordered Jolie and his brother Sam to stay inside the car just as a precaution while he checked out the house.

He swept through the downstairs, upstairs, in only moments in time, listening for thoughts and sounds that even a mouse would never hear.

The house was clear, but something was wrong. There was a lingering presence, a feeling that he could not dismiss.

He went to the bottom of the stairs and sat. He placed his hands flat on the wooden board of the first step of the staircase.

Something alive was lingering in the house. Not a person, but something left behind by a person, not physical.... Like a vapor of thought somewhere in the distance; an imaginary whisper in the wind.

His Aunt Martiel would say he was off his rocker, but this was an ethereal trail. If only it was dark. In pitch darkness he could see the faint glow of energy from where his family had walked during the day. Even the current overcast daylight would obliterate a trail.

If only....

Within minutes it would be gone and by the time it was dark the trail would be nonexistent like the vapor it was.

"It's safe...," said James a bit cautiously.

"But?" asked Jolie, trying to make him finish his thought.

"Is it that obvious?"

"You can hide your thoughts from me, but you can't hide your emotional highs and lows," said Jolie.

"Really! Something to work on."

She hit him playfully on his arm and then quickly apologized.

That simple exchange made him frown with sadness. Something about him now frightened her, something that Jolie would have to learn to live with.

"You shouldn't have been there today. I wish neither of you had seen that little tip of the iceberg."

But that wasn't the entire truth. Somewhere inside he wanted to perform, to exhibit his ability.

"Tip of the freakin' iceberg?" spat Sam. "What the heck is your encore?"

"Oh, a non-believer," said James, deliberately falling for his brothers trap.

"I didn't say that," said Sam. "Wait."

Jolie gave Sam her best scornful 'Now you've done it' look.

"Wait!" said Sam again, afraid of what Jolie was going to do to him. "It's almost three, I'm starving. You can show me later."

"Stay in the car," said James.

"James, don't do anything stupid," said Jolie. "What is it with him? It can't be male hormones."

She looked over at Sam with pinched lips, "Why couldn't you just keep quiet?"

"You heard me," begged Sam. "I tried to stop him."

James bounced to the center of the front yard. Although it had not rained all day, the sky was still baggy with clouds. While concentrating, he raised one palm high and lowered the other toward the ground.

"Look at the grass," whispered Sam.

All the fresh sprigs of St. Augustine lawn began to follow and lean toward James. Jolie could feel a static building in the air. What was *wrong* with him?

Jolie opened the car door, "James! Stop this right now!"

At once James pointed each respective hand sharply at the sky and the ground as if he were the conductor of some freakish natural concert.

Jolie felt the tiny hairs on her arms stand erect and instantly slammed the car door shut.

A hazy stream of lightning crackled from the now bagging clouds above James. Blue haze arced and sizzled with a grinding sound through his uplifted hand, passing out into the ground through his other, and then just as quickly it dissipated.

Sam heard Jolie whisper, "Aw shit," and quickly put his hand on the girl's trembling shoulder.

James hurried back over to the car, flexing his fingers into fists.

"How's that for an encore, bro?" asked James, turning back to examine the bent grass.

Sam's eyes were big as saucers and his mouth could not shut.

"I don't know what's going on with James," Sam whispered to Jolie. "I don't think we should tell anybody."

"Don't worry. Nobody would believe us," she replied.

"Okay, okay, I see you aren't impressed with my light show," James frowned. "I'm going inside."

He knew he had successfully diverted the thrust of questions that Jolie would continue to probe him with, until he gave her an answer he knew she wouldn't want to hear.

Sam carefully inched to the place where his brother had called down fire and saw a round burned spot in the green grass - Grass which incidentally was still spiraling in, forming a swirl.

"Dang, a crop circle," said Sam.

"A what?" asked Jolie.

"Do you ever watch the news?"

"Wanna see something cool?" asked James.

"No! No more," they both chimed in at once.

James nodded and placed his hand on Sam's back. The hair on his head immediately stood out in a fuzzy black halo.

"Quit that James!" said Sam, jumping away from his brother.

He tried frantically to comb his mass of black hair back down with his fingers, "You don't know what that might do to me. It..., it might neuter me or something."

Laughter finally broke the seriousness of the moment.

Jolie looked up at the porch steps and sighed tiredly, "We're still alive. Aunt BeBe is going to be so grieved over her little café."

"I think that will go away when she realizes everybody could have been killed," said Sam.

"We'll all help make it right again," said James.

Jolie didn't seem quite as convinced. It wouldn't do any good to try and discuss her thoughts with James at this point in time. He was on some kind of stupid power trip.

Jolie quickly separated herself from the boys. Apparently she was the only one that saw where all his experimentation was heading.

Away from their chatter, her heart saddened. Her father was willing to destroy the last of her family just to get what he wanted. Aunt BeBe and the last few people Jolie could call family were more precious to her than her fathers' bruised ego. What would he do next?

It was up to her to stop her father....

Her spirit was broken as she reached the foot of the stairs, then she heard something else and her blood boiled.

Fury and heat pulsed in her steps as she forced herself to walk slowly up to her bedroom.

Catherine lowered the windows in the car and crouched there, listening to seagulls cry in the distance. She could already hear Martiel and BeBe chiding her for her rudeness.

The seagulls swarming overhead seemed to be mocking her as well.

Catherine closed her eyes as tears slid down her cheeks, salty as the coastal waters somewhere nearby. She inhaled deeply at a gust of cool humid breeze whispering through the open window, helping to clear her head, helping her to think.

A list of questions began to build.

Was she stubborn? Yes, of course she was; stubborn as a rock.

Was she unwilling to know the truth? Maybe. Probably.

Was she willing to lose Sam? Stinging tears continued down her cheeks for James. But Sam? No. Absolutely not. She could send Sam back to his father where he'd be away from all this.

No. Sam would run away. He had her stubborn streak, just like James.

She silently cursed at her crowded choices, then pondered other questions....

Was this the last person her son consulted before his death?

Was the advice James received as cryptic as what she had just witnessed?

The only thing she got out of Dominique's advice was to let it all go - *Que sera sera*. It'll all work itself out in the end.

Is that what these two soothsayers told James?

Something was itching in the back of her mind, some unanswered question that refused to inch forward.

Then it surfaced.

Dominique didn't ask about James, he seemed to already know that her son was still present and interacting with the family.

That spiritual mumbo jumbo was easily explained.

BeBe had most likely told him or possibly her Aunt Martiel; further proof of his sideshow tactics.

Her husband Robert always told her she had the habit of over-thinking her situations. But that was also another tactic.

A slim smirk emerged at the corners of her mouth; it was her over-thinking had proven Robert's infidelities. She actually had spent too many hours over-thinking that subject.

Catherine sighed and looked down at her watch. It was almost four in the afternoon and she was beyond ready to leave.

What could they possibly still be talking about?

Then she posed her one last question to the deafness of the car.

"Has Aunt Martiel finally lost her mind...?"

CHAPTER 33

Jolie hurried up the stairs to her bedroom. All her senses were trained and focused as she stormed inside, almost slamming the door.

"I know you're here," she spat, immediately dropping to her knees and looking under the bed.

She jumped back up and gazed around the room. Everything was still in place, looking undisturbed. Her anger grew as she felt the violation of someone's presence.

"Come out now or I'll call my father and have him take care of you," she gritted.

"No...," begged a muffled little voice.

Jolie stormed to her walk-in closet and threw open the door.

There sat a dwarfish little man, crouched in a circle of salt, staring up at her with bushy eyebrows raised in terror. When she saw the salt, she wanted to laugh, but wondered where he had learned how to use it.

"My daddy sent you here?" she asked.

He nodded quietly, gripping the gun at his side, still in the holster.

"He's not going to stop is he?" she asked.

He lowered his eyes and shook his head.

Jolie let out a puff of anger and stalked into the closet.

"Come on," she whispered, yanking him to his feet inside the circle. "You're going to take me to see my daddy."

"But...," he stammered, pointing down at the salt.

Jolie looked lost for a moment, then stepped inside the circle of salt.

"Keep your mouth shut," she ordered. "Don't even breathe. If you say anything, I'll shove you out of the circle. And if you think Damien Dimanche is bad, you haven't met my boyfriend."

"Oh, I know about your boyfriend," he whispered. "He's gettin' more and more famous every day."

She placed a stiff finger over her lips and frowned as she tried to silence the little fool.

Jolie knew James. This would only take a moment.

Sam was busy inhaling his second sandwich between sips of Coke while watching James discharge more energy.

He faked another uncomfortable laugh, smothered by his stuffed mouth as their housecat perched himself between them on the couch.

Sam wanted to talk to James about the café, about everything that happened, but felt too uncomfortable even to mention it. Even his firm relationship with James seemed to be slipping away from him, like all the others in his family.

He cringed as James raised his fingertip and zapped at some errant bug unfortunate enough to find his way into their living room. Tommy perched himself closer and began his strange chattering cat talk and staring intently between the flapping moth and the frequency of the crackles of electricity.

Then there was a sudden silence.

A sensation not unlike cold water poured through James and he stood to rush upstairs and faded from Sam's view.

Jolie's room was empty and quiet.

He heard Sam's distant voice from somewhere downstairs call his name, but only once.

Jolie's thoughts were lingering in the air as if she was seated on the edge of her bed, frantic, angry, and in shock. There was that same other ethereal scent he detected earlier, stronger now.

But there was no one in her bedroom.

"Jolie, what's wrong?   Where are you?" he asked, vigorously searching the room for any signs of a presence.

Not again, not on his watch, this could *not* be happening.

James exploded with anger and poured through the house looking for Jolie. He circled the grounds outside looking and listening and finding nothing.

Catherine remained in private disgruntled resignation during the entire trip back to Natchez, feeling outnumbered by both friend and family over the strange meeting that day. It was just getting dark as the carload of women pulled up to the garage.

As they slowly stepped out of Martiel's BMW, they were immediately greeted by a chattering Samuel Earl, holding a shotgun like a wild-eyed vigilante.

He tried frantically to explain all that had happened over the last few hours in one long frantic blast.

"What's wrong with you?" asked Catherine. "What are you doing with that gun? Put that down."

Sam faced off with his mother, "James is looking for Jolie. I think, ...she disappeared. They both disappeared. I've searched the whole house, everywhere for the last three hours."

Sam gasped in a breath as the stress began to break him.

"We were together, right there in the living room and poof..., James jumps up and bails on me."

"Sam. Get a hold of yourself," Catherine said, grasping him by his shoulders.

"I need to tell you about the break-in," said Sam, frustrated at having to start all over.

"What break-in?" asked Martiel.

Sam grunted and lowered his head in weakened aggravation.

"Okay..., after the Cajun Café got blown away, we came back here...," he began again.

"My..., my..., *The Cajun* got blown away?" whined BeBe. "Oh God, what happened?"

"Why won't any of you listen to me?" blurted Sam.

Catherine stood back from him and stared, oblivious to his exhausted frantic effort.

"Sam, calm down. You're acting like a five year old. Get a hold of yourself," she barked.

Sam immediately shut down his effort, along with everyone else in the group, and hurried toward the house.

"The boy's about to snap...," warned Martiel. "Don't do it."

"Sam. Sam wait," said Catherine. "Where's James now? Explain what happened to Jolie."

Sam spun on his heel, "I don't care if you ground me for the rest of my life, you figure it out. I'm done."

Sam's voice was quivering inside, but strong enough that he had made his point.

"Where do you think you're going?" spat Catherine.

"James will listen to me when he gets back. I'm going inside to wait for him."

The fête along Bourbon Street was alive with elbow-to-elbow traffic. One pub barker after another waved an enticing arm at passers by, although each establishment was at an over capacity crowd.

"I see the circus never leaves town," mumbled Floyd.

He dug deep in his pocket to drag out some change and tossed it into a street musician's red velvet collection pouch.

"Wonder which church that came from?" he grunted, as he suddenly had to sidestep four teenage tap-dancers jumping in time to a boombox blaring a distorted tune.

Floyd quickly skirted several other amateur performers, ducked his head and began to walk faster through the crowd. When he looked up, he could barely see the blinking red light at the top of a tower in the distance, his chosen landmark to keep him near the hotel where he was rooming.

He quickly turned the next corner attempting to steer

himself back in that general direction, while glancing at a few faces along the way.

It was then he realized that he had unconsciously been herded into the French Quarter.

This wasn't the oblivious walk he'd planned. Now he could barely keep his eyes from window-shopping.

Inside most of the storefronts were pruriently displayed women in various stages of undress, stuffed into their glass showcase, and foisted as a cheap hat for sale. Some were writhing to the rhythm of the live band inside the pubs, others bent double while dressing and undressing. Others were perched on a tiny chair or stool; a few were gliding side to side on a swing like a child on the playground, again mostly naked.

Detective Floyd questioned the gender of some, still trying to keep his eyes and thoughts to himself.

It wasn't his first trip to New Orleans but his intended walk down Bourbon Street was not for entertainment. It wasn't even Mardi Gras and the streets were still a nightmare, thronged with a party crowd, which was initially what he wanted.

He was looking for a public place to think about today's visit to the New Orleans Federal Building and the reactions of the various people he'd met. After mulling it over several times, he was becoming convinced that James Williams or his busybody Aunt had supplied the list of names Sheriff Howard passed on to him. This was so obviously a pre-conceived trail of corrupt officials; anyone would have to be blind not to see it.

In all his years of law enforcement, he had operated

both inside and outside of the law, mostly outside. He had an intimate knowledge of the type of characters capable of hiding behind a badge and all the while garnering a separate income under the table.

That was all in his tainted past; a closed book. Recent life altering events dealing with James Earl Williams had put him on the straight and narrow.

After today's visit to Director Carmange's office, he was actually getting concerned for his own safety. Again, from personal experience, these people didn't like to be snooped on; this could turn out to be a hornet's nest. Even the Assistant Director's office was suspect.

This was why Detective Floyd had chosen a very public, very crowded place to think instead of his hotel room or some sparsely occupied hotel bar. The more public the better, believing it offered him a mode of privacy and security. He was hopelessly wishing for a bodyguard for himself and slid his hand across the holster of his hidden service revolver in hopes of some reassurance.

There were six more interviews scheduled for tomorrow, pre-approved by the Directors office as an innocent sharing of information pertaining to crime traffic in and around Natchez. After crushing several toes with his size twelve shoes today, he would be meeting stiff resistance from tomorrow's faces.

It was as if he could smell the corruption leaking from under closed doors and behind shiny badges, all with something to hide. Just the idea that they thought he was too ignorant to see past their lies made him all the more furious. But, it was such a thin line between playing dumb and asking questions; push too hard and he might end up taking a one-way ride to one of the plentiful dark swamps nearby.

Their cold answers and staring daggered eyes were more interested in what he knew. He knew exactly squat. That was the rub. He was going about this whole visit blind as a bat.

He chuckled to himself; his only leverage was their ignorance of his real intentions.

Floyd turned and slipped inside an open door and quickly sat at a vacant stool at the end of the bar.

"Beer, ...something on tap," he blurted into the squinting face of the bartender.

The blaring voice of a musician squealed over a five-dollar amplifier as a few keys on a piano began to tremble slightly off key.

Floyd threw down a ten on the bar as a tall glass dropped in front of him.

"No charge for the heat," said the bartender, sliding back his money.

He walked away before Floyd could reply. That first sip of cold beer put everything back into focus. He was a walking target. Anyone with half a eye for street business would recognize him as some form of law enforcement.

It was a hideous misjudgment, walking along the thoroughfare while in his business suit.

The comical lyrics behind the piano blurred; he had the sudden urge to find his hotel room, get inside and lock the door. Minutes later, he slid back into the throng, to do exactly that.

Everyone's mood had blackened inside the Ames Estate; avoiding each other, confronting each other, then hiding again.

Catherine was still standing outside Sam's locked door trying to talk some sense into him, chattering away in monologue as Martiel and BeBe searched the huge house for evidence of James and Jolie.

"It would have been so much easier for Sam to explain what happened," Martiel mumbled to herself with a sigh.

"I agree," answered a familiar voice from the stairs.

BeBe appeared and joined Martiel in the hallway.

Martiel was startled as she heard Catherine's voice rise and fall once again from somewhere downstairs.

BeBe put her hand on Martiel's back softly, "I think Jolie's okay. We gotta get our wits together and figure out what's happened."

Martiel nodded.

"I've checked the entire downstairs," BeBe sighed, grimacing as she heard another muffled outburst from Sam.

"I've gone through every room but Jolie's," said Martiel. "Would you join me? You'll be able to notice anything out of place whereas I wouldn't."

The two women scoured the room noticing only minute details of disturbed clothing.

"Someone could have been here besides Jolie," said BeBe. "She had little ways of doing things that she and I had in common. The way she placed things, arranged things."

Martiel walked to Jolie's closet.

All the old clothes from another era had been pushed to the back of the deep dark closet, and Jolie's few items of wardrobe were hanging on the wooden dowel nearest the door.

"It looks untouched," said BeBe.

Martiel walked toward the back of the closet and slipped on the floor almost losing her balance.

"Flip on the light please," said Martiel.

Both women looked down at a haphazard circle of white sandy grit on the floor of the closet.

"Is that salt...?" questioned Martiel.

"What is Jolie up to?" asked BeBe, angrily. "Surely she wouldn't do something that stupid."

Martiel's eyes drilled at her, waiting for an explanation.

Floyd stood in a torpid vacancy, holding onto a street-corner lamppost, and weary of the revelry of the party crowd. The smells of odd smoke, rank beer, and unknown funk was nauseating his senses. Under different circumstances he would be in the mix of the throng, numbed by the buzz of a few beers and the music; *under different circumstances*, he reminded himself.

Another set of fireworks scattered his focus and he pressed on toward his hotel.

His repetitious rehearsal and projections over the next day's visits finally caused his mind to run aground. He was tired.

The La Quinta Inn was only six city blocks away and he could feel his bed calling his name.

"Would you like some company?" asked a feminine voice.

"No thanks," was Floyds immediate response, without a glance. He had lost track of how many bawdy solicitations he had received since entering the busy thoroughfare.

When he turned to see the face of the person speaking, he was taken by surprise. All the other potential suitors had been the rough talking street workers, but this one seemed different.

The petite blond woman was dressed in a very conservative dark business suit and the red hue surrounding her green and brown speckled eyes spoke of her own need for rest. A group of sainted revelers ran roughshod past them, plastering her against him.

"I'm sorry," said Floyd, catching her shoulders. "I thought..., you were...." Then he finally smiled.

She stood back and straightened her jacket, clutching her purse tightly.

"I understand," she smiled. "It looks like your friends left and I honestly didn't like walking around here at this hour without, well..., safety in numbers. You know?"

"My friends?" asked Floyd, circling around at the crowd.

"The two gentlemen dressed like you," she said. "I just assumed that they were with you the way they were following."

"They were no friends of mine, I assure you," smiled Floyd. "And I'd be happy to escort you, but I was just about to leave this fun house and try to get some sleep."

Detective Floyd realized what a horrible mistake he was making even as the words were emanating from his mouth. It wasn't every day that someone as attractive as her walked up and started a conversation.

"You must be from out of town too," she said loudly, trying to match the din of another passing group.

He nodded, still looking warily at the mass of bobbing heads up and down the sidewalk. "And you?"

She slid her thin red lips into a smile as her answer.

"Preston Floyd," he said sticking out his hand.

"Francine Stenowski. Pleased to meet you."

"I was hoping you were leaving here, actually," she said. "I was thinking of some way to persuade you to walk me back toward my hotel."

She instantly fluoresced bright red.

"I mean. What I meant to say was...," she groaned.

Fireworks went ablaze at the next corner making them both jump.

"You meant to say that you need an escort to walk you back to your hotel so you won't get mugged by some gender confused stranger," offered Floyd.

"Yeah, that's..., that's better," she said.

They both turned and began to walk side by side in the direction of the Detective's hotel.

"These friends of mine, could you describe them?" asked Floyd.

"I can do better than that," she said.

She fumbled in her clutch purse for a few seconds and pulled out a pearl handled .25 caliber automatic pistol. It only flashed long enough for Floyd to see it, before she jammed it deep into his side; before he had time to consider that she posed a threat.

"I can almost empty the clip in you and no one will even notice," she bragged. "Now *sweetheart*, let's both take a nice stroll together."

He couldn't believe it. No one in the milling crowd saw what was happening.

"What do you want with me?" asked Floyd.

He stopped and she lovingly slid her arm underneath his suit jacket, painfully digging the barrel of the pistol into a kidney.

"As if you don't already know," she chirped almost happily. "See the trash bin in front of us? Take your service piece out where no one will notice and drop it in and keep walking to the end of the block."

He was already contemplating the best method to relieve her of the weapon and get free of her threats. He slowly reached under his jacket, grasping the handle of his gun, when he felt her pistol dig painfully deeper into his lower rib cage.

"Remember, I can completely disembowel you right here and walk away before anyone notices that you've fallen," she said. "I don't have specific orders *detective*. You choose."

Detective Floyd knew she was right. The small caliber pistol would barely rise above the noise in the crowded street. There was little chance that anyone would even notice his execution or be willing to get involved as a witness in a street killing.

They turned the corner and walked down a relatively empty alley to the next street corner where a dark blue van was idling.

CHAPTER 34

An unexplainable turbulence gusted through the streets of Natchez Mississippi. Sudden thrusts of wind rocked cars on the streets; a few were forced off the road along the highway into town and each route out.

Unwary that he was generating hurricane force winds, James was searching through each and every vehicle.

There was simply too much territory to cover. He tried to guess the distance in which a car, a fast car, could have traveled, then spiraled outward in his search, finding nothing, sensing nothing. It was a futile effort.

His body had begun a strange vibration he couldn't calm. If he were still flesh, still human, it could easily be diagnosed as a severe panic attack. Somewhere inside he had to believe that Jolie was alive and well. He believed he knew all the reasons why. It was the sins of Jolie's mother, Regina Dimanche; her sins against Damien, that was feeding this frenzy.

"Damien…," he whispered to himself.

Moments later James was anchored to a wall, *sotto voce*, listening to the transpiration of events through his invisible membrane as Damien barked and plotted multiple variations of sorties to defend his territories.

"It's all gone to hell!" yelled Damien. "I can't fix this, nobody can."

The Marrello family, which James had visited the night before, was already in the process of taking over Dimanche control of the east freight yards, key to his business operations. The retaliation had the complete approval of the *family council*.

It was done. As Damien would say - *finito*.

Damien was not invited to the council meeting; a death-blow in itself, and the decision had been made behind his back. His men were beginning to cut glances at each other in absolute silence, considering their own fates if Damien couldn't recreate solidarity among the families.

"All because some muscle claiming to be mine busted up their two-bit joint."

Damien looked around at the new faces before him. Some of the older faces were on the bottom of the lower Hudson River though no one present would admit to that knowledge. He looked out through the fractured panes of glass in his empty office, now patched and crisscrossed with supporting duct tape.

"It sounds like the same person that busted up your office," said Sticks. "Arthur says...."

"*Arthur* says..., *Arthur* says...," barked Damien. "*Arthur* isn't here is he? I don't want to hear anything else about what *Arthur* said. There is no way the same man could be here the night before Arthur's debacle, which is incidentally costing me a small fortune to clean up, and then show up thirteen hundred miles away a few hours later. My private jet can't fly that fast. It's somebody else, maybe the Marrello's did it themselves to get the sympathy of the council. I want everybody's ears to the ground. There's a group of these wise-guys."

Although Damien's office had been sanitized of all the destruction, one piece remained. It was his new focus. A piece of his old desktop had been cut out, a piece with a deep groove burned into it that read: "I'm coming."

Mildred walked through the opening where office doors once hung, with a few sheets of paper in her hand and silently offered it to Damien.

She stepped quickly out of the office, "Don't shoot the messenger."

"Look at *this* garbage," he growled.

The transcripts from the wiretap on the Ames home, the leveled café and BeBe's home, were useless. They barely used the telephone and when they did it was grocery lists and movie rentals. He angrily wadded them up and threw them on the floor.

"Somebody's feeding them our every move," he said, shaking his head. "We can't fight two wars at the same time."

The chaos that should have excited James brought him no consolation. Damien was oblivious to the fact that Jolie was missing. As James probed between the coarse linings of Damien Dimanche's thoughts, the name of a sentry, a scout, surfaced for a whisper of a moment. Damien's mind was burning so hot it was nearly impossible to follow his every retaliatory scenario.

There was one parting thought that lingered with both Damien as well as James. Damien had built his empire on blood and if that was the way he was forced to keep it..., then so be it.

Vision, however blurred, always seems to be the first thing that begins working after a hard blow to the head; then comes the ringing in the ears and pounding headache. Detective Floyd suspected that the headache was the least of his forthcoming problems. He kept his eyes closed and tried not to convey to his abductors that he was in anyway capable of listening to their conversation.

"He wasn't wearing a wire, so who sent him?" asked a voice.

He squinted his eyes to see and realized that he had been sandbagged, and the cloth over his head was too dense to see anything beyond shadowed silhouettes.

"That's what we're going to find out," answered another.

He squiggled carefully, slowly, and discovered he was in underwear and t-shirt.

"He's awake," snarled a voice.

'Crap,' he thought, 'The beginning of the end....'

A hand reached under the hood and ripped off the tape covering his mouth and all he could do was grunt as it took with it a few stray hairs missed while shaving that morning.

He slowly tested his feet to find that they were more than likely attached to whatever he was seated on.

He leaned forward only to find more restraints.

His friends would have described him as hog-tied, blinded, and waiting for the sledgehammer to fall.

"Mr. Floyd," said a new voice.

Hands slapped both sides of his face until he grunted.

"Good. Now, we have a few things to discuss," said the voice.

"You sound familiar," said Floyd. "Haven't we met?"

Pain radiated throughout the right side of his face as his head snapped to the left.

'A leftie,' thought Floyd, for future reference. He spat a familiar metallic tasting warm goo, then suddenly understood that he had no future to refer to.

This was a final exit interview.

"Yeah, I remember you," Floyd grunted. "Fifth floor...."

He wiggled his jaw softly trying to regain hearing in his right ear.

"If you intend to live past tonight, you'll spend more time listening and answering questions," said the voice.

"Listening...," sighed Floyd, as his body slumped.

"Good. Who sent you here?"

Floyd thought for a minute and to buy some time, feigned passing out. If he told them that Sheriff Howard was the origin of the list of names he was following upstream, Sheriff Howard would be the next one sitting in a seat exactly like this. If he told what he suspected, that the list originated from that busybody aunt of James Williams, either she or one of her family would be facing execution after the fact.

His feigned reluctance to answer was met with a drenching of cold water over his head. The cloth covering him, quickly absorbed the water and he snapped up in his seat, gasping for air through the tight weave of mesh molded to his face.

"Answer the question, Mr. Floyd. Who sent you and where did you get your list of names?"

"S..., Santa gave me the list," said Floyd. "Checked it twice...."

White-hot pain pierced his naked upper thigh then traveled slowly to his kneecap, and after he had exhaled the last ounce of air from his lungs in a scream, he smelled smoke and seared flesh.

"Again, answer the question," said a calm voice.

Floyd gasped for air, "The..., the Easter bunny," he wheezed.

A repeat performance ensued on his opposite thigh, resulting in a scream of threshing and gasping.

"One last chance to talk before I feed you your roasted gonads," the voice spat.

Something that was blazing hot waved in front of his covered face, still bearing the stench of his own seared flesh.

"So. You're finally getting serious," whispered Floyd. This was most likely the last time he would be able to control himself, before he spilled everything they wanted to know.

The next pain was so brilliant, so pure in its origin, he thought he heard the voice of some long past friend..., as he skated over and beyond the rim of consciousness.

"I don't believe it, but it worked," said Slinky. "Who would have thought that plain table salt could come in so handy?"

Jolie ignored Slinky as she yawned painfully, then

continued concentrating on blocking her thoughts from James. He had to be in his usual rage by now. She almost smiled at the thought.

"You need to be quiet," spat Jolie. "You're not in a circle of salt right now and if my friend finds us, you're going to wish you were back in that sewer you crawled out of."

"You mean your *boyfriend*, don't you?" asked Slinky. "And you're keepin' him from finding us? How?"

"You don't know anything," said Jolie. "Now be quiet before I have you pull up to the next dock and let me out of this junker."

The very idea of another two hours on this rotting cork of a boat made her want to lean out the window and heave.

The pitifully slow tugboat was only a few dozen yards off the bank of the Mississippi River, with a billow of oily smoke killing the mosquitoes in its wake.

Jolie was fighting sleep and after the last several hours and the already long and stressful day, she was wishing for her comfortable bed..., and James.

Slinky slid his pistol onto his lap where Jolie could see it, "Don't start getting any ideas. You're in this for the whole ride, little sister."

Jolie whipped her head to the side and laughed as she slumped tiredly against the inside cabin rail of the ugly little tugboat, "My daddy knows I'm with you now. He might not be the best father a girl could ask for, but I know what he'll do to you if I tell him you threatened me."

Slinky's face blushed, his knuckles blistered white with his grip on the wheel as the gun went back into its holster.

He reached forward and flipped off two of the forward flood lamps and sat back sulking. At least her threat made the dwarf-man shut up. What she wouldn't give for an hour's nap.

Jolie was glad that she'd insisted on calling Damien after their first three hours downstream. It was while they were refueling, after what escalated into a loud argument, Slinky finally deferred to letting her visit an outside telephone booth, handing her the phone number to Damien. Her phone call was short and to the point, hanging up when her father's attempt at small talk began; that was when her eyes noticed Slinky. Jolie spied around the corner of the riverside fuel station, watching her unwitting taxi driver meet with some men that looked as if they were poster children for the mob. They handed him some heavy cargo, but never wandered close enough for her to see their faces.

Slinky was up to something and she had at least another two hours to listen inside his miserable little head as they chugged toward the mouth of the river.

Another gust of breeze woke Jolie from her sleepy stupor and she stuck her head out the window into the night air.

Trying to relax her mind was fruitless. James was in every gust of wind and every dip and swell, causing her to gasp and search the blackness of the night air. Still trying to convince herself that if James hadn't found them yet, he wouldn't until she was ready.

How was she going to explain her reasons for leaving?

After the display of hatred on her Aunt BeBe's beloved

café, she knew it was only going to get worse.

All James had to do was think and he would know exactly why she had to leave. If she didn't settle this fight between her parents, Damien would eventually kill them all, then.... She shuddered violently as she contemplated what James would do in retaliation. She'd had a glimpse of what he was capable of.

She sat back down on the crackled vinyl seat-cushion and stared at the front window.

Slinky glanced down at his backpack close beside him, barely containing his excitement at the thought of what was hidden inside. If Jolie wasn't prize enough, that old book would get him a right hand seat of power with Damien Dimanche, if there was a seat left when the family war was over. But if not, he had a whole new world of other options.

Slinky looked over at the young girl only a few feet away, her face was frozen in concentration, but she seemed scared. Every time the boat listed, she jerked and stared out across the river.

Jolie gasped loudly once again and Slinky turned to see her glaring his direction.

"What?" he asked. "You got another problem?"

Jolie stood carefully and walked to the window on the other side of cabin.

"Hey, you go sit back over there where I can keep an eye on you," he ordered.

"What's in your backpack?"

"Personal stuff. Now go sit back down..., now."

Slinky waved his gun, motioning her to back away.

Undeterred by his threats, Jolie dropped down and grabbed the backpack, hurrying out the rear door onto the wide aft deck of the tug.

She was unzipping the backpack when she heard the engine drop from a steady hum to a putter. Her hand was inside it..., it couldn't be..., then her world went dark.

CHAPTER 35

The Garden District park bench somehow soothed the corruption of his spirit, weakening the vibrations that were threatening to dissolve his mind. James Earl stretched against the wooden slats and laid his head back looking up at the leaves twitching carelessly to the tune of a night wind. He imagined Jolie sitting beside him where she had so many times, before and after his death. Their talks always calmed him, reassured him, and gave him hope. Even after the finale of his enemies, Jolie made him believe all was not lost. How he missed his anchor to the living world.

His thoughts turned toward his aunt, and her words, 'Follow the instructions exactly.'

"Follow the list," he growled aloud.

He quickly looked around to make sure no one heard him, then realized it was nearly three in the morning and groaned. The park was abandoned by all but him.

It was such a short time ago; Jolie had almost perished. How close that had been. By a complete miracle and with the aid of a ghost, he had found Jolie. This time there were no ghosts, no miracles; he was alone and it was eating him again. There was no help above or below the horizon to come to his aid.

The serenity of their park bench was now tainted.

He stood and walked away....

The ruined Cajun Café was an empty dark hull, devoid of life and laughter. If he'd had time to search or question one of the gunmen, he might have found out something, anything. Surely they were still in the Natchez jail. He could easily manage an interview with the prisoners, but if he was seen, if someone described him it could cause another family calamity.

He laughed at the thought.

Since when had that stopped him? No. Maybe someone had called - maybe someone had heard something at home....

The forlorn faces of Martiel and BeBe told James differently.

Amazingly, everyone was still awake.

The general mood of the Ames Estate was no better than the one inside Damien's war room. It was poetic balance.

He made his presence known by thumping the door, an attempt at humanity, before breaching a conversation.

"What are you two arguing about?" he asked.

"You tell him," said Martiel. "I don't have the stomach for it."

Reluctantly BeBe tried her best to explain the circumstances that allowed Jolie to disappear like a wisp of smoke without being detected.

"Why didn't somebody tell me how salt affects me?" he gritted. His head snapped toward Martiel, answering her unspoken demand. "I am controlling myself."

His preemptive blat suggested to both of them he was fully prepared to join in with the common angst filling the house.

"I wanted to," said BeBe. "I wasn't sure about what you are, James."

He knelt humbly in front of the chair where BeBe was seated. "What else can you tell me?" he pleaded, ignoring the 'what you are' implication. "Somebody has to tell me the truth." He stopped and glared accusingly at his aunt.

"You might be able to pierce the shield of salt," said Bebe, "...in theory."

"In theory," sighed James, ducking his head.

Riddles again.

"In my grandmothers' book, it talks about someone like you. I didn't think it could be, because it spoke of a person like you as a myth, an anomaly of nature, or an immortal, almost godlike."

BeBe wasn't making the situation any calmer, but he did ask and he wanted the truth.

"I can't give you advice that might get you...," she began again.

"What? Killed?" he grinned.

"No, much worse," she answered.

James stood so quickly, both women jumped in terror.

His rolling laughter filled the house, booming into every crevice; finally morphing into a sickening hysteria. Something was breaking in him, stretched beyond its boundaries.

The house hung silent for several moments. The Ames Estate was haunted once again. Not by the Ames descendants, but by a strange new host.

Catherine and Sam carefully inched around the corner to peer into the room, their differences suddenly dissolved and they were too terrified to enter.

"I don't care about any of this. One of you..., have a vision! Roll your eyes back in your head and tell me where Jolie is!"

"I can't force a vision," said Martiel, quietly.

"Then how is it a gift?" he asked. "Isn't that what you call it? A gift? Tell me?"

His malicious grin transformed into vicious hatred. James wavered from their view and reappeared just as suddenly.

Martiel pretended not to notice, but having no answer to his demands she proffered none.

"Whoever has my baby Jolie won't take a chance at driving all the way back to New Jersey, not with Jolie, that's for sure," said BeBe. "She'd claw their eyes out the first chance she got. She's not as helpless as she looks."

James almost smiled at the mental picture of Jolie defending herself. There were no answers here, but he had one other option. There was another place to get an answer....

He left without a whisper.

Jolie's head hurt and she wanted to sleep.

The sounds of other boats and the rush of water dashing against the front bow let her know they were close to their destination.

"You awake?" asked Slinky.

Jolie muffed an angry reply against an oily tasting cloth inside her mouth sealed with duct tape.

"Yeah..., sorry about that," he mumbled.

Jolie's eyes were bulging from their sockets as she yanked at her restraints and contemplated the situation she now faced. She chewed at the filthy gag in her mouth with no success, growling as she pulled fruitlessly against her bonds.

Her eyes watered past her headache as she remembered; Slinky had her family journal, containing every family secret for generations past.

Somehow she had to contact James.

She screamed his name inside her head, answered by silence. It was still dark, a couple hours before dawn; he should be able to hear her easily no matter where he was.

She screamed his name again inside the vastness of her thoughts, then once again against her gag. Her whole body shivered as something grainy fell into her ear and she shook her head from side to side at the nuisance.

Her violent wiggle drew Slinky's attention making him chuckle.

"Yeah, I was kinda in a hurry with the salt mix. Didn't mean to get it on your head, but I don't want to take no chances with that boyfriend of yours. I read all about him in this book of yours. See, I know the Pizza Man personally, not that he was a friend by any stretch, but I don't want no part of what he got done to him."

Salt mix? A circle of red, white, and black grit surrounded her on the tugboat's cabin floor, as if traveling on a moving body of water wasn't enough.

James couldn't hear her, but her Aunt BeBe or Martiel might....

More salty grains sifted through her hair and down into her ear and she groaned and swallowed at the mawkish gag in her mouth. If her hands were only free, she wouldn't need someone to rescue her.

"You go right ahead and grunt and struggle all you like. This book and your boyfriend are gonna make me rich!" laughed Slinky.

Jolie tried to kick at the floor, scatter the circle of salt, but her feet and hands were anchored to a lanyard in the cabin deck floor.

"I know..., I know..., I probably shouldn'ta bumped you on the head, but we're on a deadline. I stopped and called your papa while you were sleepin'. He's on his way to meet us. I'm sure he'll forgive me when he sees what I have in my backpack."

His idle comments were straining her temper and the madder she got, the louder her constricted aspiration became, making her world swim.

At her boiling point, she began to flop and twist against her bonds in a grand attempt to free herself, then she swore she'd never get on another boat again as long as she lived.

Slinky locked his eyes on the horizon and swung his gun around in her face, "You settle down, little sister. The only thing keeping me from putting a hole in you is the bonus I might get for bringing you in undamaged. You keep up that noise and I'll forgo the bonus. It's not that much."

Nearly four a.m., the only light inside the Natchez County Holding Center was the square exit sign at the far end of the hallway. The basement had recently been renovated to accommodate the overflow of visitors; a side effect of the increased commerce and casinos. The natural order of gambling and alcohol produced a fresh influx of money..., and visitors to the Natchez Jail.

The one named Arthur lay sleeping, while the others in adjacent cells were tossing and turning fitfully, staring at the shadowed lines on the ceiling. Each one hoping in their own way that their future wouldn't be cut short for their failure.

His arms resembled a wrestler, or a power-lifter, matched equally by a thick chest, all suited to his profession. The others thoughts produced nothing useful that James could extract, but one thing was certain, both conceded that Arthur was their boss. They looked to his direction to keep them alive even amongst their own kind.

James whispered into Arthur's dream state, trying to inject just enough to cause a reciprocal effect. If he could pull it off, there would be no need for dramatics or the risk of exposure.

"You need to call Damien," whispered James. "You better report in."

"Stupid, I already called the boss," Arthur mumbled incoherently, but the thought was clear enough.

"Remember what the boss said to do," he whispered again.

"Keep our trap shut. That's what he said."

His semi-waking thoughts echoed their plan, while James listened. The FBI would be there the next day to extricate them from the mess they caused. Faulty handling of due process, Miranda rights, or some other loophole would have them home in a matter of days.

"Then you can drive home," whispered James.

"Fly in the boss' jet." He smiled in his sleep and turned onto his back on the cot, sighing a deep breath.

"Who you talkin' to, Ot?" asked the man in the next cell.

"Nobody. Shut up, I'm trying to get some sleep," said Arthur.

"Where's the plane?" whispered James.

"What plane? Who said that?"

So much for stealth....

James gripped Arthur's throat and covered his mouth at the same time, pinning him to the creaking bunk.

"Listen very carefully, *Ot*," said James. "I'm going to remove my hand in just a second and let you breathe. The first and only thing you're going to say is where Damien's plane is at."

James squeezed gently on Arthur's trachea, causing him to gorge. "If you say anything else, anything..., I promise I'll rip this out and lay it right beside you, understand?"

Arthur gripped at the air in a desperate attempt to force the hand holding his throat. When he found there was nothing to grip, nothing to see in the dimness of the light, he panicked.

James dropped an elbow into his sternum and loosening his handhold for an instant, forcing him to expel any air in his giant lungs.

Arthur sucked air frantically through his nostrils, on the verge of puking.

"What did I say?" said James. "One thing. Where is the jet?"

James heard him think, 'New Orleans.'

"Hey, what's going on!" yelled one of the cell mates.

The lights came on in the bunker, temporarily blinding everyone in the row of cells.

"Quiet down in there!"

Arthur had rolled to the floor gasping in sips of air and holding his throat.

"Get some help over here," yelled another.

The jailer walked the row, against the far wall, looking in each cell.

"What's wrong with you?" he asked Arthur.

A raspy voice whispered, "Somebody..., tried to..., kill me."

"You're crazy," he laughed. "I'm the only one that has a key to the door. You're not fooling anybody."

A stick banged loudly against the bars.

"Everybody quiet down! Lights out in sixty-seconds!" he yelled as he strolled back down the hall.

The closing of the door clacked loudly, instantly followed by darkness.

"What happened, Ot?" asked the other men.

"Something was in my cell," he rasped. "Somethin' bad."

Damien sat alone in the complete silence of what was left of his office, waiting for his car to arrive down front.

What a long day this had been.

He spat on the floor and slid back on a tattered couch, his hand resting nervously on his holster.

Now he was going to owe the Russian mob a favor. It didn't matter that he paid them in cash for the guns and ammunition to beef up his operation. The transaction itself was considered the favor. The one thing Damien hated more than the Russians was having circumstances force his hand.

He was a planner, a chess player with one restless King and a missing Queen.

That's what this all came down to. He couldn't let go of his hatred, his loss. If he hadn't been so blinded by revenge none of this would have happened.

He remembered his father's old saying, "If you're out for revenge…, better dig two graves."

All for the love of a woman.

"Plane's ready, boss. Car's out front."

Damien yawned…, he could sleep on the flight to New Orleans.

He looked at the photo of Jolie, only five years old, wrinkled in his wallet. Maybe something good was going to come of this mess after all.

CHAPTER 36

Cold and soaking wet, Floyd shivered and gasped in a waking breath of air. He could only hear bits and pieces through his right ear, his left ear was throbbing in pain; probably swollen shut, probably bleeding. Voices in the distance were having a heated conversation about where to dispose of his body.

'How rude,' he thought aimlessly.

Suddenly, he heard one of the people throw up their breakfast, lunch, and dinner somewhere nearby. The rife odor mixed with the latent scent of his own burning flesh, knotting his stomach tighter.

An instant later, another person behind him heaved, then all was momentarily silent.

"What the...?" said a voice from an unknown distance away.

A gunshot exploded, echoing loudly in some cavernous unknown void around Floyd. Instantly, there was more puking and a few other clanking sounds.

An eternity passed as he sat in the hush, bound and waiting for the next volley of pain. The combined stench was becoming overpowering, forcing another rising gorge of bile in his throat.

There was the slight sound of gritty feet scooting on the floor nearby and the building expectation was becoming worse than the actual pain to come.

"Just kill me and get it over with," he mumbled, then closed his eyes waiting for the next slamming blow.

It was the least he could do for Sheriff Howard and those he cared about. His life had been meaningless, useless. At least Sheriff Howard had people that he cared about and those that cared about him. If the information stopped here, it might afford everyone some time to defend themselves.

"How noble," said a new voice. "A change of heart merits mercy."

"Just finish the job!" screamed Floyd, his voice a harsh rasp. Exquisite pain unexpectedly rose upwards from his bowels conjugated by his efforts to speak. The last thing he wanted was mercy; a lingering death, or a life of immobility strapped in a wheelchair.

He felt the tape being ripped from around his ankles, then slowly one by one the rest of his bonds broke loose.

Blood rushed to his hands and they tingled in pain, then flushed into a throbbing numbness.

A hand tinged with the stench of death slowly dragged the cloth from off his head and he squinted at the intense overhead light glaring in his eyes.

A blurred silhouette stood directly in front of Detective Floyd and he knew it was now or never and swung his fist wildly at the misty target.

The person dodged and Floyd fell overbalanced onto a hard cold concrete floor, his damaged legs twitching uncontrollably, ...then came the pain.

"Is that any way to thank a friend?" said the voice again.

The voice almost sounded angry, even strangely ecstatic.

Two firm hands gripped his arms at the shoulders and lifted his two hundred pounds like an empty sack of flour, placing him back into the tortuous seat.

A cup of water was placed in his hand, but he was too weak and shaky to grip it.

"What a mess..., here...," said the new voice. The hand carefully placed the plastic cup to his lips.

Floyd drank the water and gasped for air, adding to the shards of pain from below.

His chest was aching and breathing was now a series of painful gulps of air. Thankfully, he wouldn't last much longer.

His eyes began a milky focus and he looked around, but there was only the one man with his back turned, covered in blood from elbows to hands. At some point, the person seemed satisfied with what he had found and began sifting through other items on a folding table.

"Do I thank you?" asked Floyd. "Or is this round two?"

James Earl Williams turned and looked him in the face.

"You!" he choked. "I might have known you were behind all this!" he gasped for breath.

"You've changed Floyd," said James. "It seems for the better."

"Yeah, straight as an arrow..., and all that," whispered Floyd. "Look..., where it got me."

He coughed a shallow rasp that was followed by a groan.

"Funny thing is..., I was dreading..., seeing you again..., and now I could kiss you."

The effort of talking made his head swim just past consciousness and back again.

"Well almost."

He coughed carefully, softly, avoiding any action that might constrict his diaphragm.

"You must have spent too much time in the French Quarter," said James.

"Ha, ha," said Floyd in his best smug whisper.

Floyd glanced down to the decussated twitching flesh of his legs and snubbed in some air. Thank God he couldn't feel it..., yet.

The thick meat of both his upper thighs from hip to knee was gaping open, seared flaps of meat, with sections of each femur exposed. There was very little blood due to the intense heat from the strange electrically heated blade his abductors had used. Floyd didn't dare look lower at what might or might not be left between his legs. Thankfully, there was only numbness from his waist down, no matter how temporary it was.

"Yeah, they butchered you," said James.

His voice was emotionless and cold.

"How did you find me?" whispered Floyd, turning his head away from his body's carnage.

"You probably don't believe in coincidence..., actually I was looking for..., a particular private hanger, when I heard a scream. Let's face it. There is no one that screams like you, Floyd."

"So what now? It's over for me," he said, his voice shaking, sucking in air. "Do me a favor. Don't leave me like this. Finish me quick. Please.... Hurry...."

Awkward feelings were stirring in his midsection down into his legs, quickly turning into jolts of blinding electric pain. He began floating again, as the new sensations began to register on destroyed nerve endings. It was no matter; his life was on the brink. This was the end.

"Do you trust me?" asked James.

Before Floyd could object, consciousness swam away.

James placed each hand over the long troughs of what used to be Floyd's legs and quietly went to that place inside himself that he still didn't understand; maybe the old Pastor *was* right.

CHAPTER 37

Early hours of the morning had passed and the sun was up, the only one that managed any sleep was BeBe and she had no plans for the day with her beloved restaurant demolished.

"James, I can't do this anymore," said Martiel.

James paced, threatening, waiting, hoping for some bit of information to manifest out of the ethereal. A hint. A tiny glimmer or fragment.

The rest of the family was skulking in the other recesses of the house, reluctant to show themselves while he raged on.

There were new lines forming on Martiel's face, since she came to visit her brother Martin back in June. What seemed years ago amounted to only a little over six or seven weeks, yet she was being dragged along in nature's time machine while James was forever seventeen.

"Neither of us asked for this," he sighed. "All the money in the world isn't worth this curse."

"I've tried to make sense of it," she began slowly. "All the visions, all the premonitions concerning Dimanche and his bunch were dead on. But when I started getting flooded with all the ones about you..., none of them happened the way I saw them. BeBe told me how tore up Jolie has been over her dreams."

Martiel's eyes welled with water, "James, that baby has so many regrets. If I didn't know better I'd say someone or something is salting our gifts to cause this confusion. That's crazy though, isn't it? That can't be possible, can it?"

James had drifted from following her ramblings of self doubt, and twitched inside, trying to remember the details of what had happened when he found Floyd. It was right there on the tip of his memory.... The euphoric feeling just after he discovered Detective Floyd, then..., his memory became fragmented images and thoughts.

In his next segment of memory he was standing at a table rifling through several papers, and when he turned, there was the ruined body of his old friend Detective Floyd sitting in a pool of bodily fluids, taped to a rusted chair. The blood on his hands and arms were from handling Floyd..., surely....

His memory swam again. The one thing that had proven itself a recorder was suddenly failing him. He had not lost a single second of time in his built-in recorder since his death, and now he had lost an entire segment of time.

Was he finally going insane? Or was he nearing his own end?

He had no rulebook to tell him how long he would exist. Anger swelled again as he realized that he was losing focus, yet again.

"How do I find her?" he whispered as he sat on the floor in front of his Aunt Martiel. "I checked every car going both ways on the interstate and every back road going south. I even found Dimanche's private hanger, but there was no plane inside or people I could find."

For the first time in her life, Martiel was truly afraid. Her nephew was out of control and barely listening to what she had to say. To make matters worse, she was now running on contrary advice she received from the voodoo *Oungan* Dominique and the scant information from BeBe.

"I can't trust my visions, James. They aren't reliable anymore. Maybe it's a sign they're leaving me," she rambled. "You know, it is possible. All the family spirits are gone."

"I'm going to find her," said James. "Even if I have to tear New Jersey in half, building by building. I've got nothing but time. If you can't help me find her, you'd better be prepared to spend every dime this family has on damage control. I can heap dead bodies up faster than you can pay to have them buried."

Martiel shuddered at the thought, "James, think about what you're saying."

"I have - for hours."

"I don't think Jolie's in any danger," said Martiel quietly, purposely ignoring his threats. "I'm telling you, the mess at the café was entirely meant for BeBe. By threatening her and whatever family was there, Damien meant to flush Jolie out and give her nowhere left to turn, except her mother. Damien wouldn't hurt his own daughter, James," she continued cautiously.

Martiel let the silence linger, not knowing what else to say. This was the very thing that had her terrified for days. The thought of James going on a blood rage, out of control, and she didn't want to be the trigger that set him off.

When she thought that James had calmed down enough to listen to reason, she began again....

"That's what the headaches were all about," she said. "I've been so afraid of what you might do in a situation like this."

"What *I* might do...," laughed James angrily.

Suddenly, his thoughts flashed to some missing moment of pleasure - that itching bit of lost memory, only hours ago.

"Does Jolie's disappearance have anything to do with the car from the Sheriff's department sitting in the driveway?"

"No, they don't know anything about her disappearance. They were here for hours asking BeBe questions about what happened at *The Cajun*. After they were satisfied that everybody was out of town when it happened, they decided to post a guard for a while."

"So, that's only for appearances," said James.

"That doesn't matter right now. Please, would you listen to me?" she asked. "You are the only one that can find Jolie."

James saw the fear on his aunt's face and turned his back on her, forcing himself to reconsider his options.

"You don't seem to understand. It's like she's disappeared off the face of the planet."

Martiel Ellington quietly considered her next few words, hoping and praying that there was some semblance of rational thought left in her nephew. Hoping it wasn't too late.

"James, what are you?"

"Oh hell…, another life lesson for the dead."

He began pacing a circle, feeling the same brutal frustration rising. Why couldn't he control it? Why *should* he control it?

"Well? Why don't you tell me? Get it over with."

She felt his rage returning, but trying to calm him would produce the opposite results, and plodded on.

"Think. What are you?"

"Besides dead? A spook, a ghost, a freak," said James. "I'm seventeen years down a dead end street."

Martiel wept inside, barely hiding her emotions.

"Elemental," said Martiel. "Remember? You're an elemental. You read it yourself sometime back in Jolie's family journal."

"Wow, that really clears up everything," he said mockingly. "What does that have to do with anything? I'm a freak of nature?"

"It has everything to do with you," said Martiel. "You're not a freak of nature; you're a part of nature…, of the elements. That's part of what Lyda Brown did to you."

James listened reluctantly as Martiel explained what she had recently pieced together from her lengthy talk with Dominique and what BeBe had shared.

After she had exhausted all she knew, along with her conjecture, she waited to see if James could understand; heaven knew she didn't.

"I can't believe Jolie was here all the time," said James.

"In her closet, hidden a circle of salt; an element that can control me."

"Not control you," she corrected. "Hide from you."

"Now you want to argue semantics? She was right in front of me...," he mumbled, feeling defeated.

Jolie actually had been holding part of his operating manual the whole time and she didn't even know it. Neither of them did.

"Her family journal..., where is it?" asked James.

"Gone," sighed Martiel. "I suppose with her."

"I should keep looking. If anything happens, summon me," he sighed.

He cautiously bent forward toward Martiel and placed his hands on her shoulders. "I know you're doing what you think is right," he said, his voice almost a whisper. "So am I."

Martiel felt a strange sensation, a surge of strength as her sleepless mind cleared and her body revived.

"Get some rest," he said, as he stood up.

When James left, Sam shuffled out of the circle of salt, amazed that James never knew that he was there in plain sight of their strange meeting.

The test had worked, but now Sam had a truckload of questions, beginning with - Why did Aunt Martiel let him witness their confrontation?

A knock at the door woke Floyd in his hotel room, his preferred wake up call.

"Thanks," he called out.

The key to his room was in his hand; no pain in his legs.

He instantly tested, then grasped at his crotch and breathed deeply.

"Thank God. Everything's intact!" whimpered Floyd. "I might just kiss him yet."

Then realizing how unmanly the words sounded, he laughed and turned over. He felt great, better than he had in weeks, months, then he wondered what day it was.

Beside Detective Floyd on the bed was a stack of papers. On top was a note of instructions to *study these* and with a *p.s.*:

"*Don't mention last night to anyone. Ever.*"

Through all the torture and pain, it never occurred to ask James where the rogue federal agents had disappeared to, but before he could start building a list of what-ifs, the telephone rang.

He groaned.

"I only wanted the knock on the door," he mumbled as he picked up the receiver.

"Detective Floyd?"

It was a friendly voice if ever he had heard one.

"Hello Sheriff."

"Are you okay? You sound a little strange."

"I just woke up," he answered, looking over at the bedside clock. Six a.m.

"I know it's early. I apologize. We had some excitement yesterday and this is the first chance I've had to call you."

"Excitement? Really?" said Floyd.

"That little café across from the square downtown was blasted to pieces. Thank God, no one was seriously injured."

"Any arrests?" he asked.

"Three in custody…, APB out on two more."

"Were they connected to the mob?" asked Floyd.

"Can't tell. Their lawyer has them gagged and grinning, they aren't talking. I'm thinking that whatever hornet's nest you're swatting is connected to what happened here yesterday. Floyd? You be real careful, okay?"

"My middle name," said Detective Floyd.

When the conversation ended, Floyd breathed a sigh of desperate relief. If the sheriff only knew.

Now he had to get dressed and find a typewriter…, and pray the hotel had a fax machine.

CHAPTER 38

Detective Floyd walked casually up to the information kiosk in the Federal Building wondering what surprises were lurking behind the hundreds of doors in the building above. He picked up a pamphlet, *Careers with the Federal Bureau of Investigation*, and sat down nervously watching the passing faces.

At nine o'clock sharp, he stood and announced his arrival to the friendly receptionist behind the desk.

A few moments later, he and his dangly visitors badge were being escorted to the elevator by another neatly dressed FBI clone.

Floyd noticed at least one set of eyes with a concerned stare burning his direction as the elevator doors closed with a ding.

Sixth floor came none too quickly. It felt so good to feel his legs, to feel all his body parts intact. After what he'd experienced, to actually feel anything at all was pretty damn great, even though his lip was still a little swollen.

Who was he to complain?

He forced the giddy smile from his face and entered FBI Director Carmange's office where he was cordially offered a seat.

"Good morning, Detective," said Carmange. "I trust you have had full cooperation of each of my staff. We like to keep an open line of communication with other law enforcement agencies."

Floyd opened his attaché and pulled a few new papers out along with the original list of names that he had asked to speak with.

"For now, lets just say that it's been very educational," answered Floyd.

The Director reviewed the list of interviewee's Floyd handed him, nodding at each name then slowly raised his eyebrows at the two other pages of information; he seemed to grow pale.

There were street names of informants working undercover in various organizations that had taken months or years to infiltrate.

"Where did you get these last two pages of data?" he asked coldly.

"Some of your staff were more helpful than others," said the Detective.

"The information on these two pages is highly classified. Have you been briefed as to the sensitivity of this information?"

"I was informed that I would receive a thorough *exit* debriefing," said Floyd, thinking of his past night's events.

He saw that the answer was not the one that Carmange wanted. "...after my information gathering expedition was completed."

"That's not protocol," said the Director. "I will find out how that happened, I assure you."

Floyd reached into his bag of tricks one more time and pulled out his preliminary assessment from the interviewee's already processed and handed them across the desk.

"Then I should probably go ahead and give you these. I believe you might find this information useful for your own purposes," said Floyd.

Director Carmange displayed his best poker face as he read the contents and turned to the phone behind his desk.

"Get Special Agent Piedmont on the phone and tell him it's time for his talk with our guest. Have him come to my Ready Room immediately. And while you're at it, inform the Assistant Director and Agent Whiting to drop their schedule for the rest of the day. I want them to attend."

"If you don't mind, Detective, I would like very much to sit in on the remainder of your interview process."

Calmly, Detective Floyd said, "By all means, the more the merrier."

The telephone rang and the director turned and answered, "Carmange..., - Piedmont's not in this morning? He hasn't reported in? Oh, I see. No, I want you to hold all calls until my meetings are completed today. No, I do not want to talk to the Associated Press. Tell them to set up an appointment with our public relations director."

The animated chatter continued until he cut it short.

"Just get Agent Albritten and send him up," he said, looking down at the list. "We'll be in the Ready Room. Would you have someone bring up some refreshments also?"

One by one, the next four names on the list were called in for a brief conversation. One by one, the director's secretary informed him that each had not appeared for duty, all without explanation.

Director Carmange was visibly upset with the personnel, "Tell me this then, did anyone on that task force show up for work this morning or leave any messages? Just these five."

The Director looked over at Floyd with a suspicious eye and hung up the receiver.

"Something tells me that you aren't too surprised about this," said the Director.

"I'm sure they're busy..., somewhere," he answered, pretending to be nonplussed, then offered to move on the last two names scheduled for the following day.

The door to the Ready Room opened and the Director looked down at his watch.

"Detective Floyd, this is Assistant Director Pratt." He then demanded an explanation. "Where is all your Special Crimes detail this morning?"

"I have someone looking into several missing operatives at the moment," Pratt answered.

The door opened again and a petite blond lady walked in the room.

"Ah, Carol, this is...," said Carmange.

Before he could finish, she looked at Detective Floyd, then ducked out and ran from the office at full speed.

Director Carmange grappled at the phone, "Have security stop Agent Carol Whiting and detain her. That's right, do not let her leave the building. Do it now."

"I'm sorry," said Floyd. "I don't usually have that effect on...."

"Save it!" yelled Carmange.

"Pratt, what the devil is going on?"

Assistant Director Pratt found a seat at the table and explained how several people in Special Crimes detail were under disciplinary investigation, but it was all routine. He went on to explain that he had no idea what happened with his secretary Carol or her reaction to Detective Floyd.

"Now Detective…," he said, focusing his entire attention on Floyd.

"Did you say her name was Carol?" asked Floyd, before he was thrown on the grill. He reached one last time into his resources and peeked inside. "She looks like a…, Francine Stenowski to me."

Both Directors lost their arrogant demeanor toward the Detective and looked at each other.

Carmange nodded his head toward the door and seconds later Floyd was left alone in the meeting room with a tray of donuts and fresh carafe of hot coffee.

"Chocolate Éclair's," said Floyd. "My favorite."

CHAPTER 39

The late August sun was peeking over the horizon, promising a cloudless skin-roasting day. With no breeze to push around the humidity, even the flocks of blackbirds were hurrying through the nearby fields before the morning dew evaporated.

James was still attempting to meditate on the sparse information that his Aunt Martiel tried to share with him.

His nightlong search had been fruitless.

Now he was grasping at straws, alone, while everyone else was blissfully asleep.

The very concept of something elemental was the most confusing thing James had tried to comprehend in his short lifetime. The meaning wasn't that difficult, but inserting himself into the equation was like trying to force a square peg into a round hole, with an emotional sledgehammer.

Somewhere he remembered a saying- *After eliminating all other possibilities, the remaining answer, however improbable, must be the correct answer.*

That came from his brother Sam. One of his brother's exercises in obscure philosophy or one of the many 'who-done-its' he was constantly reading.

The problem was, he had eliminated everything but himself. He didn't feel like the answer to anything.

It was messed up.

From what little folklore he could scrape from Martiel's shallow education and his memory, there were four types of elements. Earth, Water, Air, and Fire.

According to Martiel, everything originated from these four. However, that wasn't much to go on. He had no idea that an understanding of alchemy and the stories surrounding a historical quest to make gold would someday determine the basis of his existence. It was nothing more than pure mythology. But, according to BeBe, he was also a myth.

It didn't help that the Ames family journal was silent on the subject as well. And now the one journal that did have information was missing along with Jolie.

The urgency was blinding, like staring straight into the morning sun, obliterating any rational thought. Inevitably, his emotions were inflating the problem. He had no other recourse but to start looking for other possibilities and eliminate them.

First, he needed a new venue, to get away from the array of voices that would soon be chattering madly inside the house.

Flat of his back on the front lawn, he turned and noticed the odd shaped burn mark from his performance..., with the *elements*.

He was capable of playing with lightning, but not able to find the one person that had held him closest to reality. Jolie was his focus, his anchor, his only reason to hold on to sanity.

He looked longingly at the front lawn once again. The

grass in the place where he had called down lightening had resumed its diurnal path and was no longer in the spiraling circle he had created.

"So my childish ignorance is going to save the day," he mumbled sarcastically.

His senses peaked from the sweet smell of dewy summer rising from the grass and the rich earth beneath him. The damp lawn crunched against his back as he flattened out against the ground, breathing in the fresh air. Air that he didn't need to breathe. Why was that?

He was an elemental being, he was air, and for a reminder he vanished like the air, then reappeared.

He remembered something that Granny Smith taught him from her bible. "The wind comes and goes as it pleases, we can't tell where it comes from or where it's going, but we know that it exists."

He didn't need to be a rocket scientist to understand that. Then another of her sayings resurfaced, "You were made out of dirt and one day you'll turn back into dirt."

His *one day* had arrived ahead of schedule. James dug his hands into the soil beneath the grass and dispersed himself into the underground. It was disconcerting at first, and he wanted to gasp for air, but with some effort, he relaxed and suddenly felt it all.

Everything. The sensation was indescribable.

There was movement everywhere. Roots were pushing down, drawing moisture and nutrients from the soil and at the same time other things were in the last stages of decay, replacing what was being used. As he was reaching out he suddenly jerked with power and realized that he had connected with the ground around his grave, miles away. Daylight didn't diminish his strength while he was merged with the underworld. The implications amazed him, he wanted more, to try more. This was only earth; what about air or water or fire?

BeBe called it *godlike.*

What should have been fantastic jolts of elation was simply terrifying to his seventeen years of experiences.

He had two choices. He could accept it..., or run screaming.

'Cool,' he thought, laughing at himself, at how much his comment sounded like Sam.

Screaming would have to wait, until he found Jolie and made sure her life was returned to some semblance of normalcy.

'Focus James. Everybody else is made from dirt too.'

Well, basically..., just not as radically as he was.

Jolie was made from those same elements. She breathed air, her body was mostly water with chemicals from the earth, ...and as for fire, that went without saying.

"I'm close, so close," said James, rising from out of the earth onto the surface of the grass with a flop.

"It's the connection between us I'm missing," he whined.

This time when he resurfaced, he happened to notice that the sun was casting shadows from deep in the west. Time had slid across the dial like quiet moving water while he was lost in his stupor of enlightening euphoria.

"I don't know what else to do," he whispered in desperation.

"Try thinking about her," said a voice from the porch.

"That's all I've done for the last two days," said James, looking for his unwanted helpers face.

Sam was sprawled on the top step of the porch, listening to James talk to himself, and watching what he was doing.

"Oh, hey Sam What's up?" said James, knowing instantly Sam expected to be run off once again for intruding in unwarranted affairs.

Sam only nodded and set down his bottle of Coke. His thoughts were ugly and painful; unbearable. The exclusion and disconnection was ripping Sam apart inside.

Even in death, James still shared the same emotions with his younger brother.

"I guess everybody else is hiding from me?" mused James.

Sam smiled and nodded again, "You blame them? They think you're off your rocker. I'm kinda leaning that way too, bro."

"Don't give up on me Sam. I need help," mumbled James. "You've spent some time with Jolie. You know why I'm going crazy."

James watched the corner of Sam's mouth lift in a twitch. It was his poker players tell. He wasn't going anywhere, even if James was completely off the deep-end insane.

"You're an encyclopedia. Tell me what you know about the elements," said James.

Sam slid to the bottom step of the porch steps and stared off in the distance.

"First of all, there's five elements, not four," said Sam.

"Five?" mumbled James, sitting up, suddenly interested.

Sam ran through the history he remembered about the elements and alchemy, but surprisingly, he also remembered being fascinated about the alchemists' quest for the elixir of life.

"Why don't I remember any of this from school?" asked James.

Sam gave his brother the look he was expecting and twisted his head, "You were too busy keeping us from getting our ass handed to us, remember?

"Anyway, it wasn't curriculum," Sam continued. "I did a report on Nicolas Flamel, the old French dude that was supposed to have created the stuff."

"So it's possible?" asked James.

"Who knows? I think it's just a story myself. You wanna know what I think? I say you should try thinking about Jolie, details…, you know? *Real details.*"

"For some reason that's going to be hard to do with you sitting there watching me. But, I don't want you to leave or anything. Just turn off that thinking machine of yours for a few minutes so I can't hear you so loud."

James lay on his back and concentrated on Jolie. What did he remember about Jolie? He could feel her hair between his fingers, smell its scent, how soft her skin was to his touch, her breath on his cheek and the weight of her head against his chest, her fragrance. He pictured her deep blue eyes and how they unmistakably told him that she loved him without a word being spoken. The memory of her voice moved through him like water and his body quivered at the mere thought of it. He could still hear it as if it were alive inside him. The beat of her heart thumped softly inside him.

'James.'

He melted into the ground and listened to her once again, missing her. Something inside him longed for her and cried out for her warmth against him.

'James! A little help here?' she was yelling at his thoughts.

James opened his eyes and saw Jolie handcuffed to a bed frame in some tiny room.

"I found you," whispered James. "I thought I'd lost you."

Jolie readied herself for the onslaught of angry questions and accusations she expected.

James circled her with his arms and pulled her to him.

She was about to protest, flashing back to the immediate situation..., then she felt the electricity pouring off his body and into hers. She melted against him as she saw everything he had been through flooding into her mind.

In that moment of relief, James understood that he would never be afraid of losing her again.

He gently removed the tape from her mouth.

"I do that to you?" she asked.

"And more," he said, kissing the raw places left by the tape.

She gently returned his affection, "Can we go now?"

He carefully pinched the steel handcuffs from her wrists and turned around.

"What's that sound?" asked James.

"What? I can't hear anything. Can we please get out of here?"

"That ticking sound...."

James followed the sound to a heavy looking box mingled with several others by the door. It was emanating a steady click, click, click. That was not a good omen.

He slid it off the other boxes and pulled the lid open. Inside was a huge brick of stinky clayish material with a dozen or so wires pushed inside it. Each wire was running away to some type of clock device and it was counting backwards.

One hour and ten minutes and getting smaller by each second.

It didn't take a genius to know he was looking at a bomb. The box and everything in it weighed at least thirty pounds.

Jolie looked over his shoulder in recognition and disbelief.

"You're father was going to kill you," said James.

"It can't be," she said. "What would he get by killing me?"

"Hurting your mother?" asked James. "I need to get you away from here, right now."

"No! It was that man," said Jolie, anger and bitterness making her grit her teeth. "That sorry little...,"

"What about the man?" he asked.

"We stopped on the way here. I was at a payphone calling my father," she explained. "He was talking to some men. I heard the name Marchello? ...or maybe Marrello?"

"Marrello," said James. "Your father's enemy. This man was playing both sides of the field. Whichever side pays him the most gets you, and gets control of me. When is this going to end?"

The steady inaudible clicking filled the sudden silence.

"We can't leave this here. This is a hanger James. It would be a disaster."

"A hanger?" asked James. It was most likely near to where he found Detective Floyd. His built in guidance system had been on target all along, but his timing was horribly off.

"I hear someone else," whispered James.

CHAPTER 40

Voices were filtering out from a clandestine little room, littered with years of dust and only an orange trickle of sunlight filtering in from one tiny window. The room, nested above Damien's private hanger in New Orleans, was apparently seldom used, evidenced by a mass of cobwebs stringing between exposed girders and pipes.

Jolie was temporarily contained in another secluded room, connected by a grid of overhead walkways, once used as a nook where pilots could nap during a short layover.

"Slinky, you are a god," said Damien Dimanche. "Not THE God, but a god."

Damien crossed himself and looked upwards apologetically.

"There's this guy," began Slinky. "He's dead, but he's not, it's hard to explain. I don't understand it. I just know it's real, he's real. I saw him Damien, right in front of us. Me and Jolie were standing right there in her bedroom closet and he couldn't see us. Couldn't see us!"

Damien looked through the book angrily, remembering all the stories his ex-wife Regina had told him about her sister and their family. She never told him anything useful, but this book, now *it* was useful.

"This book tells more about the boy and his family," said Slinky. "Complete with pictures."

Damien lifted a photograph of James and his family standing in the sun in front of his grandparent's old home place. It was the old couple he had met standing beside a tall muscular kid.

"They're a weird bunch," said Slinky. "I'm telling you, it's like the *Adams Family* come to life, Damien."

Damien looked at the last few entries written in Jolie's own hand and looked over the top of the book at Slinky.

"Who else knows about this book and the rest of this stuff?" asked Damien.

"Just you..., and me," said Slinky, tapping his own chest.

Slinky looked nervously at his watch and placed his arms back behind him.

Damien gazed at another picture of his daughter. Jolie looked happy. She was standing beside some young punk, a head taller than her, both of them grinning like fools. Love sick, both of them. It was painted all over their faces. The last words written in her journal in her own hand said it all.

Something inside him flickered to life, if only for a moment. His daughter, his little *bambina*, was in love. He closed the book, dropping it on a little metal desk and began calculating his options.

"Okay," said Damien. "So this guy can do things, like move around like a ghost and stuff?"

"He can do a lot more than just move around," said Slinky, looking from side to side. He whispered as if someone might overhear their conversation, "This guy, he can take care of business. He's outa this world. Pizza Man thought he was the devil himself."

Slinky almost regretted using the reference to the Pizza Man as soon as it was out of his mouth. It meant that the word was really spreading quick about the Dimanche clan on the street.

"Huh…," grunted Damien. "This kid did that to the Pizza Man."

"Everything we need to know is in that book right there," said Slinky, pointing at the little metal desk.

There was a lot of business Damien needed taking care of, pressing business, life or death business.

"I was thinkin'," said Slinky. "Just thinkin' mind you. This guy, he's sweet on your daughter. Now if we hang on to her, we can force him to do us favors. Big favors, if you know what I mean."

Damien thought of the prospects and knew what was facing him upon return to his east coast war zone. If only this was real, not his child's imagination scribbled into some old rotting corpse of a book.

Damien remembered the words of Rooster after being in that family's house and especially how he acted after the second time he paid it a visit. Was it really possible?

Then there were the cryptic messages from Arthur via their lawyer about some red devil attacking them at the café.

Slinky watched Damien carefully while he let Damien consider, then cautiously checked the time once again.

"How do you propose we get this ghost to work for us? Is that in this book too?" he asked, breaking the silence.

"I was thinking..., if we wasta kinda knock the girl around some, easy like. Maybe make this guy think we was gonna hurt her," he shrugged, leaving Damien to draw his own conclusions.

Damien glanced at the book, then swiftly pulled out his .38 revolver and shot Slinky between his wooly eyebrows. His body folded into a limp heap on the floor.

"You think too damn much," said Damien. "Nobody touches my daughter."

"Nobody messes with my family either," said James.

James walked in the room and looked at the crumpled body of Damien's man Slinky. "Not much of a retirement plan."

"So you're the troublemaker," said Damien. "Let me guess. You and your Ms. Ellington are the ones that made a mess of my world. A real stinking mess."

"You haven't seen the rock that's already coming your way downhill," said James.

"If what I heard is right," Damien patted his side. "This gun is useless on you. That right?"

"Why don't you try it and find out?" asked James.

"Just hold onto your hammer," said Damien. "I've had plenty of time to think and I'm ready to make you a proposition."

"What could you possibly have to bargain with?" asked James. "I can take it *all* away faster than you can read another word in that book."

Damien slapped his hand on the old leather-bound book on the crusty desk, "You mean this book?"

He was obviously taunting James.

James walked over to take it away and hit something solid in front of the desk.

He looked down and saw a line of granules on the floor around the desk and disappearing behind Damien.

James hit an invisible wall, not hard, but he could see through this one.

It caused him bodily sensations not unlike pain, but more of a sickening weakness. This circle was made of something different than only salt. It was salt, but mixed with bright yellow and dark red dust.

"So you learned how to lay a *trick*," said James, a voodoo term he learned from his old adversary.

"Actually, I have Slinky to thank. He read most of this book and this was his idea," said Damien, looking down at the corpse.

He held up a large glass jar, shaking it gently from side to side.

"Salt, sulfur, red brick dust, and a few other odds and ends. Only in New... Orr... leeens," he laughed.

"Daddy, he's not the troublemaker."

Suddenly, Jolie was standing in the doorway staring into her fathers ice blue eyes.

There was a moment between daughter and father, a test of wills. She raced around James to force her way to her journal, but Damien blocked her path and wobbled his gun her direction.

"You'd kill me?" asked Jolie.

"*Bambina, Ti amo*," he whined. "Of course I won't kill you. But I will stop you."

Jolie slumped back behind James.

Damien sighed, "You know, I was ready to take Slinky's advice and use this book of Jolie's to make you do whatever I wanted you to do."

He turned to stare out the little porthole of a window nearest him, as if seeing something far off in the distance.

"I watched what you did to Slinky," said James. "And I know why you did it."

Damien nodded appreciatively, his eyebrows arched.

"You know of course, that I know about that little salt trick," said Damien. "I could have put it around Jolie and kept her hidden..., for a week, a month. Who knows?"

He shrugged his hands in the air to accent his meaning.

"You're saying you wanted me to come here?" asked James. "Knowing what I wanted to do to you for the trouble you've caused my family."

James slipped his arm around Jolie's waist, adding emphasis.

"To keep you from making a mistake," said Damien.

"You think that because you're Jolie's father, that I wouldn't do anything to really hurt you?" asked James.

"Huh, you *do* read minds," grinned Damien.

James listened to some other cold hard facts cascading from Damien's thoughts. They were barely whispers because of the circle of elements, but they were cruel facts.

If James killed Damien, Jolie would forgive him, probably, likely. But, somewhere down the road, she would always remember that her man, the one she loved, had been her father's executioner. No matter how evil she thought he was or how it was justified, he was still her father. There would always remain a brick between Jolie and him, a festering thorn.

"What do you propose?" asked James.

"I propose that I hang on to this little book, lets say, just for insurance purposes," said Damien. "You and Jolie go back to Podunk U.S. of A. and do whatever it is you do. But before you go, I want Regina brought to me and you put stuff back the way it was."

James stared at him for a moment, then laughed.

"Or I will sit here and read every last word of this book, and figure out how to use it. Then I'll take you and your family apart piece by piece."

"It's not that I don't believe you," said James, still laughing. "It's just that there's no way to put Humpty Dumpty back together."

"Then it's going to get really ugly between us," said Damien. "If I don't make a phone call in say...," he looked down at his gold and diamond encrusted watch, "...about 2 hours. You won't have a family to go back to."

He sat down in a little metal swivel chair and began to skim through a few pages of the journal, taunting James.

"Tick-Tock."

'Rooster?' thought James - that was the name whispered inside Damien.

He turned and walked with Jolie out of the room.

"We can leave and let him blow up with the bomb in the next room," said James.

The expression on her face answered his question.

"Okay, then tell me everything you know about elementals," said James.

CHAPTER 41

"**Where did you hear** the name, Francine Stenowski?" asked Director Carmange.

"It came out during the interview processes," said Floyd. "It's all written down in my report, in the notes. I gave you a copy."

"Are there other copies of this report?" asked the Assistant Director.

"I was instructed to fax a daily copy to my *superiors* to establish a knowledge base on the people that were muscling around in Natchez," said Floyd. "Your people gave me the information, without any restrictions."

"That is questionable," said the Director. "I've already explained that some of this information is classified."

"Like the unauthorized wiretapping of some of our residents in Natchez?" asked Floyd. "I can see where that might be a little sensitive."

The blood drained from the Assistant Director's already pale face and filled Director Carmange's, turning it fiery red.

Carmange turned to Pratt, "Can you sequester all the copies that have been distributed and do a debriefing of everyone involved?"

"That's going to be an awful lot of sequestering," said Floyd. He leaned back for the right moment to continue.

"I understand that an article has already gone to print at the local paper in Natchez this morning about some questionable activities of the FBI. I think it even hinted of some corruption in connection with the Organized Crime they were supposed to be investigating. I'm guessing the AP has probably already bought rights to reprint."

"You're going to prison for a very long time, Detective," said Pratt.

"If that's true, which I doubt, I have a feeling both of you will be in my adjoining prison cells."

The two men exited the room once again, leaving Detective Floyd staring at the walls, however this time Floyd could hear the conversation through the walls.

"This falls on your doorstep, Pratt!" yelled Carmange.

"So basically, an elemental is a mindless thing that can be ordered to do what it's told without question or conscience," said James.

"That's why I didn't think it was important," said Jolie. "You're obviously not mindless and you definitely have a will of your own."

"Was that a compliment?" he asked.

He dove into the blue of her eyes and would have drown.

"It doesn't describe the James I fell in love with."

The intensity of her thoughts began drawing him in, like flesh on flesh.

"James," said Jolie, blushing, then she spun from his arms and walked away. "I'm distracting you again. I'm being used somehow. I can feel it, but I don't understand it and I can't stop it. I wish I could explain it to you. I'm almost sure...," she lowered her head. "You might still be alive if not for me."

He was about to argue the point, but memories took over. Something she said reminded him of his struggle with the voodoo woman. Lyda Brown, if that was who she truly was, had been driven mad by her obsession over him and all the underlying powers he undoubtedly possessed.

The feeling when near his grave, the flood of strength and power, that uncontrollable drawing, presented a strong argument.

It was undeniable; there was some kind of strength there, some raw power. If that power was real, then it was certainly possible there was some other power capable of affecting Jolie.

Now was not the time to uncover that mystery.

"I've got to figure out how to get past the dog collar Damien made using your book," said James. "More trial and error."

Time was not on their side and in fact, it was quickly slipping away.

He was going to have to trust something Sam had told him.

Back in the room, a smug Damien Dimanche sat pretending to be skimming through the journal. He was holding the book like it was his perfect poker hand.

"What do you want?" asked James.

Damien closed the book and smiled.

"I knew you'd eventually see it my way."

James pushed against the invisible barrier slowly and

deliberately with no results.

"I was doing a little light reading while you consulted with Jolie. There's some interesting information having to do with what you are. I don't know about any of this..., some really weird shit if you ask me."

Damien stopped his discourse and looked at James.

"But..., here you stand."

The line formed a bubble below and above Damien. It was impenetrable as long as there wasn't a break in the line that circled him.

Damien was forcing James to play his own trump card.

"You know of course, that when I take that book away from you, we are going to have a problem," said James. "I understand that some information about your connection to the FBI has leaked out."

Damien sat back down and opened the book, smiling and ignoring James.

"You'll go to prison for a lot of years, but I guess you'll still be alive," said James. "Jolie might even be able to come see you once in a while."

"I'd rather be dead than in the joint," said Damien.

"How long did you say I have?" asked James.

"Let's see," he replied, looking at his watch. "You'll have to leave here in..., oh..., let's say about an hour to go save your family elsewhere. When you return, I'll be gone and most likely invisible to you."

He was telling the truth as he knew it, but the truth in that book was geared toward an unthinking, controllable, elemental; one without a *spirit*.

"If not, I'm sure I'll find something in here that will help me improvise what to do."

James walked out of the room and moments later walked back in with a heavily built wooden box and sat it down by the door.

"Your friend there on the floor was playing for both teams. Take a good look at what he left in the room with Jolie."

James tilted the box and watched Damien's expression turn pale as the lid opened.

"Who was he working for?" asked Damien.

"Does the name Marrello ring a bell?"

"I shoulda killed Slinky years ago."

James scooted the box a little closer to the edge of the circle of granular chemicals.

"The timer has about thirty minutes left on it, give or take. After you blow up, I'll still have more than enough time to get back and stop Rooster."

"Shut that thing off!" said Damien.

"I don't know how," said James. "It might go off if I toy with it."

"Bring it here then," said Damien. "Let me do it."

"I'll trade you the book for the bomb," said James. "That salt cocktail might keep *me* out, but this bomb isn't a ghost."

Damien thought through his options with a grimace, watching the timer counting off the seconds.

"Here," he said glumly, holding the book in front of him. "It won't do me any good if I'm dead."

It wasn't quite outside the circle and Damien panicked.

"We swap, even Steven. Same time. Hurry up!"

James slid the box to the edge of the circle.

"Back up," he said, tossing the book out of the circle.

He pulled the box carefully over the line and set it on the desk while James picked up the prized journal and handed it to Jolie. She hugged its old leather cover like a lost child.

Damien carefully examined the bomb, fitfully poking and prodding at different wires.

"Whoever made this used scrap wires," said Damien. "They're all the wrong colors."

"James," said Jolie, nudging him forward.

"Let me in," said James.

"Not on my life!" said Damien. "I'll figure it out. Take Jolie out of here."

"Don't let your pride kill you. Let James help," said Jolie.

Damien finally looked excited as he chose the wire to disarm the timer. Flicking open his knife he carefully cut a striped copper wire between the device and the timer. The timer stopped, then reset to sixty seconds, beeped and began counting down.

"Holy shit!" said Damien. "It's gonna blow!"

James lifted Jolie into his arms and evacuated the building.

As soon as he was far enough away he set her down. Jolie dropped to her knees and immediately emptied her stomach.

"It only lasts a few seconds," whispered James. "Take slow deep breaths."

The same thing happened to Floyd once upon a time.

Traveling that fast wasn't pleasant, but he knew she would recover. James got back to the hanger just as Damien was running out the door of the room and grabbed him.

"Get back in there and give me the bomb," said James.

"Let me go you fool!" yelled Damien. "There isn't time."

"Then break the circle," said James.

Damien, while forced on tiptoes by the iron grip on his arm, kicked frantically at the circle of chemicals.

"You'd better be right here where I can see you when I get back," said James.

James dropped Damien, snatched the box, and disappeared in a blast of cold air.

CHAPTER 42

The summer heat and the insects were all but unbearable, even in the cover of shade. The cedar trees Rooster was crunched under were causing the back of his neck to itch as sweat trickled down the back of his head.

This was one contract he did not want, in fact he tried his best to get out of it, but Damien Dimanche said that he didn't trust anybody else to do the job right. Rooster was his best cleaner. Any other time, Rooster would have seen the remark as a compliment. Now, he was trying to convince himself it was only a job, nothing more. He had to somehow make this a quick in and out. Everyone in the house was to disappear. The easiest of any hit he had been paid to do in several years. The place was secluded, no close neighbors, no traffic and definitely off the beaten path.

The Sheriff's County vehicle was still parked in the drive, but there had been no indication that there was actually an officer on the job. It was a small matter in either case; the hundred grand he was to receive, covered the disposal of everyone left in the house.

The activity around the place was down to a minimum. He had counted four people, four hits; three women and a boy. The hit of the boy he questioned at first, he didn't take contracts involving kids. This boy was no kid.

Rooster thought back to his own childhood. He was on the streets at age ten, made his first hit for the Dimanche's when he was twelve. Rooster pushed all the contemplation aside, too much thinking could get you killed.

The last of the scorching sun would soon disappear and so he stared at his wristwatch once again…, about thirty minutes. But something still didn't feel right.

It's just a job he told himself again, a hit was a hit. Some of his coworkers referred to it as sending their assignment on a permanent vacation. He guessed it was their way of scraping their conscience clean after dealing with dark side of the occupation.

Rooster didn't have that problem, he enjoyed his job.

After scratching the nape of his neck for the umpteenth time, he glared at the shadows of movement inside the house.

If the job was called off, the phone inside the house would ring and someone from inside would be instructed to walk outside onto the porch and wave a cloth. He took one last look at his watch and knew that the phone call from Damien would never come now.

As soon as it was dark, he would cut the phone line and slip inside.

These people had a set routine, easy to plot, easy to predict. It amused Rooster to watch people plodding along in their safe little lives. Same route to work every day, same time leaving, same time returning, same food joints, same everything. Everyone was a creature of habit, which made his job all that much easier.

Only one thing made him uneasy, that unknown element that he had encountered inside this huge old house. Maybe Damien knew something that he didn't or he had fallen into some weird superstition. He thought it was dopey to sit outside the house in a thick circle of salt. It sure didn't help with the insects.

But for a hundred grand...? He'd sit in a circle of manure.

Inside the Ames Estate, supper was done and everyone had fallen into their evening routine.

"James should have already been back," said Martiel. "I know what I told him, that I would leave it up to him. BeBe's a nervous wreck even though we both believe Jolie's in no danger."

"But you feel out of control, not calling the shots," said Catherine.

"I feel out of control, because I can't tell what's going on for sure," she spat back. "You sound like you have experience in the matter."

Catherine put away the last of the dishes and sat at the table with her aunt, ignoring the snap in her voice.

"I remember what it was like when I quit my job to become a housewife," said Catherine. "It was the most painful experience of my life up until then and not just for me. I still wanted to delegate and do, so I started in on delegating to the kids. Robert was always gone on a trip or working late, so the kids caught most of my orders."

On this, she thought for a moment.... Too much delegation and not enough love.

"Oh well," she sighed.

"Before you ask, Robert got his settlement offer," said Martiel.

Catherine waited for the rest of the story.

"He'll take it," she said, nodding drearily. "What do you plan to do when you're a free woman again?"

"I really don't know," said Catherine. "More education, teaching, I haven't had time to think about the future lately with all that's been going on."

Martiel patted Catherine's hand, "This too will pass."

The telephone rang and by the time Catherine had answered, BeBe had bounded down the stairs to find out who it was.

"Jolie!" gasped Catherine. "Are you all right?"

BeBe made frantic swishing motions asking for the receiver.

"My baby girl, you're okay. Where are you?" she asked.

"Of course, I can be there in a couple of hours," said BeBe. "Yeah, I remember where it is. Are you safe?"

There was a few moments silence, "I'm on my way."

She hung up and turned to run back upstairs, with Catherine hot on her heels.

"Is James with Jolie?" asked Catherine.

"He's going to stay with her until I get there," said BeBe. "It's a long drive, but I know all the back roads."

"I'll get my things," said Catherine.

"James asked for everybody to stay here and lock the house up tight," said BeBe. "He said to mention the name *Rooster* to Martiel. He said that she would understand."

Martiel came out of her stupor of thought, "Rooster?

He's Damien's executioner.   Why isn't James here already?"

"You'll have to ask James that," said BeBe.

"It'll be dark soon. Are you sure I can't go with you?" Catherine asked.

"Oh, I almost forgot," she said. "Tell Sam not to forget his guard duty and do just what James said until he gets here."

The house was locked up tight, especially the back storeroom door that was now barricaded. Even unlocked it would present a noisy challenge to force past.

Sam looked down at his watch. He had fifteen minutes before making another complete circuit through the house.

He fell onto the couch in the downstairs study and quickly buried himself deep into a spy novel, but his thoughts kept intruding, wandering back to his near future. Which school would he be going to now that he was living here? Would he even get to go to school? Would he see his father or did he even care to see him? He stretched out further and glanced at his shotgun propped where his mother couldn't see it.

Tommy jumped from the floor, scrunching next to Sam, then flopping on his side, he began his usual pre-nap rumble.

"You've got it made, cat," said Sam, scratching Tommy's soft round belly.

Tommy lolled his chocolate-fringed head up to Sam and slowly closed his sky-blue crossed eyes and went to sleep.

With the television and radio off, the huge house was eerily silent, but he didn't want any noisy distractions to hide a broken window or forced door.

"If you're going to be a guard, you gotta be alert. Make sure you don't get distracted."

Sam figured that was true. James had warned him to trust his instincts as well as his eyes and ears.

He dropped the book onto his lap and rubbed his eyes, checking the time again.

BeBe had flown out the door well over an hour ago to pick up Jolie from who knew where. Sam watched her drive away until the taillights of her car were out of sight.

Still, he was glad Jolie was going to be okay, even felt a little smug for getting asked to help his brother James especially after the conflict with his mother.

Much like his brother, Sam hated waiting and fought the urge to take a walk around the outside of the house. But James had said he shouldn't. James was the only one that gave Sam an ounce of respect, thus he trusted what James told him to do, to the letter.

It was a brother thing that James had earned. He had relied on James almost all of his life. Countless times James had put his own life in jeopardy to keep him from beatings at the hands of the old neighborhood and nearly went to jail the last time it happened. Sam shriveled up inside at the thought what might have happened to him if James had not shown up exactly when he did. He remembered the look on James' face when he pulled the guy off him and hit him with his fist. It was the scariest sight he could remember, and the sound of James Earl's fist shattering a jawbone was terrifying. His heart started thumping from the memory alone.

If the guy had died he would have lost James. No matter what happened now, he owed him.

Suddenly the novel seemed second rate and boring and he dropped it on the floor. His own life had more intrigue filled dangers than the imaginary fiction novel he had been lost in. That story was built from the vacuum of someone's safe imagination sitting behind a typewriter.

"Sam?" someone called.

He jumped, his hand instantly on the stock of the shotgun, with his heart thumping until he recognized that the voice was coming from his Aunt Martiel. His own buried thoughts had distorted the sound of his name, giving it a strange inflection.

"In here," said Sam, glancing at the time, almost time to walk.

Martiel sat down in the nearest chair.

"How are you holding up?" she asked.

Sam was still trying to decide if she was a friend or another nonbeliever to be shunned. He was already avoiding any type of conversation with his mother and lately his Aunt Martiel spent all her time with his mother and BeBe. It was a 'friends of my enemies' situation.

"I'm okay," he finally answered, picking up his novel from the floor; he dog-eared the page and shut it.

Tommy shifted to the other side of the couch in a backbreaking position only a cat could call comfortable.

"What are you reading?" she asked.

"Somebody's lies," said Sam, sitting up.

"Not all of it's a lie," said Martiel.

Sam pondered if she knew something that he didn't about the author or the title.

"Every book says something about the person that wrote it," she said. "Even fiction tells the story from that one person's mind's eye, from their experiences."

"Yeah? Well, this one's nothing close to what we've been through," said Sam.

"Have you considered writing something yourself?" she asked.

Sam thought for a moment and laughed.

"No one would believe anything I wrote!"

Martiel was happy that she had peeked under the first layer of the onion; her term for psychological manipulation.

"Haven't you heard that truth is sometimes stranger than fiction?"

"Strange or insane?" asked Sam, back in protective mode.

"Is there a difference?" she asked.

"Not lately," he admitted.

His thoughts wandered for a moment.

"Go ahead and ask," she said.

"Okay..., how do you do that?"

"Read your thoughts, you mean?" she asked.

"I've been wanting to know. I was afraid to ask," he said.

Martiel was amused at the parallel personalities of Sam and his grandfather, Martin Earl.

"Afraid? Ah, I see, it's kind of like seeing someone in

their underwear and turning your head," she mused.

"That's exactly it," he said.

Layer two of the onion was breached, but she had a long way to go. Sam was a very complex young man.

"It just comes natural," she began. The entire process seemed redundant after spending so much time teaching James, her star pupil.

"I just listen. Have you ever been talking to someone and while they're talking you already know what they're gonna say next?"

"Sure, all the time," said Sam.

Martiel's mind zoomed into revelry mode even though her head was beginning to hurt an all too familiar throb.

"You know that being able to do these things is hereditary?" she asked coyly.

She reeled. The bait was set. Take the bait Sam. Ask the question.

"So is it possible that I have that same thing in me?" he asked, his voice was quiet, but inside he was excited.

Layer three of the onion....

"Absolutely," she answered. "James didn't find out about his abilities until he was over seventeen and you're not far behind."

"Yeah, but he said you've been at it all your life," said Sam.

"Since I was about five years old," sighed Martiel.

"How do you turn it on? It's not some kind of witchcraft?" he asked, scooting up against the couch arm.

Tommy woke from the movement and preformed his usual disappearing act into the next room.

Martiel laughed, "You are definitely the brother of James."

"He asked the same question?"

"I hate to break up your little get together," said a voice behind them.

They both turned to see a tall, barrel-chested man with red hair standing in the doorway, pointing the biggest gun Martiel had ever seen.

"Rooster...," said Martiel.

CHAPTER 43

The temperature dropped ten degrees in the old Ames mansion as the two startled family members stared at their visitor.

"Don't do it Sam," said Martiel, all the while thinking. "James where are you?!"

Sam was already inching his arm toward the bookcase near the couch. The shotgun was propped, hidden, and within easy grasp.

Sam stopped moving.

"That's right *Sam*," said Rooster. "Better listen to the old lady."

What had she been thinking!? All her attention was focused on talking to Sam about his potential and now they were in deep trouble. At least the dull prompting headache was gone now and she felt incredibly stupid for ignoring it.

"Both of you, this way," he ordered. "Let's go get the other one."

Martiel grabbed Sam's arm and held it tight as they trudged upstairs to where Catherine had gone.

At the top of the stairs he made them stop.

"Take it nice and easy," said Rooster. "If either of you get any ideas...."

He cocked the hammer back on his revolver and gently

touched the barrel to the side of Martiel's head.

"Do we understand each other?"

They were both silent and afraid to speak.

"Especially you boy..., do you understand?"

"Yeah," whispered Sam.

"Call the other one," he nodded.

Martiel went inside Catherine's room to find it empty.

"Where's the other woman?" he asked quietly.

The bathtub water began to pour and they noticed the light coming from under the bathroom door.

"Get her out here, now," he growled.

Martiel knocked on the bathroom door and called Catherine.

There was no answer.

Apparently their captor was on a schedule and this was taking too long. He grabbed Martiel by the neck with his free hand and forced her body to the left side of the door. With the swiftness and strength of a horse, he splintered the door open with his heel.

Catherine sat up in the bathtub, then quickly turned and covered herself looking at the three faces staring at her. Sam dropped his gaze to the floor, while Rooster leered at her body.

"Get your clothes on," he barked. "Do it now."

All of Catherine's focus trained on the gun as she hurriedly rose from the water and slipped on a bathrobe, all modesty abandoned.

"Good. Now we're all going to take a walk downstairs together," he said. "Just do what I say and this won't get messy."

"You intend to kill us all anyway," said Martiel. "What does it matter where we are?"

Catherine's jaw dropped that Martiel would even think of provoking this big man, this killer, into doing his job now rather than later.

Rooster agreed with Martiel. He had already displaced all emotion in connection to his task. It was Damien's orders he was following.

"Just do what I say," he ordered again.

They all walked single file down the stairs and finally to the front door.

"Outside. You, kid, open the door and lead the way. No funny business."

Sam held the door open as the women walked out the front door and he motioned with the gun for Sam to follow.

Sam thrust the door into the man and shoved him with all his strength.

"Run!" he yelled.

Rooster was immovable as a tree. He swiftly grabbed Sam by the shoulder with his massive hand and shoved a thumb deep into the recess of his collarbone.

"I'll drop'im right here," warned Rooster.

Sam felt a sickening crunch in his shoulder and fell to his knees groaning as the two women rushed forward to help. But Rooster slid the pistol up to Sam's temple and stared at them with cold dead eyes.

"That was stupid," he said as he lifted Sam, crushing his shoulder, his thumb still anchored in the hollow of Sam's skeletal collar.

"In the yard," he grumbled, pointing with a wave of his gun. "Everybody on your knees, side by side."

The two women quickly walked down the steps while he half-carried a tiptoeing Sam.

"Hey," growled a voice.

Rooster snapped his head around to see where the other deeper voice came from, his gun following his vision.

"How's the chest?" asked James.

James had carefully followed them from upstairs, cautiously waiting for the right opportunity to prevent any of his family from getting killed.

The intensity of the wait and listening to the thoughts of Rooster had filled James with blind rage.

"I get four marks after all," grinned Rooster.

An instinct seemingly took over his actions as James grabbed and held the gun toward himself, crushing the barrel flat just as Rooster fired the gun in his direction. The .45-caliber revolver exploded in Rooster's right hand removing the ends of two fingers and burning his hand.

Rooster barely winced at the pain, but instead slid out that same silver spike James had seen and swung a calculated arc toward the side of his head.

James caught his hand and ripped the whole of it bodily from his wrist with a quick loud snapping twist.

Something cold, mindless and unfeeling took over as his family backed away from the flailing of bodies.

Rooster stood in shock and disbelief as James quietly tossed his wrenched and disembodied hand to the ground. He kicked the big mans left knee and watched as it collapsed backwards. The sound from the break echoed around the covered porch of the house like a gunshot.

Finally, there was a scream of pain from the killer as he awoke from the initial shock of the attack.

"James!" Catherine and Martiel yelled at James.

The James they knew was no longer present.

Rooster fell to the one good knee, catching himself with his burned hand. Blind confusion had taken over and he was no longer registering what was happening to him.

James kicked Rooster's quivering arm and Rooster's face plummeted to the ground. Another quick motion and James had placed a foot on in the middle of Rooster's broad back. Rooster's right arm popped from its socket accompanied by a piercing scream.

The women turned their backs to the spectacle in disgust, but Sam watched on with uncontrollable fascination, unable to believe what he was seeing.

Sam watched on as his brother dismantled the man one piece at a time until only the bare trunk of Rooster's body lay intact in a clotted quivering heap.

Satisfied that Rooster was completely eradicated, James staggered backwards, looking at his handiwork. Then just as quickly as he had dismantled the killer, he disposed of all the remains and the blood, deep into the earth, without disturbing a blade of grass. With no remaining evidence of the carnage, it was as if Rooster was nothing more than a bad nightmare that had somehow passed with only a draining memory. The usual cadence of insects gradually broke the silence of the night.

James knelt and placed both palms to the ground as if

feeling and searching, turning his head slowly, listening for any other intruders, like an enraged beast of prey.

"I've been lied to," whined Martiel. Her very voice was quivering with terror. "What we witnessed was nothing remotely human. It was unnatural, heinous, and it was what I was worried about from the very beginning."

"I don't understand," said BeBe. "Dominique has never given me bad advice."

"Well, there's always a first time," said Martiel. "James doesn't remember a thing after the gunshot. It's like some force took control over him. All this time I've been warning him not to do anything that he would have to carry with him in years to come. Dominique told me to just let him go, be who he is to become."

She waved her arms around in emphasis as she paced nervously. James had fallen into the role of the mindless elemental she had seen in several of her warning visions.

"I can give him or Ms. Dubois a call and try to find out...," said BeBe.

"No thank you. Fool me twice, shame on me," said Martiel.

"Aren't you being a little harsh?" asked BeBe. "He was only trying to help."

"Harsh?" laughed Martiel. "You didn't witness what we did or you'd be singing a different tune."

It was the first time Martiel had uttered a mean word to BeBe, and she was judging BeBe as if she had been there.

"I understand that they are your friends and you trust them," said Martiel. "But all our lives depend on using good information. I don't blame them or you. I only have myself to blame. I'm old and tired and I was looking for a quick fix instead of trusting my own intuition."

BeBe was already spinning inside, trying to understand how her trusted spiritual advisor could have been so wrong.

"Jolie was having the same dream as you, over and over," said BeBe. "It was that same darkness you were seeing and it was having the same effect on her too. She's just so young and inexperienced I didn't put much money on it."

Martiel slumped down on the couch as BeBe rose to refill their tea.

"It's like something's jumbling both Jolie's dreams and my visions," she mumbled to herself.

"Is James going to be alright?" asked Sam.

He had completely forgotten his personal grievances after witnessing his brother turn Rooster into a bloody pulp. He had been anchored to his room for several hours, unable to sleep.

"That wasn't James," said Martiel. "That was something else entirely. It was some base creature."

"Elemental," said Sam.

"I heard what happened," said Jolie. "But I don't believe it. I want to hear it from you James. I want to hear the truth."

"I..., I don't know what happened," said James. "Does it matter? Everyone is safe and he'll never hurt anyone else."

"Does it matter?" she repeated. "Are you serious James? Does it matter? Sam said you ripped the guy apart like some crazed animal."

"He was about to murder my family," spat James.

There was no remorse, no feeling in his speech. Jolie felt as if she were talking to a stranger. No, it was far beyond that; it was as if James was possessed.

She had her family journal back, her father was on his way home. Jolie had expected something far different when she and her Aunt BeBe arrived in Natchez. Now she began to wonder about the covenant between her father and James, especially the unknown conditions neither would discuss with her. James had suddenly had a change of heart and agreed to help Damien put his world back together. That in itself was surprising to Jolie, that James would consent to doing anything for Damien, nevertheless everything looked like it could potentially go back to normal.

Yet nothing was even close to being normal.

Since she had returned, everything was worse. The James she loved was now the one missing.

Did her father find something in her journal and use it against James? Was this a test to see if Damien could control James?

"I'm going to find out how to help you baby," said Jolie. "You're all I have and I've invested too much in you to just let you go to the dogs."

"There's nothing to fix," said James. "This is who I am."

Jolie leaned over to him and kissed him.

It was cold, calculated, and emotionless. The James she

knew would have accepted her invitation and it would have led to much more than the blank thoughtless stare.

"I have to go for awhile," said James. "I'll be back soon."

Before Jolie could protest, James had faded from her sight.

An immediate knock at the door made Jolie jump.

Martiel did not wait for an invitation, but hurried into the bedroom where Jolie sat crying.

"Is he here?" she asked.

Silence answered, as well as the tormented look on Jolie's face.

"Lets you and I take a good close look at that family journal of yours," said Martiel.

CHAPTER 44

Catherine was crouched in the dark by her bedroom window in a dead stare. The moonless black night poured into her room clutching at her mind.

Her bathrobe, a fresh one, one without bloody speckles and bits of flesh, was wrapped tightly around her. It did not dispel her chill, neither did the long hot bath she took cleanse her mind and body of the memories of what she had witnessed only a few hours ago.

BeBe had passed by earlier, knocked on her door and offered her company, just a friendly ear. She didn't answer. She didn't want company or counsel, especially from her new friend. After their trip to voodoo central and tonight's performance, Catherine didn't know if she could share that same closeness again.

She sighed and fought the urge to go apologize to BeBe; it was pride that was preventing her. BeBe was still the same person and nothing had changed between them, only their disagreement over her choice of advisors.

Somewhere far in the distant sky she could see the landing lights of an airplane flickering and it brought her back to the present.

It was no wonder that no one in the house was capable of sleeping. Would she ever sleep again? Catherine closed her eyes wishing for the warmth of the sun on her face but she wondered if it would bring any light inside her.

Part of the responsibility rested on her and the nurturing family life she had failed to produce. That was evidenced by how quickly Robert had signed the divorce proposal, accepting its terms. Over and over, she tried to trace back to that exact point in time where their marriage fell to pieces. Eating the breadcrumb trail back in time was not producing any answers and she shook her head.

Aunt Martiel had referred to it as a new beginning, but somehow it didn't feel that way. It might have been a relief at first, but at the moment, she would gladly settle for the cold unfeeling arms of Robert around her. *Alone* was the new word she dreaded.

She took another deep breath and stood facing the window.

No, Robert Williams had made his choices, now she had to make hers. Living in the past was simply another way of dying in the present.

"Mom?" said a voice outside her door. "Are you awake?"

Catherine started to ignore the voice. Then the very thought of her replicating that choice overwhelmed her. So many times in the past she had chosen to ignore the voices of her boys in favor of her own selfishness. Wondering how she ever gave into that disastrous trait in the first place, she walked to her door and answered.

"Come in Sam."

They sat down together on the side of the bed without words.

"Mom, I'm sorry," said Sam.

"I'm the one that should be apologizing," she replied.

"It doesn't matter who's right or wrong. James is the one that needs us."

"I don't know if there is anyway to help him," said Catherine.

"James never gave up on me and I'm not ever going to give up on him," said Sam, defiantly. "He was the one that was always saving my ass when I was a kid."

Catherine thought about a lecture on his language, but let it go.

"He was the one that always listened to me, helped me. I would have never learned algebra if it wasn't for James. I'd probably be dead or defiled if it wasn't for James. He took my beatings; he made sure I was safe...."

Sam's speech began to sound like a eulogy and he fell silent.

"All I'm saying is, it's just us now. James needs you, we both need you."

"When did you grow up on me?" she asked quietly.

"All you had to do was look. I've been here all the time," said Sam.

She started to hug him, but realized that it might be pushing her luck and that he might see it as another face she was wearing.

"Thank you Sam," she said finally. "You're a pretty smart guy."

"Is that all? Aunt Martiel just said that I'm a genius."

The very ground was rumbling and sparks of static were crackling around James as he stood statuesque atop the stone monument over his grave, basking in his own glory. He shook and swayed until the force of the power glowed translucent throughout his body. As quickly as it started, he ended it.

Somewhere in a distant thought, he remembered his agreement with Damien Dimanche and ripped through time to where he promised to meet him.

Damien was seated in his empty office in his favorite leather chair, patiently re-scanning his scribbled notes on a sheet of paper. He jumped as the air crackled, echoing loudly in the center of the emptiness.

"Hell, boy. You do know how to make an entrance," said Damien.

James could hear a multitude of voices milling around in the next room.

"Do you have the list of names?" asked James.

"Okay, right to the point. I like that," said Damien.

He handed James a list of people that were trying to control his hard won interests in the family business.

"Is this all of them?" asked James.

"Is this all, he asks," said Damien. "Isn't that enough?"

"I thought there was a whole section of your family that was giving you trouble," said James.

"Well, yeah," said Damien. "This is the list that.... Are you okay?" asked Damien. "I see you took care of Rooster. That was unfortunate. I'm gonna miss him."

There was no answer either way and something didn't seem right with how James was reacting to his small talk.

"Are you having second thoughts about taking care of this? Because we can pick up right where we left off."

"I made you a promise," said James. "But don't think I won't rid myself of you right now. Jolie will never know."

"I took precautions to make sure you didn't do something like that," said Damien, pointing at the floor.

"How did that work out for you the last time?" asked James.

"Don't be a wise guy," said Damien.

"I'm only trying to make sure that everyone on this list is who you want to disappear," said James.

"That's the list," said Damien carefully.

"I'll be back in a few minutes," said James. "Wait here."

"What? Wait here, what do you mean?" asked Damien.

The questions were still hanging fresh in the air as James disappeared.

Damien jumped away, then rubbed the back of his neck and shook his head. It seemed he owed Regina a few apologies concerning all things supernatural. She had even tried on several occasions to hint and help him with decisions, which he had ignored.

"Wait a few minutes he says."

Less than twenty minutes later, a large blood splattered mailbag fell onto Damien Dimanche's office floor.

There was total silence in the office.

Damien called out to James, but there was no answer.

He walked out of the circle he had dug into the floor and opened the mailbag. It was full of one hundred dollar bills.

"Holy mother," whispered Damien.

James appeared in front of Damien, completely soaked and sticky with blood. Damien leapt in a desperate attempt to return to his protected zone, but James caught him by the throat with one hand and slammed him backwards onto the floor.

James grabbed each of Damien's hands one at a time and wiped the blood off his body onto Damien's palms.

"Their blood is on your hands now," said James. "Our business is finished. I didn't take time to get an exact count, but there's over ten million in cash in the bag. That should more than make up for what Jolie's mother stole from you. Leave her alone. Tell everyone you found her, you took care of her, got your money back. They won't question you after they see that you now have control over your own business and the whole east end of the yard.

"The whole east end?" croaked Damien. "That would mean there's nobody left in the entire Marrello family."

"You better hire some more men to fill in the gaps," said James. "I want you to remember tonight for a long time. It took me less than twenty minutes to remove everyone on that list..., plus a few more. Now, you have enough money to more than make up for you losses."

James tightened his grip on Damien's neck and pressed him to the floor.

"I kept my promise. If you don't keep your part of the bargain and leave me, my family, Jolie and her mother alone, you will never see me coming, but you'll wish I was the devil before I get through with you."

He raised Damien's head from the floor and gently bonked it back against the marble floor. *"Capisch?"*

Before Damien could nod or answer, James vanished.

Still bathed in a fresh red slurry of blood, James returned to his grave. Some primal urge made him revel in the pungent scent of the blood engulfing him from head to feet.

James stared blankly in the distance, listening to all the random voices and thoughts, from every direction. It was a world of thought, conversations, a few prayers, some arguments, some passion, and plenty of violence and desires.

They all had one thing in common; they were all attuned to him.

Then he heard it. A call.

Someone was calling his name and he slipped away in obedience.

The room was filled with music and the rhythmic beat of drums and chanting. It was his name that was being chanted and it was intoxicating. A circle of people swayed as they worshiped him around an open pit with a post in the center. There by the post he saw a woman, chained to it, naked.

There was food and drink of all kinds on an altar, its smells pulled him closer and he put some in his mouth. For the first time since his death, he could actually taste.

James gorged hungrily on the food, amazed by the wonderful sensation of taste again, and poured a drink of hot liquid down his throat to satiate his thirst.

He turned his eyes to the woman with a new frenzy of lust. She was his gift. He crawled toward her; a half-crazed animal, and he took her....

CHAPTER 45

Detective Floyd crunched deep into the covers
of his hotel bed. The day had been grueling, but not nearly
as bad as it could have been without the documentation
that James had pilfered from the missing federal agents.
Tomorrow he would get to go home to Natchez with a
letter of accommodation in his possession, and an offer of
employment from the Director of the FBI in Washington,
D.C.

Undoubtedly, his simple line of questions, deemed an
investigation, had uncovered a deep vein of corruption
within the organization. His part had been played, but
fate was playing cruel games with his life because of his
involvement with James Earl Williams and his family.
Remarkably, all because of James, his ties with the *Bokor*
Lyda Brown had earned him a promotion instead of a
prison term or worse which he deserved; the very
definition of grace.

Now, this repetitious scenario of torment and salvation
left him owing his life to James once again.

He was as excited as he was terrified at the prospects of
leaving the security and familiarity of his position at the
Sheriff's Department. Maybe a change would be good for
him.

Floyd's initial insecurities of his duties as a detective

when he was first promoted were unfounded. Eventually he proved himself as an excellent caseworker and was already the go-to man in his department.

The fear of the unknown still weighed on his mind. All the FBI could do was fire him or give him a desk job somewhere in the organization, but that was only if the *Peter Principle* was still in use.

Detective Floyd chuckled aloud nervously.

For the first time since his ordeal ended, he wondered exactly where the missing five agents were and what had happened to them. Quite frankly he didn't care, he was alive and in one piece. He let go of the curiosity of all things strange and unexplained.

Thankful was the word of the day.

Peaceful sleep finally crept up on him.

Where was he? There was nothing but darkness and a single candle to light the room where he lay. Something had overtaken him and it felt wonderful. Was it a dream? It couldn't be a dream, he didn't sleep. The last thing he remembered was..., blood. Lots of blood..., the euphoria of its power was still flowing through him.

"I see you are back," said the voice.

Back? He had been asleep! No, it wasn't sleep, he hadn't slept since his..., "Where am I? What happened?"

"Where your destiny has brought you," answered the voice.

This person, this thing, sounded familiar, so soothing. Almost like he had heard it all his life and beyond.

Beyond...?

How could that be?

His head was aching.

"It is the pain of awakening that you feel," answered the voice. "The labor of remembering."

"Remembering what?" asked James groggily.

"Your origins," it answered. "Your power. Who you are."

"Yes, my power," said James, that much he remembered.

There was so much blood. He was bathed in it…. That was when he….

"Where is the woman?" asked James.

"She was a gift for you. She has completed her task," came the answer.

"I returned all their blood to the earth, my flesh feels alive," whispered James.

"Yes, and there will be more for you. Much more. All our enemies will be cleansed. Nothing can withstand your power in the earth," the voice whispered. "I will lead you to your destiny."

A hand came out of the dark, the arm draped in black cloth.

"Why can't I see you?" asked James. "Why is it dark?"

"All in time…. Let me see your hands."

James held them out in obedience.

The hand pointed its index finger on his right palm. The pointed nail drew a symbol in black into him.

It burned like fire and James closed his palm into a fist. Immediately came a dizzy spinning of power, almost as reeking as the blood on his flesh. Then the hand drew another black symbol in the palm of his other hand and once again like liquid fire inside him, he quaked.

"More...," whispered James, it was all he could force out.

His world was spinning and his entire body was on fire, flickering like a flame. The heat was like a thousand tongues caressing every inch of his body in both pleasure and pain.

"What is my purpose?" asked James.

"To do my will," came the answer. "You will enjoy my gifts and I will enjoy yours. You are my conduit into the earth."

There was nothing James wanted more than to perform, to be, to exist for the pleasure of this new friend.

He tried once again to pierce the darkness around him with his illuminate vision but failed.

"When can I see you?" asked James.

"Soon," came his answer.

"I have a task for you, to test your newness."

A hooded shroud of black came near to his ear and whispered.

James smiled and quickly disappeared.

It was a strange place. The plateau was high on a hillside overlooking the ocean. The gentle breeze and every lap of the waves on the beach below rippled power into James as he watched. Just ahead was his destination.

He stood invisible to all those around him. There was a large fire, dancing and festivities. A skinny man in wildly colorful attire was holding a staff in one hand and a rattle in the other and dancing around drunkenly.

James watched in awe as every shake of the rattle gave off rainbow colored lights and when he spoke, the air flowed in liquid waves in front of him. Others were standing and swaying ecstatically to the beat of drums.

He could smell their oblations to some perceived god and offering themselves for possession.

"Go," he heard inside and smiled.

The skinny man stopped and looked around him.

The drums instantly stopped.

He held out his staff and uttered some unintelligible gibberish in the direction of James. The spoken words flew past James like a mist and disappeared, causing the man to stagger.

James appeared before the whole congregation and stepped forward quickly, grasping the staff.

The practitioners fell on their faces in worship before their new visitor and an invisible wave of power poured toward him. James instantly clenched the little man in a bear hug, amused as his eyes bulged in shock.

In a violent blending of their powers, the two spun in a blur.

A centrifuge of red mist sprayed in all directions as the skinny man disintegrated upon all his followers.

It was dark again and James was back before his new friend.

"It's done," said James.

He stood dripping and covered in warm red rivulets.

"You did well," laughed the voice in a high wail. "He was my most powerful opponent."

"He was nothing but blood," said James.

"No one and nothing will be able to withstand us when you acquire the full true power of your source," he laughed. "You have already received the full essence of two powerful sorcerers. Your *ashé* grows stronger every day. Now we must make the final preparations to rejoin you to your bones immediately."

"Yes," said James, his body flickering with heat.

"I will share my blood with you when you are reunited with your source. I will teach you. I will be your master," said the voice with glee.

"Is that what I should call you?" asked James.

"Master."

"Master," repeated James.

CHAPTER 46

Once again, no one was capable of any sleep in the dreary confines of the Ames Estate. There were only short fitful episodes of restlessness, coupled with odd dreams for everyone.

"Summon him," said Martiel, frantically. "It's been two days."

"Where could he be?" asked Jolie. "It's almost three a.m.; that's not like James to be gone this long. He's usually sitting in that chair every time I wake up during the night."

"Let's try and get him here," said Martiel. "As quick as you can. Something's awful wrong."

Martiel had been afraid to summons her nephew that previous night and this night she'd tried and failed. It was after another sharing of information that she learned Jolie had been unsuccessful as well. Maybe their combined efforts would bring James Earl home to them.

Jolie sat her candle in the center of the table, concentrated on his name, and called aloud for James to come to her. Usually by the second time, he was standing across from her with a bright smile on his face.

"What am I doing wrong?" she pondered.

"Maybe it's not you," said Martiel and joined hands with Jolie.

Together they called for James.

Moments later James appeared, but it was not the sight that they were expecting.

James plopped on the bare wooden floor of Jolie's bedroom with a splat - naked, bloody, and with black tattooed markings on every inch of his body.

He crouched as quickly as he landed and stared at his new surroundings.

"James?" said Jolie, shocked at the sight of him.

"Do it now," said Martiel.

Jolie got the glass jar from the table and hurriedly ran a circle around James, with a colorful powdered material.

As soon as the ends of the circle met, James howled a blood-curdling scream.

"Why did you call me?!"

He lunged at Jolie like an attacking animal and hit an invisible wall, slamming himself back down to the floor, which he continued to repeat in several directions like a caged beast.

"Why is he naked?" asked Jolie. "What's he been doing?"

"I don't know, but we better figure this out really quick," said Martiel. "I don't know how long this circle can hold him."

Jolie knelt at the edge of the circle and watched as James finally calmed down enough to look at her in the face.

"What do you want?" he growled.

"James, don't you recognize me?" she pleaded.

"Of course I know you. I know everyone, everything.

You're Jolie Dimanche, daughter of Damien and Regina," said James. "That woman is Martiel Ellington."

"She's your Aunt, James," said Jolie.

"I'm no one's relative," said James, "...and everyone's relative."

"He's lost his mind," said Martiel. "Oh God, we may have lost James altogether."

Jolie's eyes grew wide, "What happened to his...?"

She didn't finish the sentence, turning her blushing face toward Martiel.

"The first thing we have to do is a cleansing. We have to get those marks off his body," said Jolie. "I have everything I need, but it's at my Aunt BeBe's house. I'll..., I'll have to go get it all."

At this point she was looking for any excuse to leave the room.

James twitched his head wildly and lunged in the opposite direction of the two women.

"I have to go. Let me out of here!" he yelled.

"You aren't going anywhere, mister," said Martiel.

"I have to go. I'm being called. They are calling my name!" he spat. "Let me go you whore!"

"Who is calling you?" asked Martiel, ignoring the insult.

"My followers, my people!" he yelled. "The ones you stole me from. Let me go!" he continued, spilling curses at them.

There was immediate banging on the bedroom door and Martiel hurried to catch the others before they forced their way inside.

"What's going on?" chimed BeBe and Catherine.

"You'll have to stay outside," said Martiel. "You shouldn't come in."

"BeBe, would you take Jolie to your house to get some things?" asked Martiel. "You need to get her back here as quick as you can."

"I want inside," demanded Catherine.

"That's really not a good idea," replied Martiel.

The revenant of James Earl Williams sat glaring at Martiel, his darkened eyes piercing her thoughts then turned his back on her, sulking.

She was exhausted in everyway imaginable and heartbroken for the creature in front of her and his resemblance to her niece's son.

The boy that criticized her need for counsel was in dire need of her help and she had none to give.

Martiel heard noises in the house below, then twitched and stood, fending off the sleep she so desperately needed.

Catherine and Sam were having another heated echoing conversation downstairs. It was amazing how some people overlooked the terrible and maximized the inconsequential. They were making the proverbial mountain out of a molehill; she grimaced at the saying and ducked her head.

"You have to let me go," he hissed.

"Not gonna happen," said Martiel.

Her eyes were beginning to water from lack of sleep; she had to keep this vigil and occupy herself until Jolie returned.

She pulled a chair up to the circle's edge and grabbed her notepad. She began by duplicating the drawings on his back onto its pages, until he sensed what she was doing and turned suddenly.

Martiel blushed at his nakedness and looked away.

"Would you mind putting that thing away? It's scaring me," she chided. "Have some modesty; you know better than that."

A glimmer of a moment, she sensed the mind of her James. It was only a flicker, but she lunged at the opportunity.

"James, what does this mark mean?" she asked hurriedly. She lifted the page of her drawing toward him.

He proudly turned his arm to display a duplicate of the design from his back she was offering him.

"A *Vévé*. It's not a design it's a spirit," he gleamed, his eyes distorting the light, reflecting the hue in odd colors.

"Shit," she whispered, her limp hands unconsciously dropping the pad into her lap. She studied the eye-shine for another moment and noted the oddity.

Martiel swallowed dryly.

Regaining her composure, she held up the pad once more.

"Let's start again," she managed. "Who..., is this symbol?"

"You would not understand his name," said James. "He rules over the grave."

She held up another interesting squiggly symbol.

"That one rules over the hounds of vengeance," he grinned. She could not help but notice that his voice was changing. The usual deep timbre of James was mellowing out, almost matching her own cadence. It was having a strange mesmerizing effect.

Another picture flashed up.

"Ah, the dark one," said James.

"What does that mean?" she asked, terrified of the possibilities.

"I can speak his name and he will come and answer your questions himself, but he will demand an offering," said James.

"No. No. I don't want you to call anybody or anything," said Martiel.

She held up another, "On your hand, this one."

"In your tongue, he is called *Tempest*, controlling the storm."

"What's that in the palm of your hand? Let me see," she asked.

He displayed both hands while she quickly sketched, mirrored in each were delicate twin swirls of black.

"They look the same," she muttered to herself.

"*The Eros*, god and goddess of desires," he answered proudly, then clenching his fists into hard weapons, shaking them at the air.

This version of James seemed to thoroughly enjoy his audience, as if her attentions were some type of homage or worship. Her subject began proudly rotating his naked body to expose every marking and told her each meaning, as well as whom they represented. There were dozens and her tablet was quickly filling up.

"Okay, the one on the center of your chest."

Martiel held up her sketch of the *Vèvè* etched into his skin..

"That one is not for you to know," he growled. "It is secret."

"Okay," she said. "What does he do?"

"You're trying to read my mind," he laughed. "I am many minds. That is a dangerous thing for you to do."

Too tired to be intimidated she asked, "Can you tell me anything about it?"

"He who owns me," said James. "That is all you need to know."

'Bingo,' thought Martiel.

"Let me go," he said again, almost playfully.

Her head was already getting a slow familiar throb. What was taking Jolie so long?

"Let me go," he whispered. It was hypnotic.

He held up his palms and pressed them against the invisible bubble he was trapped inside.

Her headache and lack of sleep made her eyelids drop momentarily, especially with the soft beckoning of his voice.

"You liked these above the rest, didn't you?" he asked quietly, his voice deep and alluring.

He waved his palms slowly from side to side.

"See how they match each other in every detail? Beautiful, aren't they? Powerful, yet gentle...."

Martiel's jaw went slack as her eyes flickered between his two palms, comparing their swirls and slashes.

"I can make you very, very rich," he offered.

Immediately in her minds eye flickered the vision of a

castle, filled with European antiques she had denied herself during her travels. The topmost veranda of the mansion had a view to die for, overlooking miles of beach and sky-blue water.

"I already have money," she grinned. "I could buy that if I wanted to."

"I can make you..., nineteen again," he murmured. "You enjoyed that year of your life. I can make that year last forever."

"Nobody can make me nineteen again," she smirked. Inside she remembered..., it was her most treasured year. Turning off her gifts, pushing them down, she had given herself one normal year free from her burden. One free year before she went to college.

"...and beautiful again," he promised. "You always wanted to be able to sing, but never quite had the voice. I can give you the voice of an angel and..., a talent for the..., piano. You would be the envy of everyone that listened to you play."

What was happening here? Did she really believe her nephew?

"Those men that pretended to be your suitors, desiring your family's money, pretending to love you, I can...," he snapped his fingers, "...make them disappear, or even better, make them regret ever trying to trick you into believing their lies."

She dreamily saw, that one young man, during her sophomore year, Sloan Merchner.... Oh how she had loved him, every waking thought was in anticipation of his proposal for marriage. Then she heard that awful spew come from his mind. How she wished then that she didn't have any gifts; wished that she could have gone on in the façade of him returning her love. But he was only planning to use her, already courting another young willing girl.

How he bruised her.

"Yes, that's the one," he whispered.

But it was another name she was suddenly remembering, Jonathon Ellington. That was who she really missed. The only man that ever understood her and accepted her for who she was - five years deceased.

"I could bring him to you also," he offered softly, almost as if he genuinely cared.

'He's reading my mind, ...right through my defenses,' thought Martiel.

"I believe you could do it," she said.

"Oh, I can," he smiled. "All you have to do is take one little finger and smear through the line on the floor. I give you my solemn promise."

"Nineteen," whispered Martiel, tears formed in her eyes and she fought back the ache in her heart, "...and the chance to talk to Jonathon one more time."

She closed her eyes and breathed deeply as streams flowed down her cheeks.

"I read about someone exactly like you once before," she said. Tiredly and yes..., regrettably, she got up from her chair, brushing the water from her face and picked up an old bible sitting among several books on a table near her.

She shook it at him.

"I read about you right here," she said.

She put the book back down and sat in her chair.

The soft voice disappeared from her nephew and another boomed at her.

"You let me go or when I do get free, I will make you older, broken and diseased, and I'll make sure you last another fifty years to enjoy it," he gritted. "This circle will only last a matter of hours."

Something inside Martiel said, "Fire back!"

"Now, who did you say that mark is on your chest?" she asked, holding up the notepad in his face.

Instantly James became distraught and spun on his heel, turning his ear to listen in a southerly direction.

He railed into the air, "I did not betray your name."

CHAPTER 47

The horizon was beginning to lighten when BeBe and Jolie returned from her home in Vidalia, just across the Mississippi River.

When Jolie ran into the room, she was struggling with a heavy basket full of items.

"Aunt BeBe is bringing up the rest," said Jolie, trying to catch her breath. "I didn't know for sure what I'd need so I brought everything I could think of."

She looked over at the circle where James sat.

"What's he doing?" she asked. "Eww, he stinks."

James was cowering in the only dark spot in the circle, mumbling to himself.

"How long has he been like that?" she asked.

"I'm so glad you're back," said Martiel. "I feel like I've been babysitting the devil himself."

Martiel explained about the drawings on his body and what happened when she asked about the last one.

"The markings on his body are voodoo," said Jolie, "but this is beyond anything I've heard or read."

She held up the pad, "I thought I recognized some of these from our last escapade," sighed Martiel. "We may have to make a trip back to BeBe's friend Dominique after all."

James raged at the invisible wall, clawing at the air and

fighting the impenetrable barrier.

Jolie and Martiel both jumped backwards in fear of their lives.

"How DARE you!" screamed James. It was bloodthirsty and violent. Two tight fists pounded the invisible barrier as the whole of the house shook from their impact.

"When I get free I'm going to relish destroying both of you."

BeBe walked in the room carrying the other basket of items Jolie brought with her. James and BeBe locked their eyes on each other and he quickly quieted himself.

"Tell them! Tell them they must let me go!" said James, looking at BeBe.

He fell to the floor and begged her, "Tell our master that I have not betrayed him!"

Light blossomed in the darkness.

Martiel and Jolie looked at each other and then both fixed their burning eyes on BeBe.

"That son of a bitch," whispered Martiel.

"According to what we just read, this is what we have to do," said Jolie. "Do you agree?"

Martiel only nodded faintly.

She pulled out four candles and a shock of winter white sage bound tightly with a twisted stretch of twine.

She carefully lit the bundle until the end was smoking and held the candles over them.

One at a time, she placed a candle directly on the wooden floor on the four quadrants, North, East, South, and West.

James slid away from all the candles as they were placed and finally had to retreat to the center of the circle.

"What are the four candles?" asked Martiel. "Is this witchcraft?"

"Sort of," said Jolie, "...but not entirely. James seems to have reverted to an elemental. Usually an elemental is only a single mindless force and bound to only one of the elements, but James somehow kept his own mind and personality and is..., was..., able to use all four elements at will."

This was why he was so desirable by anyone that knew how to control him. He could be used as an invincible force.

Jolie got ready to light each candle.

"Each candle represents each of the four elements. Earth, Air, Fire, and Water. Before we can do a cleansing, we have to own him."

"I don't understand any of this," said Martiel. "Isn't this like using the witch to fight the devil?"

"Yes, that's exactly what we're doing," said Jolie.

She held up the family journal and read from it, calling to the Guardians of the four quadrants and each of the elements in order as she lit the candles.

Jolie cringed inside, "If her mother could only see her now." Regina had tried her best to isolate Jolie from that part of their family, yet here she was, performing a cleansing and banishing rite.

The bundle of sage was pouring thick white smoke off its end.

She walked the circle, holding it and asking the air to

carry the smoke into the circle.

Nothing happened; the smoke swirled away and began to fill the room with a layer of choking thickness.

"I don't understand," said Jolie. "It's supposed to fill the circle."

James spat at her and lay sprawled on his back, exposing himself and laughing at the two of them, warning them to let him go.

Jolie skimmed through the book, frustrated by the lewd gyrations of James on the floor and the fowl stench from his body.

"What am I missing?" she whispered.

"So much for owning him," said Martiel.

"Oh, thank you," exclaimed Jolie. "I forgot."

"You're welcome, but for what?" asked Martiel.

Jolie pulled a needle hidden in her collar and poked a hole in her thumb.

"*I* have to own him," said Jolie.

Blood spouted to the surface and she walked back to the circle and dropped a spot of her blood over the first candle in the sequence.

James screamed and cowered against the farthest point from her as she walked the circle.

Each candle received a healthy drop of her blood.

"Now *I* own you," she spoke into the circle.

James was now cowering in a fetal position and twitching with his forehead touching the floor.

"No!" he screamed. "Stop it!"

She gently puffed the end of the sage bundle until it was glowing and spitting sparks onto the floor, then once again walked the circle. Instantly the smoke poured into the circle and filled the void like a clouded fishbowl until it was impossible to see through it or even the outline of James.

The globe of smoke hovered in the room like an odd spectacle.

The smoke in the room where they stood slowly vacuumed toward the circle until the room cleared and it became quiet.

"What now?" asked Martiel.

"We wait," said Jolie.

Their wait was short lived.

James slammed his body against the clear wall of his cage. His eyes were blazing with fear and rage.

He receded into the smoke, then burst into a bright blue flame over his entire body and screamed an unearthly wail shaking the walls of the house.

The smoke began to swirl, becoming a cyclone of power inside the circle, condensation formed against the wall and water slid down in rivulets, becoming a contained storm.

Someone was beating on the bedroom door again and yelling, demanding to get inside.

Lightening flashed inside the violent orb and slowly it began to clear until it was transparent once again.

James was gone.

Only scattered bits of muck remained around on the floor where he had been.

Jolie panicked. "Where did he go?" she asked. "Did I kill him? What have I done?"

"Will somebody let me out of here?" asked a groggy voice.

Slowly James faded into sight, clothed and in his right mind.

Before Martiel could stop her, she jumped into the circle where James was and flew into him with a kiss.

"You're back," said Jolie.

"What?" asked James.

"You smell like a new baby," she said.

Tears welled up in her eyes. She held up his arms and yanked up his t-shirt to make sure that all the markings were gone.

"What are you two talking about? I never left. What is she talking about Aunt Martiel?"

The hammering on the door finally ceased and there was mumbling in the hallway.

"It's a long, long story James," she sighed, falling backwards on top of Jolie's bed.

"I got nothing but time," said James.

CHAPTER 48

Jolie Dimanche was on the verge of the peace she had been wishing for..., for how many weeks now? James was with her, and the rest of the world was shoved into a corner while she enjoyed their solitude.

"What was it like?" asked Jolie.

"I don't remember anything," said James. "I'd say it was like falling asleep, but I don't remember what sleep feels like anymore."

Jolie snuggled deeper into his arms and breathed deeply at his clean earthy scent. The mindless bloody monster was gone and James was back; the one that she loved and more importantly, the one that loved her.

"Why don't you get some sleep?" he asked.

"Are you kidding? I don't think I'll ever be able to sleep again, not after the last twenty-four hours."

Her curiosity was burning inside and she tried to find a way to ask the questions she wanted answers to.

"James. I know you said that you don't remember anything, but when you showed up, you were covered in blood," said Jolie.

"Aunt Martiel gave me a blow by blow," said James. "Every time I let my anger loose, my...," there was that word again, "*elemental* self took over and I became its slave. When I felt the urge to butcher someone, the rage took over and I went blank. Then everything went blank."

He was glad that he couldn't remember.

"I'm not very proud of what I did. I'm sorry Jolie. I don't even know when it started. The last thing I remember was the sound of the killer's gun exploding in his own hand."

"There were other things I'd like to know, but they can wait," said Jolie.

"I don't know about that either," said James, looking away.

If he were truly flesh and blood, he would have felt a quick heat and the red flush of deep embarrassment across his cheeks.

"Aunt Martiel has always been blunt and completely honest with me - about everything."

"You were pretty scary," said Jolie. "I have to admit, I was having second thoughts about you."

He sat silently for a moment, feeling naked in her presence.

"Jolie, thank you for everything you did. For bringing me back from wherever I was. What Aunt Martiel told me..., was beyond bad. Whatever happened, whatever I did, I don't think I ever want to find out."

He wrapped his arms around her and cradled her. He believed he understood a part of how his grandparents had stayed together for so many years in such a deep committed relationship.

"Thank you, honey," he heard himself say.

Jolie smiled up at him.

"Now I'm your honey?"

"They aren't answering my telephone calls," said BeBe.

"That's no surprise," said Martiel.

"I can't believe that Dominique would have anything to do with what happened to James," said BeBe.

"I have my suspicions that he had something to do with *everything* that's happened to James from the very beginning," said Martiel.

"But I've known them and trusted them for years," whined Bebe.

"Remember when you took James to visit Dominique and he promised to help? As soon as he found out about James and his situation concerning that Lyda Brown, everything went downhill. Oh my God. That was right before he died in the accident," she moaned.

"Don't jump to conclusions," said BeBe. "It could be a coincidence."

"Jolie, how can we keep this from happening again?" asked Martiel. "How can we contain James Earl?"

"There's a hole somewhere," said Jolie, busily skipping through her journal. "A door, or something missing that's letting him be manipulated. It's got to be here somewhere." She continued to dig through page after page. "I'll find it."

"You won't find it in that book," said BeBe. "You'll have to look in mine."

Jolie looked at her aunt as if she had seen her for the first time, already angered that she had been keeping so many secrets.

"What do you mean there's a hole?" asked Martiel.

"You raised quite a stink in New Orleans," said Sheriff Howard. "You managed to uncover a mole in their organization that had been there for years. In the Directors own office, no less."

"Didn't mean for everything to go so haywire," said Floyd. "One thing led to another. It was just a chain of events."

"Speaking of a chain of events, did you see the news this morning? There's a mob war going on up on the east coast. I telephoned Director Carmange and asked him if there was a connection, but he hung up on me. I guess we wore out our interdepartmental welcome.

"That mob family that made the news a few years ago, the Marrello clan, they all disappeared in one night. No trace.

"Thank God that's for someone else to sort out."

"Agreed," said Floyd.

"I know I asked you to keep a low profile, but I think you handled the situation very well," said the sheriff.

He stood and offered his hand, which was gladly accepted.

"I don't mean to look a gift horse in the mouth, but exactly where did you come up with that list of names I started out with?"

"From a private detective agency," said the sheriff. "They've dropped information in my lap from time to time over the years and have always proven themselves reliable."

Floyd shook his head in agreement - *Martiel Ellington.*

"Is there something wrong Floyd?" the sheriff asked. "You had that *thinking-cap* look on your face again. You get that from time to time."

"No. Everything's fine."

"Well in any case, I'm glad to have you back in the office. Oh, and by the way. While you were on your way back here, Carmange's Assistant called and left a message."

He sorted through a few note pad scribbles and found the one he was looking for.

"He said that they found a body that might be one of those missing agents you were going to talk to. Pieces of a body floated up to an oil derrick out in the Gulf of Mexico. Funny thing though, they had to identify the body by partial dental records."

"P..., partial, dental, records?" stammered Floyd.

"He said the guy may have been run over by an eighteen-wheeler. Gruesome business. They don't have a clue as to how he got so far out in the Gulf of Mexico. I guess it pays not to make the wrong kind of friends *and* enemies."

BeBe handed Jolie a heavy twelve by fourteen inch book, bound in thick black leather with markings and scrolls on both front and back covers. It had a fold-over snap-lock that required a key.

"What do these mean?" asked Jolie, recognizing a few of the Vèvès similar to the ones which had adorned James Earl's body.

There was no answer.

"Do I cut the book open or is there a key?" asked Jolie sarcastically.

BeBe pulled a leather string from around her neck.

On the end dangled the little round gold talisman Jolie remembered, always around her neck, the twin of Jolie's.

Unconsciously she pressed her fingers to the one she was wearing and anger filled her once again.

Looped behind BeBe's talisman was a tiny brass key Jolie had never seen before.

BeBe hesitated then handed it all to Jolie.

"There are rules," said BeBe. "Whenever you read it, you must never open it unless you cast a circle of consecrated salt. You must never take it out of the circle unless it has been locked shut. Do we understand each other? Not even in an emergency."

Jolie looked at her aunt and wondered how this book fit into her past.

"How do I get consecrated salt?" asked Jolie.

"Blessed water..., pour in a sack of rock salt, and boil it until it's dry," said BeBe. "I have some in a sack you can use."

Jolie took an old cloth sack of salt from BeBe's hands and felt its weight before dropping it on top of the book.

"This is my book," said BeBe, "...but I've only opened it once or twice."

"I don't understand," said Jolie.

"It belonged to my grandmother," said BeBe. "The markings are for protection. If someone opens it outside our family bloodline or even outside the circle, the *wards* will rise and the *protectors* will come."

"Where's Jolie?" asked Catherine.

"Still sitting upstairs in her room reading and taking notes out of that damnable book," said Martiel. "I don't like it one bit either. That book makes my skin crawl."

"Is James there too?" she asked.

"You should know the answer to that question. They're inseparable, two peas in a pod," said Martiel. "Sam hasn't left them either. By the way, you need to talk to BeBe. She feels responsible for so much that's happened."

"It wasn't just her," said Catherine. "There were so many factors involved."

"When it rains it pours," said Martiel. "Let's pray for some sunshine?"

"I'm going to drive into town and talk to her," said Catherine. "Is she still at the café?"

"She said the insurance people were meeting her. I've got a construction crew lined up to renovate as soon as they do the appraisal," said Martiel.

"Always efficient," said Catherine.

"I don't know any better," smiled Martiel, "...can't help myself."

"Should I tell her about Dominique?" asked Catherine.

"I think I should be the one to do that," said Martiel. "She already has enough guilt about that situation as it is."

"I can't understand how they moved everybody and everything without a single trace," said Catherine.

"I've got someone looking into where they went, just in case," said Martiel.

"Just in case of what?" asked Catherine. "I can't think of

anything but good riddance."

"Which is why I should be the one to tell BeBe," said Martiel. "Ms. Dubois was a long time friend of BeBe's and even if she didn't agree with her leader Dominique, she was bound by her oath's to do whatever he said, and still is I guess."

Martiel looked for someway to quickly change the subject.

"I got a message in the classifieds today, from Martin Earl and Maime. They won't be back until September first. They want to spend another week in Fiji. I can't for the life of me figure out why."

CHAPTER 49

Some types of information about the unknown should stay unknown. That's what Sam was thinking as he sat carefully transcribing the words Jolie read to him.

After many hours of hearing her exclaim, "Oh, here's more," and spitting lists of instructions to him, he had no desire to go into the circle of salt where Jolie was resting on her stack of throw pillows.

The talisman she had faithfully worn around her neck was discarded and turning black inside a glass of consecrated salt water. It would have been so easy to soak in regret, but now that the puppet strings were cut, she needed to concentrate on righting months of wrongs.

James sat in amazement listening and committing to his meticulous memory the word for word record of his limitless capabilities, while pondering the idea that someone was willing to perform the hideous and barbaric ceremonies necessary to create such a one as himself.

These same ceremonies were nearly the same that Lyda Brown had attempted in the early 1800's with his ancestor Syrus Earl Ames and his firstborn child. She must have existed for generations, for many lives, hiding in seclusion for fear of being hunted down and killed for her practices and for her knowledge alike. If she had garnered the bones of James Earl Williams, she could have forced him to rejuvenate her for other lifetimes and used him for her every desire.

"That's it," said Jolie. "That's what we have to do."

She carefully closed the book, and locked its clasp tight and set in on the floor.

"What's it?" asked the two boys.

"It's as simple a spell as anyone can perform," she said. "Hiding in plain sight."

"Huh?" they both repeated.

"It's why none of us have been able to see the obvious," she said excitedly. "I've only read about all this. I've never used any of it," said Jolie. "My mother wanted me to be able to live a *normal* life. That's why I didn't remember it."

"Let us in on the secret," said Sam.

"Oh, I don't know what it is. We have to reverse the spell," said Jolie.

"Oh, that makes perfect sense," said James, flopping backwards in his chair. "What are you talking about?"

"After we do the spell, you'll know what to do your own self. We won't have to tell you," said Jolie, ignoring his sarcasm. "It's so powerful that you could hunt for your car keys for the rest of you life and not see them sitting right in front of you, but simple enough for a five year old to perform."

"Oh my," said Martiel. "That's going to take some doing. I had his real casket and body encased in two feet of steel reinforced concrete, six feet under."

The spell worked as simply as Jolie had described.

James had experienced an awakening of sorts.

In times of distress, in times of need, he was drawn to his grave, pulled relentlessly toward the answer, the answer he feared - the unknown.

"What will happen when he gets his bones back?" asked Catherine. Her maternal fears were that James would forever be gone. That she would have to say goodbye yet another time, permanently.

"It depends on James," said Jolie. "He gets to decide his future, but only once, then it's decided forever."

"That's easy. I want to live," said James, entering into the room.

"If this works, how are we going to explain his resurrection?" asked Catherine. "He's had a funeral, he's been buried. There's no way to reverse all that."

"Just be happy he's alive and leave that part up to me," said Martiel. "That won't be a problem."

"Money can't fix everything, Aunt Martiel," said Catherine smugly.

Martiel ignored the remark and moved on. "How far to you trust Damien Dimanche?" she asked James.

"We have a *very... clear...* understanding between each other," said James. "I trust him. There won't be any more visitations."

"You have got to be kidding!" said Sam.

Catherine nodded in assent with her younger son.

"Damien may be a cold blooded killer, but he loves Jolie," said James. "He'll leave her alone..., and us."

When Damien saw the picture of James and Jolie together, something happened inside. He would do anything for her.

"Quit changing the subject, Aunt Martiel," fussed Catherine.

"What about exhuming the body? That alone is going to take months of legal work."

"It would take me about two minutes to fix that," said James. "And that's if I take my time. I hate that big white monument. I always have."

"You have to be *given* your bones," said Jolie. There was more than a hint of desperation in her voice. "If you take them yourself, you'll be gone. End of story, no more James."

"You neglected to tell us that," said Martiel.

"Why is that a problem?" asked James.

Jolie lifted the notes transcribed by Sam.

"It says here that the closer you get to your remains, the stronger the uncontrollable urge will be to reattach to them," she explained. "It's why people like Lyda Brown were always having to redo the work lifetime after lifetime."

"Whoa, so every time some alchemy or magic was performed to do the Nicolas Flamel experiment, they ended up back in the ground," said Sam. "That's why nobody could prove he actually completed the alchemy experiment."

"I can do it," said James.

"No, you can't," said Jolie. "Not by yourself. Why do you have to be so pigheaded?"

"Do we want to take the risk?" asked Catherine. "I guess we could wait and go through the legal channels to get the grave opened?"

"Every moment we leave his body exposed, we leave the door open for people like Dominique to prepare a summons and call him and he can't refuse," said Jolie. "James will have to live inside a circle of salt to prevent him from going to wherever he's called, and we might lose him all over again."

"Bro, go sit in some salt," said Sam. "I don't want to see naked, bloody James ever again."

"If you hadn't been snooping you wouldn't have seen him the first time," chided Martiel.

"I don't want to be some bird in a cage," said James. "It's hard enough not being able to do living things."

"Aunt BeBe and I have already dumped a trail of salt around the entire house," said Jolie.

"Then it's settled," said Martiel. "Jolie and James will go tonight and excavate the casket."

"Why Jolie?" asked Catherine.

"If anybody can keep James on focus, she can," said Martiel. "Isn't that right Jolie?"

"Yep," said Jolie, smiling over at James. "I own him."

BeBe walked through the door, scooting her feet on the doormat, with a huge smile on her face.

"I have never seen so many carpenters in my life! I'm going to be able to reopen *The Cajun* in eight days and it's going to be magnificent."

Sam was stretched full length on a couch in the living room, half-asleep, with the television blaring.

"Where is everybody?" she asked, glumly. Her happy announcement had fallen on empty ears.

Sam sat up and looked groggily at her. "They're all taking a nap."

Frustrated that there was no one with which to share her good news, she prodded Sam for more information.

"I take it Jolie found what she was looking for?" she asked.

"Oh yeah," said Sam. "Hey, I think James wants to see you upstairs."

He thumbed toward the stairs and lay back down on the couch.

"At least someone isn't dead around here," she said, then laughed at the bleak irony of her statement.

Jolie was sound asleep on the bed with James lying beside her when BeBe walked in the room.

"Glad to hear about your restaurant," said James. "Someday soon I might even get to taste your food again."

"I knew I could count on you to be awake," she smiled, then frowned. "What are you doing laying there on the bed with Jolie?"

"I have to stay in the circle," he pointed toward the line on the floor. "Just to be on the safe side. In case someone breaks the one around the house by accident."

Before she could raise her eyebrows with another dart, "Jolie said to tell you thanks. Your book is over there by the window."

Atop a pillow on the floor was BeBe's inherited heavy black grimoire, locked and sealed.

"Here's the key," said James, handing her the leather cord. "I hope we never have to use it again. There's a lot of dark stuff in there."

"That's why I never read through it," said BeBe. "Gina told me to keep it away from Jolie at all cost. I guess I owe her an apology too."

Instead of turning to leave she paused where she stood, trying to generate the nerve to say what was on her mind.

"James..., I..., really didn't know," she mumbled.

"I know you didn't. You only wanted to help."

"I need to tell you how badly I feel about everything, but I suppose we both know how it feels to be used."

James let her take her time. He didn't feel it was necessary, but she needed to say it, to get it all out.

"James, I'm sorry for everything Dominique did. I had no idea what he was capable of. I still can't believe he went to such lengths to get his hands on you."

"You shouldn't apologize for him, besides it's the same with everybody. Everybody wants something," said James. "I guess he wanted it all."

She understood what he meant and stepped around to get her book.

"I suppose I should destroy this," said BeBe.

"No, I don't think so," said James. "It's a part of your family's past, a real relic. As bad as some of it is, we'd still be wondering what to do if it wasn't for your book. But..., if I were you I'd find a really good place to hide it."

CHAPTER 50

The incessant banging at the front door finally woke James from his trancelike stupor.

"Can somebody please answer the door," he mumbled.

As if it were his own heartbeat, he heard Jolie's rhythm rise for a moment, then settle back into a steady restful pace. She was breathing gently, still fast asleep and when he glanced at the window, it was obvious that the sun had run away to parts unknown.

The incessant knocking started again, louder this time.

"Oh please," sighed James.

Why couldn't anyone else hear it?

Everyone was still asleep, of course.

He tried to peer into the thoughts of his family, then to sense who was beating on the door, but the infernal circle of salt was dampening his power.

Again, the knocking.... This time it sounded like it was pounding against his head.

"Won't someone please answer the door?" he whispered.

Everyone that associated themselves with his family had a key to let themselves inside, but what if it was someone from the Sheriff's Office or from the Gazette? What if it had something to do with his grandparents..., an emergency?

James sat up on the edge of the bed, straining to hear.

"It won't hurt to listen by the door," he mumbled.

If it was important, he could wake Sam, the rest of his family desperately needed sleep after the trauma he'd put them through.

His feet touched the gritty trail of salt on the floor.

Of course the salt wasn't a trap, it was a hiding place. It was the culmination of the other minerals and additives that transformed it into a prison.

It would only take a few seconds and he could be right back beside Jolie.

There was the bang, bang, banging again.

He decided to get Sam and let him take care of it.

As soon as James stepped out of the circle, he disappeared.

On a dare, born of morbid curiosity, a trio of teenagers chattered their way to the front of the old cemetery.

Sunset had come none too soon and bolstered their courage enough to enter through the vine laced iron archway.

Heaven's Gate Cemetery had become something renowned in the area after weeks of publicity of all the grave robberies and ghosts around the area. There were already talks of secret parties to be held during the upcoming holidays among several groups in the high school.

With charcoal and a small roll of butcher paper in hand; Tom, Clay, and Emma were making rubs of the oldest gravestones, gradually watching the dates get older, the deeper they trespassed. Their rubs would be proof of their trespassing to display in their clubs, the school, even their rooms. And they were the first to come up with the idea, and the first to step inside the necropolis.

There was also another motive for their visit.

"Who's going to start?" asked Clay. "I've got your mama's instructions right here."

"Pick one Emma."

"Get one we can set the candle on," she mumbled quietly, as if someone would hear them if they spoke above a whisper.

"Start here," she said. "Just the ones with stones so I can stick the candle."

"Are you sure we won't get caught?" said Tom.

Clay laughed - a little louder than the other two expected. "Are you kidding? Look at the place. Nobody comes here."

"Mama says there's traffic here and I believe her," said Emma. "Be respectful and keep your voices down."

"Do this one first. It's shaped like somebody with a sheet over their head," Clay laughed.

"Don't you think this is wrong?" asked Tom.

"Of course it's wrong, that's why we're here!"

Their muffled laughter swam with the Spanish moss through the night air, pushed by a whisper of a breeze.

Emma jammed the wax candle on the smooth stone and scratched a match on the rough backside. She cupped her hands in a makeshift globe as the flame flickered and snapped.

All three knocked on the stone with their bare knuckles

as their friend Emma read the instructions.

"We call on thee, –insert name here- to appear before us."

"What's the name on the stone?" asked Clay.

"We call on...," they raised a lively trio chorus, inserting the name of the interred chiseled into the lichen stained granite.

They all laughed at the name, then listened intently as vampiric mosquitoes, gnats, and no-see-ums fought the breeze to feed on their fresh blood.

"Do it again," said Emma.

The repeat performance did manage to raise goosebumps on their arms. Still, their requests were met with silence.

"Guess this one's too tired to talk."

"Ssshh," spat Emma. "Mama said to be patient. Do it again."

The candle flame crackled and spat, then gave one great leap as the breeze died down.

Their second call was met with absolute silence.

"My turn to pick," said Clay somberly.

"That direction," said Emma. "It's darker over there."

"It's darker everywhere," said Tom, his head spinning back and forth.

"The older ones are off the trail," noted Clay.

"What if it works and we get a freak or a crazy person?" asked Tom.

"Or a murderer?" whispered Clay, over Tom's shoulder.

Tom spun to look around him in the near pitch-blackness.

"Maybe a demon...," hissed Clay.

Clay was beginning to believe his own press as goosebumps crawled his spine.

Tom swatted furiously at Clay's outstretched hands and walked away, glaring into the near black, looking for the trail.

"Quit being a wuss," said Emma, then she saw he was leaving.

"Wait Tom..., I'm sorry. Don't leave. You can't go. Mama said it takes three to make it work right."

Tom turned around and grunted before hovering closer to her. After all, Emma was the only reason he had agreed to this expedition in the first place.

The three shuffled through the taller grass in the dark tripping over a long flat headstone.

"Here..., this one," Clay said, after brushing the dust off the top of a cracked stone. "Wait. Let me do the rub first before you stick the candle."

The paper flapped over the stone, with several hands holding it in place with the scritch-scratch of charcoal whipping across the surface.

"Okay. Got it," said Clay, scrolling up the first rub.

Emma slammed the candle center mass, giving it a hard twist against the stone.

She lit it as quickly as she could before everyone deserted her.

The flame leapt in great gulps then settled into a swirl.

"Creepy," whispered Emma. "Check the name, let's do it while the candle's acting weird."

Their combined knocking was again met with silence.

The only thing that changed was the goosebumps they all shared.

"I think it's really working," said Clay, in a worried tone, scraping his arms.

Nearer the main road to the back, Emma saw a glowing white fixture through the bagging limbs on the trees.

"That one!" she said excitedly. "I've got a feeling that's a good one."

They ran through the dark between the other graves up to a huge white stone crypt.

"Wow, what a grave," said Tom, walking inside the covered monument. "This is bad, look at the dates."

Clay shook his head, "It's not old enough for a rub."

"He was only seventeen Clay," said Emma. "A year older than us. Fresh kill. Look when he died. Mama said that the newly dead were easier to contact."

"That's cold blooded," he replied. "Stick the candle!"

"No, I don't like this," said Tom.

The match burst to life and the scent of sulphur hovered around them.

"Write the name on here," she whispered, handing the instructions between the two boys.

The candle was barely burning, a tiny wick of flame blistering the white wax.

All three knocked their bare knuckles and repeated the phrase -

"We call on thee, James Earl Williams to appear before us."

Then they knocked again.

The ground shook under their feet.

"Oh yeah!" whispered Emma. "Did you feel that?"

She stepped outside the monument, put down all the papers and weighted them down with a rock to empty her hands.

She ran back inside and placed her palms on the stone as if listening for some answer inside, "Do it again."

They knocked and chimed in chorus.

"We call on thee, James Earl Williams to appear before us."

All three knocked again.

The ground shook again.

This time there were noises all around them in the pitch black of the cemetery.

Jolie woke and slid her arm over the pillow next to her, startled by something. James was supposed to be lying there, safe; she hurled the empty pillow aside.

"James?" she whispered.

She jumped to the edge of the bed.

"James?" she called out louder.

If he were in the house, it would only take a whisper for him to appear beside her. Jolie flicked on the lamp beside her bed and looked at the floor. The circle of salt was intact and unbroken.

So where was James?

She heard talking downstairs and jogged the steps toward the source. The tension in her body relaxed when she saw that everyone else had stirred from sleep about the same time.

"Where's James?"

Jolie's voice was much calmer than she felt.

Everyone was wobbling around in the kitchen like round bottomed stones. Martiel was looking through the cabinets for something to snack on, while Catherine was clanking at the sink.

"He's supposed to be with you," said Catherine.

She began rinsing the coffee pot under a loud stream of water.

"He's probably with Sam in the living room."

Jolie turned and yelled into the void of the next room at Sam and heard a grunt as her answer.

"What time is it?" asked Jolie, spinning toward the wall clock.

Nine-forty something, sunset was around eight-thirty.

"But James isn't answering me. He's gone," she said hysterically.

"I suggest you summon him," said Martiel. "Pretty quick. You're the one that owns him, remember?"

Suddenly her apatite disappeared and Martiel sat down. She couldn't take another nightlong battle to reclaim James like the last one.

"I already called him," said Jolie. "He didn't answer."

"Calm down honey. We'll join hands and all call him together," said Martiel.

"Oh no..., what if...?" whined Jolie, not daring to complete her dreary thought. "Should I go get the jar with our containment mix?"

Martiel nodded glumly, "Better safe than sorry."

"Surely he wouldn't try to dig up his grave alone," said Catherine.

All eyes were suddenly locked on Catherine in shock.

"Oh no...," said Jolie, as she snatched the keys to her aunts car off the kitchen counter.

"What do we do now?" asked Clay.

"How should I know?" barked Emma.

"You're mama's the one that calls herself a witch," said Clay. "Doesn't she tell you anything?"

"Where do you think I got this?" she spat back, shaking the piece of paper with the script.

James materialized on top of his crypt and sat down, instantly feeling the jolt of power.

He heard the voices below him inside the big white sepulcher, just kids maybe fifteen or sixteen years old, but what were they doing? How did he get here?

"Well, we can tell her that it sorta worked," said Clay.

"I say we get out of here now," said Tom.

"You can't leave," whispered a voice. "You called me."

"Quit it Clay," said Emma, her body shook with a rigor as she slid close to Tom.

Clay walked outside, "Hello?"

"I mean it," said Emma. "Cut it out."

Tom and Emma poked their heads outside the small opening of the crypt with nothing but shadow and starlight to offer for illumination.

"What do you want?"

"Awww, crap," said Tom. His knees buckled at the silhouette of someone seated Indian style above them.

"Can't do that," said James.

"Who are you?" asked Emma.

"Who did you call?"

"If you're really the dead guy, show yourself," said Emma, picking up a loose stone from the ground.

Unbelievable.

Thrill seekers, potentially headed for a lifetime of trouble. After everything he had been through, three kids *experimenting* with something best left alone had yanked him from Jolie's side.

Now that they knew their actions could bring results, it would never end, unless....

"Where's my gift?" asked James angrily.

"G..., gift?" asked Clay. "What gift?"

He looked at Emma, "You're mama didn't say anything about a gift?"

She shrugged, "How should I know?"

"Let's go," said Tom. "I don't like this."

"You're not a ghost," laughed Clay, backing up from the crypt to get a better look.

James faded from transparent to opaque and back before their eyes.

"Give him something!" said Emma, frantically.

"I have some money," said Tom, pulling out some change. His hand was shaking badly and his few coins jingled to the ground in the dark.

James laughed sarcastically, "What do I want with money? Where is your sacrifice? Which one of you will give me blood?"

"Sacrifice?" asked the three, almost in unison.

"If you don't pick, then I get to choose," said James.

"Let's get out of here," said Clay. "This is crazy."

"Then I choose you," said James.

"Wha..., What? No. You don't want me. Take her. She's the reason we're here," said Clay.

"The girl?" asked James. "You'll give me the girl for my sacrifice?"

Clay stared into the dark, looking at the translucent form of whoever was talking.

James laughed at them as he felt his body begin to quiver.

Trouble - that familiar intoxicating pull of his bones from deep in the ground erupted inside him. Just being here made him vulnerable to any number of deeply evil possibilities.

James heard himself hiss words at the ground around his grave. It barely crossed his mind when his body began reacting to the surge of transferring power, with the familiar glowing blue iridescence. He tried to leave, but their summons held him fast and there was only one way he knew of to end their hold on him.

He slid off the top of the crypt to stand before the three.

"W..., why do you need a sacrifice?" asked Emma.

"Not for me," said James. "For them...."

They looked where their summoned phantasm was pointing to see the gaping void faces of the nearby risen dead, listing toward them.

"Give me my sacrifice!" yelled James.

"Here! Take her!" said Tom, pushing Emma forward and holding her struggling shoulders. She chirped a short scream, as her voice caught in her throat.

The three broke into a diagonal hurdle to get away.

CHAPTER 51

Jolie and Sam ground to a stop in front of Heavens Gate Cemetery, just as a small car was zooming out of the parking lot. They heard muffled screams the moment Jolie shut off the engine.

"That's not a good sign," said Sam.

"Nope," she agreed. "But he's here, I can feel him."

They both jumped out of the car and ran toward the back of the cemetery.

The glowing body of James was reflecting off the stark white crypt and illuminating the entire area as they approached.

He was frantically taking bricks off the monument and hurling them into the wilderness behind the cemetery. One at a time, a huge block of stone would crunch loose and he would turn and sail it through the air over the cemetery's back wall.

"James!" said Jolie. "What are you doing? You promised to wait until I was here with you."

He turned to look at them, the power of death and resurrection was snapping the air.

"Did you see a car leaving?" asked James, his voice frantic.

He was suddenly still, already grasping the next stone

projectile. Before they could answer him, "It was three kids, about Sam's age. They knocked on my grave and summoned me. If three stupid kids can call me, then as long as this grave stands, it's a liability. I'll never be safe.

"I know I promised you, Jolie, but this couldn't wait. One of the kids mother is a witch. They might come back with reinforcements. Wait...."

James stopped all motion again and there was dead silence.

"Do you hear that?" he whispered.

Jolie heard it, but had dismissed it as the beating of her heart in her own ears. It was the steady distant sound of a drumbeat. The sound wasn't floating on the night breeze, it was coming from somewhere all around them.

"We don't have much time," said James.

In minutes, the monument was demolished and removed down to a flat concrete slab. James tossed the brass marker plate on the ground.

"How did you find me?" asked James, as he contemplated his next duty.

"When we found out you were missing, Catherine asked if you might try and do this alone," said Jolie. "That was when I knew where you were. I own you. I felt this is where you'd be."

"Can't think of anybody else I'd rather be owned by," he smiled.

"Better step back."

He disappeared, reached down deep into the ground and found the concrete block surrounding his coffin. The earth shook as he unearthed the massive block, heaving it on top of the ground in an explosion of dirt and debris.

"Well, there it is," said James dizzily.

His body quivered in a blue translucence.

"Any last words before I break the seal?" he asked.

"Just in case something goes wrong," said Sam. "Thanks...."

"Honor was all mine, bro," he replied. "Oh. Hey Sam, I tested your theory. You were right, as usual."

James reached down, grabbed a hand full of dirt, and crushed it in his hand.

"Here," said James. "Something to remember me by. You know, just in case."

Sam held out his hand and James dropped a single palm-shaped gold nugget into his hand.

"Whoa, dude...," whispered Sam.

"Just another reason somebody would want to use me," said James.

"James? The drumming is louder," warned Jolie.

James nodded and looked at her trying to find all the right words to say to the one he loved.

"Don't you dare. Say whatever it is to me later," she ordered.

He nodded, "Let's get this over with. Cover your faces."

His fist slammed down on the block and it shattered. Stone and steel fragmented the ground until his casket was exposed.

"That's all you are allowed to do," said Jolie, quickly. "Now you get back and let Sam and I do the rest."

"No, I..., I... t...think I can do it," said James, drunk from the power.

"James, no!" said Jolie.

He reached toward the casket to open the lid.

"James, I command you to step back," ordered Jolie.

James blankly inched backwards in an obvious fight against his will.

"Won't this be gross?" asked Sam.

"You should have thought of that before you volunteered to help me," said Jolie.

Together they forced the top half of the lid open, but it was empty, no body to be seen.

"What? I don't understand?" said Jolie.

"Don't freak out," said Sam. "James wouldn't be all *firefly* on us if something wasn't in here somewhere. Give me some help."

Together, they took hold of the other end of the fractured casket and broke it loose. There in the bottom end of the box in a crumpled stack was the bleached white skeleton of James Earl Williams.

"They're just bones," said Sam.

The instant James caught sight of his remains, only the binding command of Jolie restrained him from lurching to retrieve them.

The mere sight and presence of his physical remains caused him to transform, flowing around him was a blue flame of fire, twitching and swaying in an invisible wind.

"We have to hurry," said Jolie. "Hand me the head first."

Jolie looked past the wavering flame where James stood in a drunken stupor.

"James Earl Williams, do you wish to live?"

There was only silence as if he actually had to consider

his choices again. Would this be the end or would he choose life?

"For me?" asked Jolie.

"Yesss," a torrid voice hissed out of the cold blue flame.

The thought tormented her again. Something she'd read from the arcane grimoire of her Aunt BeBe's. It could mean everything for James..., but if he ever found out.

Should she?

She wasn't being selfish...; it had to be the reason fate had paired the two of them together from the beginning.

It was now or never. There would never be another opportunity like this in several lifetimes, possibly never again.

She took the pin always present in the collar of her blouse and poked her right index finger, hiding it from Sam in the darkness.

Blood sprouted the color of a rose against the violet luminescence.

This last minute choice would forever alter James, and her. It would have to forever remain her secret, her burden, her guilt, to her own grave.

Sam carefully handed Jolie the skull from inside the broken casket, supporting the slack jaw with both hands.

She smeared her blood on the top of the bleached white surface and handed the skull into the cold flames.

There..., the first part was done. There was no possibility of turning back. Only one more thing to do that must be done.

"James Earl Williams, as your owner, I give you your bones," said Jolie. "You may live."

One by one, Sam handed her each bone, scooping up the last, the tiniest in little handfuls. Jolie sprinkled the last few into the cold flickering blue, waiting expectantly.

Nothing happened.

The flame still quivered in front of them, with James Earl in a dead stare, encased within.

"Are you sure you got them all?" asked Jolie.

Sam scrambled through the cloth, but there were no more to be found.

She turned and faced the cold fire.

"James, come to me," said Jolie. "Remember me, please."

The fire rose upwards and extinguished into the pitch black of the night. Left standing in the darkness before her was the form of James Earl; naked as the day he was born.

The threat of the drumming dissipated back into an eerie silence.

"Sam? The clothes..., would you get them from the car...?" she asked.

"Already on it," he said, as he disappeared from her sight.

For the first time in weeks, there was complete quiet.

"James?" whispered Jolie, afraid to touch him.

James stood looking blankly then suddenly gasped, sucking air into his lungs.

"Jolie? Where am I? Is it over?" he asked.

"With me. That's all that matters now."

There were only moments before Sam returned with his clothes.

It was too late to change her mind, blood had been spilled. The task must be completed or..., she didn't want to think of the consequences. Jolie rose up on tiptoes, pulling him to meet her, then she quietly spoke the memorized rote from the black pages of her great grandmothers' grimoire into his ear.

He looked at her gently, lovingly - then it was done - there could be no turning back.

He awoke as if from some strange dream, some stupor and she held him, balanced him from falling.

Her conscience would forever have to take a back seat.

No one could ever know. No one, especially James Earl.

Their arms wrapped around each other, basking in the peace as Sam's footsteps crunched toward them in the darkness.

"I could get used to this," said James in a hazed whisper.

Jolie pressed her cheek against his chest and closed her eyes.

"I bet you could," she smiled.

Her James was back..., alive..., forever hers.

CHAPTER 52

Natchez Mississippi was mysteriously experiencing some relief from the usual end of August swelter and humidity, while the Mississippi River continued on its lazy course to the Gulf of Mexico, unobservant and quiet.

In a few weeks, the townspeople of Natchez would forget the slaughterhouse intent reigned down on the Cajun Café. A historical marker in the form of an iron plaque, stood proudly before the new storefront, recording the event as a misdirected attack against the FBI with the local police as the heroes.

Copies of the original story in the Natchez Gazette, verified by the notorious (AP) trademark, were vended just inside for a dollar.

Already, photos were being taken by huddling tourists and business was at peak capacity, much to the delight of its owner.

A young couple drew stares as they strolled past the entrance with several of their own purchases dangling from their arms.

"Don't you think we're tempting fate? Out in the open like this?" James asked.

"How often does a girl get an opportunity like this?" asked Jolie, fanning a credit card below her chin. "Besides, Martiel told me to pick out all your clothes from now on.

She says you don't have a clue what nice looks like."

"Is that why all my blue t-shirts are missing?" he asked.

"Burned them..., all of them," she smiled proudly. "Not that you didn't look good in them mind you, but a change was in order."

"A lot of changes were in order," mumbled James.

He quickly stepped in front of Jolie and kissed her burgundy lips before the flashing 'don't walk' sign on the street corner changed.

Martiel commissioned Jolie to pick out clothes for James; anything but that same ridiculous blue t-shirt he caked on every day since his death.

"So you think I look good in this?" asked James, pulling on the lapel of a sport coat.

"Mmm hmm," she answered. "I could get used to this look. But you're still allowed to wear your jeans."

She patted him on the backside of his new slacks when she was sure no one was observing.

"It's just perception James. The man inside the clothes..., now *that's* what I'm interested in," she remarked.

Her flowered dress swayed gently with her long hair as they turned toward the waterfront. Their frequent glances toward each other concealed a private conversation with each meeting of the eyes. It was a perfect day.

No death, no gloom, no destruction; at least not in their lives..., not today.

Before they could make it past the downtown lattice of streets, the bells in the church tower began to sound.

Jolie shivered at the sound and snapped her head around.

"Is everything alright?" asked James.

The bells were causing an itch in the back of her mind. Something she needed to get a handle on, someday; not today.

"Our times up. We need to get back," she sighed.

"How do you think my mother is going to take the news?" asked James.

"She's not going to like it," said Jolie. "You should know that without asking. But I think it will grow on her."

"I hope so," said James. "I told Sam. He promised to keep his lips sealed."

Jolie stopped walking and pulled James against the nearest building.

"You told Sam? And you think he can keep quiet?"

"Yeah, we're tight," said James, grinning.

Jolie laughed, dropping her concerned frown at the boyish exhibition of solidarity between the two brothers.

"Let's take a short cut," said Jolie.

She took his arm and led him toward the garden district. Her favorite place was that little bench, where they had spent their first moments falling in love.

"Do you think we'll be able to have a real life together?" asked James. "A normal one?"

"Who wants normal after everything we've seen?" asked Jolie.

"I don't know. I think I could handle boring," said James.

"Are you saying that life with me would be boring?"

James playfully circled his arm around her and hugged her close. When their eyes met, James smiled at her and she felt some of his pent up energy flow between them. Jolie gasped in a breath, then offered a misguided attempt to punch him on the shoulder, her arms laden with hoops of her shopping.

"Nah, who wants normal," said James, pulling her back into step.

"Keeping everything we know a secret, that's going to be the real challenge," said Jolie. "The world isn't ready for the new James Earl."

The unmistakable clamor of Martiel, Martin Earl, and Maime bustled into the front door to their old home place, dragging in small luggage, shopping bags and a trunk. Catherine and Sam were the first to meet them with open arms, listening to their excited discourse.

"You're back early!" said Catherine.

"Blame it on Martin Earl," said Maime. "No, don't do that. There's no place like home little girl. Besides, we've been invited back to the island in a month or so."

Catherine hadn't seen her mother look this happy in years. Her face glowed a soft brown tan with her hair pulled back behind her head.

They were interrupted by a new voice as more luggage bumped through the door. It didn't take a genius to figure out that the lady before them was Jolie's mother. Dark eyes were the only contrast, but her olive complexion and petite figure were a dead giveaway. She was Jolie twenty years into the future.

"Everybody, I'd like you to meet Regina Dimanche," said Martiel.

Her robust personality rolled out the red carpet to Catherine and Sam.

"You must be Catherine!" chirped Gina. "You're just as pretty as Martin and Maime said you were. And this is Sam? He's no boy...," she said staring straight up into Sam's face. "He's a man."

Sam blushed a healthy beet red and stuck out his hand.

Regina sidestepped it and gave him a tight hug.

"My goodness..., and solid as a rock," she mumbled, circling her arm around his waist.

"Martiel arranged for Gina to meet us on that little island," said Maime. "We have had the most fun. You wouldn't believe some of the stories she's told us."

"We did have fun didn't we?" laughed Regina. She loosed her grip on Sam and took Catherine's hand and tugged her to a seat in the living room.

Martin saw his opportunity to move past the congestion and trudged toward the couch, flopping down comfortably.

Sam saw him move out of the mainstream of conversation and joined him.

"How was your vacation, grampa?" asked Sam.

"Good, Good. My sister was right, there is more to life than Natchez," said Martin. "How are things going here?"

"Amazing," said Sam.

"Really?" asked Martin. "How is the situation with James?"

"That's a surprise," said Sam. "I promised to be quiet."

More secrets. Why should he be surprised?

"It's good to be home," said Martin, gently brushing against the arm of the couch as if it were a long lost pet.

"Sam, it's time we got back to work on that truck of yours," said Martin. "I've had way too much rest."

"Sounds good to me!" said Sam.

Regina's voice rang out above the others and Sam was thankful it was a pleasant voice instead of some grating noise.

"Where's my little girl?"

"Where's Jolie?"

"Where's that boy of yours she's so in love with?"

"What's his name? James?"

"Is he my future son-in-law yet?"

"I want to have a word with him in private if you don't care. I know he's your boy, but I want to make sure his intentions are honorable with my Jolie."

Martin rolled his eyes at Sam, "Better go find 'em. It's not going to stop."

CHAPTER 53

The immediate family were assembling in the dining room, for a surprise party. Use of the actual dining room was a surprise to the eldest of their family considering the constant use of the kitchen as dining and meeting area.

BeBe had conceded to take her sister Regina to see her renovated café and out for a tour around Natchez. Since the hounds of hell had been called off her trail, she could actually enjoy herself without a disguise, or planning every move and watching over her shoulder.

Everyone was restless and waiting as James, donning his new clothes, walked in the room locked in tow with Martiel. Jolie and Sam found a comfortable place scrubbed against each other in the corner, out of the way in case there were fireworks.

Martiel blurted out the news before thinking about the repercussions.

"Everybody, I would like to introduce to you James Earl *Ellington*."

"Ellington," said Catherine. "What's that all about?"

Martin and Maime looked at each other, flabbergasted.

"Okay, everybody put your teeth back in your mouths," said Martiel. Her backbone was already stiff and ready to war.

"Let me explain, please?" said James, looking quickly at Martiel.

"You have the floor," said Martiel. She almost said 'It's your funeral' but swallowed her words.

Instead, she took a deep breath, stepped around the long table, and began some nervous duty with plastic plates and forks.

"As you all know I died on June 26th and everyone here went to my funeral. Every one of you went through almost as much torment as I did these past weeks. But through a turn of fate, I have been given a second chance at a normal life."

He walked around the room and touched each one of his family in some way. He held some hands, touched faces, hugged others, and let them do the same.

"What I want you to understand is, I'm not some dead thing anymore."

Martin and Maime were visibly touched at the new information, fearfully clasping each other's hands, not knowing what to say.

"But the question came up, *by my mother*, concerning what we should do about this now? I can't just show back up - Oh, sorry, we were wrong. All the police reports, the coroners' reports, the county records, the funeral, the newspaper accounts; sorry it was all a mistake.

"So with some outside help, I was given the opportunity to be a real person again, *and* remain a part of this family."

He stopped for a moment and searched their faces.

"Aunt Martiel has adopted me as her son, and by doing so, making me a legitimate person and giving me a legitimate name. As you can tell I look a little different, so as long as I stay clear of anyone that the family knows personally in town, which is just about everyone, I can live a normal life."

Martiel stepped up to the plate and interrupted his speech.

"First of all, I would like to wish James a happy birthday on this twenty-eighth day of August."

Everyone clamored a moment when they realized that they had entirely forgotten that James would have been, and was now turning eighteen years old.

"Here is my present to you, James. I have here in my hand two full scholarships to Brown University which I would like to present to..., Mr. James Ellington and Ms Jolie Dimanche. They are good as long as you are in attendance for whatever major you choose."

"Me?" said Jolie. "What made you do that for me?"

"Oh please...," said Martiel. "Do you have something better to do?"

Jolie walked forward, in total shock and surprise.

"Does my mamma know?" asked Jolie.

"Yes, yes, of course she knows," said Martiel. "Regina's as nosey as I am."

James blocked Jolie's path and whispered in her ear, "I need to ask you something."

Jolie instantly became nervous, "James, it needs to wait until later."

"I guess..., sure...," he said, testing her eyes.

Jolie took the brochures and enrollment information from Martiel and thanked her.

James discretely slid his hands in his pockets and an object fell from his hand to the bottom of the pocket.

"Well..., now that we have all that out of the way, let's eat some cake and ice-cream," said Martiel.

Catherine walked quietly out of the room, remembering the words that Dominique had spoken to her.

The nighttime air was fresh with a steady breeze keeping the bugs at bay. It had been a long, long day.

Sam was enjoying being out on the front porch without fear of some dark terror lurking about, ready to slice his throat. The bruise on his collarbone was hurting and beginning to stiffen.

James walked up to him, "Reminds me of when we moved from the old neighborhood and we got to walk around the block without watching our backs."

"Yeah, that was extreme," said Sam.

"By the way, Happy Birthday bro, or is it cousin? How weird is that?"

"Nothing's changed as far as I can see," said James. "We're brothers forever."

James stuck out his fist to bump against Sam's.

"Do you think mom will recover?"

"Yeah, just give it some time," said Sam. "It's an ego thing. I'd be freaked out too if you hadn't told me ahead of time."

"It was supposed to be a surprise, not a slap in the face," mumbled James.

"Why the adoption?" asked Sam. "I thought that was a little weird."

"I had to be a legal descendant of an Ames to lawfully take control of the family finances..., that is..., when Aunt Martiel passes it on to me," said James.

"Don't you mean your adopted mother?" said Sam. "Sorry!"

Sam took a brotherly poke at James in the arm.

James reflexively tensed his arm and it felt like he had hit a concrete post.

"Ow, damn."

Sam shook his fist.

"I thought..., aren't you, you know, normal now?" he asked.

"Sure," answered James quietly.

"Look, I'm going out on a limb here. You have to promise me that this will stay just between you and me, okay?"

Sam slumped, "Just this one. I'm tired of secrets."

"Okay then. As far as everyone knows, I'm as normal as you," said James.

"Bad choice of examples," said Sam, grinning. "That's cool. That kind of makes me your side kick, now that I know."

"I'm no superhero," said James. "Get that out of your head right now. I mean it. I want to live a very..., normal..., life. So don't screw that up for me, please?"

"Bro, you ain't normal," said Sam. "You didn't flinch. That was like hitting a brick."

James gave him the brother stare until Sam nodded.

"Who else knows?" asked Sam.

"Just make like you're the only one and leave it at that."

"Whoa, does that mean that you can still...?" asked Sam.

James interrupted him, "*Normal*, Sam, leave it like that."

"Normal," said Sam. "But, hey can you help a dude out?"

Sam slowly pulled off his monogrammed t-shirt.

"Think you can fix this? It hurts like a bitch."

Sam's entire right shoulder was several hues of purple, red, yellow and green from his being carried one handed by Dimanche's hit man.

James looked around to see if they were alone.

"Yeah, I can fix it, but the bruises have to stay until they clear out on their own. Besides, it'll get you lots of sympathy with the chicks when you start school next week."

The family was finally sleeping, or at least trying to, when Jolie walked out in the front yard where James was standing. He was staring up at the stars, lost in peaceful thought as she slid her arm around his waist.

"It would have been the wrong time," said Jolie.

"Besides, you already know the answer. Yes!" she squealed, throwing her arms around his neck.

"What do you mean, the wrong time?" he snarled. "I had it all planned. I was going to spin you around and go to one knee and ask you in front of the whole family."

"Your mom would have gone off like a roman candle," said Jolie.

"She needs to get over herself anyway," said James. "Right now, you are the most important person in my life."

This earned him a well deserved kiss.

"I'm more worried that *your* mother will recognize the

ring," said James.

"My mother?" said Jolie. "What are you talking about?"

"It was one of the conditions for Damien, your father, to do the work for Martiel," he explained. "He gave me a ring to give you. It was one of the rings that he gave your mother."

"One of my mother's rings?" said Jolie. "You're kidding? Let me see."

"No," said James. "Not until the time is right."

She slapped him softly on the arm with her open palm.

"Where did Jolie go?" he asked, looking around them.

She took his face between her hands.

"It's not everyday a girl gets engaged. I can be silly."

"You're right," said James. "It's time we started acting our age isn't it? It's just.... I don't know how to say it, I feel like I'm eighteen going on forty."

"When do we tell everybody?" she asked.

"Right now if you want," said James.

"No, let everybody sleep. They've earned the rest."

CHAPTER 54

The clamor of the crowd was disconcerting. Hundreds of people were checking baggage, chatting, sitting reading newspapers, and bustling around the Dallas Love Field Airport.

"At least you got to spend a week with your family before you had to leave," said Martiel. "Quit worrying. You're mother will come around."

Martiel was fussing over James Earl's tie and as usual, grabbed a pinch of his well-groomed hair and pulled down a sprig to hang on his forehead.

"There." She patted his chest with both hands, her seal of approval.

James looked around nervously and out the window at the tarmac.

The giant metal flying toys were being pulled around by tiny little go-cart looking things.

He accidentally knocked over his luggage as Jolie and Regina walked up followed by a porter struggling with a cart of several bags. Jolie was already following his actions and looked up at him.

"What's wrong James?"

She hadn't seen him fidget like this since the very first time they met.

James leaned toward her ear, "I don't like flying."

"You are kidding, right?" She smiled vindictively.

"Four flights a year for the last four years, summers and Christmases," he said, squinting at her.

"I'll hold your hand," said Jolie.

James swallowed and stepped to her side. "Light traveler I see," he said, looking at the heaping buggy.

"We're going to be there for a while," Jolie said, frowning at his dissention.

"Are you going to watch over my little girl?" asked Regina. "My future son-in-law..., and such a handsome young man."

She gave James an approving swipe of the hands down each arm, then smiled up at him.

"You know Jolie's never been away from family for very long. She's kind of a homebody, likes her solitude and such; a little broody at times. That'll make her a good student."

She leaned toward James, "And a good wife and mother. I expect grandchildren, in due time of course."

Regina hugged him, "Jolie..., whew, this boy is solid."

Jolie pulled him away from Regina, "He's taken mama."

"Make sure that dorm room she gets is a private room. I don't want her to have to share with some neophyte groupie or.... Wait, it *is* an all girl dormitory, right baby? Not some co-ed wild bunch."

"Mama," said Jolie. "Take a breath."

She squinted her dark eyes at Jolie, "I'll go check your baggage. Might as well throw yours on here too James."

Regina wriggled her finger at the porter and glided off while the others watched.

"Is that what I've got to look forward to?" asked James.

Jolie tightened her lips into a dot and glared up at James.

"I guess I can deal with it," he smiled.

The airlines counter announced their preflight check-in.

"We'll see you Christmas break," said James. "Watch over Sam?"

"I'll make sure that he gets plenty of attention," said Martiel. "It's your mother I'm going to have to work on."

"Be easy on her, she needs you and gramma to support her until she adjusts to her new life," said James.

Martiel nodded.

"Take care of him, Jolie."

Another announcement began barking their departure.

Regina called to the group, "Come on, you'll miss your flight."

"Knock 'em dead," said Martiel. "Uh, poor choice of words."

THE END

EPILOGUE

The harsh steady wind on the beach was whipping the water into foamy spit. The inhabitants on the island of Haiti were preparing for a seasonal tropical storm that would soon arrive.

"It's good to be on home soil again," said Mambo Dubois.

"James made that possible for us," said Dominique. "All our enemies are gone. We must give thanks to him."

Their bare feet scrubbed along the gravely sand of Indigo Beach, enjoying their home island.

Oungan Dominique explained the possibilities of future events to his apprentice and how everything could still change.

"It is a shame that all our wishes did not materialize as we had hoped with young James," said Dominique.

Waves rushed up the beach, erasing their footprints in the sand behind them.

"Many changes will come as soon as the child is born."

Italian to English Insert
*Loose translations – some slang / figurative

Chapter 4
- *Signorina – young lady*
- *balordo vecchio – Old Fool*

Chapter 5
- *Mia Fiore – my flower*
- *Entrare le dannato limousine – get in the damn car*
- *sìa già – yes already*
- *Pensaci – think (remember)*
- *Tu e vostra mamma – you and your mama*
- *Ficcanaso e balordo - nosey and stupid*
- *Città – (the) city*
- *Ci Pensati – you think about it*
- *Domattina – tomorrow morning*
- *Zia – Aunt*

Chapter 6
- *capo bastone – "the boss"*

Chapter 13
- *Ingenuo scimunito! Non capisco – Naive idiot! I don't understand.*
- *semplice cosa – (a) simple thing*
- *troppo chièdere – too much to ask?*
- *infestato – possessed*
- *Esci – go (get out)*

Chapter 17
- *Bene, bene – good, good*
- *fuor di luogo – out of place*
- *Esca – bait*
- *Andiamo – let's go!*

Chapter 22
- *Esci – out (exit)*
- *Coglione – asshole*
- *Capisch – (you) understand*
- *Dono – present*
- *Personalmente – personal (leaning toward intimate)*

Chapter 27
- *Soldatos – soldiers*

Chapter 29
- *Capisch – (you) understand*

Chapter 31
- *Personalmente – personal (leaning toward intimate)*

Chapter 34
- *sotto voce – silent (like a whisper)*
- *finito – finished*

Chapter 40
- *bambina – baby girl*
- *Bambina, Ti Amo – baby girl, I love you*

Chapter 44
- *Capisch – (you) understand*

ABOUT THE AUTHOR

David Pyle is the author of several supernatural tales and short stories with a library of information for new writers on his website – www.pentwist.com.

Other recent publications available on Amazon Books and Kindle:

Between Life and Death
(Book One)
ISBN-10: 0692306234
ISBN-13: 978-0692306239

Minutes
ISBN-10: 0615860516
ISBN-13: 978-0615860510

Pitre
ISBN-10: 0615877958
ISBN-13: 978-0-615-87795-2

www.ingramcontent.com/pod-product-compliance
Lightning Source LLC
Chambersburg PA
CBHW021842010726
47493CB00005B/1518